THE
FLAGS
OF
DAWN

STANLEY FRANCIS

For Jane

My how and my why.

First published in Great Britain

Copyright © Stanley Francis

The moral right of this author has been asserted.

Editing, design, typesetting and publishing by UK Book Publishing

www.ukbookpublishing.com

ISBN: 978-1-915338-41-9

Cover photos by:
Jordan Hile, Tom Barrett and *John Adams* on Unsplash

Some of this is true

Prologue

Today – Stonefall cemetery, Harrogate Yorkshire

The gaunt figure stood alone; a chilling breeze tugged at her black fedora, which she restrained with a gloved left hand. Connie delved into her capacious handbag with her free hand in search of a smoke. Brittle snowflakes melted on touching her shivering frame, the pure whiteness forming contrasting winter patterns that shimmered on the brim of her hat and settled on the shoulder of her black quilted overcoat. Peering into the empty cigarette packet, she remembered that she had resolved to give up... completely this time.

She shuddered as an icy gust fluttered a loose thread on the seam of her black plaid shawl. Absently scuffing the freshly turned earth from the heels of her winter boots, she watched as the condensation of her sighing breath was snatched by the breeze. Partly obscured by a white rosebud in her left buttonhole was a small round pewter badge embossed with the letters 'EE'.

Connie was reflecting, struggling to contain her emotions, hiding them from herself and others. The wintry shower was beginning to ease now; as the last snowflakes melted into teardrops as they traced charcoal mascara tracks, stark against her pale features.

Two figures sat motionless in the comfort of a dark blue Lexus, unobserved but watching Connie intently from the rutted shingle which served as a car park. Outwardly, her expression revealed little, but the few who knew her well would recognise the vulnerability which she disguised behind an embroidered lace handkerchief.

But listener... I will allow Connie to tell you her story in her own words.

Introduction

My name is Connie. This is my first attempt to put words to my thoughts and give dialogue to my emotions.

I wasn't even sure that the story was mine to tell. Even if it was, how should I begin? Should it even open with me? But if not, then who else is there?

I will remain for ever indebted to each and every one of those who helped me to release this genie from its bottle. They breathed life into dialogue, brought colour and texture to each phrase, and illuminated every word. If you decide to read on, I hope that it will do the same for you.

This story has been waiting to be told, and I think the time is now, so let me tell you how it all came about.

Connie today

I treasure that Fedora more than anyone could imagine. It was a birthday gift from him, the first for 50 years. He had watched me as I placed it carefully on my head, admired it in the mirror, and adjusted its position slightly, my smile reflecting his. On this day of all days, it was the only headwear for the occasion. Okay, it wasn't black – according to the label it was 'Celtic Indigo' – but just for today none of that mattered.

As long as I can remember, I had been searching for my father, or perhaps, for the person I wanted my father to be. Or maybe I was looking for me, or the person that I wanted to be. But there I stood, somehow rooted to the spot, my mind racing, reliving over and over where and when I first met him. Even in his absence, he had been part of my life for as long as I could remember. Not only the missing piece of the incomplete jigsaw that was me, but much more. He gradually became that indispensable part of every jigsaw, the box lid, the solution, the pattern and framework upon which completion of any puzzle depends.

Often when I look back at our chance meeting, it seems like an eternity, but just now it feels like yesterday. When I first met him, he appeared to be a reclusive and vacant figure, whose unblinking gaze seemed focused somewhere in the middle distance. However, the man I came to know was very different from anyone else I had met. He was from another age. A time when young lives were measured in fleeting weeks, and the boundaries between innocence and blame, right and wrong, were twisted and indistinct. He was from the ranks of volunteers, men with courage and humour in equal measure, young men who shunned heroism but whose guile and resolve came to define their generation.

Part 1

"Remember who you were before the world with all its folly and conceit, told you who you should be"

A Manifesto for Paradise – 2016

Chapter 1

Mary

I've never met my mother, Mary. They told me that I was a new-born on the night the bombers came. In 1942, a bomb, just one bomb was enough to reduce the house in York to a smouldering pile of rubble, ending two lives and depriving me of a mother. Perhaps at my birth, in those fateful hours before the bomb, my mother and I may have introduced ourselves to each other at some primal, subliminal level, but of course, I have no recollection of forming such a bond. Of my father, I knew nothing but soon learned that the stigma accompanying that admission had other implications. If I gave it any thought at all in my early years, I assumed that my mother Mary, and my father had spent time together choosing a name for their unborn child. Little did I know that I would need those comforting daydreams of hope and optimism in the darker days to come.

Even now, it feels strange referring to my mother by her first name, but for the sake of clarity, I will continue to do so. I was painfully aware that I had missed knowing Mary as 'mother', or even just 'mum'. I felt robbed of those intimate moments, which

I would have valued beyond measure, and which I still crave to this day.

Of course, I never knew what Mary looked like, but, as a child on long, sleepless nights, I used to picture my mother's face in my mind's eye. I would screw up my eyes, see her smile, benign, beloved, feel her warming and fragrant presence close by and comforting. I have since learned that her story was short, like so many from that bygone era. It was nonetheless heart-rending, a painful nettle that I somehow had to grasp. Her stepfather deserted the family home during the bitter winter of 1929 when she was a child. Her mother succumbed to a bout of tuberculosis and died in poverty following The Great Strike.

At the age of 13, just when orphan Mary was to be made a ward of court, she was offered a room in a bedsit by an elderly aunt in York. Of course, Mary knew nothing of her ageing relative or the profound effect she would have on Mary's life.

Klara

Only in late middle age, she was older than her years. Although apparently able-bodied, Aunt Klara always seemed to need help. Mary was unlikely to forget her first impression of her estranged aunt. Klara's appearance was striking, but for all the wrong reasons. If Klara really was a long-lost relative, she could not be more different than Mary's expectations. Perhaps she had hoped for some benign and kindly benefactor, a wealthy spinster, or at worst a Miss Havisham. But Klara was none of those. Although she could not be described as Dickensian, she did share many traits with that author's more troubled characters.

To Mary, her new aunt always looked either angry or alarmed; it was difficult for her to tell which was which.

Mary decided that Klara had somehow offered to carry the world's cares and look after them as if they were her own. Or perhaps she was simply waiting for the next in a series of catastrophes to befall her. Mary was yet to learn the truth that Klara had already lived an entire lifetime, every moment of it etched upon her furrowed brow. Her face was pallid and hung in folds above thin mean lips, drawn tight in a habitual grimace. Imprisoned beneath the mesh of a tightly clamped hairnet, permed silver locks made valiant attempts at escape. Although quite capable of walking without it, she had taken to carrying a walking stick. An ornate blackthorn shillelagh which she would shake for emphasis, indicating who or what had been chosen as the focus of her wrath at the time. She came with a unique assortment of vague symptoms, undiagnosed conditions, and a general air of malaise.

Klara constantly called on Mary, demanding everything from a morning cup of tea to a milky bedtime nightcap. At 9 pm exactly every night, Klara would insist on her bedtime drink, partly to 'take away the taste of her milk of bismuth', while insisting that taken in the right doses, *Ovaltine* was a well-known antidote for insomnia. Klara had often insisted that her niece should try it, as Mary 'needed good sleep as she always looked tired'. A forlorn hope as Mary knew to her cost. Unfortunately, for both Klara and Mary, the biggest sleep of all would come soon enough. But when it did, it would take a much more sinister form than that of a warm bedtime beverage. Struggling to come to terms with her aunt's eccentricities, Mary summoned the doctor on more than one occasion. His impatient diagnosis was clear: there was nothing he could do medically to ease her condition.

"Condition – what do you mean, condition?" enquired Mary.

Closing his Gladstone bag, the doctor's reply sounded more like a rebuke than a diagnosis.

"There is nothing organically wrong with your aunt. She suffers only from a chronic case of hypochondria, young lady, and you would do well to keep that in mind before you call me again."

The doctor's words hung in the air, fading as he made a hasty exit. Mary was pretty sure that she knew what chronic meant, but she decided to look up hypochondria in the old dictionary in the parlour. After the experience with the doctor, Mary came to realise the true extent of her predicament. Increasingly cantankerous and short-tempered, Klara was confined to her room on the ground floor of the bedsit and had come to rely totally on Mary over the years.

Although she frequently complained of her afflictions, Klara was still capable of summoning help whether noon or midnight. Her gnarled knuckles were still more than capable of ringing the ornate miniature Alpine brass cowbell which she kept just within reach on her bedside table. If that failed, Klara would rap her walking stick against the ceiling. Living on the floor above, whether awake or asleep, Mary found it very tempting to ignore the incessant knocking and the reedy Alpine chimes. She would often bury her head under her pillow, a muted scream of frustration forming a scowling mask on her sleep-worn brow.

Captive and downtrodden, Mary had to discover everything the hard way, the true meaning of not only hypochondria but also servitude. Now in her late teens, her once youthful and enthusiastic responses to her aunt's demands had become muted over the years. Even though Klara provided my mother with a roof over her head, and food on the table, I've often wondered how Mary felt over those dismal days of darkness. Perhaps she felt obligation and maybe gratitude, but I'm certain she must have felt enslaved. Cornered in a gilded if tarnished cage where she had become both comforter and comforted.

Friday, 1 September 1939

Since returning from her morning shift at *Rowntree's*, Mary had lost count of how many times she had been called already that afternoon. Still washing the dinner plates, she was summoned by the bell yet again. Obedient as ever, Mary was told to switch on the ugly *Ekco* wireless which dominated the entire ground floor of the bedsit. Its imposing presence and walnut facade sneered at its audience as they waited, illuminated only by its glowing dial and valves. The veneered monster came to life just in time for the Greenwich time signal and the 6 pm News. With a cut-glass accent and crackling reception, BBC newsreader Lionel Marson announced the German invasion of Poland to a stunned audience. Having listened to the entire broadcast in silence, with one insistent gesture, Aunt Klara said,

"Shut that goddamn thing off!"

Mary obediently switched the wireless off, leaving only a combustible silence and the stale odour of scorched dust, a permanent feature of the *Ekco's* still glowing amplifier. With her collection of elusive ailments and bohemian ancestry, Aunt Klara rarely missed an opportunity to voice her outrage. Mary cringed, awaiting the inevitable onslaught.

"... Why did nobody stop that madman last year when it was possible, before it was too damn late?..."

Although her question hung in the air unanswered, Klara was right – today was a day for outrage, one which would soon be followed by even greater injustices.

"I tell you why..." Klara continued. "... that damned pacifista Chamberlain and those French spineless toads stood with one hand over their eyes and the other up their arse, while those Prussian bandits take my country...

"... You think they just stroll in and make themselves at home and sitting comfortable? That will be bad enough if you please. But no, they throw us onto the street, *violets*, and destroy everything they see. I tell you now, who will even raise the finger of objection, let alone the fist...?"

The invasion of her homeland and the prospect of another conflict in Europe proved too much for Aunt Klara. After hearing Mr Chamberlain's declaration of war on 3 September 1939, the *Ekco* was once again silenced. Aunt Klara took to her bed where she remained, issuing loud proclamations to anyone who'd listen.

"Yes, Mr Chamberlain, you know why that Hitler give you the paper in München now... you know he has signed your toilet paper!" Adding for good measure, "... Neville, you made pact with the devil, and yes you also have sold your own soul and ours, Mr Chamberlain... Idiota!..."

Mary knew from experience that it was futile to intervene with her aunt in full flow, as the rant continued.

"... Okay, you order general mobilisation, who in God's name is he? I hope he has big army; he will need one now..."

Mary interrupted, suggesting that too much excitement might be detrimental to her aunt's health. Still, Mary's well-intended advice was lost in Klara's continuing proclamation.

"... look at you, you are young, you don't know what these people will do."

"I run away from those barbarian monsters when they invade my country last time, I know what they do, who force me and my family to leave our home, go into woods where we make shelter and hide. My father gone, my brother die begging in streets of Kalisz, my sister beaten and raped, how she survive, only God knows. I bring her to this country 25 years ago. See my name... English name Marchand is not my name, my sister and I take name from the man who help us escape to England, now in prison for his good work, for God's sake. These bastards won't stop, they will do the same here as they have done to my country... you take my word... God help us all now..."

Mary interrupted her aunt again.

"I didn't know you had a sister..." she asked as Klara bridled in mid-flow at the interruption, glowering at Mary who insisted,

"... you didn't tell me that you had a sister."

"See how little you know of me, and you are family to me now..." came the reply.

"... of course I have sister, Prudenze, she have boy, what I call *dran*, what you call the child of love of course, what I call the child of hate, there is not love, just rape."

"So you have a sister and nephew; where are they now, in England?"

"Used to live here, of course, nearby Birmingham someplace, I forget. After she have son, she do her best to love him, put him in college, but she is broken woman, damage too much."

"My God, Aunt Klara is she still alive?" said Mary, transfixed.

"She wanted to start new life, start again. I don't blame her, she moved to South Africa, for God's sake, leave her son here. Anything to get away."

"Do you hear from them?"

"From him, never, no fear, he finished at Birmingham college university to be, I think dentist or some such. Last I hear he go to Poland for God's sake."

"Do you hear from your sister?"

"I have one letter from Prudenze, from South Africa, each year on St Nicholas – then no more, I can see why, she has new life and new dream to follow, I should say good luck or good riddance maybe.

"I have letters in my drawer, I show you beautiful stamp on envelopes. I will write my news to her, tell about you and the government and another bloody war. She never reply to me these days and never had much to say. Too busy liking animals and seeking her fortune."

Lefty and Mary, Spring 1942

As an orphan, Mary had been overjoyed to be offered a room in the bedsit in York. For Mary back then, a dream fulfilled, one she had secretly nurtured was coming true. In her teens, she had longed for a home, a family, the chance to live her own life, not that which was chosen for her. But in almost seven years of servitude, Mary's optimism, enthusiasm, and gratitude had dwindled to resignation, as the drudgery of day-to-day life in Laburnum Grove took its toll. Complaining of frailty and sickness, Aunt Klara had taken to her bed in the parlour on the ground floor, still demanding everything from a cup of tea to a change of clothes. Although she did her best, caring for her needy but ungrateful aunt, Mary spent what should have been her carefree years in a bleak and cheerless existence. Confined to the upstairs room of the shabby bedsit, desperately lonely, Mary daydreamed of freedom, independence, escape from the clutches of her aunt, and the dismal ramshackle apartment. With only a meagre income from her job at the Rowntree's factory, it was the only life that she could afford in the suburbs of York in the early months of 1942.

In recent weeks the landlord, Tobin, threatened to evict both Mary and her aunt, if the backlog of rent was not paid. Given to bouts of heavy drinking, Tobin had more than once cornered Mary and demanded rent or payment in kind for the privilege of allowing a sub-let. Mary faced the prospect of becoming homeless again, so she saved every penny that she could from her job.

Owing to the shortage of sugar, cocoa, and other imported products, part of the Rowntree's factory in Haxby Road had been commandeered by the War office. The production line had been converted to assembling munitions and fuses for various weapons.

After each shift, Mary had to scrub her hands with *lifebuoy* soap until her skin was red raw. It was the only way to remove the yellow stain from the explosive powder which seemed to cling to every inch of exposed skin. The odour of the factory clung to hair and clothing which inevitably became masked by the pungent aroma of carbolic soap. But as with most household items those days, soap was rationed, so Mary and her aunt had to share, which inevitably led to accusations of waste from Klara. The pay from Mary's job was still a pittance, barely enough to cover day-to-day expenses, but it did get her out of the house, and away from the constant pressures of her aunt for a few hours. However, as soon as Mary returned home, Klara would confront Mary with a backlog of demands. Determined to make Mary pay for her absence, she would condemn her careless attitude towards her 'pitiless and housebound Aunt'. Mary became convinced that Klara spent her time alone scouring her worn copy of the Polish/English dictionary, for colourful adjectives with which to punish her wayward and careless niece. Fortunately, Klara would mispronounce most of her translated insults, which lent a comic element to her otherwise caustic taunts.

It was about this time that Mary met Lefty at a dance at the Assembly Rooms in York city centre.

Lefty

Born in the summer of 1921, Donald 'Lefty' McFarland was a farm boy from Québec province. He had always been interested in machinery and was captivated by the idea of flying from an early age. Convinced that Québec, with its separatist lobby, would block Canada's referendum for conscription, he joined the Royal Air Force. Following the introduction of the British Canadian Air Commonwealth Training Plan, pilot training for the RAF included Canadian nationals.

After completing initial training, Lefty arrived at Fort Hubert Canadian Air Force Base, just outside Montréal. He was awarded his pilot wings after soloing in the Canadian-built Harvard training aircraft. He was promoted the following year and transferred to the UK. Lefty was posted to Yorkshire to train on the twin-engined *Avro Anson* in preparation for flying the newest multi-engine RAF heavy bombers. The war department strategy of 'area bombing' using state-of-the-art aircraft was a new initiative. It was claimed that bombing was the only option if 'we are to take the fight to the enemy,' and may even shorten the war or so Air Marshal Harris assured the nation. As a pilot, Lefty became part of 513 Squadron Royal Canadian Air Force based at Linton-on-Ouse just outside York.

The squadron was scheduled to be one of the first to receive the newest aircraft in the RAF inventory. Lefty was teamed with six other volunteers to form a crew to fly the latest RAF heavy bomber, the Halifax. The crew continued training while they awaited delivery of their new aircraft and soon became inseparable. On a day out in Scarborough, following a lunchtime pub visit at the Star and Garter, they visited a tattoo parlour on the high street. Defying service regulations, each had their forearm tattooed with "The Lucky Star and Horseshoe", an interpretation of the squadron motto 'Étoile Chanceuse' in deference to its Québecois origins.

On the assumption that luck is associated with actions of the right hand, each was tattooed on the right forearm. All that is apart from Lefty who announced that, as he was left-handed, he must be tattooed on the left forearm, risking accusations of jinx. When one of the gang asked Lefty if he believed in that stuff, luck from a star and horseshoe, Lefty assured them that it worked whether you believed in it or not!

Lefty would catch the bus to York, visiting Mary whenever his duties would allow. They became lovers. The tall, rangy Canadian with the features of a teenager and a ready smile, became engaged to Mary, who was expecting their child. It wasn't long before Lefty became the focus of Tobin's wrath. The feeling was mutual, and Lefty, defending Mary from the landlord's advances, had exchanged blows with Tobin more than once. At least now with Lefty's help, the rent arrears had been paid. He neither expected nor received thanks from Aunt Klara, who would claim only that she found Lefty's boyish charms irresistible. But as Mary spent more time in Lefty's company, Klara secretly nurtured a growing resentment concealed behind her artificial smile. It soon became obvious that she was unwilling to share her niece with anyone. But as far as Mary was concerned, Lefty was her saving grace when she needed it most.

The war was entering its third year, and with the newspapers full of reports of stalemate in the Western Desert and the disastrous fall of Singapore, there seemed little optimism on the streets. But at least, Lefty and Mary could get together whenever their duties would permit. Tobin once again threatened Mary with eviction after her now obvious pregnancy could no longer be disguised. Klara would attempt to defend Mary against the worst of Tobin's alcohol-fuelled threats, despite that he now knew that Lefty would intervene in any dispute involving Mary.

With her shoulder-length auburn hair, hastily constrained in an improvised bun, Mary still wore an expression of childlike naïveté which belied her distinctly feminine ways. Whatever she wore and however tired and unkempt she felt, she would turn heads. Overly self-conscious because of her pregnancy, Mary was modest and apparently totally oblivious of her effect on others.

Each time she returned home, Mary would attempt to close the front door silently with a faint click, then tiptoe past Klara's open door in order to avoid the constant demands of her aunt. Before making her way to the apartment above, Mary had to pause on the landing to draw breath before attempting the last flight of stairs.

Chapter 2

GEORGIE

On a bitter morning in the winter of 1942, Lefty and the crew clambered into the back of the RAF truck which would take them to the airfield at Preston in Lancashire. Along with his squadron colleagues, he had to collect a brand-new aircraft from the production line at Salmsbury just outside Preston. Lefty and the crew were to fly it back to Linton-on-Ouse where it would be used on operations. On arrival at the factory, he and other crews waited in the office of the English Electric Co, where they were offered tea and biscuits while waiting for the fog to disperse. The factory usually manufactured everything from household appliances to steam locomotives, but was now on a war footing. It was a hive of industry, a giant well-oiled machine, manufacturing front line aircraft for the war effort. The production line was in full swing, and with strict security regulations in force, the crews were not permitted access to the manufacturing floor.

Spectres slowly emerging from the mist – the crew caught their first glimpse of the brand-new aircraft through the window in the nearby hangar. Each bomber a glistening leviathan, a

Kraken waking from its eternal slumber ready to wreak havoc on those who would deny its lethal purpose. Cockpit crew members were given a small blue manufacturer's handbook entitled 'The Handley Page Halifax II'. Both pilots and flight engineers studied with the preoccupation of schoolboys cramming for exams.

As the sun broke through the remaining haze, a pinstriped factory manager from the English Electric Co made an appearance and shook hands with each crew member. Adding in jest that, although the aircraft was named after a city in Yorkshire, it had been hand-built by Lancashire craftsmen.

The manager added that the Halifax was the finest aircraft not only in the UK but anywhere in the free world. Cautioning the crew that 'if they looked after the aeroplane, it would look after them'. The manager presented each pilot with a small pewter lapel badge, embossed with the letters 'EE', a memento and token of good fortune from the English Electric Company. He wished them all a final farewell, still emphasising confidence in his product. As the last reluctant shrouds of mist dispersed, teacups emptied, cigarettes extinguished, they were able to get airborne from Preston for the short hop to Linton-on-Ouse.

Cruising high above the rocky outcrops of the Pennines, the sunshine exposed the forbidding stare of the slate grey tors which somehow beckoned them from beneath. Emerging from the shadows, the carpet of winter heather on the lowland moors glowed with purple hues as they continued eastward. Lefty became lost in the reverie of the moment, the pure escapism of flying, in contrast with the stark reality of war. Marvelling at the experience, Lefty recalled his boyhood heroes, aviation pioneers such as Lindbergh who had completed his solo transatlantic flight only 15 years earlier. Kindred spirits who had shared his dreams, wondered at the deep blue of the firmament, and revelled in the joy of creation. However, a voice from somewhere deep inside his soul tugged at his wistfulness, reminding Lefty that behind the illusion of freedom lurked the cold reality of menace. An unwelcome stowaway which lives for battle, thrives on darkness and dread, always eager to accompany every warrior of the night. He would engage in combat soon enough, but right here and now the prospect of warfare seemed alien, a dark and distant portent of the future. Manoeuvring the new aircraft, Lefty was pleased to discover that the controls responded well to firm inputs. The flight deck was quite cramped for his tall frame. Still, despite having to sit shoulder-to-shoulder with the flight engineer, the large aircraft was surprisingly easy to control. However, the rudder required a full stretch of Lefty's leg to be fully effective. Getting in and out of the aircraft was a tight squeeze – Lefty's six-foot frame required him to adopt a full crouch to avoid hitting his head. As they became more accustomed to the new aircraft and its operational limitations, each crew member settled readily to their tasks in the cramped confines of the fuselage. It wasn't long before they each acquired a great affection for their charge, defending 'her' from the jibes of crews from other units.

Visiting Mary the following week, Lefty spoke with youthful enthusiasm about the brand-new aircraft which had been given the squadron identification letter 'G for George'. The previous night, Lefty and the crew had held a christening party for their new aircraft. Henceforth she was to be known as 'Lucky Georgie'. The unofficial ceremony of 'wetting the baby's head' was apparently performed with beer, rather than holy water, in the best traditions of the service.

CHAPTER 2

Aware that it was only a few weeks before *her* new baby would arrive, Mary reflected that she had experienced little luck in her life. But things were changing now, she was going to be a mother soon, and part of somebody else's life, a family at last. But Lefty and Mary kept their feet firmly on the ground; they knew that their child would emerge into a changing world. A world of love and excitement, laced with uncertainty, and turmoil. Mary hid her concerns for Lefty's safety, quietly praying that 'Lucky Georgie' would bring him and his crew home safely after every mission. As an act of reassurance, Lefty pressed the 'EE' lapel badge into the palm of Mary's hand, confessing that it was the nearest that he could afford to an engagement ring at the moment. Lefty took great care to assure Mary that the day would come soon when she could choose a ring of her own.

Chapter 3

THE JOB

Lefty mentioned that the squadron was preparing for a 'job'. He and the crew knew little apart from the fact that it would take them away for a week or so. Mary's pregnancy had been difficult, and she was suffering the worst symptoms of her condition, but the midwife had been a great help to her over the period leading up to full term. Lefty promised that he would do his best to stay in touch with her. He knew full well that even if Mary could make it to the nearest public phone box, these days private calls were rarely transferred to RAF operational phone lines. With Allied forces now on the highest state of alert, military phone lines had been secured, their use strictly prohibited by private individuals. From previous experience, Lefty knew of some calls which had got through, but only those enquiries from immediate family members. All other personal calls were discouraged and politely declined by the switchboard operator. Official letters would be released to next-of-kin to keep relatives informed, if and when that became necessary.

Over the next week, although not confined to camp, Lefty and the crew were training in preparation for the impending operation. The punishing schedule demanded the full involvement of the crew, leaving little or no time for leisure. During his last visit, Lefty and Mary each bid their farewells, his warm embrace reassuring and vital. She would remember feeling his heart beating in time with her own, and her unborn child stirring in response to the rhythm. She repeated her silent prayer that he would return soon to be reunited as a family of three. They waved their farewells as Lefty stepped onto the street to catch the last bus. He blew a kiss to her, and she made a smile for him. The kind of smile which dissolved slowly behind hands cupped with anxiety, almost hiding a frown of doubt which furrowed her brow. Mary felt a single tear condense around one eyelid, a saline track across her cheek, prompting an involuntary shiver as Lefty rounded the corner and disappeared from view.

RAF Kinloss

In preparation for deployment, Lefty and the crew flew hourly missions practising low-level tactics with the new aircraft at Strensall bombing range just outside York. Leave was now embargoed until after the operation was complete.

In mid-April, the squadron was ordered to deploy to Kinloss in Scotland where they would assemble with other units to mount a raid. Lefty and the crew assumed that the target would be in the North Sea or Scandinavia. Wherever it was, it was going to be a 'big show' judging by the sheer number of aircraft on the dispersal, with more on the way. The nights were bitter in the wooden huts which served as crew accommodation at RAF Kinloss. Early spring in Yorkshire had been reasonably mild, but in northern Scotland, the weather had a distinct chill. Although Lefty was acclimatised to cold weather, this was a damp and pervasive cold unlike the dry sub-zero temperatures and blowing snow of home. Even though the Canadian winters could be bleak, Lefty recalled the warm and sultry summers in his native Québec, which seemed even more distant now. Each evening the crew sat smoking and playing cards. And each evening an easterly breeze rolled the harr in from the bitter waters of the Moray Firth, blanketing the coastline in a shallow but persistent sea fog. At each morning briefing, the met man promised clear weather, but each evening was the same. The fog seemed to cling to everything, man, and machine, as each evening the raid was postponed. There had been rumours amongst squadron crew members that the operation may have to be cancelled if it did not happen soon. There was even a joke on the squadron which suggested that Kinloss might mean Dead-loss. Lefty enjoyed the humour of the crew; he watched them as they laughed, smoked and joked. He knew that they were ready, their time was coming, their mettle would be tested. Now or never. Lefty would be flying the mission, and they would each look to him in the coming days. He would not let them down.

It was Thursday 27 April 1942, and by the previous evening, mission-essential modifications had been completed on every aircraft. The bomb bay doors had been adapted to carry the new weapon load, and classified navigation equipment had been removed from each bomber. On their first crystal clear day, G George or 'Lucky Georgie', along with sixteen other aircraft were all ordered to cockpit alert readiness. The crews knew that if the raid was to take place, it would be within the next 24 hours. The briefing for the operation was scheduled for mid-afternoon. The aircraft armed and fuelled, the details of the mission were outlined in the temporary operations building. Windows shrouded with blackout curtains; an air of anticipation pervaded the crew briefing room. Punctual as ever, the squadron commander appeared at the side entrance and marched to the front of the room. As somebody shouted "Attention!" each crew member stood, accompanied by the sound of scraping wooden chairs. At the appointed time, all doors were secured, and the crew members were ordered to sit as a topographical wall map of Norway was revealed. The operations briefing began in earnest, the audience now hushed.

Addressing the assembled company, the squadron boss levelled a billiard cue pointer at the map, indicating a fjord on the western coast of central Norway. With appropriate ceremony, he began: "Gentlemen, may I introduce you to The Beast, not my words, but those of our illustrious leader..." And after a pause for effect, "... If you're not already, you will become very familiar with this particular Scandinavian holiday resort." Once his introduction was complete, the boss handed the billiard cue over to the intelligence officer who began by pointing out the latest remarkably sharp black and white images of the Tirpitz, her dazzle camouflage paintwork specifically designed to confound any would-be attacker. Then he began to describe the target in greater detail; well-camouflaged and heavily armoured, the battleship languished on her moorings in a heavily defended fjord in central Norway. Acting as 'fleet in being', without moving from her moorings, the mere presence of the Tirpitz threatened the security of the North Sea shipping lanes, the Iceland gap, and by extension, the entire North Atlantic. Allied convoys bound for Murmansk were now forced northward into the notorious gap between northern Scotland and Iceland. To complete the tactic, the exposed and sparsely protected convoys now fell prey to silent grey wolfpacks. U-boats waited in ambush, their quarry easy pickings, while crews were preoccupied, removing heavy rime ice from exposed rigging and superstructures. Any mariner who braved those northern latitudes risked capsize due to ice or a fiery death from beneath the waves. Each fury vowed demonic vengeance and retribution upon any vessel tempted to trespass their realm by entering the notorious Gap. The Tirpitz had become a sneering and deadly manifestation of the activity and achievement paradox.

There had been several previous attempts to sink the battleship, which succeeded only in stiffening German resolve. Tirpitz was moved to more secure moorings where she could be more effectively concealed and better defended. The intelligence briefing revealed the truly daunting might of the vessel, which was equipped with numerous onboard anti-aircraft batteries, guided by sophisticated search radar. It had been decided that a high-speed, low-level aerial attack would be necessary to increase the element of surprise. The plan was to overwhelm her defences, allowing Tirpitz minimum time to react. Murmuring could be heard between crew members, and somebody near the back of the room offered a muted whistle of amazement. This would be no easy task, no 'milk run'. The elusive Tirpitz had become one of the highest priority targets hidden in one of the best camouflaged, heavily defended, and inaccessible corners of the Norwegian coast. Precipitous ramparts of granite lined the fjord, every promontory and outcrop was peppered with anti-aircraft batteries. Each vulnerable point was protected by high calibre artillery emplacements. At the first sign of threat, strategically positioned smoke generators on land and on barges were waiting to obscure her already well-camouflaged position.

The weeks of planning and preparation paid off, as every crew member in each individual aircraft in the wave had already rehearsed their role. For the navigators and pilots, meticulous calculations of payload and fuel requirements were necessary in order to safely complete the round trip. There would be a very narrow margin for error, so each crew had been selected for their night-time navigational expertise. Weather forecasts for diversion airfields were also briefed, each of which would remain open until the last straggler landed.

The scope of the operation was now very clear, for a 24-hour period all major airfields from East Anglia to Newcastle, and Carlisle to Cromarty, had been alerted to expect aircraft returning from the raid. Those unable to make it back to Kinloss because of either battle damage or fuel shortage would at least have an emergency runway if needed. It would be a close-run thing; all eyes would be on the dim glow of the fuel gauges as each aircraft headed for home.

Briefing complete, all watches synchronised, each crew member surrendered any personal items which might betray their unit identity or origin. The crew checked their aircraft and settled down to a last-minute smoke and mugs of something resembling hot cocoa from the WRVS wagon.

At dusk on 27 April, the Aldis lamp signalled a steady green light from the control tower as each aircraft departed in the prebriefed sequence of six-second intervals. Lefty, 'Lucky Georgie' and the crew would be first, leading an element of four

Halifax bombers. Rolls-Royce engines and wooden propellers strained as the heavily laden aircraft lumbered down the runway, accelerating reluctantly. Lefty's fist was pushed hard on the throttles by Roy, the flight engineer, and shoulder-to-shoulder each squeezed every ounce of energy out of the roaring Merlin engines. The end of the runway and airfield boundary fence loomed large until it appeared to fill the entire windscreen. Above the din, one of the jokers at the rear of the aircraft was humming 'For Those in Peril on the Sea' on the intercom. Once again, the air gunner's humour eased the tension. But if they didn't get airborne soon, it seemed inevitable that those aboard 'Lucky Georgie' would be added to the infamous list of aircrew who would have to swim home, having suffered the indignity of ditching in the Moray Firth, without ever getting airborne.

Chapter 4

Mary, York 1942

In direct reprisal for the RAF bombing of the historic city of
Lübeck in March, Hitler in his outrage decreed that historic
British towns were to be targeted. Using the Baedeker
guidebook, printed in Germany for tourists, the *Luftwaffe* began
selecting historical British cities and cultural centres to attack.
So it was that York Minster became a target on the night of
Wednesday 29 April at 12 40 am.

Mary shared the shabby apartment with her aunt in the York
district of Poppleton, adjacent to the main railway station in York,
and within easy reach of the RAF station at Linton-on-Ouse for
visits by Lefty. Its location was convenient enough, and despite its
small size, Mary's upstairs flat was adequate but left no privacy
when entertaining guests. However, the business of scraping
together the weekly rent meant using the last of her food coupons
just to make ends meet.

It had been a long day; still exhausted from the anguish and
trauma of the difficult birth, and the constant demands of her
new-born, Mary nursed the child. Exhausted, both mother and

baby sank into a deep sleep in the old armchair. The midwife had promised to send the district nurse to tend to Mary in the late afternoon, but those days it was not uncommon for routine appointments to be missed. In her slumbers, Mary dreamt of life in a country cottage, Lefty playing with their daughter in the dappled sunlight of a summer garden. Around midnight a mournful sound intruded on her peaceful world as she was roused from her dreams by the wail. Not the cry of a child but that of something even more primal and urgent, the air raid siren carried across the city as the stillness of the night erupted into chaos. But there was no time to prepare: drowning out the sirens the first bombs were falling. She felt rather than heard the first concussions, then the explosions crept closer and much louder. Still waking, confused and uncertain, she knew that there was no time to reach the air-raid shelter, so Mary took her child into the bedroom. Covering them both with counterpane and pillows, she took refuge as best she could, still cradling her child in her arms. Then it seemed that the entire house shook on its foundations. Mary realised that the blackout curtains above the front door had been left open, allowing light to spill from the landing onto the street below. Fragments of plaster and dust drifted down from the ceiling and Mary felt sure that with one more hit close by, the entire roof would collapse and trap them both.

Then she became aware of Aunt Klara on the floor below, who might not have heard the warning and may be unaware of any danger. But as the mournful echo of the siren subsided, it was replaced by an eerie silence. The entire city seemed to hold its breath in anxiety and disbelief. There had been several false alarms over the winter which had turned out to be drills for the civil defence and local authorities to rehearse their reaction in the event of a raid. She had been warned about showing a light on a previous occasion, when the curtain in the hallway had remained open, out of reach without standing on a chair. But this was no practice, and there had not been an all-clear from the sirens; it was not over yet. Mary became paralysed with fear as the second wave of bombardment ensued. She remained covered in the blanket with her child, aware of the distant drone of a vehicle or aircraft, sounds punctuated only by muffled explosions accompanied by the crash of shattering glass.

Chapter 5

AIRBORNE

U rged on by Lefty, 'Lucky Georgie' finally achieved take-off speed, skimming the tall pines which skirted the airfield, wheels retracting. Georgie established a shallow and shuddering climb, vivid blue exhaust plumes flickering from each engine. Their initial progress was slow – the quantity of fuel and specialised weaponry required for the mission imposed an unusually high take-off weight, resulting in a sluggish rate of climb. Over his left shoulder, Lefty watched the North bank of the Firth slip away beneath them as they continued their climb south-east of Wick. Just visible off to the North and West, the brooding and eerie spectres of Orkney and Shetland appeared as shadows in the middle distance. Beyond, suspended high in the gathering dusk, Polaris, the North Star, glowed. The guiding star which the navigator would use to plot their heading and make corrections to their course. Adjusting the trim of the aircraft, Lefty hoped it would be their lucky star tonight. They would certainly need all the luck they could get on this mission: no rabbit's foot, no talisman or trinkets, Lucky Georgie would see them through, a sentiment acknowledged by all on the intercom.

Following the waxing moon eastward in formation, the dark expanse of the North Sea became all-consuming as they struggled to maintain their position in the formation. Finally reaching their operational altitude, the gunners cleared and fired their weapons, followed by an eerie silence broken only by clicks of background static. There was little conversation on the intercom, each crew member straining to optimise their night vision. With the absence of landmarks and the horizon indistinct, they were each left to their thoughts, each resisting the temptation to drink from their thermos flasks. Being a superstitious bunch, they always left their hot drink untouched until they were established homeward bound after a mission. The heady reek of new paint, engine oil, and leather pervaded their world. To accommodate the load of four 1000 lb naval mines, the bomb bay doors on the Halifax were unable to fully close, making the cabin unusually noisy, draughty, and uncomfortable. Strict radio silence was observed by each crew, but silence is not only the absence of sound, because there was more than enough noise to go round. There was something else, something that went unspoken but nonetheless tangible, visceral, an itch that could not be scratched. Not an odour but a taste, an oxidised rust of fear which coated each tongue. A hint of freshly spilt blood, the essence of a nightmare, and the tang of death. Each tongue a cloying mat clinging to the roof of each bone-dry mouth. No crew member would find the words to express it, but the emotion was engraved on each darkened countenance. They each knew this would be their first contact with the enemy and they were risking everything. Whispered prayers, or maybe just pleas to which no one gave voice, but which each of them harboured in the dark and fearful realms before night-time combat.

Commencing a slow and deliberate descent, they skimmed through layers of spilt milk. Shallow opaque clouds which formed water droplets on the aircraft windscreen obscuring the horizon. For the moment, the crew was forced to fly on instruments only, wings level, following the compass.

As snatches of the Norwegian coastline came into view, they continued their descent, the navigator skilfully guiding them towards the mouth of Trondheim fjord at the predetermined speed and altitude. Passing through 500 to 400 feet, they were met with the full force of the Nazi reception committee reserved especially for an incoming bombing raid. Streams of fire snaked up towards them as it rapidly became apparent that the planned element of surprise was in vain. The night sky was torn apart by incandescent flashing tracer fire, not only from the Tirpitz but from the surrounding peaks of the rocky fjord. Menacing outcrops passed perilously close to the port wingtip, as a hailstorm of shrapnel rattled against the aluminium skin of the airframe. 'Lucky Georgie' absorbed the punishment of multicoloured tracer fire from all sides, a roaring primaeval moth, trapped in the beam of a thousand distant suns. It was with great relief that the crew heard the bomb aimer shout the much anticipated 'bombs gone' above the din, as the aerial mines were released. Relieved of her heavy load, 'Lucky Georgie' reared up like an unruly steed, all four engines protesting. Full power was needed now to clear the high ground at the eastern end of the fjord. As Lefty heaved on the controls, banking south while the bomb bay doors closed, a bright explosion illuminated the entire aircraft as the starboard outer Merlin engine burst into flames.

Chapter 6

Mary, York – April 29th, 1942

More explosions reverberated across the city, like an approaching thunderstorm. The closer the bombs came, the closer Mary clutched her child. Close and yet closer. Terrified, she clung to her child, counting out the rhythm of her pounding heart. Flash... one umbrella... two umbrella, three umbrella, as if the storm of steel would pass harmlessly overhead. Then, just as she thought the worst of the onslaught was over, a blinding flash and deafening roar tore Mary's world apart. Collapsing masonry, tiles, brickwork, and shattered glass, the sound was deafening, but Mary didn't hear any of it. The next thing she was aware of was looking up at the star-filled night sky. Bewildered, deafened, covered in dust, her lower body seemed immobile under fallen brickwork and masonry. Unaware of the passage of time, senses numbed, ears ringing, Mary became aware of an insistent voice somewhere below her. "Is there anyone there..." And again, louder this time "... anyone in the house?" Mary heard herself reply in a voice she didn't recognise "I'm here with my baby, please help me".

What was left of the main structure of the house was balanced precariously on the only remaining supporting wall. Mary heard the scuffling sound of loose brickwork. As if from nowhere, a middle-aged man in a boiler suit appeared. Covered from head to foot in brick dust, the ARP warden reached out towards her across the collapsing remains of the upper storey and bedroom.

Noticing that Mary had been trapped by the legs beneath a fallen lintel, the warden said, "Stay put, love, and stay calm; I will get help." Mary's urgent response was "please, PLEASE take my Child". The warden stretched out again; reaching across the rubble, he grasped what appeared to be a dusty, stained bundle, rolled up in a counterpane. Reassuring Mary, the warden said, "Don't worry, love, we will look after him for you until we can get you out of here."

"It's *HER*, not him," replied Mary instinctively. The murmurs of the wakeful child subsided, and the uncanny silence returned as the shuffling sound of the crawling warden faded.

Her awareness starting to return, Mary became conscious of the numbing pain in her legs and realised that she was completely trapped. Above her, the sky was a deep and inky black, scintillating stars pinpoints of light. She became aware of the fading sound of droning engines above, and then a strange tinkling sound like falling icicles or a dropped pencil. A metallic tube landed on the exposed woodwork, close to Mary's elbow. Instinctively she reached out as it rolled slowly away from her along the fractured wooden beam which had once been a rafter. At first, distracted and mystified by the object, she winced with pain and frowned as she watched the progress of the metal tube. But then the reality dawned on her as it continued its fall. Like a struck match, the magnesium ignited as the incendiary continued downward on its quest for destruction. Mary knew then that it was the end. As the fire took hold on the lower floor, her last thoughts were for her daughter's safety, Aunt Klara on the floor below, and her fiancé, Lefty. Her last words formed soundless on her lips like a whispered dream: "dear Don... Please help me now... I've left our daughter in safe hands, but I'm her mother, and I've let her down..." Then the noxious but merciful fumes deprived her of her senses as she was shrouded by unconsciousness and swallowed by all-consuming tongues of fire.

Chapter 7

HOKLINGEN NORWAY

On board the stricken aircraft, the flight engineer reached over Lefty's shoulder, grasping at the throttles in an attempt to shut down the blazing number 4 engine. Lefty's training instantly kicked in. Recalling 'dead engine, dead foot', Lefty extended his leg, pushing hard on the rudder pedal to counteract the increasing yaw, as the fire threatened to engulf the main fuel tank in the starboard wing. With little time and fewer options, Lefty banked South and prepared for the worst. Unable to maintain altitude, he desperately sought a suitable place to safely perform an emergency landing. As the aircraft started to sink below 200 feet, the flight engineer pointed out a smooth snowfield that had been mentioned in the pre-flight briefing. Barely discernible in the pale moonlight slightly to the right of their track, surrounded on all sides by woodland, the smooth open snowfield became the only option. Lefty nodded in agreement as he trimmed the aircraft up for the approach, telling the crew to execute the emergency landing drills.

On first contact with the ground, the initial impact was much heavier than Lefty had anticipated, his mind raced from the responsibility of destroying a brand-new aeroplane to the overwhelming necessity of safeguarding his crew. The Halifax acted like a snowplough, touching down wings level, it gouged a huge swathe through the snow, eventually coming to a halt, with the fire partly extinguished but still smouldering, threatening to engulf the entire airframe. The ensuing silence was profound, broken only by echoes of distant gunfire and the drone of throbbing Merlin engines as the other aircraft turned for home. Creaking and clicking, resigned to its fate, Georgie's tortured airframe settled, partly covered in a shroud of white, the shattered stumps of wooden propeller blades grotesquely suggestive of broken limbs.

In his haste to retain control of the aeroplane, Lefty's harness straps had not been tightened. As the aircraft absorbed the first concussive impact, his forehead and temple struck the cockpit coaming above the instrument panel, leaving him dazed and lightheaded. Roy, the flight engineer, helped him through the escape hatch, as blood from Lefty's head wound seeped into his left eye, adding to his state of stunned confusion. Sliding out of the aircraft and into the night, Lefty collapsed in the snow, his head and shoulders propped against the port wing as he lapsed in and out of consciousness.

The last thing he remembered was thoughts of Mary somehow interspersed with sounds of distant barking and faint voices.

Sensation returning, Lefty became aware of gently falling snowflakes melting on the side of his face, kaleidoscopic colours pervading his senses. In a dream, he had fallen from his wooden toboggan in his boyhood winters on the frozen surface of the

Lachine Canal in his native Montréal. His consciousness subsided again as he dreamt of throwing snowballs and gathering around the log fire on the canal towpath to the sound of boyish laughter. Somehow the throbbing in his head would distract him in his reverie without allowing him to surface to full consciousness. Lefty was oblivious of the figure treading carefully through the snow towards him, the breath of a panting husky turning into freezing vapour. Dragging Lefty's unconscious body across the snowfield and into a thicket, the stranger propped him against a small stand of birch while attempting to distract him. Life seemed to be seeping from Lefty's youthful, punished, and unresponsive frame. He retreated once again to the dream-haunted world of his childhood.

As the first light of dawn broke over the crash site, the wreckage of the aircraft had already begun to sink slowly from view. What had appeared from the air to be a snow-covered field was a frozen lake. Early-morning gusts blew snaking trails of snow across the frozen surface of the lake until all evidence of the fateful events of the previous night had been erased. The fickle star of fortune bore witness from its lofty perch, conspiring to hide its followers and any trace of their presence. 'Lucky Georgie' had sunk from view and now resided in the slumbering embrace of the deep. Aeons of silence disturbed only by the soundless but graceful glide of the lifeless hulk as she settled softly on the lakebed, Georgie's final destination, a silent water world of permanent twilight and sedimentary silt.

The lake had played host to many others from the distant past, providing both cushion and crypt, exclusive accommodation for all its ageless victims.

Chapter 8

WALTER

L efty was roused to partial consciousness as he dreamt, the loyal family husky of his childhood gambolled with him in the snow. He was waking now from a deep freeze slumber, his feet and hands so cold that they had no sensation at all. His leather flying helmet had been partially removed, and dried blood caked his face, obstructing his vision. But the husky was there now, in front of him, its warm breath condensing a few inches from his shoulder. Lefty now inhabited that twilight world somewhere between daydream and reality, as he instinctively reached out his left hand towards the attentive dog. In the background, he thought he heard a murmur, not English, not the Québécois of his boyhood, but nonetheless reassuring and comforting.

Resuming his search in the grey light of morning, Walter and Tojo the husky returned to the spot by the frozen lake where they had left the airman. The German search parties who had interrupted his earlier rescue attempts had long since returned to their base, so now it was safe for Walter to help in any way he could. To his amazement, the wreckage in the middle of the lake had disappeared completely. The dry blowing snow had drawn a white veil over the night's proceedings; the only footprints in the fresh snow were the farmer's own and the pawprints of the husky. Had Walter dreamed the whole thing? Retracing his steps, the farmer and his dog returned to the lakeside, searching for the spot where they had left the semiconscious airman. Bounding over the snowdrifts, Tojo was the first to find Lefty in the small birch thicket where he had been concealed. Enlisting help from a farmworker who was snow clearing, they carried the inert body into one of the farm outbuildings, to provide shelter from the elements and concealment from prying eyes. Walter anticipated that search parties would resume their quest for aircraft wreckage and were no doubt actively looking for any evidence of downed airmen in the locality. The farm was remote and stood at the end of a long unpaved drive, well rutted with years of use, mud showing through the recent snowfall. At least the farmhouse offered a clear view of the main road, so any vehicle approaching would allow the farmer time to conceal the airman.

At dusk, Lefty was taken into the farmhouse now that his body had partly recovered from the cold. His condition improved markedly, as Lefty was plied with warm drinks and wrapped in blankets. While Walter and his wife prepared hot food for supper, Tojo's insistent barking alerted them to the vehicle. The German truck drew to an abrupt halt outside the farm, breaks squealing, tyres crunching and headlights shining a narrow beam across the drive. It was followed by a stern rapping on the farmhouse door. Walter and his wife exchanged anxious glances; their fear palpable as the door was answered, revealing the unmistakable silhouette of a German officer. In an adjacent room, Lefty had been hurriedly taken out of the rear stairs into the storage area where he hid behind stacks of stored wood and sacks of dried animal food. This time the search party was not satisfied by just questioning Walter and the family; they insisted on a search of the farmhouse. The reluctant searchers impatiently moved round to the farm outbuildings, but frustrated by the tedious and unproductive task, their search of the farm was cursory at best. The farmer's protestations of innocence had been so convincing that Lefty went undiscovered. Following this close call, the family in their dilemma decided that, if found, Lefty's discovery would put all their lives at risk, but they were determined to care for their very own airman. Over the next few days, injuries dressed, Lefty's circulation and general condition had returned to normal, and he was recovering well. It became necessary to destroy Lefty's RAF uniform, which, if discovered, would obviously betray them all.

What few possessions remained including every item of Lefty's clothing was destroyed. That which could not be buried was burned, along with any trace of his nationality. Lefty now wore a new disguise and became dressed in the garb of a local Scandinavian farmworker. The only conspicuous signs remaining were a scar above his left eye and his tattoo, so he became accustomed to wearing a cap while keeping his forearms covered.

Word came of the rest of the crew from 'Lucky Georgie'. Luckily, the others had received only minor injuries during the forced landing. While three had been caught and imprisoned, others had evaded detection and headed for neutral Sweden with the help of partisans. Walter and the farmhands spoke little English, but they established a dialogue that consisted of hand signals, pencil sketches, and Walter's schoolboy English. To Lefty's disappointment, Walter was able to explain that all the battleships in Trondheimfjord remained on their moorings, apparently undamaged, despite the intensity of the raid. After all the preparation planning and training, Lefty felt sure that some damage must have been inflicted on Tirpitz. If only by sheer numbers of bombs dropped, there must have been some good hits. But the outcome of the operation was confirmed by local resistance members. The sustained air attacks over 48 hours prompted the German high command to move Tirpitz. After minor repairs, she would remain out of harm's way in an even more remote location deeper in the Trondheimfjord. If there was a successful outcome of the raid, it was not the anticipated one. On her new mooring, the Tirpitz would have to perform additional, complicated manoeuvres before heading out towards the mouth of the fjord. Valuable time for the resistance to pass on an early warning of the battleship's movements and possible intentions.

Although perceived as an advantage by allied intelligence, it would be short-lived. Nazi High Command was already planning to move Tirpitz further north to Narvik or Tromso.

Lefty was told that he would be safe with the family for the time being, so long as he did not betray himself by speaking English. He was to be accompanied by Tojo during daylight hours, the dog acting as both defender and sentry. Discouraged from talking at all, Lefty was put to work chopping firewood, feeding the livestock, and clearing snow. When asked in broken English about his star-tattooed arm, Lefty provided an explanation. However, Walter thought that Lefty may be mistaken for a Jew with the star so apparent on his skin. By gestures, they again warned him not to reveal his bare forearms as there was a group of quislings known to be active in the locality. If the family was betrayed, and the German authorities in Trondheim alerted, the discovery of a British airman would be a valuable trophy for the collaborators. Narrowly escaping detection during subsequent searches, Lefty became acutely aware of the risk to Walter and his family. He resolved to make his own plans to escape and remove the family from any danger.

While a small number of RAF crew members from a previous raid on Tirpitz had avoided capture, a few were believed to be at large in central Norway. Others less fortunate had been captured or turned in by fearful locals.

Brutal reprisals against both partisans and innocent civilians were now the ugly and inevitable consequence of any form of civil disobedience or opposition to the Nazi cause. To make matters worse, news filtered through of an incident that occurred just outside Bergen in the spring of 1942. The sleepy town of Telvåg became the target for the full ferocity of German vengeance. While attempting to arrest suspected partisans, two German officers were shot by the resistance. In their wrath, the Gestapo rounded up the entire population of Telvåg, razed every building to the ground, and either executed or imprisoned every man, woman, and child.

The shockwaves from this outrage sent ripples far and wide, sending an unambiguous message to every neighbourhood from the Skagerrak to the North Cape. In one fell swoop, every dissenter, every would-be resistance fighter was compelled to review their ambitions, curtail their activities and in some cases abandon the partisan cause altogether.

Over the next few weeks, Walter and his wife knew that they must rethink their plans for concealing Lefty. During long and sometimes heated arguments, it became obvious to Lefty that the farmer's wife was now desperately concerned. Not only for their own safety but that of their extended family in Trondheim. Despite their hospitality and courage, Lefty understood that he had to go. But go where? Access to the nearby border with neutral Sweden was the most obvious escape route. Although tempting, the option was no longer viable with the recent introduction of roadblocks and military checkpoints. Any attempt at escape across the border to Sweden was now regarded as impossible; consequently, other options, no matter how impractical, had to be considered. However, events were to take their own course.

Chapter 9

RESISTANCE

I t happened in late May; Lefty was busy clearing ground in a paddock on the eastern boundary of the farm property, while Walter made his routine trip into town. It was an onerous task in the pasture removing a stubborn patch of thatch, and the day was unusually warm and sultry. Lefty resisted the urge to remove his jacket and roll up his sleeves, as Walter had warned him not to expose either his tattoo or the scar across his left eyebrow – each was still conspicuous and needed to be kept hidden at all times. Although it was thirsty work, wearing both cap and jacket, Lefty persevered; it was not in his makeup to give up or take a break. He would have regarded any lapse as a betrayal of the trust, hospitality, and pure courage that Walter's family had shown him.

Nevertheless, as he worked, the hairs on the back of his neck began to bristle and he became aware of the familiar and unsettling feeling of being watched. He always trusted his instincts, and cautiously surveyed his immediate surroundings to see if he was alone. There was no vehicle on the farmhouse drive; besides, he would have heard it arrive. Stopping as if to draw breath, Lefty leaned casually on the rake and absently pushed back the peak of his cap while drawing the sleeve of his jacket across his brow. He looked around the paddock in each direction, scanning the woodland to his right. Unseen, the stranger continued watching him, half-hidden in the woodland brush, the man was scrutinising Lefty, examining his every move. Lefty was caught off-guard when the dishevelled figure finally emerged from the undergrowth about 100m away. Startled by the sudden intrusion, Lefty's immediate impulse was to run. Still, taking deep breaths, he regained his composure and carefully considered his options. If he sprinted back to the farmhouse that action may be regarded as suspicious, and if this was indeed a threat, he had to assume that the man may not be alone.

What's more, Lefty knew that there were several groups of quislings active in the greater Trondheim municipality, and he could not afford to attract their attention. He had been warned about the armed gangs who conspired with the Gestapo, and that they were to be feared, more than any of the other threats. Still considering fleeing, Lefty watched as the figure beckoned him, back towards the treeline. Looking over his shoulder for help, he remembered that Tojo the husky had accompanied Walter on his Saturday trip to town. He had little option but to comply. Without the dog, Lefty was acutely aware of his vulnerability. Despite his furtive gestures, the man appeared to be alone. If this was some sort of trap, it was either very elaborate and contrived, or just spontaneous and harmless. If push came to shove, Lefty was always prepared to defend himself, but the only weapon to hand was the wooden grass rake which he decided would be of little use. Propping the rake against a fence, Lefty cautiously approached the figure. As he got closer, Lefty thought he was a worker from a nearby farm. But no, this was a stranger. The man wore some sort of military tunic which had all rank and unit markings removed, leaving only ragged stitching visible. Besides, Lefty noticed that the man's scuffed boots had not seen polish for years. His overall appearance reminded Lefty of a tramp, but as he was about to find out, this was no vagrant. Cautiously approaching the treeline, Lefty was suddenly grabbed from behind and dragged bodily into the woodland, his arms pinned behind his back. Pushed roughly by unseen hands, Lefty was propped against the trunk of a spruce, his mind racing. This was not a German; the man before him wore the swarthy complexion and stocky physique of a local. Lefty sensed rather than saw movement behind him; he turned his head slowly as his nose rested inches from the stock of a Luger pistol, its muzzle levelled at his temple.

Taken to a derelict barn beyond the clearing, Lefty was questioned in broken English overnight and well into the next day. His captors said they would release him once convinced of his identity, on the condition that he would work for the anti-Nazi cause of the resistance. If he betrayed them, it was made clear to him that he would be hunted down and executed.

As the weeks passed, the long Norwegian days offered little in the way of concealment in broad daylight. Lefty knew that any prospects of escape and repatriation would have been shelved until darker evenings returned. With little option, he resigned himself to accept whatever tasks the resistance gave him. Back at the farm, Walter had been informed that Lefty was now working with the resistance. Walter's family knew that the airman was no longer their responsibility. Now that all evidence of Lefty had been destroyed, the farmer and his family could deny any connection with either the resistance or downed airmen.

However, it had been Walter's detailed description of Lefty's tattoo which finally released the farmer and his family from any further connection with, and knowledge of, the resistance. Once the airman's identity had been confirmed, the resistance group decided to arrange for Lefty's repatriation at the first opportunity. The resistance leaders knew the value of experienced aircrew to the Allied war effort. Still, any attempt at repatriation during the Nordic summer would be suicidal and could even put invaluable partisan intelligence sources at risk. In the meantime, Lefty was put to work, monitoring *Luftwaffe* activity at the nearby airfield, observing any construction work, and noting any significant operational deployments. Coordinated by SOE, the Special Operations Executive in London, resistance groups throughout occupied Europe and Scandinavia required the official sanction of SOE before any operation was approved. Like much of Whitehall, their wheels turned slowly and preparations were made long before any allied operations could be planned. SOE prided themselves on their intelligence-gathering which had become their speciality and without which they would be 'fighting in the dark'. They groomed agents in the field and recruited the best and most trustworthy resistance workers. The work was especially valued in remote areas and those which were difficult to assess by aerial reconnaissance. Of particular interest to the allies was the aerial defences in the Trondheim area, where all activities were closely monitored, including the airfield at Lade on the outskirts of the city. The runway at Lade had suffered damage during an attack by the RAF earlier in the year. Since then, repair work had been completed, and the runway had been temporarily paved with wooden planking. Although the allies regarded the attack on Lade as successful, damaging both airfield infrastructure and parked aircraft, it had been costly. The RAF suffered significant losses of both experienced aircrew and valuable aircraft, so any plans for hit and run raids were shelved unless there was an overriding need. Even then, permission was required directly from Whitehall, who would only sanction vital, intelligence-led operations.

Of more immediate concern, was the construction work at Vaernes air station located at Stjordals, 30 km north of Trondheim. Additional runways and the extension of the existing landing strip would make Vaernes the principal *Luftwaffe* airfield in the region. With its commanding position, the airfield would provide air superiority over the already much-militarised fjord and berths. There was further concern caused by the construction of another airfield adjacent to new submarine pens at Dora in Trondheimfjord.

Working from an improvised hide, a derelict wooden hut, about 1 km from the airfield at Vaernes, Lefty provided regular updates to SOE via resistance channels, while trying to remain undetected. Noting that construction work was nearing completion, Lefty concluded that the new runways and upgraded facilities at Vaernes could easily accommodate fighters, bombers, or heavy transport aircraft. Although absorbed in the task, the prospect of capture or evasion was never far from Lefty's mind, and he took care to keep his escape options open. While submitting surveillance reports, Lefty had crossed the path of the dentist known as Dr Rathke several times. Acting as handler for resistance agents, Rathke inhabited a shadowy world. He claimed wide-ranging contacts within occupied Norway, and access to many high-grade intelligence sources. As such, Rathke was deemed trustworthy by both SOE and *Abwehr* intelligence services alike. But Lefty found him shifty, noting that the dentist would avoid eye contact with anybody, a man with something to hide. However, Lefty was determined to grasp any opportunity for either escape or repatriation, acknowledging that he may have no choice but to trust Rathke, his contacts, and his secretive manner. Something about the dentist's clumsy, self-serving way was unsettling, as if he was hiding much darker secrets. Lefty felt distinctly uncomfortable in Rathke's presence, and resolved to keep all contact with the dentist to a minimum.

As youthful as he was, Lefty had learned discretion the hard way, he trusted his best hunches, a trait that had alerted him to danger, and served him well so far, and he did not trust Rathke. No, this man fostered doubts that burrowed much deeper, primal, and somehow malevolent. A face that Lefty would be unlikely to forget.

On clear nights, working only with a pair of field glasses, it was risky and monotonous work for Lefty. He could readily identify the different aircraft types which used the airfield at Vaernes, recalled from the recognition silhouettes, memorised during squadron basic training in the UK. So long as he could remain undetected during his periods of surveillance, he felt safe. So far, compiling and submitting reports to the resistance had become routine. Routine, that was, up until now. The current directive from SOE was relatively straightforward. It required agents to identify types and numbers of *Luftwaffe* aircraft at Vaernes. But the new directive went one step further, adding new challenges to intelligence gathering. The main focus of SOE efforts in central Norway was to accurately assess the enemy's disposition and strategy in the area. From now on the type and identity of individual aircraft would need to be recorded and, in particular, specific unit or squadron markings. To comply with the new requirement, Lefty would have to get much closer to the airfield if he was to accurately identify every aircraft, its paint scheme and configuration. He knew that the resistance cell had been promised a set of Barr and Stroud binoculars which would have been ideal for the new task, but for the moment Lefty would have to manage with what he had. He used field glasses intended only for pre-war civilian use, and even with quality Zeiss optics, they were inadequate in lowlight conditions.

Even after midnight with the curfew enforced, he had to get closer to the airfield boundary... much closer.

As the first phase of runway construction was nearing completion, aircraft activity at Vaernes gradually increased. The second phase of runway construction was already underway, part of which would be extended on pilings out into the fjord. When complete, Lefty estimated that it would increase the useful landing and take-off distance by almost 25%. Concluding his weekly summary to SOE, he noted that the upgrade could potentially accommodate all aircraft types in the current *Luftwaffe* inventory.

Construction work at the airfield usually ceased around 7 or 8 pm, after which the hangars and dispersal areas were illuminated only by sparse pools of security lighting. But at the first sign of an air raid, the entire airfield would be blacked out. Although the darkness offered a degree of concealment, Lefty knew that security patrols with dogs were a major threat when working close to the airfield perimeter.

He frequently heard barking and was aware that sentries were posted at the main entrance and exit points, and armed vehicles regularly patrolled airfield taxiways. He reported that his observations were often interrupted by airfield perimeter guards forcing him to hide. But in true Aryan tradition, most foot patrols took place at frequent intervals, especially during the hours of darkness. In an earlier report to SOE, Lefty confirmed that while the airfield security did use guard dogs, resistance sources suggested the airfield was not allocated the same security status as other military units in the region, despite its strategic significance. One report from within the airport garrison maintained that the resident *Luftwaffe* units were not a high priority when it came to guard dog selection. The airfield guard commanders were often left to choose from what remained after the *Kriegsmarine* and Gestapo had taken the most prized and best trained pure-bred German shepherds. Consequently, they were often left with less suitable male crossbreeds, once described as a quarrelsome pack of mongrels. The report added that many of the dogs were incapable of locating their own *bälle* to lick in broad daylight, let alone find a stranger after dark. In conclusion, the report stated that if let off the leash, many of the dogs would be more of a danger to their handlers than any would-be intruder.

Although the hounds' bark may be worse than their bite, Lefty was not prepared to put that to the test. He had watched them at a safe distance on one occasion, snarling and straining on chain leashes. He knew to avoid them at all costs and became accustomed to remaining downwind of them during his night-time excursions. The limitation restricted Lefty's activities, but whenever the wind was favourable, Lefty used an improvised hide. A derelict wooden shed that overlooked the airfield perimeter offered a good overall view of the airfield while remaining concealed. The neglected plot had been used as a strawberry field, but this year's crop would have been sold at Trondheim market weeks earlier, so he was unlikely to be disturbed. Although the location was very close to the airfield dispersal, in late summer the plot became overgrown with weeds and briars, providing additional cover for Lefty. So long as he could remain concealed and silent, he felt safe; but each night, he would need to break cover and return to the safe house before dawn. Lefty's weekly intelligence summaries became indispensable and included assessments of airfield defences, aircraft movements, and troop transports. His contribution to SOE intelligence in the region assisted the allies, who were drafting a battle plan for central Norway. Following heavy losses on previous air attacks, the allies would only resume raids on the deep-water moorings used by the Tirpitz and other capital ships if losses could be kept to an 'acceptable level'. Other priority targets were the U-boat pens just outside Trondheim. Lefty's report warned that the reinforced concrete structures may be operational in two to three months if construction work was left uninterrupted.

Chapter 10

PRISON

The incident occurred in mid-August 1942. After a frustrating night of surveillance with no significant activity to report, he was returning to the safe house in the early hours when Lefty's luck finally ran out.

Having successfully evaded detection during his intelligence-gathering excursions, so far, so good. But he was unaware of the trap which had been laid for him. A quisling had informed the authorities in Trondheim of suspicious activities at the safe house, and whether true or not mattered little to the Nazis. The *Abwehr* thoroughly searched the safe house, but finding little they ransacked the place while waiting for the occupier to return. Lefty's suspicions were aroused as he observed the safe house while crouched in the treeline, his vision sharp and accustomed to the twilight. There appeared to be a vehicle partly concealed behind the barn, adjacent to the farmhouse. Certain that he had seen movement or shadow at an upstairs window, Lefty remained unobserved, while he hid the field glasses in nearby shrubbery. Creeping stealthily around the side of the house, he was suddenly grasped from behind by strong arms. As rough hands frisked him for weapons, a green-grey staff car pulled up abruptly, while two *Abwehr* officers manhandled him into the rear seat. Driven at speed through the first light of dawn, he recognised the sleepy village of Ekne, not far from Walter and the farm. Lefty was seized by a sudden dread – what if he was being taken there and Walter and his family had been captured? Even worse, would the farmer's family blame Lefty for betraying them?

To his relief, they passed the junction which led to Hocklingen and the farm, but a new fear seized Lefty as the car forked left and jolted down a narrow unlit lane. Devoid of any signposts, the track led deep into pine-clad woodland. Without warning, the vehicle pulled up on the front drive of an imposing building. Rectangular in layout with a central clock tower above the main entrance, the entire place looked deserted. The faded brickwork facade gave it the appearance of a dilapidated apartment block or a rundown college campus. Seized by unseen arms, Lefty was snatched from the vehicle as he instinctively looked up and grabbed what he thought might be his last view of the outside world. There was no evidence of any habitation besides the sounds of distant voices echoing from within the hallway, and sinister shadows cast across a floodlit forecourt and perimeter fence.

Jostled through the wood-panelled doors at the main entrance, Lefty was struck by a sense of foreboding, an unmistakable air of desperation that permeated the entire building. Falstad school was in desperate need of refurbishment. Requisitioned by the Nazis, it now served as an interrogation and detention centre.

The reform school and dormitory was chosen for its seclusion and was considered the ideal location for the custody and processing of the growing numbers of political prisoners in the Trondheim area.

Thrown into an empty cell, Lefty was held for questioning by the SS, and he had time to consider his predicament as his eyes adjusted to the confines of the damp, dark, echo chamber of his cell. When conducting surveillance at the airfield, Lefty had covered his tracks carefully, especially during prolonged periods of absence from the safe house. He knew that if he left the slightest clue of his presence, the outcome would mean the difference between life and death. By now, the Nazis would have scoured every room in the safe house searching for incriminating evidence before they razed the building to the ground.

Subjected to prolonged periods of interrogation, Lefty reluctantly revealed his true identity, but divulged only name, rank, and number. Left in solitary confinement, he resigned himself to his fate, knowing full well that those accused of espionage would be executed. Many before him had suffered the same fate, agonising periods of freezing confinement, followed by prolonged bouts of torture. Despite the dim prospect of survival, Lefty resolved to reveal nothing of use to his captors for as long as he could.

It was not until the last week of August that Lefty's capture came to the attention of Rathke. The dentist had concocted a plan, but in order for it to succeed, he needed the cooperation of a scapegoat. If approved by the SS, Rathke's plan was to foil SOE operations while subverting resistance activities in Central Norway. Unaware of the double agent's treachery, Lefty was destined to become the bait in Rathke's elaborate trap. Meanwhile, with ready access to so many subjects, the dentist had been experimenting with novel methods of interrogation in a disused classroom along the corridor from Lefty's prison cell, from where Lefty could hear the anguish of fellow prisoners. He knew little Norwegian, but Lefty certainly recognised the repeated cries of "*Nie*". He guessed that the desperate plea of "*Mamma*" would have universal recognition whether whispered or screamed. After a while, Lefty found it impossible to distinguish between man, woman or child. Each voice declaring its own level of despair, each sharing the same fate, their very own personal purgatory. The anticipation of torture itself was horror enough, the dread, the desperation, then the reality of agony. A world of despair—the final numbing silence of resignation and submission. Death would do, anything to hasten the end, *anything* that would offer release from the inquisition and the living nightmare.

He listened as different individuals tolerated different levels of pain. Some would give in easily, within an hour or less; others lasted for days, praying aloud, screaming at their gods for salvation or death, or begging mercy from their captors— innocents with nothing to offer, no secrets to reveal, just victims. Lefty was left to wonder how long he would survive when subjected to the same treatment. How long before he would cry out for his mamma; too far away, she would never hear her stepson in his hour of need. But, perhaps she never would have, wherever she was and whoever she was now.

However, the dentist had his own agenda, an ambitious plan, one which may allow Lefty a stay of execution, a reprieve. But in the long run, Lefty would only be permitted to survive as long as he remained of use. He was to be assigned to a party of gravediggers where, resourceful as ever, he would be allowed to concoct his own escape plan.

The SS was aware of the Shetland Bus operation – the SOE organised a number of fishing boats operating between the Shetland Isles and Norwegian coastal fjords in support of resistance activities. Rathke had convinced the SS of his plan to allow the airman's escape without raising suspicions on either side. The whole plot to subvert the Shetland Bus hinged on the understanding that the SOE and resistance would be convinced of the need for Lefty's repatriation and his bid for freedom was genuine. If there was even the slightest hint of German involvement or the participation of a double agent, the entire plan would collapse.

Apart from dissenters and resistance members, the prison at Falstad played its own part in the Nazi programme of ethnic cleansing – '*Das Ungezieferder*' or vermin were to be eradicated from every corner of occupied Scandinavia and beyond. They kept meticulous records; Slavs, Magyars, Romanies, Zionists, all were being wiped from the face of the earth in preparation for the thousand-year Reich, and Norway was no exception. Not names, just numbers; not people, just statistics; no memorials, only ditches; not humanity, just scum.

So far as the German high command was concerned, who would notice or even care if one or two more '*Untermenschen*' joined the mounting toll of those who would have no place in the new order. If left unchecked, the vermin would pollute the populace of the new Aryan utopia. In fact, the SS at Falstad prison decreed that any gravedigger who had outlived their usefulness would be destined to fashion their own tomb in the nearby woodland.

However, negotiations between the dentist and the resistance had been fraught with uncertainty. If Lefty did manage to escape, where would he go? The obvious refuge would be to return to the farm at Hoklingen. But would he be able to find his way there, and if so, would Walter be prepared to take the risk of concealing him again; and what of the risk of reprisals?

The nearby forest at Falstadskogen had become an execution and burial site, as the regime in Trondheim murdered their victims, the accused and the blameless – guilt or innocence was irrelevant to them, body count the only measure of effectiveness.

The tranquillity of the forest would be shattered by the echo of gunfire. A cloud of starlings disturbed by the clamour, would rise briefly, and settle again in a nearby roost. Lefty came to know these days as his outdoor days. Grateful for the respite from the airless confines of his cell at Falstad, Lefty could savour the aroma of the pines. He inhaled deeply as he remembered the fragrant Douglas Firs in the woodlands of his boyhood in Québec. After digging was complete, it would start. Today it was a single truckload with only six or eight, it was difficult to count them owing to the terrible contortions of the cadavers. The previous day there had been more; quislings, Nazi collaborators and their gangs had obviously been busy.

Lefty and another prisoner carried the dead, their bodies unceremoniously dumped into the pit. Some buried alive would have been better off dead, others led their children by the hand; all knew that their fate was sealed. The unmistakable sound of a Luger pistol and its punctuated reports would fill the tranquil woodland, and the inevitable carnage would begin.

Once used for cultivation, the killing field formed a stark rectangular clearing in the pine forest which doubled as a makeshift cemetery. More a Nazi refuse tip for their grisly by-products, the freshly turned earth marked the last resting place for the mortal remains of their victims. Those whose only crime was being in the wrong place at the wrong time, others, whose beliefs were not shared by the new order, some although innocent, were labelled as guilty. There were times when Lefty wondered if any would be spared before this evil regime finally ended. Loving families shared these hastily dug trenches, the young, the old, and the infirm, distinguished professors alongside street worn tramps. Each shared the same fate.

Today an early evening drizzle added its own tears of pity to the carnage, turning earth and blood into cloying mud. Lefty and the other gravedigger had completed another day's work, covering any evidence of the misdeed. Hidden from sight maybe, but the crime would be etched deep in the perpetrators' dark hearts forever. Other than the guards, the gravediggers would be the only ones to return from the clearing alive, reprieved for another day. Each knew that all too soon it would be their turn, into the pit, dead or alive. Lefty surreptitiously observed the guards; they were not the mindless thugs who usually accompanied the party.

What's more, they shared only one rifle between two on this particular day. Although each would have sidearms, Lefty knew that withdrawing a pistol from its holster beneath a bulky standard-issue woollen greatcoat would take about 10 seconds for an alert sentry. Even allowing two more seconds to cock the pistol, take aim and fire the first round, a total of 12 priceless seconds.

Lefty knew that he could run at 8 mph, which would take him 13 seconds to cover 50 yards, more than halfway to the tree line and the sanctuary of the dense woodland beyond. Although he knew that he would still be in range for a Luger pistol shot, Lefty had watched the guards earlier as they smoked. The rifleman, in particular, appeared lethargic and overweight, uneasy in his heavy woollen greatcoat. Carefully considering his options, Lefty knew that he would present an easy target for an alert guard armed with the Mauser rifle, but that was a risk Lefty had to take. He prepared himself to actively look for an opportunity, a distraction before he would attempt the sprint across open ground towards the beckoning woodland. With the weapon slung carelessly over his left shoulder, the rifleman did not possess the awareness of a marksman. No, this man bore all the hallmarks of a foot soldier, and what's more, one who had spent too long on guard duty. Lefty reckoned that he could make the dash of around 100 yards to the tree line in the time it took for the rifleman to act, ready the rifle, and chamber a round. That would take, at best, five seconds. Releasing the safety catch, taking aim, and firing the first shot would take another four or five seconds. The sanctuary of the spruce woodland beckoned, Lefty would have a chance of escape, a slim chance but a chance, nevertheless. Assumptions are well and good and maybe the risk was too great, but aware that he was only a mile or so from Walter's farm at Hoklingen, and the possibility of refuge, Lefty had nothing to lose.

He watched the guards carefully as they conversed in German; they appeared to be arguing. On the far side of the freshly dug earth, the guard with the rifle was summoned to the rear of the vehicle, as the truck appeared to have a flat tyre. Inexplicably, the guard removed the rifle by the sling and placed the Mauser inside the cab of the truck. The rifleman moved to the rear of the truck, looking under the vehicle from the rear. While one guard struggled to find the wheel jack, the other released the spare wheel from the truck's underside, leaving the gravediggers unsupervised. An adrenaline surge shot through Lefty – he knew that it was now or never. Summoning up all his courage, Lefty flung down his shovel and ran for all he was worth. In the fading light, a voice cried out behind him in German, ordering him to halt, only 300 feet from the tree line. In a clumsy attempt to grasp the rifle from the truck's cabin, the startled guard threw aside his Luger pistol and grabbed the rifle. But by this time Lefty was just 200 feet from the cover of the woodland. Crouching on one knee, the guard fired a well-aimed rifle shot which seared a burning path past Lefty's ear. Loading another round into the chamber of the Mauser, the guard closed the range, stumbling forwards towards the tree line through the mud and freshly dug earth. By the time the guard fired a second round, Lefty was plunging headlong into the woodland, and the shot shattered the bark of a spruce, showering splinters over Lefty's head which scattered in his hair as he ran.

Chapter 11

FUGITIVE

The border crossing between Norway and Sweden was the most obvious and most direct route for those attempting to escape Nazi-occupied central Norway. However, since the recent attacks on the Tirpitz, German patrols had been reinforced with extra checkpoints manned by armed guards on the main road 14. Now all traffic travelling in and out of central Norway was being stopped and identities checked.

Although the pine forests of the Nord Trondelag region offered a permanent evergreen canopy for would-be fugitives, the Germans imposed a strict curfew in areas of known resistance activity. Adjacent to the secure berth for the Tirpitz in Trondheimfjord, frequent armed foot patrols with dogs controlled all access to the fjord, and the adjoining coastline. All travel was strictly monitored, especially access to and from the Swedish border. Since the Nazi occupation of Norway, many had attempted to flee to the neutrality of the neighbouring country. Most had been shot or captured in the attempt. The fate of each individual was uncertain – some faced execution, many others swelled the ever-increasing ranks of the 'missing, presumed dead'. Other partisans had taken their own lives rather than face the prospect of incarceration and a lingering death at the hands of their brutal captors. A similar fate had befallen many innocent civilians throughout occupied Europe, exposed and helpless in the face of Nazi domination. Powerful deterrents, not only to fugitives, but also those who offered them help or sanctuary. Reports had been received of some local resistance fighters who had successfully used the shortcut from Trondheim across the Swedish border to Åre. But that option would be far too hazardous for Lefty's escape.

There was, however, an alternative.

The Shetland bus, a clandestine unit, operated a fleet of small Norwegian fishing vessels and their crews. They braved the North Sea from Scotland to the numerous inlets and islands along the western coastline of Norway. Each crew required an exceptional level of local knowledge, expertise, and courage in no small measure. Known as the 'The Bus' to the resistance, the intelligence-led operation had successfully infiltrated and evacuated agents, supplied weapons and equipment to encourage organised resistance and incite subversion. Repatriating Lefty would be problematic, and even if he was approved by London, each mission was fraught with uncertainty and risk. The local resistance network in Trondheim would arrange to contact the UK, requesting permission for Lefty's repatriation utilising the so-called 'bus route'. In recent months, the Germans had become aware of clandestine activities around the Norwegian coastline. But, as always, the primary commitment of the *Kriegsmarine* was defending the Tirpitz and other capital ships at anchor. The main threats were allied submarine activity and air attacks, each of which had been attempted in the past. So any plans to use valuable resources searching the entire Norwegian herring fleet for a floating needle in a haystack of ocean was seen as futile.

Any change to existing *Kriegsmarine* standing orders would not be received well by local commanders and would require direct authority from Berlin.

However, German high command orders were under review. New priorities and rules of engagement had been received by the *Kriegsmarine*. They would be tasked to undertake joint operations with the *Luftwaffe*, in order to crush Shetland bus activities in the area.

With this in mind, the Nazis reinforced their units in the area with additional armed fast coastal patrol boats, shore batteries, and spotter aircraft. The constant threat of the Nazi war machine in Trondheimfjord and the local area represented a formidable challenge to any allied activities, covert or otherwise. However, the Shetland bus crews also faced the notoriously unpredictable North Sea weather, adding further risk to each hazardous operation. More than one otherwise successful mission had fallen victim to the storms and extreme sea states prevalent in the area.

Chapter 12

JUDAS

An appointment with the dentist.

Late in the summer of 1942, during one of his weekly trips to Trondheim, Walter visited his friend Dr Rathke, who ran a dental practice in an apartment adjacent to the Sandgata in central Trondheim. Rathke befriended Walter, on the face of it, an innocent enough relationship, but as a farmer, Walter enjoyed a wide circle of friends locally, and unwittingly became a source of interest, an intelligence asset to the dentist. They met most Saturdays when Rathke bought Walter's produce in the local market.

The son of a Polish immigrant, the man who now called himself Dr Rathke had been educated in the UK in the name of Faber. He was tutored in both English and Polish by his mother. After arranging a scholarship for her son at Birmingham University, she emigrated to South Africa.

Impulsive and independent, Faber enrolled as a dental student where his progress was described as 'uninspiring' by his tutor. A fellow student observed that Faber was a loner who seemed to be attracted to dentistry by the opportunity to exploit the vulnerable. He enjoyed inflicting fear and pain rather than a chance to treat and heal. He apparently enjoyed subduing his fellow students, demonstrating that many patients secretly enjoyed fear, making them easy targets for manipulation. He also appeared to enjoy close physical contact with patients of either sex, where he could use fear or favour to influence and control. He described his victims as sheep, weak-minded masochists ripe for extortion. A perceptive tutor had remarked that Faber demonstrated 'Jekyll & Hyde' tendencies bordering on breaches of patient trust, especially when it came to practical exercises in clinical care. Rather than a worthwhile and fulfilling career, Faber seemed to regard the profession as some sort of self-indulgence. More worryingly, he appeared to derive some level of personal gratification when dealing with patients, showing little or no regard for either best practice or empathy. Faber soon became restless and frustrated by the 'endless demands of bookwork', especially when it came to the level of study required in finals year. It was clear now that Faber's prospect of successfully graduating was slim, having demonstrated little application to his studies. By mutual agreement with his tutor, he withdrew from university and was advised to 'choose a less demanding career path, one that better suited his temperament and inclination'.

Undeterred, Faber applied to the British Dental Association to register as an unqualified practitioner. He was provisionally accepted, but when BDA checked his student records with Birmingham University, he was deemed an 'unsuitable candidate' and his application was rejected.

Throughout his boyhood, Faber nurtured a misplaced loyalty to his mother's homeland and he decided to see it for himself. With no formal dental qualifications, Faber obtained a forged diploma and applied to join a dental partnership with a practice in Danzig. Dr Rathke, the elderly owner of the surgery, lived alone. He was approaching retirement age and was committed to finding a younger partner to take on the practice, allowing him, Rathke, to sell the business and retire on the proceeds. After initially accepting Faber as a junior partner, Rathke began to have doubts about his new understudy. Responding to patient enquiries, Faber had claimed to be Rathke's cousin and furthermore asserted his entitlement to a fair share of the practice income and assets. Aware of Faber's poor performance, and ambitions, Rathke became suspicious and questioned Faber closely about his employment history and qualifications. After discovering a letter addressed to Dr Rathke from the British Dental Association, Faber realised that his practice partner had been checking on his qualifications. Something had to be done. Faber could not afford to be exposed as a charlatan, so he needed to act swiftly. He had already planned to betray his partner and appropriate the practice for himself, but now that Rathke had forced his hand, the deed must be done sooner rather than later.

With time running out, and the deteriorating situation in Poland following German occupation, Faber decided to take matters into his own hands. He concocted false allegations, accusing Rathke of voicing Zionist, anti-Nazi opinions. Rathke denied the allegations, while Faber used extortion and threat to acquire a greater share of the business. The man who had spent a lifetime creating a respectable dental practice, Rathke, was arrested and interrogated by the Gestapo. Still insisting his innocence, the hard-working and blameless widower was deported to Stutthof internment camp, never to be heard of again.

It was time for the second part of his plan. Using falsified documentation, Faber employed his practice partner's identity, now calling *himself* Dr Rathke. He had managed to acquire the dental practice, his partner's passport, and identity, and his full set of dental instruments and equipment. Unable to sell the business on, Faber locked the surgery in Danzig and let the remaining apartments to rent. Pocketing the proceeds, he moved to Norway and opened his own practice in Trondheim under the assumed identity of Dr Rathke.

Eager to promote himself as a respected member of the local community, the dentist applied to become a member of the prestigious Trondheimfjord yacht club with its clubhouse next to his surgery by the quayside. If accepted, members enjoyed access to sailing ketches in the marina and throughout the fjord. But since the occupation, with the arrival of Tirpitz and other capital ships, martial law was declared along with a strict curfew. All private moorings in the dockyard and adjacent fjord were commandeered by the *Kriegsmarine*, who imposed severe restrictions, limiting civilian access. Employing forced labour for the construction of U-boat pens on the fjord, Trondheim was rapidly becoming one of the most militarised ports in northern Europe. With his multilingual skills and local contacts, Rathke was recruited as a British agent and was employed as an intermediary between SOE and the Norwegian resistance. As a British agent, Rathke obtained intelligence by working in close cooperation with German authorities and claimed to collaborate as part of his deep cover. However, the dentist was being drawn closer and closer to the Nazi cause. Despite the obvious risks, the dentist still had access to both SOE operations and Nazi ambitions in and around Trondheimfjord.

Armed guards controlled all access to the waterfront, and civilian activity was restricted to the local herring fleet. Fishing skippers had been issued with individual permits for crew members, and their craft used the quays under the strict scrutiny of the *Kriegsmarine*. Waterborne patrols regularly checked harbour permits and would enforce curfews, effectively closing off the fjord with little or no notice. However, the fleet of smacks provided a ready food supply for the locals although they only benefited from what remained of the catch after the Nazis had taken their quota.

Avoiding suspicion, Rathke had managed to hide his duplicity from his entire network of contacts, and particularly his friend Walter. During a routine dental inspection, Walter managed to ask the dentist whether he still had access to his boat, or if he knew of any other means of escape. In response, the dentist confided in Walter that he had heard of small fishing vessels that crossed the North Sea in support of Norwegian resistance workers, and promised to find out more.

Henry Rinnan and The Kiss of Judas

Working in his surgery behind closed doors allowed Rathke privacy and the invaluable opportunity to converse without being overheard. The dentist took on the role of intelligence clearinghouse for local resistance groups, while claiming that he was frightened of betrayal and feared that the telephone line in his surgery was being monitored. Rathke admitted to the resistance leaders that he was now obliged to treat German patients, stating that discouraging them or attempting to deny treatment to the occupying forces would raise suspicions.

Trondheim was rapidly becoming an extremely dangerous place. Uncertain who to trust, its citizens were being drawn into a twilight world of quislings, informants, and organised pro-German gangs. One notorious local pro-Nazi group was organised by Henry Rinnan, a local man turned collaborator. Known as *Sonderabteilung Lola*, Rinnan and his gang operated with impunity, ruthlessly crushing any opposition to Nazi occupation, with resistance sympathisers singled out for special attention. *The Rinnanbanden*, as they were known, would dupe innocent locals into expressing anti-Nazi opinions, then abduct the victims including women and children, who were imprisoned and tortured into betraying others, including those who had no connections with the resistance.

In the dark and fearful world of Nazi-dominated Trondheim, the new Judas could assume many guises. That 'dependable' uncle, the angry neighbour, the disgruntled heir, the jealous mistress, and even the trusted dental practitioner and family friend.

Locally, old scores were settled, and new, malignant alliances were forged. The once-proud Nordic municipality had become a vortex of fear, a focal point for paranoia and treachery, opposite sides of the same ugly and bloodstained coin.

Chapter 13

DECEIT

The dentist told Walter that he had been approached before about arranging escapes but said that he was reluctant to get involved following a spate of local purges. He finally agreed, saying that he would make an exception for his friend and offered to get details of a fellow yachtsman who may be willing to help.

Accepting the offer, Walter was asked to return for a follow-up appointment later in the month. If all went according to plan, Lefty was to have a clandestine rendezvous with a local partisan and traitor using the code name 'King', another of Rathke's henchmen.

Resistance leaders were aware of the risks, so Walter and Lefty were warned not to jeopardise the escape plan, or compromise Norwegian nationals in any way. If they did, those implicated would deny any involvement, and Lefty would be on his own.

In fact, the dentist, known to the resistance as Rathke and to UK SOE as Osprey, had been turned, and now had a foot in both camps. He was about to serve two masters as he took his first steps on the path to greater treachery.

Early in 1942, Rathke came to the attention of the intelligence arm of the *Waffen SS*. In the early hours, he was woken by an insistent pounding on the door of his apartment next to his practice in Trondheim. In his second year as an Allied agent, Rathke thought he had become accustomed to the possibility of compromise or betrayal. He had rehearsed his response to any inquisitor time and again, and thought he had prepared himself well. But suddenly roused from his slumbers, an ice-cold spasm galvanised his entire frame. He had memorised his credible cover stories which he knew he could relate if accusers came calling. Deep in his core at this early hour, the dentist felt the dread of a child woken by a nightmare, as a deep fear welled up from some dark corner of his being.

On a previous occasion, the Gestapo had questioned him regarding his dealings with the SOE and Milorg, the partisan organisation which coordinated Norwegian resistance activity. On that occasion, he knew that he had convinced them that his connections within the resistance community had provided invaluable intelligence for the Nazis. An avid follower of Sun Tzu, Rathke knew that in the world of espionage the inscrutable teachings of 500 BC held true to this very day. He had learned to keep his friends close and his enemies closer. In the murky world of the double agent, the ability to distinguish between friend and foe meant the difference between life and death.

However, this time it was different. In a personal testimony, a female Gestapo agent claimed to have evidence regarding the dentist's abuse of controlled drugs, including nitrous oxide. He was confined to a cell and interrogated by some of Rinnan's thugs. Under duress, Rathke eventually admitted to his addiction to hard liquor, but denied allegations of helping himself to various drugs from the dispensary in his own practice.

In fact, the dentist had consumed cocktails of various controlled drugs and alcohol since German occupation had restricted access to his usual pharmaceutical suppliers. In desperation, he had turned to the only available alternative, the Scandinavian illicit markets notorious for their high prices and low quality. He admitted to himself that he had used excessive doses of nitrous oxide gas on some of his female patients for his own gratification.

Hiding his secrets, Rathke managed to convince his captors of his Nazi allegiances, but as further proof of his loyalties, he was forced to become an active member of their evil fraternity. Harbouring some misgivings, he complied and quickly became part of their activities. Taking comfort from his drug dependency and perverse activities, Rathke became accustomed to the gang's brutalities, finally becoming a willing accomplice. Encouraged by the more deviant members of Rinnen's gang, he began to employ a hypodermic syringe around a victim's eyes and other sensitive parts of the anatomy. Experimenting with new methods of interrogation, Rathke began to administer increasing doses of controlled drugs to his victims, recording each individual's reaction and tolerances. He impressed some of the senior gang members after demonstrating that he could prolong a victim's suffering, thus weakening their resolve. Morally bankrupt, Rathke barely recognised the bloated features and haunted expression that stared back at him from the shaving mirror each morning.

Treacherous and unprincipled, the dentist no longer recognised himself as the young undergraduate called Faber. As Rathke, he had become a hideous caricature of a monster who lurked in the shadows of his '*Zmierzch*' or twilight path of no return. Somehow the single syllable in Polish served to emphasise the dentist's level of depravity which he now regarded as normal.

Rathke dreaded the prospect of Allied victory, deemed impossible only a year ago, but things were changing rapidly. With America in the west and Russia in the east, both giants mobilised, the Nazi's biggest challenge was yet to unfold. Rathke knew that if defeated, the Nazis would become scapegoats, leaving sympathisers and collaborators exposed. It would be difficult to deny the testimony from dozens of victims and their witnesses, each with first-hand accounts of his atrocities. Such quantities of evidence would be impossible to hide from fervent Allied investigators, baying for blame, driven by the vengeful. The very conflict that had granted him his new and evil identity might well be his downfall. Rathke began to rationalise his behaviour, regarding his actions as acceptable 'necessary evils', including his treachery and appalling interrogation methods. Somewhere during that process, he had lost any vestiges of conscience or moral value that he may once have had.

As an impostor, Rathke knew that he could keep up the pretence and pass himself off as a responsible medical practitioner. But possessing the very last vestiges of morality, the dentist had little time to waste, pondering the civilised luxuries of conscience and scruple, that was for others, not those destined for Office in The New Order.

No, Rathke had bigger fish to fry. He was to set a trap using the British airman as bait. The dentist was to arrange for Lefty's 'escape', he would be aided by King, a quisling posing as an accomplice, King would deliver Lefty and the SOE agents to

a rendezvous with the Gestapo. With no consideration of the
risk to his friend Walter the farmer, Rathke decided that one
more betrayal would not matter, the means justified the end. As
usual, Rathke decided that his plan was a masterpiece, he would
ensure that it would be an outstanding success despite the cost;
what's more, the prospect of closing the Shetland bus operation
once and for all would be too tempting for the SS to ignore.
If they were convinced of the value of using a sprat to catch a
mackerel, the plan promised to be an outstanding success and
coup for the dentist. Previously the Gestapo had insisted that the
British cared little for the exfiltration of Norwegian nationals,
but he knew that they could be convinced of the value of using
the British pilot as bait. Acting on intelligence provided by the
Abwehr, the SS had been informed of an impending Shetland bus
mission. Although German intelligence agencies had succeeded
in deciphering encrypted SOE messages, the information
revealed only approximate dates and no coordinates of the
landing point. All the SS knew was of a planned operation for
the second week in September with a possible location in central
Norway. During the first few months of 1942, there had been
several attempts by the SS to put paid to SOE operations in the
area. But with new intelligence, the participation of a quisling,
and the unwitting Lefty, the SS considered that they finally had
an opportunity to capture SOE agents while gaining a priceless
treasure trove of Allied intelligence. This time, a Gestapo shore
patrol would intercept the Shetland bus, capturing agents and
those waiting in the landing party. Rathke knew that if he made
a strong enough case to the British, the pilot, Lefty, would be
considered important enough to risk extraction by the SOE.
Rathke persuaded the SS that once the trap was sprung, none

of the Allied agents would make the return journey to Shetland, and none would escape the inquisition which awaited them. None should expect mercy, no quarter would be asked for or given.

None would be spared.

For the trap to be successful, the plan would require the close cooperation of several different German units and departments, who traditionally worked independently. Each had been reluctant to share intelligence in the past. Inevitably, the plan would involve the *Kriegsmarine*, the *Luftwaffe*, the *Abwehr*, and quislings, let alone the participation of a double agent, all under the unblinking eye of the SS. Using intelligence obtained from official sources and information extracted by quislings, success hinged on the close liaison and cooperation of all those involved. However, each department was assigned different priorities and resources to the plan. Therefore, the task was often delegated to junior officers who had files full of potential threats, some more credible than others. Some overworked Nazi commanders claimed higher priorities than that of 'chasing fishing boats'. But the dentist was ambitious. He hoped to further his own ambitions, along with those of the Nazis when credited with the elimination of the Shetland bus operation. He would also claim another personal victory: exposing and crushing the largest and most active resistance movement in the area.

Although a last-minute decrypt revising details of the rendezvous was received by the *Abwehr*, it was too little and too late. Only partly decoded, the message revealed little specific information of use to the Nazis. The updated details, such as they were, suggested a new location and time for the operation. The ambiguous information was passed on to cascade down to the units involved. Each would require close cooperation to guarantee a successful outcome. So far, the strategy of *Blitzkrieg* had worked well for the German high command, but joint tactical ventures in occupied countries were problematic. When it came to high priority short-term operations, Nazi shortcomings were those which dogged many large organisations – namely bureaucracy, rivalry, and in-fighting.

On the Allied side, SOE was responding to urgent requests for weapons and the infiltration of Allied agents. The latest Shetland bus mission would be landing on a remote island in the archipelago to the north-east of Trondheimfjord. SOE had agreed to extract Lefty so long as he could meet the trawler at the given rendezvous point, well outside the mouth of the fjord and away from prying eyes. For the bus to escape with Lefty under cover of darkness, there was no room for error.

This Bus would not wait, and there was to be no relief service.

Lefty's extraction was low priority, very much a sideshow for the SOE. It was made clear to all that the primary mission would go ahead with or without him. The bus was on her way, passwords and identities confirmed, their purpose clear, the outcome uncertain.

The heedless and indifferent fog of war enveloped all its victims. Tonight, some would be accompanied by the star of fortune, some would not, and some would pay the ultimate price.

Chapter 14

ESCAPE

O n the previous day, Lefty had successfully escaped from the Falstadskogen killing ground and managed to elude capture in the forest, but it had been a close-run thing. Probing torch beams from armed patrols came perilously close as he hid, panting and motionless, with only bracken and pine needles as camouflage. In the confusion, Lefty had become disorientated attempting to find his way through the darkened maze of the Trondelag woodland. Skirting open meadows and keeping to the sparse tree line, although stealthy he felt extremely exposed. Expecting to be picked out by a sudden beam of torchlight, Lefty's heart pounded a drumbeat as he listened, alert for any activity. He crossed the curfew-darkened road near the village of Ronglan. Glancing at the night sky, he crouched by the roadside, drew breath, and took a moment to re-orientate himself. The gap in the evergreen canopy offered an unobstructed view of the heavens now that the rain had cleared. The seven stars of the great bear constellation appeared over his shoulder. Without either map or compass, glimpses of the heavens through the darkened branches were sufficient to allow Lefty to get his bearings. Keeping undercover, he traced woodland trails through the undergrowth of stinging briar tripwires and bracken covered ditches. Polaris behind him, he knew he was moving in a southerly direction. After what felt like hours, cold, hungry, and exhausted, he finally stumbled upon the farm.

The first Walter and family knew of Lefty's escape was when the farmer answered a persistent knocking at the rear door of the farmhouse. In the pale light of dawn, after weeks of absence, the family was alarmed at the sudden appearance of a dishevelled and haunted figure in the early hours, and Lefty was greeted with mixed emotions. Although Walter had been told of some arrangements to evacuate Lefty, the resistance knew little of the airman's whereabouts, only that he might seek refuge at the farm. Walter had been willing to help Lefty, but the farmer's wife had witnessed Rinnen's ruthless thugs in action and was only too aware of the fate of those accused of helping the resistance. She had become overly anxious and reluctant to expose the family to any further risk. Meanwhile, Rathke, who had contrived Lefty's prison break, now had to rely on the support of others. He had been advised of a last-minute report – the timing of the Shetland bus operation had been brought forward by one week at the request of SOE. In fact, unbeknown to Lefty, the boat was about to leave Shetland, heading for a rendezvous somewhere in central Norway.

Now Rathke had to hastily arrange a follow-up appointment for Walter, who duly returned for 'urgent treatment' the following day. This time the dentist secreted a folded slip of surgical paper behind the farmer's teeth. He warned Walter that in the event of capture or compromise, he was to swallow the piece of paper, emphasising that the dentist would deny any involvement. The farmer knew nothing of Rathke's loyalties, and despite the

82

obvious risks, he always assumed that he could trust the dentist. Arriving home, having kept the folded paper safely in his mouth, Walter passed it on to Lefty who had been waiting anxiously for the farmer's return.

Having spent the day concealed in a barn, Lefty was befriended by a feral cat with whom he shared both cat naps and meagre scraps from the farmer's kitchen. Walter gratefully released the damp rice paper from its hiding place and handed over to Lefty who scanned the hastily scribbled note; Lefty memorised its scant contents. In pencilled scrawl was the name 'King', the location of a bridge at nearby Hammervatnet, and a fishing ketch named 'Slyngel' or 'Rascal' moored near Vikhammer. With no detailed information regarding the hasty rendezvous, Lefty had few options, so he prepared himself for the coming hours and the prospect of freedom or death.

The bus crew were ready, the time had come, and it was now or never for Lefty. After dark, he would leave his hideaway and become the hunters' quarry once again.

The legendary Norse god Odin was reputed to dispatch the Valkyries to accompany warriors on their quests. As 'choosers of the slain' these battle maidens were said to protect those who acted with valour and virtue. But above all, they favoured the courage of the warrior. All too soon, there would be courage aplenty, but would the fates intercede with triumph or tragedy, Valhalla, or oblivion? Only time would tell.

Perhaps 'The Rascal' would live up to her name, and perhaps attempting escape was futile. But despite the risks, the cause of freedom could only be furthered by the courageous, those who were prepared to risk all, undaunted by the odds.

At the farm in Hoklingen, now that darkness finally returned, Lefty cautiously emerged from his hiding place in the barn and silently closed the gate at the rear of the paddock. He edged down across the fields towards the cover of the hedgerows which skirted the lake. Although grateful for the farmer's help, Lefty was aware that it was only a matter of time before search parties would check the farm again, and every moment he stayed in hiding subjected Walter and his family to additional risk. But any delay now was a waste of valuable time, Lefty knew how important it was to seize the opportunity and make the rendezvous with the Shetland bus. SOE would need to take full advantage of autumn and its lengthening hours of darkness to complete a successful mission while minimising risk. Lefty estimated that it would take four hours of footslog to reach Vikhammer, including the rendezvous with King, and time was not on his side.

He knew that it would take a while for the rod cells in his eyes to adjust, as he crept his way through the deep and bewildering cloak of the Norwegian autumnal night. Carefully placing each footfall, he moved at a stealthy pace, stooping low through the shrubbery. Skirting the northern bank of Lake Hoklingen, he became more aware of the landscape and its features, as his eyes adjusted to the deep vault of the Nordic night. The stars in their scintillating constellations gradually resolved themselves against the inky backdrop. Lefty recalled from the farmers' almanac that the waxing moon would not rise until the early hours of the following morning. The shortening September days would allow him to wear the mantle of night-time for only a few hours. With little time for preparation, the escape plan and rendezvous arrangements were unavoidably brief. Lefty had become accustomed to the detailed and disciplined planning of the military mind, and initially found himself questioning the hasty plan. However, with all its shortcomings and uncertainties, the plan offered Lefty his only hope of freedom, repatriation, and home. The one opportunity for escape was within his grasp, and the more he considered the plan, the more he found the prospect of freedom irresistible, an undeniable urge. He knew this may be his only chance. In an alien world, in the middle of an ugly war far from home, Lefty would see this through, whatever it took and whatever the outcome.

Senses taut as a bowstring, he surveyed the heavens for the celestial signposts which would guide him on his way. Startled by his movements, a small creature rustled in the undergrowth nearby, causing Lefty to freeze. Rooted to the spot and as still as a statue, he became aware of the profound serenity of the scene. Lefty had always felt at home in darkness and loved the night; it offered a solace and seclusion rarely found in the full light of day. Gazing skyward briefly, he felt the cool night breeze of the lake as it herded the last tenuous wisps of low scudding clouds onwards, ever onwards. Onwards, to the horizon, onwards towards freedom, towards liberty – towards home.

Brushing a damp cobweb from his face, Lefty shook his head to clear his mind of distractions. There may be time later for thoughts of home across the Atlantic, Mary across the North Sea, and the child he longed to see. Right now, nothing else mattered other than escape; every footfall carefully placed, one step in front of the other, one cautious stride at a time. Wary of undue haste, Lefty knew that so far his progress was too slow; he needed to quicken his pace if he was going to make the rendezvous. Skirting a small thicket, he became more and more uncomfortable about the idea of King. He felt uneasy about the vagueness of the meeting point and the woeful lack of information about his accomplice. Would he be expected to help King? If he was vital to the plan, surely King would be an asset rather than a hindrance. Nevertheless, Lefty began to entertain thoughts of going it alone, finding his own way to the mooring at Vikhammer. But maybe, just maybe, King had more information; some vital clue or password that Lefty was unaware of.

Polaris emerged as the sky cleared; the unmistakable blue-white beacon gleamed motionless over Lefty's right shoulder. The nocturnal watchman's compass, the lodestar of antiquity guided him now as he orientated himself moving steadily westward.

The deep stillness of the night was broken only by the occasional mournful call of an owl and his own deliberate and muted footfalls. Reflections danced in the ripples of the quicksilvered lake, the same lake that Lefty had chosen as an emergency landing field months earlier. A sanctuary which now played host to Lucky Georgie and held her in its deep embrace, embalmed for posterity.

Meeting the junction of the tributary at Fossingelva, Lefty crouched in the undergrowth by the small drainage sluice used to control outflow from the lake. His progress halted now by the sound of barking and faint voices in the middle distance. His breath condensed around him in small clouds as he listened for any sign of threat. Resuming his journey, he made slow progress and was extra vigilant. He followed the narrow sinews of the tributary, as it rushed over the pebble-strewn bed, which created just enough background noise to mask any that he might make. Ahead, he could just make out the main road as it snaked towards the narrow bridge just north of the small town of Åsen. Alarmed by the sound of approaching traffic, Lefty froze. Crouching close now, the bushes providing inadequate camouflage, beams from slotted headlights skimmed the hedgerow just above Lefty's head, as the vehicle rounded the bend travelling southward towards the bridge. Aware of the strict night-time curfew restrictions, Lefty assumed the worst, that this was a German patrol. Feeling exposed, he edged closer into the chilled water, wincing as he felt its icy grip around his ankles, clenching his calves, numbing his legs, and permeating his very soul. The small truck slowed as it crossed the bridge, brakes squealing as it drew to a halt no more than 50 yards from Lefty. In the cab, the solitary occupant appeared to be studying the terrain, as a small cloud of tobacco smoke issued through the driver's open window. Lefty could just make out an epaulette on his shoulder and *Wehrmacht* markings on the door of the truck. He fully expected an armed troop of soldiers to suddenly emerge, leaping over the tailgate, weapons at the ready. Instead, all that emerged from the cab was the muted barking of a dog, followed by what sounded like a loud curse in German to silence the animal. Feeling exposed in his ill-concealed hiding place, Lefty watched intently. He suppressed the impulse to run, getaway across the open fields, but he knew full well that if the dog didn't catch him, a well-aimed rifle shot might. The moments passed as Lefty's heartbeat resounded in his ears, counting off each agonising second. To his relief, a discarded cigarette stub was ejected from the cab. It made a cascade of red sparks as it impacted the paving and bounced over the kerb, while the truck accelerated away. Driver and dog continued their journey, oblivious of the encounter.

Chapter 15

KING

The incident served as a wake-up call. Lefty was unlikely to forget the taste of fear which had accompanied his intelligence gathering forays months earlier. He knew from the resistance that there was a shortage of trained dogs, not enough to accompany every German foot patrol. He had witnessed the animals at the *Luftwaffe* base first-hand. They were vicious beasts, several of which could only be restrained with vigorous use of choke chains. Lefty considered that they were certainly no less of a deterrent for being untrained.

Now bitterly cold, feet squelching softly within his boots, Lefty waited for long minutes after the red lights of the truck finally receded into the distance. The deep silence of the night returned, consuming him in its autumnal grip. Without a sound, he approached the narrow road bridge, crouching beneath it, grateful for its shelter. Lefty edged deeper in towards the gaping shadow of the concrete abutment, startling a pigeon which clattered noisily from its roost. Alarmed by the sudden disturbance, Lefty gathered his wits as he contemplated his rendezvous with 'King'. A deep shiver of fear chilled him as his mind raced with the consequences if the whole thing was yet another elaborate trap. Although there was no moonlight, to Lefty's relief, thin wisps of mist now served to deepen any shadows, offering some refuge for the hunted. The atmosphere beneath the bridge was fetid and dank, the smell of rust and the odour of desperation and decay seemed to seep into everything. Lefty waited impatiently, watching his breath condensing, and listening for any sign of movement along the riverbank to his left, but none came. Beneath the concrete abutment, even the smallest sound reverberated alarmingly from within the dark and cavernous echo chamber of the bridge. Every so often, Lefty offered the code word 'King' tentatively into the darkness, which only returned to him as an empty and desolate echo. After what seemed like an hour, resisting the temptation to return to the comfort of the log fire in the farmhouse, Lefty abandoned what little shelter the bridge offered, and resolved to continue his journey alone. He knew that on reaching the mouth of the tributary, keeping the fjord to his right, he would be travelling west. So long as he kept his bearings, he would reach the outskirts of the village of Adalasskogen. Beyond that lay the most perilous and exposed part of the journey to the small inlet east of Vikhammer.

Suddenly, he was alerted by the snap of a breaking twig. Crouching stock still against the backdrop of the hedgerow, Lefty froze, startled and vulnerable, acutely aware of every breath condensing around him in the gathering mist, betraying his presence. A bone-chilling fear gripped him, an involuntary shiver shook every nerve and sinew as a single drip of condensation ran down his face, an icy and unwelcome tear. Alert to every sound in the darkness, Lefty strained his eyes against the shadowed undergrowth which shrouded the far entrance below the bridge. Ahead of him, he sensed rather than saw crawling in the shadows, movements stealthy but nonetheless deliberate and human. The mist was condensing into shallow tendrils of fog which rolled in from the adjacent fjord, as the most malevolent game of hide and seek began. Neither pursuer nor pursued wishing to be ambushed here in this, the darkest and most forbidding trap.

Then the small and tentative word "George" was whispered, a single syllable carried along by, and almost lost in the sound of the river, a remote and indistinct murmur. Summoning up what remained of his courage, Lefty offered the agreed response "King". As he watched intently, a small portion of the deepest shadow at the far end of the bridge moved. At first hesitant, the wraith-like figure slowly emerged. Meeting for the first time, each cloaked in darkness, they conversed briefly in hushed voices; King warned Lefty to stay close. They agreed to continue to the next rendezvous with renewed resolve, King making insistent gestures urging Lefty to continue onwards towards the fjord.

Passing the dark mouth of the river on their right, Lefty could just discern the open fjord, its dark expanse blanketed in a shallow fog. Small lapping waves made liquid sounds, as a faint breeze carried the dense salt-laden air onshore, partly obscuring their path. Hugging the shoreline, they made slow progress with King dragging along behind. Lefty waited impatiently for him to catch up, both now moving in close to the bank of the fjord in the direction of Vikhammer and the 'Rascal'.

The lamps at the *Luftwaffe* base at Værnes were visible ahead, cutting a swathe of light into the gloom, directly across their intended route. On the horizon, searchlights attempted to pierce the fog, adding a surreal and disorientating glow to the stone-strewn shoreline. To their right on the north-eastern edges of the fjord, muted shafts of light scoured the floating booms which protected the approaches to the Tirpitz's mooring. King gestured, pointing at his watch; they both knew that only a few hours of precious darkness remained. In hushed tones, Lefty agreed that whatever the outcome, they were committed, there would be no turning back now. Cocooned in wreath-like swathes of much denser fog which shrouded the southern bank of the fjord, their progress was slow. Cautiously, they approached the extended perimeter track of the *Luftwaffe* base at Værnes. They planned to skirt the airfield and work their way stealthily between the approach lights and runway threshold.

In contrast to its normal noisy daytime operation, the airfield appeared quiet and deserted. The runway side lights were dimmed; each yellow ember formed a small halo in the opaque eddies of the white shroud. Edging past the airport perimeter, they kept low along the rocky beach beyond the runway threshold, wading slowly and carefully around the posts of the darkened runway approach lights. Even the small lapping sounds of their progress through the water seemed amplified in the all-encompassing stillness of the night. As they paused again and listened intently, each group of runway lights was progressively extinguished, and the deep darkness of the night returned once again. From his observations of the previous weeks, Lefty was very aware of the threat posed by the recent arrival of a *Luftwaffe* BF 109 fighter wing at Værnes. Whilst the aircraft were a constant threat in daylight, Lefty knew well that they were not yet equipped for night operations. He remembered his final intelligence report, which stated that many of the aircraft at Værnes were grounded awaiting modification before deployment further north.

Although the airfield would be closed for normal operations, there was a small active *Luftwaffe* unit on permanent standby dedicated to airfield defence and combat alert 24-hours a day. But with the prevailing weather conditions and reduced risk of air attack, they would probably be stood down. In recent weeks, night raids on Tirpitz had become less frequent, and tonight with their target obscured, any allied air raids would have to be postponed until the weather cleared.

As their eyes adjusted to the deeper darkness, the two resumed their trek westward towards Vikhammer. Irritated at their lack of progress, Lefty now urged King onwards. At that moment, King lost his footing and stumbled forward into the water, uttering a muffled curse as he fell. Helping King to regain his footing, Lefty lowered him to a sitting position behind a small rocky outcrop. As King struggled to regain his balance, they were both transfixed by the sound of barking dogs in the middle distance. They froze in their steps, crouching low, as the ferocious barking slowly subsided. Then the sky lit up above them and somewhere in the middle distance a siren wailed. All the airfield perimeter security lights were illuminated, accompanied by renewed bouts of barking, which sounded much closer now. Although fog would favour the fugitives and hinder search attempts, torch lights attempted to pierce the gloom as the dogs pursued their quarry. Instinctively, Lefty and King took flight, crouching, splashing and stumbling as they went. Still recovering from his fall, King was only able to move slowly now and was shivering, drenched from head to foot.

German voices urged the dogs onward, accompanied by incessant barking. In the haste and confusion, King stumbled and fell again. Lefty spun round to help him, only to recognise the impossibility of the situation. Playing on King's back, the torch beams were now just a few metres away, gasps of breath condensing around him in the dancing shafts of light. Whether prompted by desperation or instinct, Lefty fled headlong into the gloom and was swallowed by the night.

Chapter 16

A PLACE CALLED HELL

Lefty avoided the rock-strewn beach; taking greater care he moved silently, up to his calves in the freezing margins of the fjord. He knew that if he waded slowly and deliberately, the dogs would be less able to detect him in the fog. As a child in Canada, Lefty had grown up with working dogs and knew them well. He was aware that although most will react to any disturbance by barking, some breeds commonly used as guard dogs were often those least able to effectively follow a scent and were rarely trained to track. Enveloped now in the cloying saline air, Lefty strived to put more distance between himself and his pursuers. With every footfall he hoped that the humid air would disperse his scent, further hampering any efforts to track. He crept towards the bank carefully now, keeping low, seeking what little concealment the pine trees offered. Every sound muted in the gathering fog, the voices and barking were becoming more distant. On reaching the mouth of the river Stjordals to the south of the airfield, Lefty became aware of a towering silhouette looming above him. Squinting, he could just make out the concrete arch and parapet of the river bridge which carried the main coastal railway south towards Trondheim. His mind racing, Lefty knew that with King's capture, it would only be a matter of time before his fellow fugitive would be forced to reveal his own identity and that of his accomplice. Although Lefty and King had had little time to converse, the thought of abandoning King to the mercy of the enemy was alien to Lefty. He would allow himself the luxury of guilt later, but the incident served to provide a greater urgency to Lefty's escape, and the absolute necessity of making the rendezvous with the bus. With survival uppermost in his mind, no distractions, no going back, Lefty had to concentrate now, his only thoughts fixed on finding the Rascal.

The bridge was completely shrouded in fog, but with each step he made, he knew that he might easily stumble into a railway checkpoint, security patrol or sentry. Carefully clambering onto the slick surface of the concrete parapet, Lefty stayed low, aware of even the slightest sound. With heightened alertness, he felt extremely vulnerable and conspicuous as the cold and damp of the concrete sank further into his core. Finally, Lefty rounded the end of the bridge, creeping stealthily along the railway siding, his progress hidden by a screen of empty rolling stock and tanker trucks. To his relief, he could see no foot patrols or sentries posted on the western end of the bridge. It was with great relief that he let himself slide down the slippery concrete towards the shoreline again. In his haste, Lefty stumbled against a rusting enamel signpost which bore the single word 'Hell'; the bitter irony of the village name was not lost on Lefty. Brushing past low-lying shrubbery, he reached a small inlet and could just make out the silhouette of two small drifters moored to buoys, a few metres into a sheltered bay, partly concealed by a small birch copse. Lefty's eyes narrowed as he strained against the gloom of the chilling fjord. Squinting, he could just see a small group of dinghies, as he crouched low again, hiding and listening for signs of life. More in desperation than hope, Lefty waded into the freezing water as the first vestiges of dawn appeared above the mist. He approached the first boat; its wooden hull discoloured, and paintwork blistered, there was no evidence of a name on the transom. He ran his hand over the faded and flaking paintwork of the hull, now desperate for food and shelter. Lefty was running on empty, utilising what remained of his resolve. He moved on to the next dinghy, silent ripples from his wading spreading across the mirrored surface of the bay. Once more searching for the Norwegian name, he had remembered 'Rascal', but he struggled to recall the spelling in Norwegian, was it 'single' or 'slinger'? Shivering conspired to confuse his already numbed and fearful mind. Frustrated, he resolved to get out of the icy water, seek shelter and whatever warmth he could in amongst the pines and birches which lined the shore. Turning awkwardly, Lefty's knee knocked against a second dinghy, a tender which bobbed slowly on its painter, thudding gently against the woodwork of a fishing boat's hull. Then he saw it, barely visible in the half-light the name 'Slyngel' on the faded paintwork of the small trawler. He had found The Rascal! With great relief, Lefty hauled himself along the painter to the small fishing vessel. Finally boarding with considerable exertion, he collapsed onto the decking, exhausted.

Chapter 17

THE RASCAL

Recovering from the exertion, Lefty crawled across the planking towards the bow of the vessel where he found a square hatch in the decking, which he slid open, revealing a stowage compartment. With dawn about to break, he slithered into the narrow storage area where he covered himself with well-used fishing nets. Closing the hatch above him, he lapsed into a fitful and restless sleep, his nostrils filled with the smell of diesel oil and the sour and pungent reek of stale fish.

He was woken suddenly, roused by the sound of footfalls on the deck above. Feeling conspicuous, he pulled more netting over himself, burying his head completely under a foul-smelling tarpaulin. Lefty knew little Norwegian but listening intently to the insistent tone of the conversation, he found it calm and somehow reassuring. Still, he waited and listened; the voices were directly above him now. Then the hatch slid open, and in half-whispered broken English he heard, "Is the king here?"

Still, Lefty remained hidden expecting the worst, then:

"... if you can hear me, conceal yourself, and later tonight we will bring you to Hitra". Then, after pausing came the repeated enquiry:

"Is the king there?"

With all the courage that he could muster, Lefty offered a muffled Norwegian "Ja," followed by a "yes" for good measure.

He had decided that that the crew could not know that he wasn't King; then, as the hatch cover was closed, he started at the sound of an object falling onto the net close beside him as the footsteps retreated. Venturing his hand, he reached out in the darkened hold and grasped a small paper bag. To Lefty's delight, the bag contained a banquet consisting of three oatmeal biscuits and an apple.

Laying low, Lefty eagerly consumed the modest rations, and late into the afternoon sleep found him once again, and once again he willingly gave in to it.

Alarmed by footfalls on the deck above, Lefty was woken again. Having lost all track of time, cold and confused, he strained to hear Norwegian voices in the hushed tones of casual conversation. Having established Lefty's identity, the crew of two reminded him to remain below decks out of sight during the journey until they arrived at the fishing grounds off the island of Hitra. He was told to expect further instructions once they were underway. Lefty began to relax, expecting to hear the engine spring to life at any moment. He did hear an engine, but it was not the Rascal's pounding diesel.

He became aware of insistent German voices as they hailed The Rascal from the middle distance. Lefty froze as the pulsing reverberations of a motorboat echoed throughout the hull of the trawler. Engines stopped, the craft drew alongside accompanied by the scraping sounds of fenders being lowered. Then the sound of more footfalls on the deck above and new voices, questions; some in German others in stilted Norwegian. The boarders walked around the deck, conversing with the crew. Although he remained hidden, Lefty detected what sounded like a tone of enquiry rather than demand. Suddenly the hatchway above him was opened, and a torch beam probed the darkness below decks, moving across the netting and reaching deeper into the shadowy recesses of the hold. Lefty held his breath. Discouraged by the stench of stale fish, the search party re-closed the hatch as the conversation resumed in broken Norwegian. The motorboat engine started again, and the patrol boat moved off the fender, the reverberations slowly fading in the distance. Shortly after, the Rascal's engine roared into life and much to Lefty's relief, she slipped her moorings and was underway. As Lefty listened to the reassuring sound of water lapping against the wooden hull, a feeling of elation swept through him. He exhaled long and hard; his desperate bid for freedom now seemed within his grasp. Finally leaving the tyranny and brutality of Nazi occupation, he allowed himself brief thoughts of hearth and home. But Lefty knew that the next steps on the path to liberty would be fraught with risk. This was the second day, the day of the rendezvous at Hitra. In the darkness of the hold, Lefty knew the "Ifs" only too well. He reviewed each of them in anticipation of the perils ahead.

If they managed to make the rendezvous at Hitra, and *if* he could successfully board the bus, all well and good. But *If* King had been forced to reveal their plans following his capture, the Nazis may already be in pursuit. Even *If* they could avoid each of those hazards, almost 300 miles of North Sea lay between them and safe haven at Shetland.

PART 1

As the last vestiges of daylight finally faded, Lefty moved from his cramped and confined hiding place. Remaining below decks, Lefty stretched his limbs in the darkness as he listened to the comforting rhythm of the trawler's throbbing diesel engine. Pulling out into the channel passing Trondheim, the Rascal made slow but resolute progress through the darkness, her navigation lights reflecting in the stillness of the night-hushed waters of the fjord.

Turning south by the headland with Selva light to port, the Rascal bore out into deeper waters. In preparation for the night's fishing, the nets which had provided Lefty's hiding place were now needed on deck. Lefty started as the hatch cover slid back, and a tall, swarthy figure reached in and offered his hand, beckoning Lefty onto the deck. Emerging from the hold into the still night of the fjord, Lefty gratefully inhaled the cool salt-laden air.

He found himself alone on the decking, surrounded only by the deep darkness of the Nordic night. He was approached by a deckhand wearing a weather-beaten fisherman's smock, a woollen cap pulled low over his ears and a hood which partly disguised mahogany creased features. The crew was now busy preparing the nets for a night of fishing in the open sound. The reach would cover the deep productive herring grounds to the North and East of the island of Hitra. Once the nets were set, Lefty was taken to the small wheelhouse where he was given dry clothing and a welcome mug of hot cocoa. Warming his fingers, both hands clutched around the enamel mug, Lefty savoured his first sip of cocoa since leaving Scotland. He recalled crews and aircraft waiting in anticipation and the haunting remoteness of the concrete dispersal at Kinloss. In September, April felt equally remote, as did Mary, their child and even his last drink of cocoa from the NAAFI wagon.

Kinloss, York, Montréal. Each felt remote, half a world away both in space and time.

Crouched in the light of the single lamp, he was shown the rendezvous point indicated on a nautical chart with a gesture from a well-worn pencil. In broken English without preliminaries, the captain detailed the impending rendezvous. He revealed that the brush with the Germans on the mooring before departure, was not unusual. The skipper of The Rascal was well-known by the German patrol boat crew who were assured of a supply of fresh fish on their return the following morning.

With the recent arrival of another heavy cruiser and two destroyers on the moorings adjacent to Tirpitz, security in the area had been enhanced. Reinforced concrete revetments were still under construction in Trondheim Harbour, and a squadron of *Kriegsmarine* craft regularly patrolled the sound from Hasslevik, Trondheim, and beyond to Flattenfjiord. The armed patrol boats were fitted with powerful searchlights and presented a constant threat. Nightly excursions by small trawlers in the area were generally left alone; however, the threat remained and any vessel could be subjected to random inspection at any time. The captain of the Rascal was aware that German patrols were always on alert, searching for suspected agents or resistance workers in the area. Tracking towards the Hestvika light, the sky wore a high milky overcast, the improving visibility permitting better identification of lighted landmarks and channel marker buoys in the sound. The Rascal passed abeam the well-lit construction works at Brekstad, on the northern side of the fjord, floodlights glistening in the distance. The strategic installation included an airfield and a menacing triple barrelled shore battery which dominated the approaches to Trondheim fjord, shielding the moored Tirpitz.

Chapter 18

THE SHETLAND BUS

Rounding the small island of Sorleksa, concealed by its low, rugged silhouette, the Rascal was brought to slow ahead as the engine idled and the fishing nets were hauled aboard. To the north, the dark and forbidding Norwegian Sea brooded on the horizon. The captain strained night-widened eyes in an apparent scanning motion when, slightly to port, a dim orange lamp, and the running lights of a larger craft appeared. Its navigation lights blinked twice before being extinguished as the craft drew closer. Aboard the Rascal, crew members were busy transferring the catch into wooden boxes in the hold. Above the noise, in muffled Norwegian, a voice hailed the Rascal; the captain responded by displaying another orange lamp which he positioned on the forward deck. Releasing her fenders, now darkened throughout, the silhouette of the larger ship loomed as she drew gently alongside Rascal. Lefty was urged forward to the stem, as he snatched at the bigger ship's bow rails. Tumbling over its deep gunwales in his haste, he was dragged bodily aboard the darkened vessel by firm but unseen hands. At that moment, a gunshot rang out from across the channel echoing from the rocky shoreline beyond. Muffled curses and a new sense of urgency took hold of the crew. Transferral complete, as Lefty looked over his shoulder, The Rascal slipped away quickly vanishing into the darkness, setting her nets for the next run eastward.

A second more distant shot rang out, and at that, the crew of the darkened and more powerful vessel swung her head around, opened her throttle, and headed northward towards the sanctuary of the open sea. Firm hands urged Lefty to be silent; index finger to lips, he was guided along the decking towards the cabin of the new and larger boat. Along with Norwegian, he was sure that he could distinguish urgent conversation in a hushed Scottish brogue. Lights extinguished; the new trawler was running at speed – with only a few hours left until dawn, the 'bus' needed to make a clean escape. Hushed again, Lefty was taken to the dimly lit cabin. Two crew members sat crouched in the space below the deckhead, each unshaven face lined with anxiety and fatigue. Silence on the 'bus' prevailed, broken only by the rhythmic bass pulse of her diesel-powered heart. Glances were exchanged as Lefty was briskly manhandled, outer clothing removed and inspected, in search of anything which might confirm his identity or raise suspicion. Finally, in a whispered gesture, he was offered a blunt pencil and told to print his name on an empty cigarette packet. In a shaky hand, Lefty wrote the words King and George, which he offered to the crew. They grudgingly accepted his response, each exchanging conspiratorial glances. Lefty's whispered questions were hushed more severely now, a calloused hand clamped firmly over his lips, as the ketch rolled gently on the swell, into the Nordic night.

Chapter 19

A PAINTED SHIP UPON
A PAINTED OCEAN

F irst light revealed calm seas, enveloped in a shallow mist. A high milky overcast warned of changing weather and the scattered rays of morning sunlight were muted by an opaque halo. Although there was no sign of land to the east, daylight now instilled the dread of exposure with no possibility of refuge. The cloak of darkness had served the fugitives well, and there had been few sights and sounds of other vessels as they made good their escape. Following the dawn 'stand to', the lookouts changed watch on the main deck, with the captain accompanied by one crew member seated in the close confines of the aft cabin. Observing that the glass was falling, the captain emphasised that they were extremely vulnerable until the forecast weather front arrived. The occlusion with associated squalls, reduced cloud base and rainfall would be the sailors' friend today, but it could be a couple of hours before they met it as they progressed westward. Having completed only the first third of their journey, they were intensely aware of their conspicuous presence on the open sea. All were very mindful of the fact that they were still within the range of patrolling aircraft from airfields on the Western Norwegian coast. Extra vigilance was necessary now, and the lookouts doubled, one on the port quarter, another on the starboard. Lefty was questioned now that silent routine was suspended. He described his own narrow escape, including the incident at Værnes airfield leading to King's capture, and the encounter on The Rascal the previous day.

Lefty was eager to ask his own questions, but before he could speak, he was told in broken English that they did not want to know any more about him, nor was he to know any more of the captain, the crew, or the mission. On the need-to-know basis, the understanding was that if anyone aboard is captured, they will have little or no information to divulge. Apart from the ship's name 'Røta' displayed on the front of the wheelhouse, no names, no ranks and no destination, and only vital equipment aboard. No one and nothing to betray them, or their true intentions. If capture or compromise looked inevitable, all charts and classified documents would be secured in a weighted bag specifically designed for the purpose. When there was no alternative, the bag along with its secrets could be consigned to the deep beyond retrieval. Lefty was told to surrender any personal items, anything which could compromise security in the wrong hands.

But his pockets were empty, no wristwatch, no money, no possessions. Nothing apart from his tattoo, and he had plenty of practice at hiding that. Even the clothes he stood up in were not his own.

Following a lunch of sea biscuit, washed down with tepid tap water, the atmosphere on deck slightly relaxed as clouds began to gather and the wind increased from the north and west. With the headwind producing a calculated speed of six knots, after almost 12 hours the crew calculated that they had completed the most hazardous portion of their return journey. But their hasty departure from Hitra at 12:40 am required high-power settings from the engine overnight, eating into their reserves of diesel oil. Under sail, but with fuel tanks now half-empty, it became necessary to steer the most direct course to Shetland. So far, their south-westerly track had taken them almost parallel to the Norwegian coast before reaching the relative safety of the open North Sea. Although the gathering clouds offered some concealment, everyone aboard the 'Røta' remained at heightened alertness as they still had several hours of daylight remaining. Until then, they would be exposed, sitting ducks fleeing before the storm, seeking the cover of darkness and a safe passage to sanctuary.

Chapter 20

ATTACK

With the swell building and the cloud broken only by one shaft of late afternoon sunlight, the first of several attacks began with shouting from the lookouts. The JU88 bomber came in low and fast from the East in an apparent attempt to confirm the ship's identity. Then, in a steep, aggressive turn, the leading aircraft set up the first run of attack, dropping a stick of four bombs which straddled the *Røta* as she weaved her evasive manoeuvres. The lookouts struggled to arm their weapons, losing their footing on the decking, now drenched with salt and spray. A second bombing run was accompanied by a staccato burst of machine-gun fire from the aircraft. Once again, the bombs fell wide, but the nose gunner found his mark, stitching a line of splintered holes along the ship's starboard hull and smashing the glass on one side of the wheelhouse. In a climbing turn to the south and east, the aircraft made no further attempts to attack. But on-board the ship, relief was brief as the ominous atmosphere of concern and anticipation was written on every face. Although the lone attacker had disappeared into the lowering cloud base, the *Røta*'s course and location had doubtless been reported back. Lefty and the crew knew that once their exact position and track had been determined, it would be child's play to plan and direct follow-up raids.

Suffering only minor damage, the small ship ploughed on in the face of a building swell and a darkening cloud bank to the west. Then in the half-light of dusk, under brooding skies, a more concerted air attack came. Two medium bombers commenced their run, one after the other releasing their bombs as they passed low overhead. Onboard the *Røta*, there was little alternative but to continue defensive manoeuvres in the hope of avoiding damage. From mid-ships two crew members each manned the Lewis guns, mounted on the deck. They fired defensive bursts at the attackers in an attempt to distract the bomb aimers. Once again, returned fire from the aircraft straddled the decking, injuring one crew member and starting a small fire aft of the hatch cover. With the ship now releasing a conspicuous smoke trail, one aircraft broke off the attack and turned eastward, leaving the remaining bomber to finish the ship off.

In the maelstrom of the final bombing run, a huge explosion raised the entire stern of the *Røta*, accompanied by splintered wood and debris which showered the aft decking. Stem down, the ship wallowed as she absorbed the punishment, the crew struggling to regain their footing. Still defiant, but now resigned to her fate, *Røta* struggled onward. Too dark to press home the attack, the remaining JU88 turned away and climbed to the north-east as the first heavy drops of rain peppered the remaining windows of the wheelhouse, a prelude of the squall to come.

One more well-placed bomb would have finished the ship for good, but the coup de grâce never came. Securing the vessel and checking for damage or injury, the skipper applied first aid to the crewman with a shoulder wound, stabilising the injury with a first aid field dressing. The small fire on the hatch cover had been extinguished by sea spray, and it seemed as if *Røta* had again escaped serious damage. However, in the mounting sea, the fractured after-mast broke, resting at an awkward angle across the forward hatch and decking, shattered wood like splintered limbs. In the wheelhouse, voices were raised above the tumult, as the helmsman struggled to regain control of the vessel. The steering mechanism flailed wildly, as the boat's wheel began to spin clockwise then back again as the ship pitched and heaved erratically in the swell.

Chapter 21

HARD ON THE HELM

A sluggish response from the helm rendered any attempt to maintain a consistent bearing futile. Any rudder movement was restricted and jammed intermittently. In the starless rainy night, a heavy swell took hold, as the compass card in the binnacle slewed back and forth from north-west to south-west. The wild deviations were so misleading that the crew had to rely on dead- reckoning and their own instincts as the only aids to navigation. The *Røta* settled lower in the water as the crew attempted to bail the seawater rapidly accumulating in her bilges. Still making headway, but drifting and unable to maintain a steady heading, the crew nurtured *Røta*, urging her onwards towards Shetland and the promise of sanctuary.

In the wheelhouse, a crew member struggled with the helm while Lefty and the captain pored over the Admiralty charts, attempting to establish a fix for the vessel's position. Dead reckoning was even more of a challenge now with headway much reduced and little usable information from the log. The crew were painfully aware that the drift would be taking them off course south-westwards. The captain plotted an offset course to compensate for the discrepancy; he knew they must avoid the perilous Easter Skerries shoals. Aware that they must expect landfall soon, the captain warned all crew members to maintain a good lookout, in an effort to avoid the rocky shoals which stretched eastward from the Shetlands into the North Sea. Both wind and tide conspired to impede their progress, all eyes alert for any sign of the East Skerries light which should appear to starboard. Although thankful of the throbbing beat of her engine, the crew knew that *Røta* would go wherever the squalls would take her now. Named after the Norse goddess of storm and snow, they would need all the good fortune that *Røta* the Valkyrie, or any other deity, would offer.

Without warning, the vigilant crew started at the sharp snap of splintered timber, the crack of greenwood on an open fire. The ship lurched to port as storm-driven spray and gouts of water rushed over the gunwales, threatening to capsize her. Muted words of alarm lost amongst the maelstrom; the crew manhandled the port lifeboat from her davits. Drawn by wave and tide, the stricken ship foundered on the treacherous granite shoals of Muckle Fladdiecap. Realising that the boat was lost, the crew abandoned *Røta* to her fate. On-board the ship Lefty had gone below with a lifejacket, attempting to save the injured crewman. Suddenly without warning *Røta* started to disintegrate, her mainmast heeled over, trapping those below decks. Lefty was thrown clear but, losing his footing, he fell into the dark and turmoil, tumbling uncontrollably into the heavy wooden planking of the lifeboat and slid into unconsciousness at the height of the storm. A sudden gust washed towering waves which broke over her gunwales now as *Røta* slowly capsized and submerged in the maelstrom.

The sirens of the deep welcomed *Røta* and her gallant souls, each destined to become a votive offering, a vow of consecration fulfilled, the final act as the Fates were appeased.

Chapter 22

DRYLAND

As the storm started to abate, the flood tide carried the lifeboat before it with Lefty and only one crewman, each strewn unconscious across the centre thwart of the dinghy. The storm's energy began to dissipate, but the relentless pull of the tide swept the dinghy away as darkness and rain filled their world. When consciousness finally returned, Lefty found himself alone. The lifeboat's broken hull was stranded, partially embedded in the heavy flint shingle of the beach, and partly shrouded in kelp fronds thrown up by the storm. In the calm gloaming of first light, Lefty began to waken. Disorientated, he slowly rolled onto his back while gathering his senses. Painfully raising his hand to wipe the salt from his eyes, Lefty glanced around for other crewmen. Without any sign of life, he sank back with his shoulders propped against the planking of the lifeboat's fractured hull. As he did so, his upturned face caught sight of the ragged remnants of the storm clouds as they sped towards the horizon, the first vestiges of a pastel dawn now visible in the East. Slowly rolling his head to ease the nagging tautness of his neck, Lefty glanced skyward. Over his left shoulder, he marvelled at the constellation of the Great Bear as it glistened to the north, with the Pole Star beyond. As sensation and dream mingled, his last conscious thought was of Mary and the Lucky Star, the '*Étoile Chanceuse*'.

Later that day Lefty's inert body was recovered from the deserted beach adjacent to Mail and Cunningsburgh on the eastern coast of Shetland. Suffering from dehydration and exposure, Lefty's semiconscious form was lifted into a truck from the nearby Royal Navy base and carried off to the Gilbert Bain Hospital in Lerwick. On the ward, his progress was slow but, encouraged with the offer of sweet tea and biscuits from a WRVS volunteer, Lefty began to recover. In his more lucid moments, he became aware of a figure sitting patiently outside the nurses' office. Distracted only by people entering and leaving the ward, the figure reminded Lefty of a Highland gamekeeper. He appeared to be absorbed in studying a creased copy of 'Highland News'. Every so often the bearded figure would peer furtively over the top of the newspaper at any sign of activity. Occasionally, Lefty looked up and caught the gamekeeper glancing in his direction. Lefty sensed foreboding in the stranger's dour manner and furtive glances. Lefty asked the WRVS ward volunteer, as she served hot drinks, about the visitor. All she could offer was her own opinion that he was from the mainland, probably one of those plainclothes policemen. In the same breath, she warned Lefty that the stranger wanted to question him as soon as he awoke. Unsure why anyone would have such an urgent need to question him confounded Lefty and left him with a vague feeling of unease.

Over the next week, the doctor was satisfied with the improvement in Lefty's condition for him to be transferred to the mainland. Accompanied by the gamekeeper, he was escorted on a fishing boat to Peterhead. During the journey, his escort remained silent and evasive when questioned regarding their destination and purpose. On arrival, Lefty was detained in a dilapidated building at Port Henry overlooking Peterhead harbour. But he was bemused by the order to produce formal means of identification – they knew full well that he had none, they had had plenty of opportunities to search his clothing while he was in hospital. With only the clothes he stood up in, and his story to relate, Lefty was challenged to give a detailed account of himself and his unexplained appearance on the beach in Shetland. After countless repetitions, his statement was typed up and read aloud to him after he was cautioned to tell the absolute truth, which he duly did. His interrogators were obviously unsatisfied with Lefty's explanation and stated that they needed to make enquiries to determine that he was who he claimed to be. Had he been planted in the vicinity of a classified War Office unit, with the purpose of reporting back to his handlers in occupied Europe? They explained that 'The Robinson Crusoe method' had been employed by "our own War office to infiltrate some of the more difficult targets in occupied Europe with the purpose of spreading disinformation and encouraging subversion". If found guilty, the offence would be regarded as a deliberate breach of the Geneva Accords. As a traitor, he could expect a maximum penalty of capital punishment following wartime protocols.

Still recovering and bemused by his captors' questioning, Lefty asked to be returned to his unit once his identity had been confirmed. Surely that would be a formality which could be cleared up by one phone call to his squadron, or so he thought. For prolonged periods Lefty was left in solitary confinement, while his captors attempted to verify his identity. Any enquiry with the War Ministry or RAF unit records would confirm his story and verify his identity. It would be straightforward, just a matter of procedure, and Lefty had nothing to hide. Having related the same story time after tedious time, Lefty began to doubt his own version of events. Whoever they were, his inquisitors twisted and turned his words, applying ever-increasing levels of mental pressure. It seemed to Lefty that they were determined to find him guilty for some reason.

On being woken early one morning, he was told that he was to be transferred while remaining under military detention. A clerk issued a rail warrant for two single fares to King's Cross London with a further onwards connection to Goring in Oxfordshire. Enquiring about their destination, all Lefty was told was that he was to be returned to his unit. But before that, he would have to undergo a thorough medical examination and be measured for a new uniform. Still accompanied by a plainclothes policeman, he was driven at speed to Dyce railway station just north of Aberdeen. At the ticket office, the policeman snatched the ticket from the bemused booking clerk before it reached Lefty's hand.

Boarding the train, wearing a smug expression, the policeman sat in silence for the entire journey, occasionally eyeing Lefty with an expression of both suspicion and disdain.

During one of the stops on the interminable journey, Lefty did consider the option of escape. He noticed that the carriage door next to the toilet was in use and obviously unlocked. As tempting as it was, he dismissed the idea, reminding himself of the fact that he was returning home. Perhaps now was the time to relax, to shake off the paranoia of his time in Norway, to stop instinctively searching for any opportunity to flee.

With the benefit of hindsight, Lefty's urge to escape was not so misguided, but at the time, he could not have known that this was just one more journey that would terminate in yet another dead end.

Camp 020r, Nuffield Oxfordshire.

Lefty became preoccupied at the prospect of returning to operational flying at Linton-on-Ouse, being reunited with Mary and meeting his new child for the first time. Then he became puzzled as he saw that the train was on a different route. Yes, it was going southbound, but on a different line – they should have stopped at York at least half an hour ago.

Perhaps this route would take them to another station closer to both Mary and Linton-on-Ouse. But they had passed Sheffield and would soon be out of Yorkshire altogether. Remembering that he was to have a medical examination, a new RAF uniform and identity pass, mere formalities, or so he assumed. Sometimes it seemed to Lefty that the modern military machine relied on bureaucracy as much as bullets.

It came as no surprise to him that there would be a mountain of paperwork to be completed before he could return to his first loves, flying and Mary, each a vital and burning passion from deep within, driving him onward.

Met by an anonymous olive-green staff car at Goring railway station, Lefty and his escort were driven briskly down leafy Oxfordshire lanes. After the monotonous train journey from Scotland in the company of his surly guard, Lefty found little cause for optimism. However, he started to relax and look forward to the prospect of new-found freedom.

Lefty's daydreams were suddenly interrupted as the car came to an abrupt halt outside a rambling country mansion, brakes squealing and tyres crunching on the gravel drive. Lefty noticed security barriers and high barbed wire fencing which surrounded the entire perimeter. Measures which seemed out of place, at odds with the fine Gothic architecture of what might be a typical English stately home. Lefty became filled with a familiar sense of foreboding, the same instinct that had kept him alive in Norway. Now back in the UK, he hoped he may never be exposed to such threats again. Certainly not here, in rural Oxfordshire, but nevertheless, Lefty's instincts served him well and were rarely misplaced.

Lefty and his escort were met at the impressive main entrance and challenged by an armed guard in uniform. Hushed preliminaries exchanged, his escort handed over paperwork and Lefty was led away to a cramped, musty prefabricated annexe at the rear of the building. The shabbiness of the room was relieved only by a trestle table accompanied by two folding wooden chairs. The only small window was partially covered by a blackout blind, the metal frame exposing peeling paintwork and glasswork crisscrossed with peeling strips of paper tape, an optimistic precaution against flying glass in the event of an air raid.

Following unspoken directions and glances of contempt from an armed guard, Lefty obediently occupied one of the chairs and sat alone in the room awaiting further events.

Lefty's statement was once again reviewed in detail by a well-dressed but curt clerk. Finishing his duties, the clerk stood up, closed the folder, and left the room. The file was left closed on the table before him. Tempted to open it, Lefty noticed the pink colour of the folder which revealed little apart from the red stamp which announced the contents to be Secret. Although he was in the room alone, Lefty knew better than to open a folder of that classification without proper authority. To do so would have exposed him to suspicion and further interrogation. Soon after, a stranger entered the room. A tall, gaunt figure with a comical music hall appearance, reminiscent of a smartly dressed, if sombre, Charlie Chaplin. It soon became apparent to Lefty that any attempt at humour would not be appreciated.

Scraping the wooden chair against the worn brown lino, and without the courtesy of introduction, the man seated himself opposite Lefty. During the prolonged silence that followed, the officer felt in the pockets of his ill-fitting jacket and positioned an oblong tobacco tin in the centre of the table with the precision of a practised chess player. Lefty studied the silent stranger who ignored him completely. As he watched, the stranger conjured a box of Swan Vestas which he carefully positioned alongside the tobacco tin. Reluctant to be the first to speak, Lefty watched as the officer drummed a monotonous tone with his left hand on the tabletop. He carefully removed a rosewood pipe from another pocket, which he placed in front of the tobacco tin.

Lefty's frustration grew as he waited, wondering if the tobacco tin contained some sort of device or was it just full of Ogden's St Bruno rough cut. But he waited patiently nevertheless, not wanting to give any cause for suspicion or delay to his return to York.

After a while, without any preliminaries, the questions began in a more ominous tone this time.

"Right. Now, sergeant err..."

PART 1

"McFarlane," Lefty offered to the officer who removed his horn-rimmed glasses to better observe his subject.

"Yes... You see we are faced with quite a dilemma here... sergeant," he said. The questioner somehow managed to emphasise the word sergeant, injecting both sarcasm, and conceit into each syllable.

"Exactly what dilemma?" asked Lefty indignantly. "Look, I was told that I was brought here for a medical and to collect a new uniform." Curbing his anger, Lefty added: "I don't know who you are, but this certainly doesn't look like clothing stores, let alone a medical centre to me!"

"Shall we get one thing straight, sergeant" was the indignant response, "I am asking the questions here, and you will oblige us with the truth."

"I'll give you my inside leg measurement if it gets me out of here and back to my squadron, which, incidentally, is where I belong, my parent unit!" Lefty replied.

The retort came swiftly with the spectacles hastily removed again for emphasis. "You think this is funny then, sergeant? Let me tell you that while you claimed to be in the enemy embrace in Norway, we have been fighting our own war here, safeguarding the nation from the Nazi hordes. Our remit includes the interrogation, detention, and internment of aliens, collaborators, and quislings as it happens..."

And without stopping for breath, "... If we are convinced that your written statement is at odds with the official account of events, we have unrestricted authority to take what action we see fit to contain and/or neutralise any individual or group which we deem to be a threat to the realm... Do I make myself clear?"

"Crystal." Lefty managed to stop himself from saying the word aloud as he gathered his composure.

Obviously satisfied with his performance, the officer appeared to relax. He produced a small pocketknife from somewhere in the depths of his ill-fitting 50-shilling suit and slowly reclined in his seat.

Quoting King's regulations, Lefty stated that his response to any further questions would be restricted to number, rank and name only, as he regarded himself as being under interrogation.

Considering his response carefully, the officer opened the penknife and began reaming out the charred bowl of his pipe. The performance finished as the officer tapped the pipe noisily against the steel waste bin, the only additional piece of furniture in the room. Then, without warning, the barked response was indignant:

"Don't you dare have the temerity to quote King's regulations at me, sergeant, and don't think that the Geneva Convention, that cosy little retreat of the traitor, applies here... the Red Cross does not deliver parcels here, and I can tell you now that you probably won't get a birthday card from your mother! Nobody knows we exist here, and that's just how we like it."

Lefty remained silent during the entire tirade.

In a more reasonable tone, the officer continued. "You see, your squadron has you listed as missing in action nearly six months ago, rather a long while to be languishing in an occupied country. And guess what, while you were enjoying your Scandinavian holiday, some of our high-value assets in Norway were compromised. The very same assets which were put in place to assist the repatriation of downed airmen and the ex-filtration of agents. What we would really like to know is how you negotiated your release from your captors in Norway?"

More urgently now with clenched fists: "What did they offer you in exchange for your freedom – perhaps the acquisition of a few tasty snippets of information to be passed on to some of Adolf's friends, or the betrayal of more of our prize assets?"

"So, surviving a crash landing, being half frozen to death and then shipwrecked during my escape was not convincing enough for you?" enquired Lefty in frustration.

The officer suddenly appeared to relax again; leaning back, he shuffled absently at the papers in front of him. Then, in a sham of informality, he continued, "I've always been a devotee of acting, amateur dramatics that sort of thing, how about you?"

Adding, without waiting for a response, "... you know what the most difficult part of acting is? Winning the trust of the audience, being plausible, executing an authentic, well-practised routine of deception." The questioner met Lefty's gaze as he recharged his pipe with St Bruno. In a well-rehearsed and affected manner, the officer made a second attempt to light the brimming pipe with another Swan Vesta. Then, leaning forward, he exhaled a stream of fresh blue tobacco smoke directly at Lefty. After another pause, he continued. "The difficulty lies in remembering your lines on the night, get one word or one syllable wrong, and you've betrayed the trust of that audience. They will doubt you from thereon in until the last curtain call..." He continued, "... Now perhaps you can see how important it is for us to establish the facts. You see, we know all about the dentist in Trondheim, but we think he may belong to *them* as well as *us*, and he too is committed to subverting SOE operations."

Lefty responded, "Look, as far as I knew the dentist was a member of the resistance, Rathke claimed to have had sources within the Gestapo who he relied upon when gathering intelligence. He offered me a means of escape, an offer which I could not refuse; in fact, it was my duty to accept...

"... If you suspect the dentist of collaborating with the Germans rather than the resistance, are you seriously suggesting that I was part of some conspiracy? If there was a trap, then I was the stooge, the victim, the bait. How many of your people have spent prolonged periods in an occupied country? I can tell you here and now what it is like, and you have no right to refer to it as a holiday. It involves day-to-day survival, sleeping with your ears and eyes open, never knowing who you can trust. I know nothing more of the arrangements for my escape other than the rendezvous with King... Put that in your St Bruno and smoke it!"

Dismissing the taunt, the officer wafted the smoke away with his right hand and continued... "Ah yes, King..." came the response. "Perhaps you'd like to explain the disappearance of your alleged accomplice?"

"I can add no more than I have told you in my statement, you know about the rendezvous, you know about the 'Rascal' ... For heaven's sake, when you organise these so-called Shetland missions, don't you people even know the identity of those to be repatriated? I didn't know King; I had never met him before the rendezvous and his capture by the airfield at Vaernes."

"Ah yes, so you chose to abandon King to his fate and beat a hasty retreat, and then what?"

At that moment came a knock on the office door. "Come!" barked the officer, annoyed at the intrusion.

A messenger in a grey uniform nervously pushed the door ajar and passed a document in a file marked urgent to the interrogating officer. After signing a receipt, without looking up, the officer dismissed the messenger with an impatient gesture.

The file carried the caveat 'Most Secret' stamped on its pink cardboard folder which the interrogating officer opened with a practised hand. Releasing the security tag, he scanned the covering text on the single sheet of A4 paper.

The file contained an SOE intelligence report, including an accurate account of the Shetland mission, including Lefty's name and a meteorological analysis of the storm which had sealed the fate of the '*Røta*' and her crew. The report concluded with a detailed analysis of the security implications pending inquiry.

Chapter 23

INQUISITION

H e had lost track of the days or was it weeks? The same questions came day after day, and Lefty was becoming more and more indignant. He was continually threatened with extended periods of solitary confinement if he persisted in his "obstinate and insubordinate" manner.

When Lefty asked the identity of his inquisitors, the only response came in the form of a warning: "we are posing the questions, your only task is to respond with the whole truth." Sinister overtones, and veiled threats, the consequences of non-compliance.

More days passed into weeks. Lefty was spending more prolonged periods in solitary confinement, with no opportunity for exercise or communication with the outside world. Since his escape from Norway, Lefty had become aware of spasmodic dizzy spells, which, although infrequent, were causing him concern. He was not to know that his detention at Nuffield, or Camp 020 as it was known to the intelligence world, was to be over sooner rather than later. Following another inquisition, where considerable pressure was exerted on Lefty, he experienced what he would later describe as a blackout.

Woken abruptly by the matron, Lefty had been dozing in bed on the ward at St Hugh's College Hospital on the outskirts of Oxford. He was informed that it was time to make himself presentable for the morning ward rounds. Introducing himself by name, the young doctor closed the curtain around Lefty's bed. Although it was easy to hear any conversation on the ward, the screen gave the illusion of privacy.

In his best bedside manner, the well-spoken doctor told Lefty that he had a relatively rare syndrome. A form of reflex epilepsy that can be caused by outside stimuli such as loud noises, flashing lights and other stress-inducing triggers. Lefty was encouraged to hear that the condition was treatable. As long as he took the required dosage at the correct time, the medication would help prevent the onset of further episodes.

As the doctor continued his rounds Lefty felt relieved, looked around the ward; the plainclothes policeman who had become his shadow had finally disappeared. Perhaps Lefty had finally escaped the clutches of his 'Special Branch' minders. His thoughts now turned to Mary, the child he had never met, and life on the squadron. But there was one other concern: his aircrew medical certificate. If his new condition came to the notice of the RAF medical branch, his fitness to fly status would be reviewed. Medical officers in the Forces were all-powerful with a well-earned reputation for being over cautious. Along with the squadron commander, only they had the authority to relegate aircrew to ground duties. Lefty had known them to suspend the flying categories of fellow squadron members with relatively trivial medical conditions. Possession being nine-tenths of the law, it could be a lengthy process, convincing them that you were fit to fly again.

With the war dragging on into its fourth year, Lefty, along with every experienced aircrew member, would be desperately needed, and he was anxious to return to flying duties as soon as possible. He also knew that he must retain his aircrew status, or he might end up in some monotonous office job, a fate which all aircrew were desperate to avoid. Depending on whom you listened to, the war would be over soon, but no matter whether it took one month, one year or a decade, Lefty was more determined than ever that the Nazis must be crushed. He had seen their inhuman practices first-hand and knew that the Allies must emerge as victors. Since Japan had joined the Axis powers, it was time to take a stand, defend the free world and release the occupied countries from tyranny and slavery. When it was all over, Lefty would apply to become a UK citizen, marry his fiancée, and create a new life for himself and his family. With few possessions and only the clothes he stood up in, he was discharged and instructed to return to his unit. After collecting his prescription and rail warrant from the medical orderly, Lefty was officially discharged from hospital. He was driven to Oxford railway station, where a stern clerk at the ticket desk threw a scowl at Lefty, scanned the rail warrant, and checked the document as if he had never seen one before. With only a few minutes before the train was scheduled to arrive, the clerk turned the document over as if examining it for fingerprints, before grudgingly issuing a single ticket to York.

Chapter 24

RETURN TO THE FOLD

During his prolonged absence from England and subsequent detention, Lefty had held his concern for Mary in check, hoping that she was safe; now the first thing he would do was to propose to her, ring, or no ring. Their child would be a one-year-old by now, boy or girl he wondered, secretly confessing that he was hoping for a boy who would share his interests and passions, but no matter what, along with Mary, the child remained his most cherished longing. Lefty's head nodded as he felt the warmth and rhythm of the train, a soothing lullaby which surrounded him, dispelling the frustration and fatigue of recent days and weeks.

Lefty dozed fitfully, dreaming of family life with Mary, ambling through sun-drenched summer meadows. His left hand of love wrapped around hers, warm and reassuring, a tiny hand cupped safely in hers. He daydreamed of domestic bliss with Mary in an idyllic post-war world. Any thoughts of Canada and his stepmother seemed now but distant memories, a world away, another lifetime.

Stop start, stop start, the journey seemed endless with its inevitable wartime delays. The train slowed once again and finally lurched to a halt with a metallic clang, rousing Lefty from his catnap. He blinked and cupped a hand above his brow; peering through the grime of the carriage window, he could just make out the name Selby on the station sign. Smoke from the stationary engine drifted on the breeze enveloping the carriage and obscured the entire platform. A harassed guard strode along the platform announcing to passengers that the train was to terminate here, and alternative transport would be arranged to York city centre. There was an audible sigh of frustration from the carriage as passengers stood and collected their luggage. A soldier in uniform silenced the complainers with, "there is a war on y' know, what do you expect? ... ow many bloody trains do you think there was at Dunkirk?"

Stepping from the train, Lefty headed for the station forecourt where he joined a throng of dejected passengers queueing for the bus. A voice in the crowd declared "it's only half an hour to York city centre, won't take long". The ill-tempered and impatient bus driver disagreed, muttering "you'll be lucky"! Grumbling resumed as passengers boarded the bus and struggled to find a vacant seat, while the driver announced "standing room only" with officious indifference.

As the bus approached the outskirts of York, Lefty blinked and surveyed the scene before him. In the middle distance several buildings were damaged with workmen clearing away rubble and filling trucks with masonry and brickwork. So much had happened during his absence, Lefty had heard little of air raids in Britain since the Blitz of 1940 which targeted major ports like London, Bristol, and Liverpool. Lefty began to realise how out of touch he was; it seemed like he had been out of the UK for years rather than months. But why the city of York? Surely it had little strategic value as a target when there were so many rich pickings to be had further south.

On the overcrowded bus, Lefty lowered his head in an attempt to see beyond a haze of blue tobacco smoke. Opposite him was a passenger whose features were hidden behind a copy of the Daily Mail which rustled noisily as each page was turned and folded. Lefty hadn't had an opportunity to read the newspapers for many weeks and could not ignore the column in front of him. In bold lettering he read "Total War – latest devastating attack on Aberdeen", quoting significant loss of life. Apparently, the *Luftwaffe*'s twin-engined bombers were now able to operate over the UK with impunity, despite their limited endurance and minimal fighter cover. The entire landscape of the war was changing rapidly.

Through the windows, he recognised some of the familiar landmarks of the city, but streets adjacent to the station had been completely demolished. York Railway Station itself had suffered severe damage and looked as if it might collapse completely at any moment. The iron buttresses and masonry were open to the elements, revealing the full extent of the damage. Skylight panes smashed, enamel signs bearing platform numbers buckled and rusting, the ornate steel framework charred and exposed like the ribs of some long-dead whale. Once busy platforms were littered with the debris of war, with extensive fire damage evident from station approach to the main entrance. The waiting room door had been blown off its hinges and the ticket office, although unattended, had one window open for enquiries. But with the main platform straddled by the remains of a huge locomotive blown from its rails, capsized, and covered in rubble, no trains would be leaving York any time soon.

A scene of complete devastation; every pane of glass in the station was broken, leaving unsightly gaps where windows had once been. Partly delaminated after recent rain, cheap plywood covered every aperture, a hasty and inadequate attempt to secure what was left of the building. With repairs to twisted railway tracks underway, and partially assembled scaffolding supporting the main structure, Prosser's once proud 'monument to extravagance' had become a playground for children. Girls and boys played truant from ruined classrooms to clamber through mounds of limestone, brick, and steel, searching for prized war trophies.

Any fragments of shrapnel were prized trophies in class or playground and always in demand, especially one of 'theirs'. But there again, its origin didn't matter, the mere mention of "Jerry shrapnel" became the "gold standard" in the playground and fetched the highest values, the most valuable collateral when negotiating 'swaps'. Young treasure seekers seemed undeterred by threats from workmen or the temporary notice which warned *"LNER Property, Keep out – Thieves Will Be Prosecuted"*. It didn't matter, bomb fragments could be easily hidden in pockets, when it was time to run home and begin negotiations.

Consulting an emergency timetable on an improvised notice board outside the station, Lefty realised that he would have a long wait for the Easingwold bus. Nothing seemed to be running on time at the moment, and unless there was a relief, only one bus an hour operated on the service which would take him to the gates of RAF Linton-on-Ouse. Standing on the Lendal river bridge, Lefty paused to take in the scene before him and began to grasp the full extent of the damage to the city. Just visible was the remains of the Guildhall which had obviously taken a direct hit, leaving only an ugly and lifeless shell. Lefty got his bearings and quickened his pace towards Laburnum Grove, Mary, the new baby, and the bedsit he left so many weeks ago. Aware that he wasn't expected at the RAF base until the next day, Lefty decided to walk to the bus stop outside the city centre; he knew he could resume his journey from there.

Turning right onto Wellington Row, he followed Leeman Road under the railway arch. Enjoying his new-found liberty, he decided to take the river towpath. Since leaving Norway, he had been cooped up for so long that he had almost forgotten the scent of clean fresh air. Air untainted by tobacco smoke, stale sweat, or dread. The heady aroma of freedom.

As he inhaled deeply, savouring the cool breeze from the water, Lefty noticed that the Rowntree's factory had been hit, and was reminded again of Mary, hoping that she was safe in amongst all this destruction. The relief landing ground at Clifton looked unusable, ugly craters pockmarked the once manicured lush green of the private airfield. Summoning up as much optimism as he could, Lefty hoped that the city suburbs had escaped the worst of the raid.

After all, hadn't he and the crew been trained to avoid bombing urban areas, deliberately minimising needless harm to 'innocent' civilians. RAF crews were briefed to attack only legitimate targets, armament factories and other installations, and only those deemed to be strategically important. Any raid in occupied Europe would be cancelled if there was significant risk to the civilian population. In emergency, squadron op orders required them to jettison any 'hang-ups' over water or fetch unprimed weapons home rather than drop them indiscriminately.

In the residential streets of York, the clean-up operation had been thorough. Here and there individual houses had disappeared like missing teeth in the perennial smile of the suburbs. Surely fate could not be so fickle as to take the lives of one family and spare that of neighbours. But still, as he continued his journey, the destruction was evident across Bismarck Street and onto Boroughbridge Road. Lefty could feel every sinew in his body tense as he turned the corner into Laburnum Grove; he stood rooted to the spot in disbelief. He searched desperately for the house, but the street had changed, the familiar scene now somehow unfamiliar. An ugly crater suggested a direct hit to the eastern end of the Grove. Lefty counted the house numbers from the corner of the street. Some had suffered relatively minor damage, while others were missing completely, but only a scorched and rubble-strewn gap remained of what had once been number 11.

The street was desolate and lifeless.

Somewhere nearby, a song thrush offered its own solitary laments perched in a lofty sycamore. Perhaps it sang of new life, hope, and optimism, amid devastation and destruction.

No sign of life, the bedsit, or Mary.

After checking with what few neighbours remained, he discovered that most of the adjacent houses were unsound and not safe for occupation. The popular and friendly Laburnum Grove bore silent witness to its fate, regarding the destruction with unseeing eyes from its blinkered and boarded windows. Mary must have survived; she must be with friends or neighbours who may have taken her in. Overwhelmed by emotion he searched for neighbours, but then stood as he gazed at the scene before him.

There was no activity at all, he stumbled on the broken paving aimlessly. Amongst the desolation there was movement, a figure scrabbling amongst the brickwork of the collapsed wall. The man raised his arm as Lefty wandered past.

Lefty couldn't bring himself to acknowledge. Ambling slowly towards the entrance to Laburnum Grove, he finally found himself at the bus shelter on Boroughbridge road.

He was about to sit on the wooden bench when a voice addressed him from behind.

"... Lefty, isn't it? I thought it was you, I almost didn't recognise you without your uniform..."

The man was unshaven and dishevelled and appeared close to tears. Lefty managed to ask ... "Sorry, what did you say?"

"... I'm Reg, number 17, or what's left of it. The missus is in Doncaster infirmary with serious burns. She hasn't woken yet..."

"What happened here?" said Lefty.

"Good job you missed it..." said Reg. "I've been trying to find anything to salvage from what's left of the house, but last time I came they were seeing off looters, and you couldn't even get in the Street. You looking for Mary from number 11? They've gone, mate, all gone. Last time I saw Mary she was expecting, but what exactly happened I don't know, but the building was burnt out when I saw it... Perhaps she's been taken in somewhere, but somehow, I doubt it. But the Fire Brigade and the ARP wardens looked for days, and one or two had just gone... disappeared in the blink of an eye. Once the water mains and the gas were fractured the whole street was evacuated, it's been like this for months..."

As he spoke, the Easingwold bus approached. Lefty remained seated as if he didn't notice. When the bus drew to a halt, the driver shouted... "Standing room only, move along please, plenty of room upstairs..." adding ... "Are you pair just gonna stand there gawping or are you getting on?"

"Hold on!" shouted Reg. "I'm helping this chap..."

"Well, where is 'e going then, because you're each about to become pedestrians shortly! If you're both coming, get on! Either that or kiss, hug and say farewell, just make up your bloody minds..."

"You going to the RAF camp, Lefty?" said Reg.

Lefty nodded vacantly in response, and asked, "Is there a later bus?"

"In an hour and half there is a relief, but it won't be stopping at the RAF Camp. Look, I'm already late, are you young lovers getting on or not?"... as the conductor raised his arm to ring the bell.

Reflective and sombre, it seemed to Lefty that the rules of war had changed during his absence. Was everybody now a potential target? Men, women, and children, were they all now the latest victims in some sort of random, and macabre twist of fate?

But if their target was the RAF Base, the German crew's navigation was pretty poor. They must have been almost 10 miles off-course.

Lefty recalled his training days on the bomber squadron; between them they had all made some pretty bad errors, but the navigator had never been that far off target even on his worst days.

With the recent introduction of the new, highly classified 'Gee' electronic navigation equipment, RAF bombing accuracy statistics had improved dramatically. It seemed to Lefty that the enemy was unable to keep pace with Allied technology. Perhaps the self-proclaimed master race was fallible after all.

One thing was sure, his quest for Mary would have to wait.

Stepping down from the bus, Lefty arrived at the airfield's main gate, the light blue sign proudly declared 'RAF Linton-on-Ouse'. Challenged at the gate by an armed sentry, he was escorted to the guardroom with only a temporary identity pass and a used rail warrant – Lefty needed somebody on the station to vouch for him. Surely some of his old squadron comrades were still around, but arriving at the guardroom wearing only civilian clothes, Lefty's reception was less than welcoming. At the desk the duty NCO frowned at him and unceremoniously directed him to Station Headquarters adjacent to the main entrance. As he approached the impressive ivy-clad brick building, he noticed a freshly painted sign which proudly announced: '62 Beaver Operational Station (RCAF)'.

Lefty realised that the long-promised operational Canadian bomber squadrons had finally arrived at Linton-on-Ouse during his absence. Although located on an active RAF station, the new unit would be under the direct control and administration of the Royal Canadian Air Force. Same king, different boss.

During his aircrew medical, the tattoo on his left forearm was noted by the doctor, who said nothing but regarded Lefty with a mixture of condemnation and distaste.

Physical examination complete, the doctor turned his attention to Lefty's medical record. Scrutinising his diagnosis and prescription, the doctor coiled his stethoscope and placed it carefully on the desk before him.

Looking Lefty straight in the eye, the doctor announced that "it was highly unlikely that he would be returned to full aircrew duties given his medical condition..." adding, "... that is my medical opinion, but your flying category will be reviewed, and the final decision will rest with your squadron commander, not me."

As he made his way around the familiar airfield to the Squadron buildings, he noticed that the entire complex had escaped any damage from the bombing raids. Lefty contemplated the consequences of the air war and its effect on the vulnerable and blameless. Had he inflicted the same on the targets that he and his crew had bombed? Perhaps the *Luftwaffe* intelligence had learned of the wartime significance of the Rowntree's factory, but that seemed so unlikely as to be absurd. Surely even the krauts weren't daft enough to target a chocolate factory.

Remembering his time in Norway, the constant dread of betrayal and capture, Lefty came to realise that in the 20th century, we had invented so many new ways to inflict suffering and death on each other. Were the virtues of innocence and mercy now just peacetime luxuries? Or had they only been put aside for the time being to make way for the new priorities of war, defeat or victory, guilt or innocence, the living, or the dead?

Chapter 25

MISSING

On arrival at the Squadron hangar, the 'boss' summoned Lefty to his office. Before his deployment to Kinloss and Norway, the senior officer had been a member of the Royal Air Force, a veteran of World War I. But all that had changed; a varnished wooden plaque on the door identified the occupant as the new Squadron Commander. The office door was ajar, and as Lefty was about to knock, a voice from within said "come!".

Determined to make a positive first impression, Lefty strode smartly in, and was directed to sit with an urgent gesture as the boss finished a phone call and replaced the receiver on its cradle.

Lefty was pleasantly surprised to meet a young and enthusiastic Canadian officer, with the firm handshake of a taskmaster and an unmistakable expression of sincerity and determination.

"Welcome to the Squadron, or should I say welcome back, sergeant, good to see you...

"... How are you, I think your squadron name is Lefty, am I right?"

Lefty nodded in confirmation as the boss continued. "So are you raring to go, Lefty?" He smiled.

"To be honest, sir, I am fine, it is just a matter of convincing the medics that I am okay. They have already told me that until my medication is reduced, I won't be able to fly."

"I understand that, and we need you back on flying duties as soon as possible."

The boss explained his own predicament; right now, the unit was at full stretch, totally committed to "Operation Pointblank", the Allied bomber offensive and number one priority for every single crewmember, every aircraft, and every squadron at the base.

"I am told that my personal jeep is at the bottom of the Atlantic at the moment, but if and when I get a new one, I will need wings on that as well!" he joked.

"We will hit the Hun where it hurts, draw their fighters into battle and destroy his ability to build more."

Lefty listened intently to his new boss. Not only an inspiring leader but a man preoccupied with one objective, one ideal, a young face furrowed by the relentless pressures that wartime imposes on all.

"We got a lot of new guys on the unit at the moment, and we need experienced pilots like you to help lick them into shape, but you will only be driving a desk for the moment, I'm afraid." He went on to reassure Lefty that he would be returned to 'ops' as soon as his medical category could be reviewed and revised. Until that time he was to help out in the operations building, vital war work involving the planning and execution of raids into occupied Europe.

The conversation ended abruptly as the squadron commander's phone rang again. He extended one arm towards the receiver, saying to Lefty, "Okay, well I think you're expected in the planning room for tomorrow's briefing, so, see the adjutant on your way out, sergeant, he will get the ball rolling with my express authority, we will do everything within our powers to get you back in the air."

To Lefty's relief, there was no mention of his Norway mission or his time in custody; the boss wasn't looking for explanations, those would have to wait; right now there was a war to fight.

Although officially grounded, Lefty's tasks would be pressured and precise, leaving little opportunity for leave of absence. So far as 24-hour leave passes were concerned, each was privileged, allocated only to those in bereavement or in need of compassionate leave.

Seizing every opportunity, Lefty would take the bus to York, continuing his search for Mary, and the fate of the child that he had never met. His search led him to the office of civil defence in the city centre. He attempted to contact the chief ARP warden who was on duty at the time of the raid, hoping to establish the whereabouts of Mary and his child. Progress was slow and painstaking. So far, all he had discovered was the fate of the wardens who had attended the public incident at Laburnum Grove, one of whom had been fatally injured, and the other killed during a later raid on the city. After several unproductive meetings with Civil Defence officials, Lefty was eventually granted access to the relevant civic records, and with the grudging cooperation of a junior town hall clerk, Lefty found the appropriate file.

He scanned the handwritten log until he came to the section for April, and a paragraph grimly entitled 'The Night of the

Incendiaries'. The record showed that an infant was recovered from the arms of her dying mother at number 11 Laburnum Grove. Trapped in the burning ruins, beyond all hope of rescue, the mother had perished along with an elderly lady whose remains were found huddled in the ruins of the ground floor. The record included a short passage covering the evacuation of Laburnum Grove owing to a fractured gas main.

The warden had duly registered the deaths with the coroner, and the child was put in the care of the nearby Red Cross shelter while bodies were recovered. Giving brief details of first aid administration and feeding, the record showed that the new-born baby girl had been put in the care of the local authorities, while next-of-kin details were established.

Beyond that, it became increasingly difficult for Lefty to make any progress. Without any documentation, he could not prove any family connection with Mary apart from his informal declaration. He had given up any thoughts of attempting to contact Tobin, the landlord of the pile of rubble which had once been number 11. He feared that any contact with Tobin would only hinder his enquiries rather than help. But now he was running out of options; however, against his better judgement, Lefty decided to visit Tobin at his home in Osbaldswick to the east of York city centre.

Still harbouring doubts, Lefty rapped firmly on the front door in Bad Borrow Lane. Reeking of whiskey, Tobin eventually answered the front door, while a small boy of three or four tugged at his unbuttoned cardigan. Tobin eyed Lefty with suspicion, blinking twice from behind a bleary and absent gaze. With the door ajar, Tobin propped himself precariously on the woodwork of the front porch. He stood in the open doorway, speechless, apparently not recognising his visitor. Then turning to the persistent child, he applied a firm backhand slap to the side of the boy's face and barked "get back indoors where you belong". As Lefty flinched at the assault, Tobin recovered from the exertion and leered at Lefty, addressing him as that bloody 'Yank', and in the same breath demanding rent arrears. After being corrected Tobin said, "Yank, lumberjack, you're all the bloody same..." adding "... if there's more of your lot coming to win the war, God help us all." Ignoring the taunt, Lefty asked him if he knew more of Mary, and the child recovered from the rubble of Laburnum Grove. Tobin managed to exclaim, "That little scrubber, you mean? ... Good riddance to bad rubbish, that's what I say."

Ignoring the outburst, Lefty patiently repeated the question, which Tobin took as a prompt to continue.

"Ay they say that there was a bairn, I wouldn't be surprised, she would take up with anything in trousers that one, especially Yanks, the little slut."

Finally giving way to his anger, Lefty responded with a reflex action. He grabbed Tobin by the shirt collar but somehow resisted the urge to deliver the satisfying blow to put paid to the man's smug and scornful leer. Raising his fist, Lefty noticed the child cowering behind the hall door, a shock of red curls damp with tears stark against the flushed and stinging face. Taking pity on the boy, Lefty released his grip on Tobin's collar, causing the drunkard to overbalance and stumble backwards.

Half sprawling on the hallway floor, Tobin continued his tirade. "You mean the bairn is yours? God help you if you think you can find that little homeless bastard. I would get going while the going is good if I were you, son." As he returned to his feet, the young boy ran out of the house towards Lefty. Close-up, Lefty thought the boy looked like a pathetic Dickensian waif, his face tearstained and grimy, a mask of desperation and neglect. At that moment with small arm outstretched, he asked Lefty for "a tanner or even a three-penny bit". Before Lefty could answer, a voice from indoors shouted: "Get in here now, Gregory, how many times do I have to tell you, I'll fetch you one when I get hold of you, then you'll have something to cry about, you miserable little sod."

Tobin reached out and jerked the sobbing child by one ear; while stumbling, he said to Lefty "You can take this little wretch while you're at it. We don't know who his father is either."

At which the boy's sobbing became a shrill and piercing cry. Then turning to Lefty, Tobin added, "Bloody foreigner, I'll get you for this, I'll get the law on you... You owe me rent, I'll get you for assault, you see if I don't."

Ignoring the goads, Lefty strode away as Tobin barked further orders at the young boy, pushing him further into the hallway, accompanied by the sound of another slap.

The landlord's reputation as an alcoholic hothead with a tendency to violence was well-known locally. Lefty knew that little credibility could be placed on any statement that Tobin may or may not make regarding Mary or the fate of her child. The only option for Lefty was to continue to pursue official records in his off-duty time.

Any enquiries at York Guildhall were frustrating experiences, mainly due to the city of York and its impenetrable civic bureaucracy. All records about war orphans were held centrally at the Home Office and remained a matter of confidentiality. Those remaining had not been adequately collated, and many had been spoiled when the Guildhall was damaged in a later air raid. Pursuing his enquiries with the Red Cross, he found a nurse who had looked after the baby during its brief stay at their post. In a second meeting over weak tea and stale Red Cross biscuits, Lefty learned little of any use. However, he had discovered that some war orphans had been transferred to the Dr Barnardo's home at Robert Memorial Hall near Harrogate. Visiting the home, Lefty's enquiries were decidedly unwelcome and particularly unhelpful. This time Lefty was dismissed because of lack of appropriate ID and was warned that he would be reported if he persisted in his enquiries. Lefty knew that the consequences of that would be taken very seriously if it came to the attention of the RAF.

Perhaps a return to Canada may be the only option, to give up on the daughter that he hadn't met, a prospect which he knew would haunt him to the end of his days, wherever he chose to live.

End of Part one

Part 2

Chapter 1

Lefty Linton-on-Ouse 1945

At war's end, the Royal Canadian Air Force No. 6 Bomber Group began the process of handing back the airfield at Linton-on-Ouse to its former owners; 6 group were to return to Canada and form a new unit dedicated to training bomber aircrew.

To continue his search for his daughter, Lefty had applied to remain at the station, rather than take another posting or the option of repatriation. Even so, he knew full well that if accepted, he may be limited to only ground duties, and working at the airfield would be quite different from his former role of bomber pilot. The post-war RAF was changing, and so was the role of the base at Linton-on-Ouse. The airfield was undergoing a transformation while adapting to the new and more mundane peacetime duties of the newly formed Transport Command. As he feared, Lefty's new duties involved far more office work than flying. Frustrated by the fruitless search for his daughter, Lefty knew that he may be forced to reconsider repatriation and return to Canada. This morning at his desk, he was considering his next

146

move in the quest for his daughter. Minding his own business, he checked his watch then turned his attention reluctantly back to the paperwork in front of him. Hearing the murmur of conversation at adjacent desks, he looked up to see the familiar, grey-clad messenger, later than usual for the morning rounds. What mail there was usually consisted of an uninspiring selection of internal memos, only relieved by the occasional personal letter. Exactly why this daily occurrence prompted an air of anticipation in the office, remained a mystery to Lefty. This morning, all Lefty was interested in was escaping the shackles of office bondage.

With all the dexterity of a bad croupier, the messenger carelessly aimed an envelope towards Lefty's desk while summoning up his best sarcastic tone: "A personal letter from the King for you, mate... You aven't been chasing after 'is daughter as well, 'ave ya?"

The envelope skimmed across the desk, landing on the floor beside Lefty, who replied, "Sleep in again, Flash?"

The messenger managed to throw Lefty a scowl accompanied by a two-fingered salute as he headed for the exit.

Marked 'On His Majesty's Service', the brown envelope would be the response to his application to resume flying duties, Lefty knew. Until now, Lefty's medical category restricted him to ground duties only, and hampered his ambitions to fly again. Nevertheless, Lefty persevered, but after two outright rejections, he knew that if unsuccessful this time, he may have to seriously consider the option of repatriation. Although the opportunities for flying may be more favourable in Canada, he did not want to give up the quest for his daughter. Sliding the tip of the pointed aluminium letter opener with his left hand, Lefty opened the envelope hesitantly. He withdrew the letter and slowly unfolded the foolscap page. Scanning the single typed paragraph, he read the words 'return to flying status as supernumerary aircrew only'. After studying each word carefully and reading it through twice more, Lefty placed the letter back into its envelope. As the reality sunk in, Lefty was ecstatic.

This was it, his key to escape a deskbound existence, to fly again...

As soon as it had arrived, the fleeting moment disappeared when Lefty was interrupted. Without the courtesy of a knock on the door, the squadron adjutant barged into the cramped office. He slapped a file marked restricted in front of Lefty, adding impatiently,

"I can't rely on you for anything; these figures are incomplete. I need them updated and on my desk by Friday morning for the C.O.'s weekly briefing..." he barked. Then after a short pause for effect, "... If you are finding the task too difficult, then I will give it to somebody else. You may think you are God's gift to flying, but you need to buck your ideas up, lad. I don't know how they work in Canada, but if you are planning to resume your flying career or God forbid work in an office, either way, you need to move at our speed, not yours...

"... Your constant applications for 48-hour passes, your frequent unexplained absences and lack of application have not gone unnoticed. The chief clerk has got you in his sights, so get a grip, lad, and get down to work." Scowling at Lefty, the adjutant stormed out as hastily as he had arrived.

Slowly and deliberately, Lefty raised himself to his full height, the grip on the hilt of the stiletto letter opener now a clenched fist. He exhaled a long sigh, and in one move kicked the office door closed with his right foot, causing it to slam. The startling sound reverberated around the office and caused a loose glass door panel to rattle alarmingly.

But now officially able to resume aircrew duties, he would pursue every opportunity for flying which came his way. Although Lefty had applied to stay in Yorkshire and continue searching for his daughter, he knew that would limit his options for flying. The post-war RAF was shrinking drastically. As units reverted to peacetime roles, many airfields were decommissioned, the land returned to its former owners, or relinquished to local authorities. Lefty would need to be patient and wait for the War Office wheels to turn, before he was finally returned to flying duties.

1946 – Be careful what you wish for! RAF Lindholme

Lefty had applied to stay at an active duty flying unit in Yorkshire. When his posting came through, although still in Yorkshire, RAF Lindholme was a bleak and unrewarding posting for Lefty. Perched on the edge of the Yorkshire Moors, Lindholme airfield seemed like a bit of a backwater to Lefty. Officially on secondary flying duties, some of his time was spent at Squadron headquarters compiling monthly statistics. At least he was able to fly several times a month. He had flown the Anson aircraft when he first arrived in the UK and was familiar with the old Aggie. Despite his experience, he found himself an Anson aircrew odd-job man. While waiting to return to full flying duties, Lefty had to content himself with mundane tasks such as loading and unloading freight, and ensuring that the aircraft remained within its performance limits.

There was always his favourite task, listening to complaining passengers. According to some, the aircraft was either too hot at the front, too cold at the rear, or just too noisy and uncomfortable. In 1935 when Avro designed the Anson as a small airliner, passenger appeal had been an important consideration. However, when war was declared it was produced in quantity under Air Ministry contract, the cabin interior became strictly utility, redesigned to meet wartime requirements, leaving few if any luxuries.

With only a thermos flask for catering, there was always the old favourite passenger gripe: the hot drinks were stale and lukewarm, and the cold drinks had no ice. Mind you, Lefty had to agree about the chicory coffee, it was virtually undrinkable at any temperature especially with the addition of tinned evaporated milk. Although most flights were under two hours in duration, Lefty admitted to praying for turbulence when serving drinks to the most disagreeable passengers, the ideal opportunity for accidental spillage. Still, on second thoughts it would give them something else to complain about!

On the odd occasion when he was assigned as co-pilot, he would have to take orders from whoever was delegated as Duty Pilot that particular day. In the right-hand seat, the co-pilot's job required few if any flying skills and mainly involved retracting or lowering the undercarriage of the lumbering Anson. Lefty knew it took 150 turns of the handle for the undercarriage to fully extend to the down and locked position. The practice had to be performed in reverse to allow the undercarriage to fully retract. Many of the trips involved training new aircrew and ferrying officials around the UK and Northern Europe. Although grateful for the opportunity to fly again, Lefty was driven by the need to be at the controls. At the moment, most of his duty time was spent either on-call or just standing by to cover sickness and leave.

Chapter 2

September 1945 Osprey

Having just emerged from the morning briefing, Lefty's morning routine was interrupted by the sudden appearance of the duty airman from the guardroom. Unsure whether to salute or not, the airmen hastily propped his cycle against the ops room door where it promptly fell, wheels spinning over concrete paving. Still flustered, the young lad informed Lefty that he was wanted by the station orderly officer. The duty airman was to accompany Lefty to ensure that he arrived at the guardroom promptly. Lefty looked at his watch, realising that he couldn't afford the time. It was another full flying day, and the squadron was shorthanded since the first wave of RAF conscripts had been 'demobilised' and returned to civvy street.

"Did you say the orderly officer?" asked Lefty as the young man nodded, adding "Or the duty NCO, there is somebody with them in the guardroom, Sarge".

"That doesn't sound like an opportunity for career advancement to me! What do you think?" But Lefty's humour fell on deaf ears.

Lefty admitted that his relationship with the squadron boss could be better at the moment. He wanted to avoid another opportunity to incur his displeasure. Punctuality and absenteeism were the boss's pet hates.

The young airman recovered his bike, still wearing an earnest frown as he pushed his bike, escorting Lefty as ordered. Then with a look of genuine concern, the young airman exclaimed, "Do you think you are in trouble then, Sarge?"

To which Lefty replied, "Well, I don't know about you, but I never go looking for trouble these days, but it has an uncanny knack of finding me!"

To which the young airman allowed himself a brief smile, adding, "He did ask for you by name, Sarge, and he was in an awful hurry. I think it's urgent, we need to get a move on, Sarge."

As far as the airman knew, the visitor was "some civvy who looked like a copper in plain clothes". Walking past station headquarters, Lefty felt a familiar and ominous foreboding. He had escaped the clutches of the authorities after his repatriation more than two years earlier. Since then, he had kept hoping that the past wasn't catching up with him, while reminding himself that he had nothing to hide.

Arriving at the guardroom, Lefty was confronted with a reluctant duty NCO. Without looking up from his desk, the corporal jerked his pencil towards a cramped room with the ominous words 'Defaulters Cell' painted on the door. Inside, a slight figure in an ill-fitting suit closed the door behind Lefty and presented an upturned palm, inviting him to sit opposite. The stranger cleared his throat whilst using his index finger to loosen the knot of his tie. He somehow looked out of place, uncomfortable and certainly overdressed for such a warm day. Something about the stranger reminded Lefty of the so-called escort that had accompanied him on his train journey to Oxford.

"I won't mince my words, sergeant..." said the stranger by way of introduction. Glancing at his watch, he continued, "... I have little time to spare and what I have to say is in the strictest confidence. I represent the chief investigator for the Allied war crimes tribunal. We need your help to trace a war criminal who you will have met in Norway."

"Let me guess... Special Branch, I can tell by the demob suit. What on earth makes you think I can help now?" Lefty replied, adding indignantly, "... If I had known it was you people, I would not have agreed to see you. Look, I have got a full flying day ahead of me, I can't spend time sitting around answering your absurd questions."

In response, the stranger said, "I understand that you have been trying to trace your daughter who you believe to be a survivor of an air raid in York... Am I correct?"

"What I have been doing in my off-duty time is no concern of yours," said Lefty. "I am a member of the Royal Canadian Air Force and a Commonwealth citizen serving in the UK with all the rights that go with it."

"Oh, how rude of me I almost forgot. May I congratulate you on the reinstatement of your aircrew medical," was the officer's response.

"So, you have followed my career, such as it is, so what?..."

Before Lefty had time to reply, the officer's tone changed as his gaze met Lefty's. "I don't think I've made myself clear, sergeant, we have the authority to act with impunity, we can promote careers and can be very generous to those who help us.

But we reserve the right to use alternative methods to deal with the unfortunate minority who refuse to cooperate.

"We act swiftly, in the blink of an eye... sergeant. Admittedly, we are reluctant to add to the list of missing persons, but that doesn't mean that we are not prepared to exercise the sanction, especially on foreign nationals, if you get my meaning, sergeant."

Then with the menacing tone suppressed, "It just so happens that you are in a position to help us. We have a long reach and a longer memory, sergeant, I would advise you to take our 'suggestions' seriously." Adding with direct eye contact, "Make no mistake, sergeant, we are serious, deadly serious. "

A diluted shaft of sunlight leaked into the room from the high single-paned window. Frosted glass secured with iron bars, mottled reflections from the single vent added an air of dejection to the cramped and airless room.

"There is nothing that I can add to the statement that I gave you over two years ago. Study your records more thoroughly, you will see that I do not respond to threats, either direct or implied."

Ignoring Lefty's plea, while glancing at his watch, the officer continued, "Let's get back to the matter in hand. Our subject of interest is 'Osprey', the dentist in Trondheim known as Rathke, a traitor and known double agent."

After a short pause for thought, Lefty replied, "As I said in my statement, I know nothing more of the dentist, so why don't you just leave me alone, go and catch criminals or whatever it is that you are paid to do."

"Ah, would that it was so straightforward..." came the reply. "... However, these things rarely are, sergeant. May I remind you that as a serving member of His Majesty's Armed Forces you are under the direct command of the War Ministry, still subject to the exigencies of King's Regulations, and the official secrets act, and as such you will do as His Majesty bids."

Standing up to his full height, pipe clenched between his teeth, the officer glared at Lefty as he continued. "Let me explain in words of one syllable, as part of a post-war Allied investigation and tribunal process, a traitor who has occasioned such damaging acts of betrayal as Osprey must be brought to account."

"If you can't find him, how do you expect me to?" offered Lefty.

Then pausing for effect, the officer continued in his patronising tone, "A history lesson for you – after the invasion of Poland, Rathke's practice partner in Danzig disappeared in mysterious circumstances, conveniently leaving him the sole owner of the practice. His command of English, German, and Polish and other languages made him an invaluable asset to us. His Majesty's Government helped finance Rathke's dental practice in Trondheim, in return for high-value intelligence with particular regard to German activities and ambitions in central Norway. Whilst working for us, his codename was 'Osprey' as I have mentioned before, which leads me neatly back to the subject at hand..."

The lecture continued... "... We have received reports of the dentist known to you as Dr Rathke. He abandoned his practice in Trondheim before he could be apprehended. He is now thought to be languishing somewhere in the Fatherland, or what remains of it. If he is in hiding in Danzig, we need to get him before the entire area is overrun by the Red Army."

A smug, self-satisfied smirk crossed the officer's face, who aimed it directly at Lefty, who replied.

"And exactly how do I fit into your intriguing little plot?" said Lefty. "I don't care for your implications. Do you actually believe that I somehow joined forces with Rathke, Ostrich, or whatever you call him? Do you think that I could be persuaded to conspire with the Nazis and subvert the allied war effort, is that what you really think?"

"What I think is immaterial, sergeant..." Then, looking at his watch... "Let's move on, shall we?"

The officer's lecture immediately changed tack. "It's *'Osprey'*, sounds like you need to brush up on your ornithology ... Well let me put you in the picture, and you can take that bewildered expression off your face right now, sergeant."

Bemused and frustrated by the apparent change of subject, Lefty shrugged as the officer continued his unnecessary repetition. "The dentist known as Osprey was serving two masters, us and the Gestapo... Okay so far?"

Without waiting for a response, the officer continued his talk in the condescending manner of a tiresome schoolmaster, pleased with the sound of his own voice.

"Fact... during the breeding season, the male Osprey, as with other migratory species, may fertilise more than one female, and dutifully provide for the offspring of each. When the climate no longer suits him, he will up-sticks and leave for more suitable climes. Deserted, abandoned, dependents are left to their own devices resigned to whatever fate awaits them... Many would die quickly, others may survive for a while, left to wither on the cruel and fruitless vine of neglect. Without conscience or remorse, the Osprey will leave them to perish, while he will prosper, go on to live a charmed life, cushioned from the grim realities of life, choosing never to return."

Deliberately interrupting, Lefty asked, "I didn't know at the time, how could I? I was in an occupied country; it was my duty to escape. Rathke offered me that chance, the only option I had. I trusted him. With hindsight, you may accuse me of naivety, but never treachery, and I resent the implication."

Ignoring Lefty's comment, the officer continued:

"Our particular Osprey not only neglected his responsibilities but saw fit to subvert the very habitat which nurtured him. This man is responsible for both the planning and compromise of your escape attempt from Norway. Not satisfied with that, he has single-handedly jeopardised the lives of scores of Allied agents and continued to do so since his untimely departure."

"I understand treachery, abandonment and neglect, I have seen the results first-hand – have you?" said Lefty.

"I am speaking, sergeant, you are listening" came the reply.

"Okay, have it your way, but what exactly do you expect from me?" said Lefty.

"Now we are getting somewhere," said the officer with smug impatience. Then through steepled fingers, leaning closer to Lefty to better observe his prey, the officer continued in his practised patronising tone.

"You will recall the farm near Trondheim where you claim to have spent a considerable period in the protective custody of the Norwegian resistance. You are to go back to Hocklingen, contact the farmer who we believe was a friend of the dentist and may know his whereabouts.

"Under the auspices of a debt of gratitude, you will re-establish your friendship with the farmer and by discreet enquiries, determine the whereabouts of Osprey. We will identify Rathke and bring him to book, and when we have finished with him, he will need to face the war crimes tribunal in Norway."

"Why me?" Lefty exclaimed. "This sounds like cloak and dagger stuff to me? I thought you people would have experienced professional operatives at your beck and call, rather than a reluctant amateur like me."

The officer adjusted his sitting position on the uncomfortable tubular metal chair whilst he considered his response. "I understand that you have had little success in your quest to trace your daughter, whom you believe to be a survivor of an air raid in York... As an incentive, and token of goodwill, I am authorised to offer you my department's assistance in tracing your daughter, if she does indeed exist."

Lefty carefully considered his options. The idea of tracing and prosecuting a war criminal, and the offer of help in tracing his daughter was too tempting to ignore.

"Who are you, and what exactly is your department?" Lefty enquired.

"We are your new friends, that is all you have to know of us," said the officer.

"So how do I know that I can trust your word when I don't know your name or who you work for?" enquired Lefty.

"It appears to me that you have little choice. I will walk out of here right now and there will be no record of my visit. You will do your duty, return to your career such as it is, and never mention this conversation to a soul, is that clear? Then you can go about your sordid little life, going round and round in ever-decreasing circles, without ever finding a single trace of your daughter. Let me see, she will be a playful three-year-old by now – wouldn't you like to give her a gift in person on her next birthday?"

Getting to his feet, the officer continued, "You will sign for your travel documents from the duty clerk in Station Headquarters, and upon arrival in Norway you will address any communication to us through the Norwegian Embassy, using the code name Osprey, is that clear?" Tidying up the paperwork on the desk, the officer returned the file to his briefcase, the hasp closing with a metallic click.

Addressing Lefty again he said, "Your department here will be told that you have been seconded to the new British Air Attaché's office in Oslo as from today. The appropriate paperwork is being raised as we speak. We will see to it that any enquiries regarding your whereabouts will be referred to us via the Station Commander. All that remains is for you to go and pack your bags... Any questions?"

Without waiting for a response, the officer opened the cell door and strode off along the corridor. Lefty hoped that it was the last he would see of the unwelcome visitor. Nevertheless, he had been puzzled by the strange encounter. He watched with curiosity as the officer marched out of the main gates, clutching a small briefcase as if it contained his life savings. All the stranger left behind was his lingering air of self-importance and the unseemly haste of somebody with a train to catch.

Return to Norway, Summer 1946

Lefty struggled to get a seat on one of the bare wooden benches in the ship's cafeteria – there was only room on his lap for his battered suitcase. Arriving at Newcastle on the overnight train from Doncaster, Lefty saw the port of Newcastle for the first time from the train windows. Although the bomb damage had been extensive, most of the loose rubble had been cleared away. The main quayside was still intact, the ferry port and terminal appeared to be functioning normally.

Lefty attempted to make himself comfortable aboard the 'Stella Polaris'. The ferry, a pre-war cruise ship, had obviously seen better days. Her once opulent furnishings and fittings lay thread-bare and unoccupied, a vision of past glories. Ghostly ball-gowned sirens waltzed in perfect time with partners, spectres in tuxedoes. Lefty fancied that he could hear the strains of the Vienna waltz, echoing across the distant hallway, keeping just out of sight, and destined to remain consigned to the shadows until relieved by a new generation of well-heeled revellers.

Even the benches in the cafeteria looked in urgent need of repair, as Lefty seated himself by one of the larger portholes while sipping at a welcome mug of coffee. Rust streaks from her anchor ports and corroded davits did little to relieve Lefty's qualms regarding the ship's serviceability, as he observed the worsening weather conditions.

Blowing steam from the rim of his coffee mug, Lefty savoured its warmth as he watched the gulls. He admired how they seemed able to sustain a precarious hover, suspended on buffeting gusts, jostled by the gale. Others perhaps more prudent were perched on the deck, feathers ruffled by the wind while taking shelter from the gathering storm. Today would be a day when wise birds would be walking.

Making full steam, the ferry slipped her moorings; released by the tugs, she headed out into the North Sea, directly into the teeth of a bitter north-easterly gale. According to the timetable, the trip from Newcastle to Bergen would take 18 hours, but with the prevailing weather, it would take more like 24. The strong swell in the North Sea accompanied them for the entire journey. Lefty already nurtured qualms about the whole idea of tracing Rathke, let alone the rough ferry crossing which added nausea to his already uneasy sensations.

The ferry's delayed arrival meant that Lefty had to spend the night in Bergen railway station, waiting for his onward journey to Trondheim. Sleeping rough in the terminal on an uncomfortable metal bench, Lefty dozed fitfully as he waited for the first signs of daylight.

A coastal mail ship plied the fjords of Norway's western coast connecting cities, towns and villages on each return trip. Aboard the '*Midnatsol*', Lefty took in the sights as he marvelled at the Fjords from the main deck. He could not help comparing this journey with his previous time in Norway and his skin-of-the-teeth escape four years earlier. This time he was able to absorb the spectacular scenery of post-war Norway and breathe its bracing and untainted air. The landscape appeared pristine, unblemished by years of Nazi occupation, or any evidence of the numerous Allied attacks. Here and there concrete bunkers and fortifications dotted the landscape as they gazed out onto an empty scene. Silent witnesses to so many unspeakable and outrageous acts of war.

But there were unseen scars, wounds which may never heal, and some which would remain deeply ingrained in the psyche of an enslaved and tortured Scandinavia. Scars which could neither be ignored nor tended, and whose wearers waited their fate in silence. Those who had been shown no mercy would demand justice or they would seek their own retribution, repayment of outstanding debt.

On arrival at Trondheim, Lefty hesitated for a moment on the quayside as memories of his earlier experiences flooded back. He recognised the abandoned U-boat pens on the North bank of the fjord, the waterfront and marina from his previous visit. Back then he had been warned to avoid the town centre at all costs, wary of the Gestapo or, worse yet, the treacherous quislings. But today the scene was alive and bustling, a peacetime city going about its daily routine. He made his way to the town centre and caught the bus out to the north-east of the city towards Levanger. The bus kicked up clouds of dust on the unmade road, just as Lefty remembered it. At the helpful driver's suggestion, he left the bus at the village of Åsen and continued his journey on foot. Overnight case in hand, Lefty made his way to the village of Hocklingen. The scene was both familiar and somehow unfamiliar. He remembered his night-time escape, the bridge and the river which now looked calm and tranquil in the stark light of day. As he walked, Lefty considered how he would tackle the rest of his task and wondered how he would be received at the farm. He was painfully aware that it wasn't the first time he had arrived unannounced at the farmer's front door.

Although Walter, the farmer, received Lefty with his customary firm handshake, Lefty thought he detected a tinge of caution in that warm, reassuring smile. The two were soon sitting drinking coffee and catching up on old times.

At first helpful, Walter gradually became more evasive when Lefty enquired about the dentist. Apparently, in 1944 the dentist had locked his premises in Trondheim and disappeared overnight. All the indications led to the conclusion that he had escaped to Sweden and effectively vanished...

Walter seemed either unable or unwilling to provide any more information on the whereabouts of his friend. After some persuasion, the farmer reluctantly agreed that even if the dentist remained elusive, his wartime henchmen, who were still at large, needed to be exposed. Walter further revealed there were others in the Trondheim area looking for the dentist, two of whom had died in mysterious circumstances. Even now, almost eighteen months after liberation, there remained sinister overtones in post-war Trondheim which lurked like veiled threats. However, the farmer did take Lefty to the main post office in Trondheim in order to establish a forwarding address for the dentist. At the desk, the nervous post office clerk was extremely reluctant to discuss the subject of local mail arrangements with a foreigner, let alone enquiries about redirected mail for the dental practice in Trondheim.

Overhearing the conversation, an elderly man emerged from the living room which served as the postmaster's office. In hushed tones, the senior postmaster agreed to meet Lefty at a cafe in the town centre the following morning. Over coffee, the old man eventually relaxed and began to unburden himself to Lefty. He spoke of his family's experience at the hands of their captors, describing some of the worst atrocities perpetrated by Rinnen and his gang on behalf of the Nazis, his own personal nightmares, first-hand accounts from an eyewitness.

In hushed tones the postmaster confided that his daughter had been abducted by Rinnen and his gang in 1942 and was never seen again, adding, "At least that animal has finally been locked up for good."

Then, glancing around him at the other customers in the busy cafe, the old man whispered, "Wherever the dentist is hiding, as one of Rinnen's henchmen he must not escape punishment, even though his thugs seem to be somehow protecting him still."

"Do you know what name he is using?" said Lefty.

"As postmaster, I have been warned never to mention that name to anybody, but he has done his damage here. If it helps to bring him to justice, I will do this one thing for a friend of Walter."

Then after hesitating, he added, "But you must assure me that you will tell no one in this city or even mention his name. The dentist still has friends here, thugs who will protect him at all costs." Pausing again, the old man regarded Lefty with both fear and suspicion. Small chestnut eyes clouded by opaque halos, darkened lower eyelids revealed the tarnish of fearful and sleepless nights. The postmaster frowned as he studied Lefty from beneath an anxious and furrowed brow. After more hesitation, he opened his neatly folded newspaper and produced a scrap of paper torn from the flap of a Manila envelope. Hand trembling, he surreptitiously passed the note under the wrought iron table to Lefty. Hastily scribbled in the corner was the number of a post office box in Danzig and the name Mikolaj Faber. Either Rathke's real name or some other assumed name, but this was definitely Rathke, the postmaster insisted. Apparently unwilling to discuss the matter any further, the old man stood up slowly, folded the newspaper under his arm, gestured farewell to Lefty and walked slowly back to his daily routine at the post office.

In 1946, rumours were rife in Trondheim regarding the fate of Pro-Nazi thugs and collaborators. Many had fled to Sweden to avoid capture, and if they had managed to hide out or disappear, surely, the dentist could do the same, with or without help. He had left his own trail of deception, calculated to lead any investigator to the same conclusion. Almost 18 months before the liberation of Norway, it was obvious that the dentist had fled. Not to Sweden where his deceptive forensic trail suggested, but to Poland. But why Danzig?... He may have returned to the dental practice.

Even so, Danzig seemed an unlikely refuge for Rathke. However, with limited options, he may have needed to return, grab whatever he could from the practice in Danzig and move on. Rathke had become a fugitive, but as either Faber or Rathke, he knew that he was still wanted in connection with criminal activities in pre-war Danzig.

Before moving to Norway, the dentist, then known as Faber, had been implicated in the disappearance of Rathke, his partner in the practice. The deliberate betrayal of an honest man whose livelihood and identity were both stolen by Faber. But whatever name he was using now, Rathke or Faber, whether in Danzig or not, he was undoubtedly cunning and resourceful. After all, it was SOE who had taught him how to avoid detection, deny accusation and survive interrogation.

If he was using the assumed identity of his practice partner, Rathke might still be in hiding in Danzig. But with the purges of the Soviet army in liberated Poland, he may well need to flee again. For Rathke, seeking sanctuary was fraught with risk, and he knew he must stay one step ahead of the Allies if he was to survive. Accustomed to the role of the hunter, the dentist had become the quarry.

Reporting in

After getting local help with translating Norwegian phone directories, eventually, Lefty was able to contact the office of the British Air attaché in Oslo. Using the agreed code word 'Osprey', Lefty confirmed the forwarding address of the dentist, emphasising that he may be using the name Rathke rather than Faber. They were particularly interested in details of the post office box number in Danzig, which he duly gave them. They pressured Lefty for more information, but he could provide nothing more, explaining that it had been difficult enough to discover that much. All that remained was for Oslo to pass on the message to the UK authorities. Lefty was informed that this phase of his task was complete, so he boarded the ship at Bergen. After arriving at Newcastle, he caught the train for his return trip to Yorkshire.

It had been several weeks since Lefty's return from Norway. His repeated attempts to contact Special Branch, using the agreed code word Osprey, amounted to nothing. Lefty planned to pick up his life, not just from where he left off, but with renewed optimism, convinced that he would find his daughter. He recalled the promise of the anonymous officer from the equally anonymous organisation who promised to help trace his daughter. Lefty had kept his side of the bargain, helping to trace Rathke. Now it was time for the officer to make good the agreement. If the promise of help in tracing Lefty's daughter was genuine, it must surely have revealed something by now. If experienced detectives were unable to trace her, what chance would he have? He was left to consider what value could be placed on promises from a person whose name you do not know, and whose organisation didn't exist. He had confirmed the name and last known movements of the dentist; he now needed details of his daughter's name and whereabouts in return. He attempted to leave messages on the only number he had, which rang constantly without answer. After a week without response, Lefty was about to give up, when the phone was eventually answered by an anonymous and officious female who would only identify herself as 'the secretary'.

More in hope than optimism, Lefty passed on the message using the code word Osprey, but none of his calls were returned and not one of his messages was answered. No contact from the officer or even a cryptic clue or message. Nothing. Lefty came to the inevitable conclusion that his report from Norway was too vague to be of use in the hunt for Osprey.

Nevertheless, Lefty resented the officer's empty promises and resolved to continue his own search for his daughter whenever his free time would allow. By now Lefty had exhausted most of his contacts and enquiries and was running out of ideas. It seemed that wherever his leads would take him, each compounded his frustration resulting in either a misleading distraction or just another dead end.

Chapter 3

Danzig – The Three Alls

The city of Danzig lay in ruins, the charred remnants of the Soviet assault and subsequent liberation. Unbeknown to Lefty, agents from UK intelligence authorities had been deployed weeks earlier to locate Rathke and apprehend him if possible. They were observing activity in the vicinity of one of the few intact buildings in the city centre that had, by accident or design, escaped with only minor damage. The name and box number provided by Lefty had been passed on from Norway to UK intelligence agencies. A 24-hour observation post had been set up in the centre of Danzig. British agents had chosen a vantage point which allowed observation of both the central railway station and the adjoining post office; the only building in the city which housed secure mailboxes. Throughout the city in every direction, Danzig was desolate. No matter where you looked, the debris and mutilation of war was evident. Displaced children seeking parents, families seeking food and shelter, others, apparently dazed, wandered the streets aimlessly. The Russian infantry had paid dearly for every blood-stained kilometre in their quest to liberate the eastern provinces of Poland. They had been the first to encounter Nazi death camps. Facing inevitable defeat, Himmler decreed that all evidence of the extermination camps and their inmates should be obliterated. The pitiless wretches who were unable to walk were executed. Some were burned alive along with the camp huts, now reduced to rubble and smouldering embers. Those still able to walk were herded westward on foot, the majority dying of malnutrition and mindless brutality on the way. The soldiers of the Red Army had been hardened by weeks of slaughter and hand-to-hand fighting. Each soldier ready for revenge and yet more bloodshed.

After overrunning another concentration camp at Stutthof on the outskirts of the city, Red Army soldiers went to work on the citizens of Danzig with ruthless brutality. With little restraint from their commanders, soldiers took anything of value, destroying any person or obstacle which stood in their way. Since the 'liberation' of East Prussia, the red Army systematically purged each province of any ethnic Germans as they went.

In 1945, following the German military withdrawal, the citizens of Danzig became victims of a campaign even more brutal than that inflicted by the Nazis.

Driven by the Communist doctrine of 'The Three Alls':

Kill all,
Burn all,
Loot all,

Mobs of Bolshevik Polish and Soviet militia indiscriminately sacked, tortured, and raped their way through Danzig, seeking out young women and any remaining German officials for special attention. As panic gripped the city, many attempted to flee westward to avoid the same fate. Men, women, and children became refugees, carrying with them pathetic bundles of belongings, some slow and stumbling, others with sticks of furniture hastily tied to donkey carts. The once beautiful city of Gdansk was in ruins, a burned-out German tank blocked the main thoroughfare. Derailed trams lay on their side like giant paralysed insects, entangled forever in webs of overhead cables. So far, attempts to trace the owner of box number 4469 had proved frustrating. However, on one occasion, a vigilant watcher observed a furtive dishevelled figure who entered the building, successfully accessed box 4469 then promptly disappeared. The detective on watch dispatched an agent in a bid to shadow the suspect. The pursuer had been briefed only to follow, report back, and otherwise remain undetected so as not to arouse suspicion. Oblivious of his pursuer, the suspect left the building by the station exit and made good his escape, simply merging with the seething knot of refugees on the crowded station concourse. The agent in pursuit was left bewildered, scratching his head beneath his woollen homburg.

In hiding just outside the city centre, Rathke was cautious and would never check the PO box in person, but employed runners on his behalf. However, in recent weeks, the city centre had become extremely dangerous, even for a petty criminal-turned-messenger, who knew every byway and passageway through the city ruins. Discouraged by the danger and the mean financial rewards offered by the dentist, the messenger's visits had become less frequent. Officially, entry to the building required proof of identity, but the PO boxes were in the lobby each secured with lock and key. After each visit, the runner simply disappeared after yet another futile inspection of the empty box. So far, every attempt to apprehend the dentist had failed. It was as if he had been tipped off, warned of the agents' presence, or spotted by a messenger, neither of which seemed likely. However, Rathke was either skilful or lucky; either way, he seemed able to stay one step ahead of his watchers.

The Allies would need another plan.

A trap

Motivated by greed and opportunity, some obstinate vermin have to be enticed out before they can be caught, a common practice used in the extermination of rodents; and one which just might expose the dentist, a ploy which may succeed where other methods had not.

So, a subtle plot was hatched involving the intelligence services in coordination with special branch and the Danish authorities. A very carefully forged letter was concocted to tempt Rathke with an irresistible bait, an opportunity that he could not refuse. The time was right, a last chance to reveal Osprey in the cold light of day.

Typed on headed paper provided by Copenhagen University, addressed to Doktor Rathke at his post office box in Danzig, the letter contained a personal invitation to a fictitious seminar. Entitled 'Restorative and Aesthetic Dentistry – The implementation of standardised ethical dental practice in post-war Europe', the fictional seminar was to be held at the University of Copenhagen Department of Odontology in just over six weeks, giving Rathke ample time to make his way to Denmark where the trap would be sprung.

For his part, Osprey, known as the dentist Rathke, had become desperate to escape Danzig and the Soviet purges, and was now willing to seize any opportunity to leave Poland. A drowning man, clutching at a straw. Before the letter arrived, he had already begun to plan his own escape. Now, letter in hand he had a lifeline, he would make his way to Copenhagen without any intention of attending the seminar. Once on Danish soil, he would make his way to the port and escape westward towards the Iberian Peninsula or South America. Although Rathke had forged identity papers and passport, he kept his name and title which he hoped might open doors. Yet he still felt vulnerable, not knowing who to trust.

As the Red Army continued its quest to eliminate any remaining pro-Nazi support in the area, Rathke knew he must leave soon, before he too was caught up in their purge.

He had anticipated the need for escape and prepared for a hasty departure. Rathke had taken several slim wafer ingots of high quality 22 karats dental gold from the safe in his practice in Danzig. The small ingots contained not only refined gold but also platinum, further enhancing their value. Every gram had been wrenched from the jaws of prisoners at Stutthof extermination camp on the outskirts of Danzig. After extraction, gold dental work was immersed in acid to remove any residue of bone or flesh. The remaining gold would be melted into anonymous slim wafers, still highly valued but easy to hide. The processed gold had been kept in Rathke's safe, awaiting collection by the central Reichsbank in Berlin. However, any Nazis who had been account holders at the Reichsbank would have long since gone to ground, leaving the gold ingots in Danzig, valuable, untraceable and literally unaccountable. Despite Nazi thoroughness, the dentist knew there would be no Reichsbank auditors queueing at his door to collect the ingots any time soon. If any official did appear before he left, however unlikely, Rathke was prepared to deal with them the only way he knew how.

Owing to their small size, the ingots were easy to hide, and Rathke was able to stitch the wafers into the hem of his woollen overcoat along with five 'discarded' gold dental crowns, acquired during his time at the extermination camp.

Whether he ever reflected on this shameful period of his life seems doubtful, as Rathke never showed even the slightest shred of remorse or pity for his victims. But given his duplicity, active support of the Nazi cause, and apparent pleasure in brutality, it seems that his corruption was complete. Although he may be able to deny even the most plausible accusations of his accusers, his victims, broken and scarred would never be able to forgive his outrageous cruelty. In their desire for retribution, some would hunt him down remorselessly until vengeance was theirs. In the deep dark recesses of his being, a hidden fear which would plague Rathke and the tattered shreds of his conscience until the end.

As his only means of contact with the outside world, Rathke resolved to check box 4469 in-person in a final bid to flee the title wave of treachery and violence which threatened to engulf the entire city.

Leaving Danzig for the last time, Rathke paid a final visit to the post office box. He hastily snatched the envelope which contained his counterfeit identification papers, passport, and the letter of invitation to the conference at the University of

Copenhagen. Glancing furtively over his shoulder, he carefully secreted each item in the inside pocket of his jacket. Rathke abandoned the post office box, leaving it empty and unlocked, the door swinging open as he made his exit. He knew that his luck was running out, and if he was to escape the inevitable onslaught, it was now or never.

His worn Gladstone bag clutched under his elbow, the dentist had salvaged what few possessions he could from his grimy apartment in the suburbs of Danzig. Rathke had become just another fugitive, but driven by renewed optimism, he had new purpose and resolve in every stride.

Hiding small denomination Danzig Gulden and Reichsmarks, he carefully distributed the used banknotes throughout his clothing. Now Rathke had only one goal: to reach Denmark and the opportunity that could determine his whole future. The dentist found the prospect of escape intoxicating. He might escape the clutches of the Red Army, and also evade the Allies, but he had to assume that both were already in pursuit. Once out of Poland he knew that Allied agents would pose the greatest threat.

All routes out of Danzig were crowded with refugees clutching their pathetic belongings, men and women, young and old, improvised transport with wheelbarrows, hand- and horse-drawn carts. Silent and expressionless, drawn, and dejected, living ghosts trudging westward ever westward. A flight from fear to hope, from slavery to liberty, from death to salvation. A desperate rout of mankind.

Knowing that the port of Danzig was running a limited ferry service, Rathke joined the crowds in their desperate attempt to escape to other destinations on the Baltic. Anything to get

CHAPTER 3

away from the inexorable tide of Soviet oppression. Pushing his way through the crowded quayside, ignoring the protests from frightened families and shrill cries of downtrodden children, the dentist elbowed his way onto the overcrowded ferry. Destined originally for Stettin, the overloaded ferry only managed to limp as far as the island of Hela in the Bay of Danzig. All passengers were ordered to disembark amid further confusion and rumour. Despondent passengers listened as an official announced that the Rostock ferry was on its way, most words drowned out by the clamour of the crowd and cries of hungry children. Rathke was painfully aware that his options were few, now that he had lost any alternative means of making his way to Copenhagen. The prospect of joining the throngs attempting the 350 km overland trek to either Stettin or Rostock would certainly be his last option. It would undoubtedly take longer and be much more dangerous, with no guarantee of onward passage to Denmark.

In 1945 as the Nazi high command in Berlin faced the inevitable prospect of defeat, many high-ranking SS officers and Gestapo members had been helped to escape the clutches of justice by fleeing overseas. But as an active sympathiser and quisling, Rathke had been left to his own devices. As a double agent, the dentist had gained the trust of the Nazis, whilst enjoying access to UK highly classified war plans. Had he not sacrificed his own safety, disrupting the Allied war effort, helping the Nazi cause in occupied Norway? And what of the high-grade allied intelligence he had passed on to the Gestapo? Had he not been instrumental in undermining SOE operations in central Norway at great personal risk? Had it all been for nought?

Mindful of the fact that those arrested for war crimes were already facing reprisals by the Soviets, Rathke knew that the few who did survive faced capture, arrest, and trial by an Allied court. The dentist considered his own crimes; he was even reluctant to use the word crime when describing his own activities. He felt no guilt, no shame – why should he? After all, he was no common criminal, was he?

In the twisted maze of his mind, Rathke now saw *himself* as a victim. He knew that the majority of the members of the Rinnen gang had been captured. He also knew it was only a matter of time before he himself was compromised. Whether gang member or victim, each would tell any lie, stretch any truth to save their own skin or condemn others. From his Gestapo handlers, he had learned of the gang's impressive success record, infiltrating, and breaking up resistance groups. He regarded their methods as legitimate, necessary evils to be dealt with in a professional manner. At first, he had managed to avoid any involvement with Rinnan's notorious gang of ruthless henchmen and sadistic misfits. The gang's well-earned reputation for violence was well-known in every household, not just in Trondheim, but throughout central Norway. It wasn't long before Rathke became a willing member of Rinnan's gang of thugs, enjoying their perverse and depraved methods and barbaric treatment of innocent victims. Although Rathke knew that Rinnan and his men had been rounded up during the Allied purge, there were still some gang members who may betray him, if tempted with plea-bargain.

He was relieved that he had escaped Norway long before liberation. Although his self-imposed exile in Danzig seemed the best option at the time, since the fall of the Third Reich, the constant checking of his post office box for notification of an assisted passage had been frustrating. Had his service to the Gestapo been forgotten? Before he left Poland, he had little option but to use the forwarding address of his dental practice entrusted only to the postmaster in Trondheim. In his desperation, trapped in Danzig, he became convinced that he had been overlooked and was forced to improvise his own escape plans. During his time in Trondheim, he had served two masters, both Nazi and Allied, at great personal risk. But he now felt abandoned, his only companion the constant spectre of betrayal which haunted every traitor's waking hours. The misery which he had inflicted on others was now his very own torment as he became increasingly bitter and resentful at his predicament.

Chapter 4

DENMARK, CAT AND MOUSE

Having bribed and bullied his passage on the ferry from Stettin, apart from the hold-up at Danzig, so far Rathke considered that his escape plan had been successful, and he was finally arriving at the port of Copenhagen. Apart from a handful of uniformed officials, there appeared to be little to concern him as he made his way to the gangway. He had considered whether he should carry a concealed firearm with him on his journey if only to coerce and deter. But he had weighed the options and decided that, if discovered, a gun would arouse suspicion, so he consigned it to the depths of the Baltic. But Rathke was a pragmatist; he had had the presence of mind to bring his small hunting knife tucked in his coat pocket where it could be easily concealed or disposed of.

He started to allow himself a small measure of conceit. Since leaving Danzig, Rathke had come close to compromise more than once, but by using bribery, brutality and cunning, he had managed to outwit officialdom on his bid for freedom. Surely now his reward was close at hand. The dentist was fond of the old quote 'Fortune favours the bold'. Perhaps this invitation was

... a very timely opportunity for his own exodus. Unfortunately for him, the trap was set, the bait irresistible, a slick masterpiece of deception, involving close cooperation of both the UK intelligence services and the Danish authorities.

Although the main British garrison had been withdrawn from Denmark by war's end, there remained a small but significant military presence at the British Air Attaché office at Bredgade in central Copenhagen. The military police at the embassy had been alerted to expect the dentist and had organised an appropriate reception committee in anticipation of Rathke's arrival. Cautious but unwitting, Rathke had been traced leaving Danzig on the ferry to Stettin several days before the fictitious seminar enrolment date. Mingling with the crowds, he eluded his watchers after boarding the transfer ferry onwards to Copenhagen.

Danish customs had been briefed to question Rathke on arrival at Copenhagen as they would have done for all arrivals from foreign ports. Rathke manufactured a smile as he approached the immigration desk, forged passport and letter of invitation at the ready. He decided that he needed to present himself as a confident and relaxed professional, despite the nagging doubts and anxiety which haunted him. Always wary, but growing in confidence, the dentist presented his passport and the letter as proof of identity. Oblivious of the plan for his capture, Rathke had unwittingly sprung his own trap. He performed his disarming smile again, remaining silent and avoiding eye contact with the customs officer. He waited patiently as he was given a brief personal search that revealed little apart from the knife in his coat pocket. In order not to arouse his suspicions, his woollen coat was returned to him after a cursory touch search. The dentist smirked to himself, relieved that he had escaped detection, relief that would be short-lived. Although the hunting knife had been confiscated, the rest of Rathke's property was returned to him in order to avoid suspicion. Checking his coat, he smiled again visualising the hidden gold wafers, the trove of bullion which remained undetected in the lining of his coat.

Bag inspected, Rathke cleared customs without incident. He replaced his worn homburg, tipping it at a jaunty angle as he joined the knot of passengers heading towards the terminal concourse, all following a white enamel sign that gave directions to Copenhagen Centrum. Once clear of the station, he would make his way back to the docks to find passage or stowaway on any ship which may offer his best chance of escape.

Left arm outstretched, the dentist was pushing the door marked terminal exit when he was distracted by a plainclothes policeman who asked him for the time. A discreet nod from the policeman was all it took.

As if from nowhere, Rathke was suddenly seized by both arms. Uniformed guards briskly ushered him to an adjacent office where he was detained by the Danish authorities while his identity was checked.

Following Danish protocol, appropriate paperwork had to be completed and identity documents confirmed before Rathke could be handed over for lawful extradition to the UK. Rarely noted for their haste, the wheels of Whitehall bureaucracy turned slowly in keeping with their tradition. But on this day when time was of the essence, it appeared that Copenhagen was suffering from the same affliction.

It was early afternoon when Rathke was bundled into a waiting staff car by armed guards and driven to the airport at Kastrup on the outskirts of Copenhagen. Awaiting approval from Whitehall, an RAF aircraft would be dispatched to collect the dentist and return him to the UK. Rathke was cautioned and warned of his impending investigation on suspicion of war crimes. On arrival in the UK, he was to be detained for questioning at Latchmere House in Surrey where the Home Office and MI6 would confront Rathke with irrefutable evidence of his wartime activities. He would be advised that he was to face charges of treason in the UK before being handed over to Norway to face further charges of war crimes.

Chapter 5

1946 – LEFTY – SPECIAL OPERATIONS FLIGHT

RAF Lindholme slumbered on with indifference, apparently reluctant to face the new day. It was peacetime and Lefty was up early on a beautiful Yorkshire morning.

It had been a very frustrating week, but, ever the optimist, Lefty hoped that good weather would herald a day when things would get better. As he walked to the Squadron, Lefty glanced knowingly at the early morning sky. This was definitely a day for flying. The only clouds to be seen were distant mare's tails threaded with gold, opaque wisps of high cloud barely visible in the south-west, carried aloft, scattered across a deep cobalt horizon.

Growing up in a country with big skies and distant horizons, Lefty had been taught to read the sky and watch for the changing of the seasons. From antiquity, outdoorsmen had learned those lessons the hard way, and were eager to pass on their wisdom to each new generation. They were men who knew when to sow, when to reap, and when to store silage for the long Canadian winters.

Like them, Lefty understood clouds and knew them for what they were: distant messengers bearing signposts and warnings. But today any signs of change looked destined for others elsewhere; not here and not now.

A shaft of sunlight found its way through the open hangar doors and shone a spectrum of coloured light that burst on the highly polished metal fuselage. Lefty was on a step ladder performing a routine pre-flight inspection of one of the squadron aircraft for a task later in the day. As usual, the hangar was a hive of activity.

Whirling propellers chopped each word of the tannoy message into disjointed syllables, and what was left was successfully drowned out by a chorus of roaring engines and power tools. The announcement specifically intended for Lefty was left for others to pass on.

The first he knew was when an engineer whistled and shouted: "Hoi Lefty, you deaf, mate?"

"Not yet!" shouted Lefty with a smile as he secured the engine oil filler cap.

The engineer raised his voice above the din in the echo chamber of the Squadron hangar.

"That's what wrong with this man's air force ... leaving a deaf, left-handed pilot doing the job of a qualified technician!"

""I would like to see one of your cack-handed grease monkeys try to land a Halifax," replied Lefty, enjoying the banter.

"Good point!" said the engineer. "Anyway didn't you hear the tannoy announcement?"

"What announcement?" said Lefty.

"Yeah, a tannoy especially for you, 'flight Sgt McFarland' by name."

"No, don't tell me, the Scharnhorst's come up again, and I've got to go and sink it single-handed!"

"Correct, genius, but in your case, it would be left-handed!"

"Well you go and tell whoever it is, that sounds like a job for the Navy. I thought they made a pretty good job of it the first time! ... Anyway, I'm busy, I've got an air test to do!"

"Gawd 'elp us all! – You air crew never cease to amaze me, when did you learn left from right, I don't know how you pilots do it!" said the engineer, adding "... anyway, you'd better get going, Lefty, somebody wants you in the adjutant's office pronto, you lucky boy!"

With a wry smile of resignation, Lefty wiped any remaining engine oil from his fingers, and dropped the oil rag onto the engineer's head. He climbed down the ladder, secured the aircraft, and made his way across the hangar to the Squadron offices.

His mind focused on the busy day ahead, Lefty was taken aback, he wasn't accustomed to seeing the door to the adjutant's office wide open, the revered oak panelling of the inner sanctum revealed to an unwashed world.

What's more, it looked empty. And it was empty – apart from the stern-faced station security officer, lurking in one corner.

An old war horse who wore a permanent frown of pessimism, the security officer waited impatiently for Lefty. With an air of conspiracy and anticipation, he gestured for Lefty to wait inside, as he glanced up and down the corridor before closing the door behind him.

Lefty was given a brief overview of an unscheduled mission. He was told that he would be collected by an Anson aircraft which was scheduled to land at Lindholme at 11:32 am. Owing to the urgent nature of the task, any further briefing would be provided when airborne. There may not be time for the aircraft to shut down engines and refuel before its onward journey to Denmark, but Lefty was warned not to intervene, as the sponsors had said that they "may have to play it by ear". All Lefty was told was that the flight had originally been planned to go from RAF Northolt in west London, direct to the military airfield at Copenhagen. Familiar with the Anson aircraft's operational performance, Lefty suggested that if there was no time to refuel the aircraft at Lindholme, they would need to refuel at the airfield in Denmark before returning to Kenley in Surrey. It soon became clear that there was little time and even less information. He was told to prepare immediately as the sponsors of the flight in London emphasised the urgency of the task. Lefty got the message: the fewer questions he asked, the better. The task outline was vague, but as far as Lefty was concerned, he would not even have time to pack an overnight bag even if he needed one. All he knew was that the flight would be going onward to Copenhagen to collect an individual needed for questioning in the UK. The Danish authorities insisted on the correct documents and procedures to permit extradition of an individual they regarded as a 'refugee'. Realising that he had little option, Lefty resigned himself to the task, without voicing any of his own misgivings.

Although the authorities in Copenhagen were holding the suspect on behalf of the UK government, the detainee had committed no crime on Danish soil. Furthermore, they would require a minimum of one eyewitness before he could be released.

Insisting that Rathke was their man, the Home Office had only agreed to send Lefty in a last-ditch attempt to satisfy Copenhagen's diplomatic bureaucracy. The appropriate documentation would be dispatched on the Anson in the safe hands of a security agent acting on behalf of the UK diplomatic service. Landing in Denmark, the appropriate paperwork was to be exchanged, but according to Copenhagen, documentation alone would be insufficient. To confirm the identity of Rathke, they also required corroboration from an independent witness; then and only then would they permit his release in to UK custody.

In London, protracted telephone conversations between the Home Office, the Provost Marshall's office, and the authorities in Copenhagen all conspired to delay the departure of the aircraft from RAF Northolt, near London.

Squadron Leader Green DFC was head of the special flight detachment at Northolt and was their most senior captain, with a distinguished wartime record, having completed 119 bombing missions. At peacetime Northolt, he had a well-earned reputation as one of the most experienced pilots on the unit, but was equally renowned for his lack of patience. Sitting around doing nothing was not his favourite occupation, and it showed. Nominated as duty captain for the flight, Green was becoming impatient. He and his co-pilot had been told to prepare for immediate take-off more than an hour ago, but here they were, still sitting on the tarmac at RAF Northolt, waiting. For Green, the morning had been frustrating, a typical example of bureaucratic hysteria; hurry up to slow down best described the captain's day so far. The aircraft had been prepared, a flight plan filed in accordance with international rules, and the co-pilot had grabbed the latest weather forecast for the route.

The insistent ringing of the secure phone in the Lindholme operations room was answered by the duty officer. The call was from the special duty flight commander at RAF Northolt who expressly asked for the Wing Commander in charge of flight operations. Acting as supernumerary aircrew, Lefty was to accompany the arresting party on the flight. His only order was described as a formality, confirming the identity of the suspect.

The Whitehall security guards finally arrived at Northolt, one carrying a secure document pouch. Each looked uncomfortable in their loose-fitting suits, and both were obviously armed. The time for discussion and updated crew briefing would have to wait. Any further issues would be dealt with en route; they were already almost two hours behind schedule.

After taking off from RAF Northolt to the west of London, the flight was to collect Lefty from Lindholme in Yorkshire and take him to Copenhagen. Once Lefty had formally identified Rathke, the flight was to take the suspect to RAF Kenley in Surrey. On arrival, the flight would be met by security guards who would take Rathke to the detention centre at Latchmere House.

With the engines running, Lefty leapt aboard the taxiing RAF Anson aircraft, which headed for the main runway ready for immediate departure from RAF Lindholme. The captain, squadron leader Green, was in a hurry, telling Lefty and the crew that they needed to make up time. After leaving Denmark, they must arrive at their final destination, RAF Kenley, during daylight hours as there was minimal lighting at the airfield and no facilities for night operations. Furthermore, once the transaction was complete, it was expressly forbidden for either the aircraft or suspect to remain overnight on Danish soil.

To satisfy extradition requirements a prompt turnaround had been planned at Kastrup airfield near Copenhagen with an expeditious return to the UK before nightfall.

The outward journey from Lindholme to Denmark was uneventful; however, time was pressing now with only a few hours of daylight left. On-board, the two security officers sat quietly in the rear of the cabin. But when prompted by the captain, all they would reveal was that the hold-up had been at Whitehall. Apparently, there had been difficulty obtaining permission to access security service records. Only they knew that flight sergeant Donald McFarland was the only "admissible" eyewitness who could identify the dentist, especially if Rathke was in disguise. Lefty acted as supernumerary crew member along with two pilots, accompanied by the two armed civilian escorts. After arrival at the military airfield at Kastrup, just outside Copenhagen, the aircraft taxied to the ramp and the engines were shut down. The captain released his seatbelt and, addressing all on board, turned, and pointed to his watch, emphasising urgency, and the need for a rapid pickup from the Danish airbase. The co-pilot was the only crew member to remain on the aircraft, while Lefty, the captain, and the two escorts were directed to a small annexe adjacent to the control tower. Before the captain left the aircraft, an animated discussion ensued between him and the co-pilot who emphasised the necessity to refuel and obtain an updated weather briefing before the return flight.

During face-to-face discussions with the Danish authorities, the validity of both the documentation and the witness's testimony were called into question. Before leaving Lindholme, Lefty had been warned by the station security officer that whatever doubts Lefty may have regarding the identity of Rathke, he was to keep them to himself. But it only took a brief moment for Lefty to recognise the dentist and formally identify him. Once the handover was complete and the aircraft had arrived at RAF Kenley, the armed escorts would disembark along with Rathke, mission complete. The aircraft was then to return to base at RAF Northolt, leaving Lefty to make his way back from London to Lindholme by train.

After further delays, the Danish authorities produced the incriminating letter, with Rathke's name on it, inviting him to the seminar in Copenhagen. With letter and suspect on board the aircraft, Rathke was secured in the cabin and handcuffed to an armed guard. The flight was finally cleared to depart for the return trip to the UK. It was now late afternoon and, under leaden skies, the co-pilot completed the cockpit checks. The original task had called for a routine daytime round-trip, but amid the confusion and haste, the mission was rapidly turning into a challenging night flight, in an aircraft that was ill-equipped for the hazards ahead. Frustrated by Danish bureaucracy in general, and the airport authorities at Kastrup in particular, Squadron Leader Green returned to the flight deck of the Anson. He heaved an impatient sigh of relief as he clambered into the left-hand seat, replaced his headset, and instructed the co-pilot to prepare for immediate departure. Both engines came to life as the crew prepared for the journey to RAF Kenley in Surrey. As captain, Green had flown many wartime missions and had become accustomed to dealing with well-planned sorties, which, like many, went wrong after first contact with the enemy, and right now the enemy was time. He was familiar with the confusion of combat. He had trained to anticipate those times when unforeseen circumstances and limited options could be a lethal combination. Times when initiative and improvisation were your only allies.

Green didn't know it, but it wouldn't be long before those skills would be needed again. Right now, as far as the captain was concerned, they were late. Once again, the main enemy was that old familiar tyrant, time, but there was a conspiracy of elements becoming involved, factors way beyond his control, lying in wait to disrupt the best-laid plans of men. As Green taxied the Anson towards the runway at Kastrup, he glanced at his watch; it was early evening already. They should have landed at the RAF station at Kenley 2½ hours ago, the aircraft should have been 'put to bed' in the hangar, and the crew should have been relaxing with the mission complete.

Above all, the captain knew aviation was an unforgiving occupation; even the smallest of oversights could be fatal. One of the cardinal sins in flying was haste. Undue haste could jeopardise any mission, no matter how well-planned, but nevertheless, the nagging urgency of the task gnawed at the captain's senses. But not just the captain, the entire crew would need all their wit and resourcefulness if they were to survive the coming hours. This day wasn't over yet, not by a long chalk. If it was the gods who were to blame, they had been mocking the task from the start, and if it was demons, they hadn't finished toying with the mission yet.

In the right-hand seat, the co-pilot was much younger than the captain and acutely aware of their predicament. As with all juniors, unfortunately, it was the co-pilot who bore the brunt of the captain's frustrations.

Before leaving the UK, the captain had requested that the co-pilot plan for a straightforward round trip, one that was becoming more problematic with each minute that passed.

The airfield at Kastrup was closing for normal operations shortly after they landed. After repeated requests, the co-pilot was able to get a weather forecast, but the airport authority was not prepared to provide refuelling for the return trip to the UK.

The co-pilot was concerned about the lack of fuel and current weather forecast, and briefly discussed his misgivings with Lefty. It was Lefty who resolved to tell the captain that the only available weather forecast was out of date, emphasising the urgent need to top up the fuel tanks.

But right now, the captain was focused, preoccupied with the urgency of the task. His word was final and would override any observations from other crew members. Driven by his autocratic manner, insisting that the urgency of the task was of overriding importance, they were on their way. As captain and war veteran, squadron leader Green knew that the task sponsors would not tolerate peacetime delays, no matter what the circumstances.

After all, it was Green who would have to face the music, the debrief by hard taskmasters who would not accept explanations which they would dismiss as excuses. They may understand why take-off was delayed initially, but exactly why the mission was behind schedule and why it was falling further and further behind, were questions that would need to be answered.

They were the last flight to leave Kastrup that day, and every minute wasted would be a minute lost. As far as the captain was concerned, the war was over, but to him, the newly formed MoD was either still at war, or looking for a new one. Green understood the need for security, but exactly why they were obsessed with timing and punctuality only the Security Services knew. Somebody obviously didn't liaise thoroughly enough with the authorities at Kastrup, who seemed more concerned with closing on time than remaining open for a special task. Some of the UK security service officers were even worse than the MoD, demigods who lived in some shady post-war world of permanent paranoia.

Climbing towards a lowering cloud base and reduced visibility, the crew were familiar with most of the airfields adjacent to their return route, but were unaware which, if any, would have conspicuous airfield lighting. The captain checked the fuel gauges again, cursing under his breath, accusing the co-pilot of missing the opportunity to refuel. He would 'have words' after they returned to base. The option of diversion had not been considered as the crew was under strict instructions to deliver the suspect directly to RAF Kenley for detention at Latchmere House.

The crew eased the Anson onwards, now cloaked in disorienting twilight as rain streamed down the windscreen, reducing forward visibility. All eyes strained, peering over the instrument panel for any recognisable landmark. The aircraft was equipped with radio direction-finding RDF equipment to aid navigation, but 30 miles ahead of them, an electrical storm was building. The radio compass, which they had come to depend on, switched first this way, then that. From Southwest to Northwest, the RDF was tracking distant bolts of lightning rather than their selected radio beacon at Detling on the Kent coast. Acting as lookout, Lefty moved from the flight deck and positioned himself in the vacant air gunner's turret, using the transparent dome as an observation port. The aircraft descended slowly in an attempt to remain clear of cloud and insight of the surface. In preparation for peacetime roles, the single Vickers machine gun had been removed from the dorsal turret of most of the early model Anson aircraft.

Owing to the hasty modification, weatherproofing seemed to have been overlooked, allowing a constant trickle of rain into the cabin. As the weather closed in, the night became an inky black void; in the distance to the west, lightning pierced the heavens as the storm built in intensity. A punishing headwind heralded the leading edge of the squall and further impeded their progress. The rain was now extremely heavy, accompanied by hail showers, the sound reverberating throughout the flight deck as it drummed against the outer skin of the fuselage. From his vantage point, Lefty glimpsed snapshots of coastline to the north, but just how far they had progressed became increasingly difficult to determine. Peals of thunder and driving rain reverberated throughout the entire aircraft. The noise level in the cabin was so intense that Lefty found it difficult to think straight, let alone concentrate. On the cramped flight deck, torrents of rain began to overwhelm the inadequate windshield wipers, severely restricting forward visibility. As the storm intensified, each crew member blinked at every salvo of dazzling lightning bolts, the involuntary reaction tearing at each retina stripping away any remnants of night vision. Every kaleidoscopic flash of brilliant Indigo punched holes in the towering clouds, night turned into day in the blink of an eye. Billowing turbulence tugged at the airframe as unseen hands rocked the wings of the Anson first this way, then that, as the storm increased in momentum with each violent discharge.

PART 2

In the cramped cabin, the armed escorts, aware of the developing situation, observed activities on the flight deck with apparent indifference. With Rathke securely handcuffed to a metal seat support, there was little left for them to do before landing in the UK, so each took turns, periodically checking the restrained prisoner. On the flight deck intercom, the pilots discussed the deteriorating weather conditions, the lack of options for diversion airfields, and the rapidly diminishing supply of petrol in the reserve fuel tanks. The captain, adamant that they should comply with their orders, would not consider the option of diversion, or any deviation from their flight plan.

Looking at the fuel gauges, the co-pilot urged the captain to refuel, but his words went unheeded or overruled, every suggestion ignored by the captain who was determined to press on. Three pairs of eyes strained, widened without night-vision, looking forward, two over the instrument panel, and Lefty, connected to the intercom in the mid upper turret. All searching for any landmark, indication of a horizon or any other feature through the darkened storm-laden squall. In the captain's bid to avoid the worst of the storm, he had deliberately deviated to the left of their intended track. But in fact, the aircraft had continued a gradual left-hand turn which took them towards the Belgian coast to the west of the Scheldt estuary, ending up on a northerly heading. Once Lefty realised the discrepancy, he advised the crew who attempted to compensate for the error, returning to a more southerly heading. The lightning was so intense now that on the flight deck, night vision had been completely compromised. The co-pilot's head was down now attempting to read the heading from the standby E2 magnetic compass, but only illuminated by a dim red light; it was all they had, even so, the instrument was

194

proving all but impossible to read. Lefty had briefly glimpsed coastal lights off the right-wing, but as they corrected their track, the lights disappeared. Static hissed and crackled, suppressing both onboard radio receivers and intercom. On the flight deck, keeping one eye on the storm, the captain consulted the charts, leaving the co-pilot to maintain control of the aircraft. Lefty needed all his concentration, searching in vain for any recognisable visual cue or waypoint.

Cruising at reduced speed only 200 feet above the waves, the only option for navigation was dead reckoning with no discernible horizon. All eyes scanned the seascape, Lefty felt the knot in his stomach tighten as disorientation plucked at the periphery of his overworked vision. Above the din, the co-pilot updated the fuel state on the intercom more frequently now. Glancing at his watch, it only took a quick mental calculation for Lefty to realise the gravity of the situation, and immediately recognised the anxious tone in the pilot's voice. Paying homage to the god of hindsight, Lefty reflected that there would have been plenty of time to refuel the aircraft on the ground at Kastrup owing to their delayed departure. Although the military base had closed shortly after their late arrival, the crew had anticipated an expeditious engines-running pickup. They had missed the narrow window of opportunity to refuel. But what Lefty could not know was that owing to the urgent nature of the task, the option of refuelling the aircraft at Kastrup had been declined by flight operations before they had even left the UK.

Post-war, the RAF operated the Anson on short hops mainly within the UK. In its day it was a serviceable enough aircraft, but now the twin-engined Aggie was beginning to show her age. The gauges on the Anson's gravity-fed fuel system were notoriously unreliable, a fact which only served to heighten the growing feeling of anxiety on the cramped flight deck.

It was obvious now, the crew knew that they must land very soon or risk ditching, a prospect that nobody relished and was only to be considered as a last resort. The captain went through the options once more. With the storm still at its height, the prospect of executing a safe water landing in the North Sea looked all but impossible. But he knew that the longer the decision was put off, the closer those roaring storm-tossed waves crept closer, ever closer.

In the cabin, the suspect and escorts were fleetingly illuminated by vivid blue flashes of lightning which lit up the entire interior of the aircraft. Each expression revealed its own level of anxiety.

The cabin windows now rivulets in the rainstorm, overwhelmed the inadequate windscreen wipers of the Anson. The only surface features which could be distinguished from the aircraft were glimpses of the crests of windblown white-capped waves, in electric blue relief, beckoning the aircraft closer, ever closer to its indigo-grey embrace.

Onboard, the crew ran through the emergency checklist and prepared for ditching. In accordance with procedure, Rathke's handcuffs remained secure, but the armed escort prepared the Mae West lifejackets and readied the keys in order to ensure that Rathke would not drown in the event of ditching. Securing the keys, and feeling for his holstered firearm, the senior escort was now mindful of saving his own skin, let alone that of the dentist. On the flight deck and in the cabin, crew and passengers both knew that they would carry out their duties, each that was apart from Rathke. But if the aircraft had to ditch, each also secretly knew that it would be every man for himself, a fact which was uppermost in every mind, especially that of Rathke. Cruising at low altitude, Lefty watched for any sign of the Cork lightship to the east of Harwich or even the Barrow Deep in the Thames estuary. However, the intensity of the storm would only permit fleeting glimpses of distant lights from the cabin windows. The forward visibility was too poor to recognise any vessel, let alone identify any landmarks on the coast. Confused and fighting disorientation, Lefty suddenly glimpsed beckoning beams in his 10 o'clock position, on the southwest horizon. After a brief discussion, the crew agreed that the only light of that intensity must be the Trinity house light at North Foreland, perched on the cliffs of the Isle of Thanet, the northern coast of Kent.

Just as it seemed that salvation was assured, the number one engine misfired, coughed, and shut down, a deadweight, its propeller a useless windmill. There was no time to hesitate or plan. The crew executed the well-practised routine, turning off fuel cock and feathering the spinning propeller blades. Each crew member made preparations; there was no discussion, they had run out of options. Lefty scrambled down from the turret, returned to the flight deck, and re-fastened his seatbelt. Estimating their position to be somewhere off the Essex coast, the crew nurtured the Anson into a shallow right-hand bank. In the tense moments that followed, Lefty made a sudden announcement on the intercom, "Coastline dead ahead, captain, looks like Southend." The co-pilot was using every ounce of concentration and announced that "it could be Rochester".

Above the noise, Lefty replied, "No, I'm sure we're not that far South, we haven't passed the Thames estuary yet."

Lefty was correct.

In fact, they crossed the coast just north of Foulness, as the aircraft became increasingly unstable with only one engine running. The co-pilot asked Lefty to start lowering the landing gear, but over the noisy intercom Lefty declared that there was no time for that, "we should prepare for a wheels up forced landing". Response from the controls was sluggish as the aircraft descended to treetop height with the second engine losing power. Lefty glimpsed a subdued glow reflected on the underside of the cloud deck just above an opaque horizon. Indicating an area in the middle distance, slightly right of track, Lefty's outstretched arm reached over the co-pilot's left shoulder, just as the view was obstructed again. Any suggestion of light was enveloped in the gloom of the next heavy downpour. The Anson descended slowly, becoming an unwieldy glider as the second engine fell silent. In the middle of the deluge, Lefty caught sight of the confluence of the rivers Crouch and Roach. Southend would be somewhere dead ahead, but visibility was still very poor. All eyes scanned the landscape ahead, each searching the surface for whatever lay in front of them, a flat and featureless void. As the dark expanse of RAF Rochford emerged slightly left of their track, the captain inched the stricken aircraft towards the unlit runway. They were so low that it was impossible to make out the airfield layout but, however indistinct, it was there, terra firma; right under the nose...

The crew braced themselves for the inevitable heavy landing. Under the influence of gravity and good fortune, the crew executed a textbook wheels-up landing on the grass airfield. The Anson bounced twice as it contacted with the ground, then careened across the sodden grass runway of Southend Rochford Airport. After reducing a wooden runway control cabin to firewood and gouging out temporary lighting, the aircraft slid uncontrollably for what seemed like a mile, before coming to rest with a sudden jolt as it struck the boundary fence at the distant end of the airfield.

For a split second, aircraft and occupants sat in total silence, while the airframe ticked and creaked, enveloped in the darkness. It was Rathke's guards who reacted first, while Lefty reached for the emergency handle of the cabin exit door.

In their haste to evacuate the aircraft, one of the agents lost his footing allowing Rathke the opportunity to grab the key. In a desperate bid for freedom, Rathke deftly released his handcuffs, while the other agent withdrew his pistol in an attempt to prevent the dentist's escape. In the darkened cabin, a desperate struggle took place as each agent grappled with the dentist. In a split second, a shot rang out, and an agent collapsed as Rathke made good his escape through the aircraft hatch, now in possession of a 9mm pistol. Brandishing the weapon and threatening the second agent, a glancing warning shot was fired in Lefty's direction, which ricocheted around the aircraft cabin. In the blink of an eye, Rathke melted away into the stormy night, pursued by the second agent who fired poorly-aimed shots of desperation in the general direction of his quarry. That was the last those aboard the aircraft would see of the dentist as he crashed desperately through the storm-tossed brambles and undergrowth towards the dimly-lit main road.

Inside the cabin of the aircraft, Lefty administered an improvised tourniquet to the injured agent who had received a gunshot wound to the leg, while the remaining crew members attempted to alert the emergency services.

When questioned by the local customs officer the following morning, all the captain would divulge was that they "had been on a night navigation exercise and had become temporarily disorientated". Out of earshot, the captain reminded the crew of the mission outline, emphasising that they had been tasked by the Home Office on a strictly need-to-know basis. No crew member was at liberty to discuss the matter with civilian authorities, adding as far as Southend is concerned this was a training mission only. The captain nominated Lefty to stand by the phone in the control tower while the crew prepared for transport back to base.

"Hold on, we've got our job to do as well, you know."

The voice came from a dour well-built individual who wore a gabardine mac and an air of jaded officialdom. He carefully placed his damp trilby on the desk next to the phone, as he addressed the crew. All three crew members, including Lefty, wore flight jackets over their uniform, revealing no evidence of identity or rank.

"My name is Squadron Leader Green..." announced the captain, adding, "... and who exactly are you... sir?"

"My name is Matthews," came the reply "... I am deputy airport manager, which gives me responsibility for the security of this airport; that includes customs, health, and immigration."

"This incident is a Ministry of Defence matter only and as such is no concern of yours, Mr Matthews..." came the captain's response.

There was a pause as Matthews gathered his thoughts beneath his furrowed brow.

"Now let me see, since when did an RAF night navigation training exercise carry two armed civilians, one of whom has been injured, with no evidence of documentation?"

The rhetorical question hung in the air before Matthews continued. "... I would say this is not just a customs, health and immigration issue, but also a crime scene, not to mention the damage you've caused to my airfield, who is going to pay for that?, I think that makes it very much my concern."

"Let me make myself clear to you, Mr Matthews..." said the captain with his customary air of authority. "... Mr Matthews, I would advise you to leave this matter with me. If you insist on exercising your authority, you will very soon get out of your depth..." adding "... Any further communication regarding the flight or circumstances should be addressed to the duty officer at Whitehall. You can find the number in the telephone book," he added with a hint of sarcasm.

"Well, Squadron Leader, Whitehall or no Whitehall, *my* airfield is officially the location of an aircraft accident, and also a potential crime scene; as such, I assume jurisdiction of the incident from here on in."

Undeterred, Squadron Leader Green continued: "Until our transport arrives, my aircraft and my crew remain my sole responsibility. From this moment on, the aircraft will be impounded and will be guarded by Flight Sgt McFarland here–" pointing at Lefty.

Thinking quickly, Lefty added in an assertive tone, "I will only allow access to the aircraft by authorised military personnel until any live ammunition on board can be made safe."

The captain nodded approval of Lefty's statement, adding his own endorsement: "Just to avoid any misunderstanding, until the aircraft has been recovered, only military agencies will have access to the aircraft to the exclusion of all others."

Interrupting, Matthews said, "Surely that does not include my team and me?"

With an air of satisfaction, the captain replied, "That means *especially* you and your team, Mr Matthews."

At that moment, an RAF staff car drew up in front of the building; the crew collected their belongings and headed for the exit.

Matthews re-joined with "not so fast..." and turning to Lefty said "... Laddie, you don't sound British to me, do you have any formal identification? As you haven't given us your point of departure, I insist on a name for processing any non-British nationals for immigration purposes."

Impatiently the captain said to Matthews, "Flight Sgt McFarland is with us. I will personally vouch for him..." Then, sensing that Matthews was going to intervene again, the captain turned to Lefty saying "... just give them your best autograph, Don, and we will get out of here. I'm going to leave you in charge, Flight Sgt McFarland."

With that, the captain and co-pilot walked out to the staff car as Lefty posted two burly RAF policeman out on the airfield as sentries guarding the entrance hatch of the damaged Anson.

Finally boarding the train to York, Lefty reflected on the events of the past two days. He thought of Matthews, 'just doing his job', the captain, Squadron Leader Green, and his order to describe the mission as a training exercise. Although it might be a plausible cover story in the event of compromise, anyone connected with the armed forces would see straight through that press statement. His own improvised warning regarding live ammunition, although exaggerated, was correct. However, the only munitions remaining on board the aircraft were pyrotechnic signal flare cartridges, safely enclosed in a metal box in the aircraft cabin. Although strictly described as a firearm, the accompanying Very signalling pistol was used in emergencies only, and not generally regarded as a weapon.

"Here!" Matthews had barked impatiently, presenting an immigration pad while thrusting a pen at Lefty, "... number, rank, full name and Nationality..." adding "... don't forget the duplicate, and sign here!" Matthews continued, "You lot are worse than the Germans, at least we knew who the enemy was back then, you lot think you are above the law." Matthews' last words lodged in Lefty's memory, "This isn't the last you've heard of this, you mark my words..."

Half smiling, Lefty murmured to himself, "Oh, yes, it is, Mr Matthews, oh yes, it is. You don't know the half of it!"

On the train to Doncaster, Lefty relaxed, enjoying the comforting rhythm and warmth of the empty compartment. He imagined the inevitable board of inquiry and secretly hoped that he would not be called to give evidence. He didn't want any prolonged interruptions once he had returned to Yorkshire, as he planned to resume the search for his daughter, hoping to have some new leads to follow.

Having applied first aid, Lefty had accompanied the injured armed-officer to Southend hospital, and the patient had been left in the best medical hands. But what about Rathke? Perhaps the second armed agent had caught up with Rathke. So far as Lefty was concerned, there had been no mention of the fate of pursuer or pursued, and neither was heard of again.

The aircraft recovery team arrived at Rochford later that morning, and Lefty officially handed responsibility to a senior engineer. Hands on hips, the technician surveyed the damaged aircraft and the engineer seemed unenthused by the task ahead, implying that Lefty had been responsible for the entire incident.

There was nothing more to be done so far as Lefty was concerned. But the circumstances surrounding the disappearance of Rathke would remain an embarrassment to officialdom for years to come. Of one thing Lefty was sure, in the corridors of power and in their private clubs, Home Office mandarins, and Colonel Blimps in the War Office would certainly want to be spared the embarrassment of that escapade. If the newspapers got hold of it, they would have a field day, but Lefty felt sure the whole thing would be consigned to the archives especially reserved for the collective amnesia of Whitehall, and conveniently forgotten.

Chapter 6

BERLIN 1948

Following a further succession of dead-end searches for his only child, Lefty was considering returning to Canada and making a fresh start. During his time in the UK, he had written to his stepmother in Montréal on several occasions without any reply. Each time Lefty had collected together the money for passage to Canada, he hesitated; he could not rest until he had satisfied himself of the fate of his daughter.

Some of his ex-forces friends from the squadron had found jobs in the new post-war civil aviation business which had gained a new lease of life using modified war surplus bombers as commercial passenger aircraft.

Lefty applied for work with Eagle Aviation who were flying freighters from Wunsdorf near Hamburg as the Berlin airlift was starting in earnest. Once again, Lefty found himself categorised as supernumerary aircrew and spent most of his time loading and unloading cargo rather than being engaged directly on flying duties.

During his time at Wunsdorf, he got to know crews from British South American Airlines – BSAA – who were fully committed to the Berlin operations in a similar sanction-busting role. On discovering that the pay and conditions were much better than he could expect from his present job, Lefty resolved to escape from the permanently cash-strapped Eagle Airways and apply to BSAA for a full flying position.

Early in 1949 Lefty completed the formal application as BSAA had begun recruiting pilots to boost their post-war long-haul operations. However, in compliance with the Air Corporations Act, BSAA and the British Overseas Airways Corporation were amalgamated in the spring of 1949 and effectively became a government-owned corporation. Despite persistent applications to the aircrew recruiting department, most of the aircrew slots had already been filled by the influx of those who held wartime posts as either captain, first officer, navigator, or flight engineer. Despite Lefty's considerable wartime flying experience and excellent letter of recommendation, as a Canadian with dual nationality inexplicably he was not even offered the courtesy of a reply, let alone an interview. After persistent enquiries, the airline board invited him to an interview as a trainee junior purser, which he politely declined, citing his flying experience and employment potential as a pilot.

After returning to the UK, Lefty found casual work as a part-time instructor at a flying school in Kent. Although the school was run on a shoestring, there was a steady stream of instruction work for Lefty, flying surplus ex-RAF Tiger Moth aircraft, and giving lectures to students. Lefty found the work tedious at times, but he needed the income, however modest. At least his free time did allow him to pursue the relentless search for his daughter, as ever, his sole preoccupation.

During one of his annual medical checks, it became clear that some of his recurring symptoms began to resurface and after further medical tests, his flying licence was suspended.

From then on, Lefty continued to suffer occasional bouts and was referred for further medical examinations. Eventually, he was diagnosed as having amnesia complicated by random epileptic episodes. He was transferred to a specialist hospital in Sussex to treat his condition after he suffered a suspected stroke.

In early 1991, when the welfare system was about to give up on him, a local social services worker referred him to the Cranbourne Foundation home for Veterans where he became a resident. With regular meals and a warm and comfortable environment, Lefty began to improve. But with hearing difficulties and memory lapses, he kept himself to himself, reluctant to join in with activities at the care home.

Introverted and withdrawn, Lefty was slowly being absorbed into a caring but inadequate system. With only dementia sufferers for company, he lacked the interaction that he needed to reverse his regression.

Unless somebody took the trouble to engage with Lefty, he would be unable to avoid the same fate as many of his generation. He would be left to swell the ranks of a new legion, the displaced, confused, and dispossessed.

Only time would tell.

Part 3

Chapter 1

YORK ORPHAN CONNIE

The ceramic wash basin was lying at an awkward angle, balanced precariously on broken tiles and brickwork. Water would never flow from its dismembered taps again. Torn remnants of floral wallpaper flapped, cheerless, in the breeze. The scorched remains of what once was an Ascot water heater lay on its side, its enamelled casing creased and cracked. The resulting gas leak had caused the evacuation of the entire street, a stark scene of devastation and desertion, captured by a photographer from the Yorkshire Post a few days after the raid. An indelible black-and-white image seared on my brain, a somewhat bizarre sight, against the backdrop of death and destruction.

The memory can play tricks, especially with younger minds. But as soon as I was old enough, I resolved to make sense of my life, fill the vacancy left by the absence of family, an aching loneliness that haunted me every waking hour.

I made up my mind to solve the riddle of my existence; I yearned to discover exactly who my parents were before I could form an adult authentic and meaningful relationship with me.

From the beginning, I felt a deep and urgent drive, a need to make sense of my life, and my mother's untimely death. But if I was going to be successful, I would need to start at the beginning, blending my earliest memories with the bigger reality of my place in the world. So I took the first hesitant steps on the long journey of self-discovery.

According to what remained of official records from April 1942, the fire which destroyed number 11 Laburnum Grove had been extinguished by daybreak the following day. But all that remained of the structure had been reduced to smouldering embers and rubble. A photograph from the Yorkshire Post taken 24 hours after the raid showed a scene of devastation with a ceramic washbasin lying at an awkward angle balanced on broken bricks, the image stark and vivid nearly 50 years later. According to the official report, after my rescue from the remains of the bedsit by an air raid warden, I was taken to the local Salvation Army first aid shelter. However, after that, there was little further official information regarding my fate as a babe in arms.

I eventually discovered that I had been transferred to a convent orphanage, the only remaining option for 'homeless waifs and strays'.

Inevitably my earliest childhood memories are vague. But the convent robbed me of my early years; at least that's how I felt. Although well-intentioned, the sisters at the orphanage imposed a strict puritanical lifestyle of self-denial. By the time I was old enough to realise, I suppose that I assumed all children were treated that way. As an orphan, what more could I expect? I was made to feel guilty, unwanted, illegitimate offspring, somehow responsible for my own predicament.

CHAPTER 1

They even gave me the name, Constance, which I decided to consider a compliment.

The sisters influenced every aspect of my formative years. It was not until I was much older that it finally dawned on me that I could form my own opinions, discover my own aspirations, exercise my own judgement. However, those opinions often seemed at odds with those ingrained in me at the convent. In retrospect, I owe the sisters much, but their indoctrination left little or no room for my own personality to emerge. The relentless routine of daily life crowded out any time for leisure or recreation. In the immediate post-war years, along with the rest of the country, Yorkshire attempted to find its way back to normality after six years of disruption and dislocation. Rationing and general shortages were still commonplace, adding to the cheerless austerity of the daily routine.

Like other orphans, any knowledge of family background was either vague or non-existent. A few pathetic tokens remained from those days, kept for me in an old red metal container similar to the old Oxo tins. But this tin was unusual: its discoloured paintwork revealed evidence of both scorching and water damage. It bore the stern warning 'Look after Your Gas Mask' in large letters on the lid. The rather pathetic contents consisted of a faded blue leaflet, a water-stained envelope containing a small black-and-white photograph, a perished child's gas mask, and a small round tarnished lapel badge bearing a stylised 'EE' emblem, the only mementoes of a previous life.

Just when I didn't think the red tin could reveal any vital clues, hidden inside the concertina folds of a blue leaflet entitled 'Rowntree's Employees –*Important Notice, Air Raids*', there was an envelope with a colourful South African postage stamp. The

Springbok returned my stare from across the years. The letter had been franked, but the imprint was smudged and indistinct. Even with the aid of a magnifying glass, it was unclear, but if you studied it carefully, it did reveal what looked like the name Witwaterstrand, but the date was completely illegible. It had a return name and address on the flap of the envelope, but the handwriting was an ornate script and difficult to read. Apart from admiring the image of the gazelle, as a child, I gave it no further thought.

At that time, just after the war, they were looking to relocate war orphans to Australia. Several of us from the orphanage were taken by train to Liverpool docks awaiting transportation. However, considered too young and frail to withstand a lengthy sea journey, I was moved to a nearby convent school to learn the basics to equip me for life. Not studious by nature, I began to play truant, but soon discovered the consequences of my actions. It wasn't long before I realised how harsh the judgement of the Reverent Mother was, and how obedient and how eager the sisters were to administer punishment. Long hours were spent reading Scripture, poetry and memorising the Catechism, along with learning how to tell right from wrong, good from evil. I came to fear divine retribution much less than the wrath of the sisters. Arriving at the convent, the first impression that visitors would get was of a picturesque country mansion. Its impressive but austere facade led to the main entrance and a simply furnished waiting area with the unmistakable odour of fresh floor polish.

To the casual visitor, the convent was home to a caring and contrite community, qualities only to be expected of the devout. But, behind closed doors was another matter entirely, another world, set aside for sinners. It was different for us, especially those found guilty of the cardinal sins of disobedience, disruption, or blasphemy. Such transgressions would attract the most severe penalties. On one occasion, I was forced to wear the black habit of shame. Taken by nuns to a chamber at one end of a cloister, I was confined there for what must have been days but felt more like weeks. Given menial make-work from dawn to dusk, I was fed on bread and water only. The sisters' rule of silence was strictly enforced, and it was expressly forbidden to speak to the wearer of the black habit. My hair was cut short with rusty scissors from the kitchen, and I was once whacked with a cane when I broke the silence rule, objecting to my harsh treatment.

Initially slow on the uptake, I did learn one thing quickly: how to take the easy route while keeping my big mouth shut. I managed to learn how to keep myself to myself, although I knew that I was not alone in my suffering. Despite many setbacks, I eventually gained a pass in my school certificate exam and did my best to search for gainful employment. With few opportunities in early 1960s Yorkshire, there was little that was open to me with my lack of qualifications and timid demeanour. Lonely and disillusioned, I drifted from job to job, with no real prospect of a fulfilling career and no relationships other than grubby, groping one-night stands. It's just as well that the sisters couldn't see me then.

Somehow, I instinctively knew that it was wrong to keep the company of some of my layabout friends from the youth hostel, especially those who had learned to smoke and date boys, years before I had considered either. At the Odeon, it seemed to me that all the most glamorous film stars smoked and looked cool in the process, so I resolved to take up the habit at the first opportunity. It wasn't long before I was offered my first cigarette in what became known in smoking circles as 'Crash the Ash' or sharing your smokes with others. Back then, those who could afford them carried a pack of five Woodbines in a pocket or handbag. After lighting it I posed, with the cigarette holder in the style of Audrey Hepburn in Breakfast at Tiffany's. I pretended to admire my untidy manicure as I watched the blue smoke curling up in a satisfying plume. After I was mocked for not inhaling, I took a deep breath, swallowed hard, and suffered what all would-be smokers must endure for the first time. The experience left me with tears streaming down my face following a thoroughly unpleasant bout of choking and coughing, much to the entertainment of the others, most of whom had already become hardened smokers.

I grew up painfully introverted with low self-esteem; I came to envy those who enjoyed a wide circle of friends, the same friends who never seemed to include me. As a teenager, I am the first to admit I was no oil painting. Having grown up in the all-female environment of the convent, I had little interest and less knowledge of the opposite sex. I found them to be self-centred, coarse, and immature, but with hindsight, I suppose in some perverse way that was part of their appeal. It seemed that the more I attempted to befriend boys, the more they would avoid me with my plain appearance and lacklustre personality. Casual jobs came and went with equally casual relationships. I had survived my teenage years, thanks to the sisters at the orphanage. But entering the adult world was a completely new experience, I found it hard to get work of any kind, but managed on the dole thanks to Mr Beveridge's National Assistance and the generosity of the welfare state. I felt alone in my clean but ramshackle flat, overlooking the ruins of a bomb-damaged York, with little money and fewer prospects.

Chapter 2

HOPE AND REDEMPTION

As with many aspects of life, events in distant lands and across generations can stitch together tenuous, unknowing strands, lives that become inextricably entwined with others. A combination of circumstances, a conspiracy of vibrant threads, a tapestry waiting for a weaver. Only those who knew the unique pattern, the warp and weft, could add colour to the otherwise monochrome fabric of lives such as mine . Living histories of families torn apart by war, a war which left the enduring legacy of a displaced generation in its aftermath, fading silhouettes in the afterglow of peace.

Connie Yorkshire 1987

Working at the North Riding Council offices in Harrogate, I had come to hate the daily bus journey almost as much as my job. It came as a great relief when I heard the news that my department was to relocate to the Guildhall in York city centre following a local council reshuffle. It was great to be within walking distance of work, and my life was at last beginning to take shape, or so I thought. The Guildhall had been restored after the bomb damage from the Second World War – a few traces remained if you knew where to look, but for a passer-by they were barely noticeable. But many of us had damage of some sort, apparent or not; the war had left its indelible stain on more than one generation.

My work as a junior clerk was unrewarding, but there seemed little prospect for career progression in any occupation in the brave new world of 1980s Yorkshire. Better late than never, I decided it was time for me to become more sociable. I enrolled for evening classes at Wakefield College, studying ancestry, with the forlorn hope of tracing any of my own family history. I nurtured a few self-inflicted ailments, but that particular ache was still lodged in every fibre of my being, seared into every sinew and bone.

Gregory

I was offered a lift from a man that I met in York library while making more futile attempts to trace my family history.

Gregory was kindly and sympathetic; more importantly, he had a car and offered to take me to evening classes at the college just outside Wakefield. It was only half an hour by car, but much longer by public transport. Even if you were patient enough to wait for the bus, as a smoker I would be banished to the top deck, frowned upon by self-righteous and intolerant non-smokers. They were not too posh to use the bus, but posh enough to look down upon others with pity and contempt. Those who were weak, unable to resist disgusting habits, especially those acquired by working-class women.

My job included centralising of county council records which I found time-consuming and tedious. All my enquiries up until now had drawn a blank regarding any information about my family. I decided that the entire undertaking was so depressing that I needed a new focus, a new me. On the crowded bus, I must have looked a sight; I had forgotten my brolly again and had to shake the drops off my transparent plastic rain bonnet before finding a vacant seat. The woman beside me was reading the latest issue of Cosmopolitan. According to the front page, glamour was in again – I wasn't aware that it had been out. It must have gone missing for a while when I was not watching.

Painfully aware that I was now in my forties and still unattached, I resolved to make myself more presentable. I began by making yet another concerted effort to give up smoking. I had unsuccessfully attempted to quit so many times, but this time I would do it, or so I managed to convince myself.

I set my mind to an even more ambitious task, the midlife makeover. I hoped it would improve my image while boosting my self-esteem. Yet another valiant attempt to console my under-confident self, the me which lingered just out of sight, below the surface.

Gregory was a lecturer at Wakefield College and lived on his own in York following his divorce. At first, he struck me as kindly and generous. But occasionally I would glimpse a different side of him – his tone could quickly turn unpleasant if he felt slighted or if anyone had the nerve to address him as Greg or anything other than Gregory. He was middle-aged, but I guess approaching 50; the first silver threads were showing entwined with copper locks at his temple. He had asked me out socially once or twice, where he was courteous and kind. Although amicable, there was something rather cold and distant in his manner.

The relationship prompted me to think again about my personal appearance. I became aware that I had drifted into the middle-aged dowdy look, 'more C&A than Dotty Perkins' according to one of the office fashion fascists. The insult did sting, but there was, unfortunately, a home truth there. I checked when I got home; lo and behold, without realising I had accumulated far more easy-care crimplene than floaty floral. What was worse, the whole lot was crammed together on wire coat hangers in my inadequate wardrobe. Although I was earning only junior clerk wages, I decided to renew my efforts, change my wardrobe and dress in a manner which I considered more becoming. I even thought I might shorten my hemline a bit and emphasise what modest figure remained. On one occasion, admiring myself in the full-length mirror in the hall, I turned this way and that, while observing my reflection from the corner of my eye. What on earth was I thinking, who did I think I was? Some teenage tart with a school gymslip hoiked up too far? ... And just how high can you wear a push up bra before the wired contraption becomes so uncomfortable as to be useless? However, common sense prevailed, and I did manage to curb my enthusiasm before the overall effect became cheap and provocative, a disaster waiting to happen. I'm sure that if I had parents, they would have grounded me at school age... but I did get some glances in the office that I certainly hadn't noticed before.

I distinctly remember the first time Gregory hit me. It was one evening when I was staying at his semi in Middlethorpe. For me it was just a weekend away, an experiment.

Soon that weekend turned into a month, and I only went back to my flat occasionally if I needed more clothes. Everything seemed to be working out fine; he would drop me off on his way to work, a comfortable and predictable routine. I admit that often it felt like it was some sort of amicable agreement rather than the romance that I had hoped for, but I suppose I was happy to settle for that. All went well at first, and I permitted myself a luxurious notion of homeliness. Perhaps this is it, I thought, my first taste of security. I had a regular income, and Gregory had his College pay which allowed for a comfortable enough existence and a level of stability that I had only dreamt of. Gregory never used the word marriage, partly because of his divorce, I assumed, but the only thing lacking in our relationship was commitment, commitment on his behalf; without that, I began to feel exposed and vulnerable.

It was Wednesday and I used my accumulated flexitime to take an impromptu afternoon off. On my way to the bus stop I thought I saw Gregory through the window of the local pizza restaurant. It couldn't be him surely – he was at work, or so I thought. But I caught a glimpse as I walked past; hesitating, I retraced my steps. I found myself peering through the window from behind a poster which promoted the unrivalled flavours of the thin and crispy pepperoni, whatever that was. Partly hidden from view, I could observe the table more clearly from a different angle. It *was* him. He was engaged in what appeared to be an urgent conversation with a younger woman. She wore an earnest expression, as she peered at Gregory over the rim of a half-empty coffee cup. I thought I caught a glimpse of a thin gold band on her ring finger, but I couldn't be sure. But I sensed rather than saw Gregory's mood, jaw set, and brow deeply furrowed. An expression that I'd never seen him wear before, the middle-ground between anger and concern, whitened knuckles, clenched fists gripping a crumpled paper napkin.

Walking home from the bus stop I became pensive and preoccupied. In the time that I had known Gregory, he had never mentioned family apart from passing references to a divorced wife. If the woman was a friend or someone from his office, despite my insecurities, I suppose I could cope with that. But there was something about their demeanour and her body language which caused me an involuntary shiver long after I had shut the door and put the kettle on.

I find it hard to explain to people how I was back then. I can't expect others to understand me if I have trouble understanding myself. The only way that I can explain it is by example.

I was vacantly searching the TV channels a few weeks ago, when I came upon a documentary about the dairy industry. Apparently, cheesemakers use this little gadget called a cheese trier, a tool used to scoop out a sample from a cylindrical wheel of cheese. The sharp hollow stiletto will penetrate from the rind to the very core, to test for maturity.

The cheese plug can be replaced once the test is over, but the damage, the violation of the hidden inner core, may never completely heal, even if the exterior appears unblemished.

It wasn't until a week or so later that I plucked up enough courage to mention the pizza restaurant encounter to Gregory. I chose my moment and couched my words in a tone more as an enquiry than a challenge. That was when things started to unravel. Things changed for the worse in our relationship. He said the woman was his ex-wife and it was no business of mine. He said that he resented being 'spied upon' and continued impatiently, saying they had 'outstanding issues' regarding the divorce settlement which had to be sorted. Following this revelation, the more distant he became, as the stranger within him gradually came to the fore. As time progressed, he became absent for longer and longer periods, and it didn't take me long to learn the truth.

I decided to make my own discreet enquiries. My searches revealed that Gregory had inherited entitlement to a property from his father, Tobin Pyle, who had died several years ago. As part of the divorce settlement, Gregory's ex-wife had staked a claim to her share of the inheritance from the sale of the vacant plot on Laburnum Grove.

Gregory became increasingly defensive if I even raised the most innocent enquiry, culminating in an outburst during which he struck me several times. More of a slap than a punch, but nonetheless stinging and humiliating.

I was determined not to cry; for goodness' sake, I was grown-up, and us grown-ups keep our emotions in check, don't we?

But I did need to weep sometimes, some sort of safety valve I suppose. Not a full-blown howl, you understand, but I knew from experience that silent tears were never enough to quench the restless cinders of emptiness that still glowed within me. Apart from that, I didn't want to allow Gregory the satisfaction of seeing my tears. On one occasion, I locked myself in the bedroom to avoid further mistreatment, using a handkerchief to stem a nosebleed.

I began to feel the same old feeling, but this time my inner being felt more like an oyster being prepared for the table. Once the knife is inserted, twisted, and slid upwards, the muscle which holds the shell closed is severed, leaving the live flesh exposed and vulnerable. Once removed, snatched from its protective shell, it can never be satisfactorily replaced. The damage is done—no pearl, and in my case, not even mother of pearl.

There was an uncomfortable reconciliation the following day. Gregory offered an apology which I took to be genuine, one of our more constructive conversations. He explained that his father had owned property in York before the Second World War and was still waiting for full compensation after one had been destroyed in an air raid. I trusted Gregory to stick to his word, but it inevitably ended up with me on the receiving end of pushing and punching and being locked away again. The experience reminded me of my time in the convent, and I became more and more concerned for my own safety if I stayed with him.

A late claim

It turned out that Gregory's father, Tobin, had been the landlord of a semi-detached property in Poppleton which had been 'destroyed by enemy action'. Immediately after the war, claims could be submitted to the War Damages Commission for compensation of bomb damage to private property. The document revealed that no claim was received in respect of the property at Laburnum Grove. Reading further, I discovered a copy of an office memo which stated that following Tobin Pyle's release from custody in 1950, he had submitted a claim after the deadline when no further applications were considered by the government.

I became intrigued. It appeared that Tobin, Gregory's father, had been in prison after the war. As a result, Gregory apparently inherited entitlement to the deeds of a property that no longer existed. He never spoke about his parents, which I had thought strange, but now I knew why. For several reasons, I decided not to mention it to him, but to pursue that line of enquiry myself, knowing that Gregory could be a very private and secretive person. During one of my visits to the Civic Hall in York, I discovered that in 1931, the property in question had been let to a Ms Klarans Marchand, an elderly lady who had died in an air raid in 1942. The property was so badly damaged that it had to be demolished.

I visited the archive several times and looked for any hint or mention of my mother, who may have lived at the house on Laburnum Grove at the time of its destruction. The rent book for 11 Laburnum Grove had been kept in an archive and gave the address and the tenant's name, but unsurprisingly no mention of any other occupants. I made a note of the name Marchand. I'm not sure why, but I think it was my yearning to find even the most unlikely connection with any living relative.

Strangely enough, I stumbled on a connection by complete accident. A page entitled 'The Night of the Incendiaries' was a handwritten report by an air raid warden in 1942. The ARP warden who attended the incident at Laburnum Grove had been killed during a later raid on York on the 2nd of August 1942. After several unproductive meetings with civic officials, I was eventually granted access to the records of the earlier raid in April of that year.

In the presence of a sullen town hall clerk, I scanned the handwritten log until I came to the section for April, and a paragraph grimly entitled 'The Night of the Incendiaries'. The record showed that an infant was recovered from the arms of her dying mother. Trapped in the blazing ruins of the house in Laburnum Grove, beyond all hope of rescue, the mother, Miss M Collins, perished along with the tenant, an elderly lady Ms K Marchant who lived on the floor below. The warden had duly registered the child at the nearby Red Cross shelter where *her* condition was described as in 'good order and uninjured' thanks to the prompt action of the authorities.

I think that was the first time I'd seen my mother's name in print. Described as a 'Miss', the undertones were there, intentional, or otherwise. I resolved to make my own enquiries now that I had a second name.

Things fall apart

Anyway, so far as Gregory's inheritance was concerned, I decided that it was none of my business and maybe he would tell me if he wanted me to know. I decided to persevere and give the relationship another chance. Perhaps Gregory would get his inheritance and settle down with his ex-wife again. At least I would have known where I stood. I was beyond caring and certainly didn't want any money from him.

Once again, I was forced to look at my options if the worst came to the worst. If my relationship with Gregory was indeed doomed, there were few affordable flats for rent locally, and fewer attractive employment opportunities. So I expanded my search at the local jobcentre to cover a wider area. There seemed to be more jobs and more money down south anyway.

I didn't have to wait long; the decision was being made for me. The College made Gregory's post part-time, and he shut me out of his life and turned to the bottle for solace, becoming even more unpredictable with violent mood swings.

Life with Gregory had now become intolerable. His absences, his addictions, and his wayward manner were each slowly destroying what was left of my self-respect. Defensive battlements that I had spent years constructing were being demolished brick by brick, and I felt more and more exposed.

I spent more time in the Civic Library, looking through newspaper articles, phone directories, or any other source that might come to hand. Luckily, back then, the library used to keep copies of British Telecom phone directories for other counties, so I filled my time searching in vain. I was about to give up the search for good when I stumbled on a very tenuous link. I found the name of Ms P Marchand in an out-of-date directory for Surrey, I made a note of the number, and resolved to give it a try. The phone rang in the semi in Croydon and was answered by a kindly and well-spoken lady with a helpful tone. I asked after Marchand, but the name drew a blank – "nobody here of that name". But before she hung up, she hesitated, and she did, however, remember the lady who had moved out several years ago now. She said that she used to have a forwarding address for mail redirection and would search for it if I wished, so I gave her my work telephone number hoping against hope for a call. After a week or so with no reply, I decided to call her back. The lady apologised, explaining that she was in the habit of keeping track of forwarding addresses, but the property had been let to other tenants over recent years. But she did vaguely remember the lady, a smoker who was foreign, perhaps Australian. She added that she felt sure the name was Merchant or similar and the address somewhere in Hastings. I thanked her for her help and renewed my search efforts.

Certainly, the name Marchand was distinctive enough but, I could find no one of that name in Hastings no matter how hard I tried. It was then that I remembered the red tin box and the envelope with the colourful stamp. I looked at it again with fresh eyes. It had been addressed to a Ms K Marchand, but what was not scorched, was water stained and barely legible. On the rear flap in faded ink was written a return address Ms P Faber and address and postal district in Johannesburg SA. Perhaps this lady was the missing link, a relative? Maybe she had also been a Marchand at some stage, so I resolved to extend my search to include P Faber as well just in case she was still using that name.

Hastings 1991

It was a longshot, but at the time it seemed like an excellent excuse to spend a long weekend at the seaside. So, I took the plunge and caught the train to Hastings, where I hoped to find Ms Marchand, or maybe P Faber, and learn more about her locally. I placed the envelope in a clear plastic sleeve, in the vain hope that the colourful stamp and faded handwriting might rekindle some distant memory. Perhaps I was clutching at straws, but I felt that I was being led by my best instincts. Anyway, this was certainly as close a link as I had discovered so far. Yes, you could say that my motives were selfish, but I felt that I could justify my quest, believing that the search for any blood relative was a worthy, selfless, and maybe even moral obligation. Lord knows I had little else to do with my time now that I had escaped from Gregory's excesses. It had taken me long enough to get the message. Although he hadn't said so in as many words, Gregory's behaviour made it very clear that I was no longer part of his life. I'd had enough of him and his violent, petty, and self-absorbed world.

Arriving at Hastings, I thumbed through the local telephone directory in a kiosk at the station entrance. Grubby from overuse and smelling musty, the directory had been damaged by prolonged exposure to the humid, salt-laden atmosphere. I thumbed each musty page carefully but drew a blank in the both the Fs and the Ms; however, I decided that I would look around town anyway. In my search for an up-to-date telephone directory, I walked into the small well-kept library at the top of the high street.

I asked for an up-to-date local telephone directory and was given a reference copy which I studied, grateful for the relative peace of the library reference section. There was March, Marchant, and Markham, but no Mrs P Marchand or Mrs P Faber. Running out of ideas, I returned the directory to the elderly assistant who politely asked me if I had found what I was looking for. I said that it was a long shot, adding that it was a pleasant enough day, and I was considering taking a stroll on the promenade. After looking up from her work, the library assistant removed her glasses and took the phonebook from me. She carefully replaced the directory in the correct reference section, and politely enquired if I was looking for somebody local. I said that I had been, but so far, my search was in vain, adding that it's an unusual name and I had thought it might be easy to find.

"What name were you looking for?" the assistant asked as I turned towards the exit. I thanked her for her help finding the directory, but I was off to have a cup of tea in the early autumn sunshine. The assistant said that the library cards held information about members, and she offered to have a quick look there If I would like.

Why not, I thought, and said Marchand, P Marchand to be precise. The assistant thumbed through the card index but looked blank, so I thought I would try P Faber. Suddenly the elderly assistant became animated and said, "I think you mean Pruda."

"Who?" I enquired.

"Her name is Ms Faber, Prudence I think, but she pronounces it differently; I think she prefers Pruda; she is not one to stand on ceremony! Quite a colourful character, she lives on Coronation Lane, the card says number 43, but please don't tell her that you got the number from me – library records are supposed to be confidential."

I thanked her and looked for Coronation Lane on the street map in the library entrance. I decided to stay the night at a local bed and breakfast and resume my search in the morning. It was getting late so I thought that I would spend the evening in my room, rehearsing what I would say if I did find her.

Pruda... I turned that name over and over in my mind as I absentmindedly watched the black-and-white image on the small TV in my room.

CHAPTER 2

1991 – The Empty Envelope.

In a strange bed with only the overnight chill of early autumn for company, I tried to make myself comfortable in the cramped bedsit. But even with an extra pillow and blanket, the tired divan stubbornly resisted all my attempts at sleep. The bright red digits on the alarm clock proudly announced that it was 2:18 am. It wouldn't be long now; I knew that very soon the warm tears would come. It's funny, I never used to weep at all, even in the toughest of times, but more often now in the dead of night, my emotions would overwhelm me. That hollow stiletto pierced my deepest soul again, leaving me spent, the shadow that was me. I had become a dry leaf, swept across some nameless deserted street, the chilled Northwind rustling through dry husks of winter wheat. I harboured a persistent yearning, an ache for something just out of reach, which neither I nor anyone else could explain, let alone satisfy. I was a sponge, porous and thirsty. No matter how hard I tried, or what extremes I was prepared to endure, the thirst stubbornly denied every effort to quench it. Maybe it was more than that, a quest to affirm the stranger that was me. Some futile attempt to discover who I was, or perhaps it was a quest for the person I wanted to be? But just now, I decided to pull a sheet over my head and ignore the digits on the clock before they scorched themselves onto my brain.

It must've been around 3:30 am that I somehow lapsed into a restless and dream-haunted doze, only to be woken again by a vivid replay of my time with Gregory. Waiting impatiently for dawn, I became plagued by doubt, wondering if I would ever be able to give up the quest to find my father. Perhaps I would have to be satisfied with a compromise; maybe just finding a distant relative would have to do. On my pilgrimage of self-discovery, if I couldn't find the destination, I may have to content myself with a signpost, or even a rumour, anything that would give me a shred of hope.

The next morning, I decided that I would find my way to Coronation Lane with new optimism, excited at the prospect of meeting Pruda. I've always been intrigued by the possibility of meeting someone who has been described as 'colourful'. I suppose we have all secretly hoped that we could meet somebody, anybody, who has been described as colourful. Once you got to know them, perhaps they could be persuaded to share their vibrant colours with us. A very attractive proposition for those of us with only a monochrome mosaic that we called life.

After breakfast and my first coffee I was in a more buoyant mood, and with new resolve I made my way to Coronation Lane and knocked tentatively on the door of number 43. In a moment of doubt, I secretly hoped that there was nobody in, and even if there was what on earth should I say to a perfect stranger by way of introduction? Just as I was about to lose courage and walk away, the front door creaked open. As a cloud of blue cigarette smoke issued through the narrow gap, a cat darted out, followed by a shout of exclamation and threat from a voice inside. Peering at me through the smoke was a diminutive lady whose tired features were obviously unaccustomed to smiling. From her lips hung a cigarette which was almost smoked down to the filter, ash dropping on what had once been a stylish tweed hacking jacket. Her mahogany features were deeply wrinkled in what looked like a habitual frown as she brushed off an accumulation of cat hair and ash before studying me up and down. Her silvered curls were matted into unkempt dreadlocks which reflected tinges of lilac in the bright sunlight. As I opened my mouth to introduce myself, I was met with a tirade of abuse with what I would later recognise as a distinctive Afrikaans twang.

"I don't care what the hell you're peddling, but at my age, I've either had it, got it, or I don't need it..." Adding "... if you know what's good for you, you'll piss off and leave me to myself...

"... bloody interfering busybodies, can't you see that I just want peace and quiet, so bugger off where you came from before I set the mastiff on you. Then we will have some entertainment, see who can run fastest."

Undeterred by the warning, I pressed an open palm onto the faded paintwork of the front door to prevent it from being slammed in my face. Despite the warning, there was no barking, no evidence of a high-speed hound. But despite my efforts, the door was firmly slammed from the inside as I considered my misplaced optimism. What was I thinking? Assuming that this was the right address, was I expecting to be welcomed with open arms? Yet another dead end. On impulse, I lifted the lid on the letterbox, peered in and said in my best voice: "I have something here that may have been yours, and I would like to return it to you."

I could neither hear, nor see very far inside the house, but I could just make out the base of an elephant's foot umbrella stand, and a worn doormat partly obscured by junk mail. As I waited for a reply or any sound of recognition, I opened my handbag and fished out the envelope, hoping against hope for some acknowledgement from within. If this was Pruda, surely she would recognise her own handwriting? If not, the postage stamp with the distinctive Springbok image must jog her memory. I tentatively offered the envelope halfway through the letterbox, while hanging on to it with forefinger and thumb. I desperately hoped that no dog was waiting to snatch the envelope from my quivering hand.

I waited as long as I could and was about to withdraw the envelope and consider my next move. It was just then that I was taken completely by surprise. The envelope was snatched from my grasp. I could hear wheezing as the voice inside suddenly demanded: "Where did you get this?"

All I was able to stammer in reply was "Pruda, if you let me in... I need to talk to you, I can explain... Please let me in." I waited hopefully for a response, but all I could hear was more wheezing.

Eventually, my patience was rewarded, and the front door opened slowly. A beckoning hand was my only reply, so I followed Pruda into the hallway. She trudged her way through an obstacle course consisting of accumulated domestic litter, inquisitive cats, and several overflowing plastic bin liners. For some reason, both cats and garbage had been overlooked; neither had quite made it as far as the open kitchen door and freedom. The untidy hallway led to a room that was now used as a lounge. It reeked of stale air, urine, cigarette smoke, and accumulated refuse. Pruda shuffled as much as walked, right arm extended against any convenient item of furniture, to keep her balance. She sat down heavily in her fireside chair, indicating for me to sit opposite.

"So, who the hell are you again?" she enquired between bouts of breathlessness.

Attempting my most courteous manner, I somehow managed to say, "My name is Connie; shall I call you Pruda, or would you prefer Mrs Faber or Marchand?"

"Never mind that bullshit," said Pruda, studying the envelope more closely this time. She obviously recognised her own handwriting and looked inside for the letter, but the empty envelope yawned back at her. "Where did you get this?" Pruda said indignantly. "This is my letter, my handwriting, it is private, personal."

I told her what had brought me here and the fate of her sister in 1942. I explained that my mother, Mary, shared the bedsit in York with Klara, and they had both been killed the same night. The envelope was with my mother's belongings and was kept for me years ago.

I politely asked after her sister to which she replied, "You mean Klara, what about her?", lighting another Rothmans king-size and wheezing while waving away the smoke with her free hand.

I guessed that Pruda was in her late sixties or early seventies and obviously found difficulty in walking.

As I waited patiently for another bout of hacking smokers' cough to subside, I studied Pruda closely; her small hazel eyes were watery from coughing. Her gaze slightly hooded by a frowning brow, thin lips revealed a slight wince of either discomfort or displeasure, perhaps both.

"What do you want, Ronnie or whatever you name is?"

I replied, "Don't you see? If the envelope is yours, my mother Mary lived with your sister in York, that would make you my great-aunt!"

With outstretched arm and open palm, I attempted to introduce myself again, but this time with a bit more ceremony.

"Pruda, my name is Connie..."

As I stood up and moved slowly towards Pruda, hoping for my first family hug, the ginger cat on her lap was showered with cigarette ash which bounced off one ear. The unfortunate animal hissed in protest, scuttled across the lounge, and skulked beneath the stained woodwork of a coffee table. Peering over a stack of old newspapers and magazines, the cat continued to eye Pruda with suspicion while licking a paw and trying to wash the ash from its head.

The moment that I had always dreamt of was lost in Pruda's outburst.

"Stupid animal, you should have been drowned as a kitten. You are just one snarl away from the street where you came from with those other spiteful freeloading scroungers."

The ginger tom looked on while blinking with smug indifference.

I waited, watching as Pruda picked up her half-finished drink. Without using the handle, she gripped the Royal Doulton cup and lifted it hesitantly to her lips. Her face immediately formed a frown as she cursed under her breath at the taste of cold tea. While lowering the cup, she used it as an ashtray, successfully extinguishing the stub of her latest cigarette in what liquid remained.

Although the kitchen door was wide open, there was no ventilation in the lounge. With the curtains drawn, the stale smell of several house cats and a permanent blue overcast of cigarette smoke seemed to hover just below the ceiling. I was starting to find the atmosphere oppressive. I suppose Pruda had not much to add to my one-sided dialogue. I was disappointed. I had been unprepared for that extreme spectrum of 'colour'. More of a shadow than a rainbow.

Just as I was considering how to excuse myself, there was a tap on the front door – the girl from the care agency had arrived. She was greeted with the same reception as mine, so I thought it might be time for me to leave. I thanked Pruda, who appeared to be dozing but surprised me with "if you want to come tomorrow, I will tell you more, much use may it do you". That was the first time I caught a glimpse of what I recognised as a mischievous smile from behind the Rothmans king-size. The carer stood in the hallway with one hand on the front door handle, apparently waiting for me to follow. Neither of us spoke, but the young carer met my gaze and shook her head knowingly as if we both shared a secret.

As I walked back to my holiday bed-and-breakfast, I thought of the carer's gesture – did she mean to imply that Pruda's condition was much worse than I had assumed? I could deal with her offhand manner, but besides that, she seemed okay, especially after the mischievous grin. I took her offer of a return visit at face value. I decided to start a diary of events during my next visit. So on my way to see Pruda, I bought a clerical notepad from WHSmith; I didn't want to overlook even the smallest detail of any conversation. Armed with biro and notepad, I set off to visit Pruda the following morning.

Knocking on the front door, I was suddenly seized by the dread that she would have forgotten me entirely overnight. Would I have to go through the same rigmarole as yesterday? But, like most of my fears, my concerns were completely unfounded. Pruda *did* remember me from the day before, and she invited me in again. This time I was received more like a daughter than a stranger.

PART 3

I felt the warmth and welcome of an aunt on a level that I had never experienced. Perhaps it was the gift, the two packs of Rothmans king-size, a peace offering which I presented at the door. Pruda did remember writing the letter and recalled mention of a niece called Mary in Klara's reply. I asked Pruda if she had any other family, but she said no, Klara was her only relative. She seemed proud of the fact that she had lived alone since her return from South Africa. With the age difference between Pruda and Klara, there had been little contact after she emigrated.

As she was speaking it occurred to me that Pruda was holding back, hiding something; perhaps she thought that I was after her money. It took me a while to convince her that I was not interested in money. I just wanted to know more about her family and my past. What Pruda and I really needed was time. Time to talk, time to share. From the hidden depths of my soul, I really needed to know her as a family member, not just the eccentric acquaintance from Sussex. Not just another name on the Christmas card list, or some friend from bygone years whom I may never hear from again. If Pruda really and truly was my mother's aunt, this is the day I had always dreamt of. Even if she had never met either of my parents, she was a blood relative. In my mind's eye, I pictured those distant genes that Pruda and I shared, the essence which coursed through every artery and vein, irrevocable, hereditary, *ours*. At last, I started to feel that I belonged, the deep, long-nurtured ache in my being was thus soothed.

I desperately wanted to stay in Hastings, to be within easy reach of my great-aunt. But I knew that for the time being at least I would have to get on with my life in York. I promised to call Pruda and meet with her again. Back in York, it didn't take

236

long before I was overcome by my loneliness and my desire to see Pruda again. The strange, dishevelled little being was slowly taking over my life, my visits to Hastings were becoming more frequent. On a previous occasion, I found her face down amongst the litter on the lounge floor. She had been there for at least 24-hours. She was dehydrated and distressed, her only company, her favourite feline, the tabby which dozed in the crook of her outstretched arm. The more I got to know Pruda, the more I thought she needed full-time care in a house desperately in need of a good spring clean. I asked her if the carers had been, but she had 'sent them packing'. I later discovered that the company had refused to come anymore because of unpaid bills.

Besides work, there was nothing to keep me in York. I was already looking for an excuse to get away from my dismal flat and escape the unwanted advances of Gregory with his drinking and violent mood swings. That relationship, such as it was, had certainly run its course. So I plucked up the courage and offered to stay in Hastings and look after Pruda; she readily agreed.

I managed to get everything in my car, including my sewing machine and a table lamp on the passenger seat. I could hardly see out of the rear-view mirror, but I didn't care. I was so relieved after rescuing the last of my things and not even bothered that I couldn't see York in the rear-view mirror. I cleared up the outstanding lease on my flat – it was due for renewal anyway. They could keep it as far as I was concerned. I had never been so sure of what I wanted. But I knew that I wouldn't find it in Yorkshire, and it wouldn't happen at all without my freedom; no commitment, no complications, I was truly free. I took a payoff from my job, and along with my small pension and my modest savings, I resolved to move to Hastings and immerse myself in the world that was Pruda. I was well aware that she could be forthright and quite intimidating at times; even so, she was my only living relative and that was all that mattered right now. Pruda just needed an opportunity to talk to somebody. I could be that somebody.

I asked her if the care company still provided help.

"I got rid of the carers, they say I owe them money, but they think I am rich, I have gold."

I had to ask, "Pruda, why do they think you have gold?"

"I don't know, rumour, just rumour. One of the carers said so. When I returned from South Africa, I worked as a clerk in the Goldsmith Assay office in the city of London." She added: "There is no gold if that's what you are here for... Just like the last lot, money, money, money, and I have got no goddamn gold! I sent the carers away; I didn't trust them in my house no more and told them to shake off, *fok voort* and not cast a shadow on my doors again. They think I am just senile old woman, what do they know? One of them was even from Ukraine, for God's sake. My ancestors were proud Carpathian peasants, they have nothing, they were persecuted minority in their own homeland. Like them, those Huns, barbarians forced us to leave. They just came and turned us out of our homes and onto the street."

She told me of the abduction of her parents, and the death of her younger brother. I was shocked when she told me that she had been raped when she was just a child. I held back my tears as she recounted her escape with her older sister, Klara. Just children, innocent refugees, fleeing from the uprising in the new Polish Republic and the desecration of their homeland. Pruda was only 16 when her illegitimate son was born just a few weeks after her arrival in England.

"I was too young; I did not know how to be a mother. Right from the beginning, he would not even take my milk. I did the best I could with him, but he was an ungrateful and spiteful child.

"I named him Mikolaj – in my home country means child of the Wolf. Each time I look into his baby blue eyes, I can only see the eyes of that wolf. Feel the pain, the shame the fear and disgust of a child – *panna, maagt, virgin*, the same in any language.

"His father stole my soul, that animal. How can I forget? Klara hated the boy, not for himself, but who he was, what he represents. I did not visit her again after he won a scholarship. I have more than enough problems of my own, let alone Klara and her opinion. Advice from a sister that I could easily do without!

"I wanted to shake off my old life; the boy was a product of despair, a constant reminder of violence, he was the result of anger and hatred. In Birmingham, I work all hours God sends just to put him through college. So help me. I did the best I could for him, but I could not love him no more than I could love his father, for god's sake. Klara called him Dran – the bastard child of the wolfsbane, the father who goes on to spread his poison, maim, torture and rape. That nightmare replayed a thousand times inside my head. It will never go away."

"Do you know what happened to your son?"

"Last I heard Miko as he called himself, had qualified as a dentist and moved to Poland, for pity's sake I tell you, Poland! But, despite my best efforts, Klara had been right when she said no good will come of him. I pray that he would change, mend his ways, God only knows."

"What did you do, have you tried to contact him?"

"No, I just wanted to get away, but I know now that I'm attempting to run away from myself, my son and nightmares of my past. In 1940, I applied for passage to Durban in South Africa. I emigrated and found work in the gold belt near Johannesburg."

I had to ask: "On the envelope in your handwriting, you also used the name Marchand?"

"I did that because I thought that my family name of Faber sounded too Afrikaans."

I also had to ask, "Is that what made you return to England?"

"At first, I enjoyed a comfortable life in Witwatersrand not far from Johannesburg. I earned much more money than I could hope for in UK, but after the end of World War II, more conflict. I could see the way South Africa was going, and I didn't like it one bit.

"I had my fill of torture, exploitation and abuse in my youth. I saw the same thing, the effects of apartheid and the way the black schoolchildren were treated. Blood was on the hands of the *blankes*. This was not the freedom that we were promised, just oppression by another name – evil bigots.

"I was ashamed to be white, it made me sick to my stomach. After Soweto riot, I said to myself that's it, enough, I will return to England, while I still have a shred of human dignity left."

Connie – 1998

After 43 Coronation Lane was put up for sale, I was at a bit of a loss, so I applied to be a care worker on the south coast, tending to those less fortunate than me. I recall it was a Thursday morning in mid-November. My ageing Morris Marina had let me down again, refusing to start. Apart from numerous mechanical problems, the MOT certificate was about to expire, and I had just about given up on it. Doors that did not latch properly, threadbare tyres and decaying bodywork: the Marina was a wreck. The car was slowly corroding, the effect of the salt air which swept across the lane from the beach. After slamming a door impatiently, and resisting the urge to kick the damned thing, I did not even bother locking it up. If anyone really wanted to steal it, they would be more than welcome to it. I thrust the keys impatiently into my handbag and continued the journey on foot in the stinging wind-blown spray. Autumn had been relatively mild, but it seemed to me that most of early winter Shorehampton was slowly succumbing to the elements. Everywhere I looked, there was evidence of neglect, wind and water, rot, and rust had taken their toll. Wondering whether I should keep the car, or just abandon it, I trudged along Seaward Lane feeling frustrated. I was also distracted as I harboured a nervous unease at the thought of starting my first session as a care worker.

Leaving Hastings had been quite a wrench after my time with Pruda. I had come to love her and missed her and her endearing eccentricities. For all her strange ways, I admired her sheer courage and even her forthright manner. I would dearly have loved to possess her unambiguous people skills and her unique ability to welcome and condemn in the same breath. Many times since, I have wished that I had her courage when I had to confront that dangerous driver or unscrupulous garage owner. I found her certainty and frankness refreshing after Gregory's lethal mixture of violence and deceit. After she was admitted to hospital earlier in the year, there was little more that I could do for Pruda. I felt distraught. I had spent most of the previous year tending to Pruda's needs as both great-niece and carer. Washing her, dressing her, feeding her, cleaning up the house and making it presentable. In exchange, she provided me with a roof over my head and her stories of upheaval in Europe and her time in South Africa. She could be very lively company, but after her admission to the Conquest Hospital in Hastings, she suffered the recurrence of an earlier tumour. She finally succumbed to a bad reaction to chemotherapy and died 10 days later.

Keeping one hand free to restrain my headscarf, I braced myself against the gusts which tugged incessantly at my faded red duffel coat. Although it was my only protection from the elements, the coat had long ceased to be windproof, let alone waterproof. I guess it would soon be consigned to the local charity shop in the hope that I could replace it with something better. But on reflection, I knew that the coat was actually past the point where it would be of use to even a street person. Heaven knows I had been close enough to being homeless myself in the past. The persistent, raucous cries of the seagulls jarred my senses and weakened my resolve. As I passed number 14, the wrought iron gate was ajar; it rattled and squeaked on its rusted hinges, painted scrollwork peeled to reveal the inevitable corrosion beneath. It was caught by a gust and closed suddenly with an alarming metallic crash. There was a finality to that dismal sound, a jailer's last scornful act, slamming the gate, turning the key, locking you up as you start your first day in a life sentence. The ultimate dread, not death but permanent incarceration.

I was in the wrong frame of mind, so why was I even bothering? Why on earth was I inflicting this new daunting and nerve wracking venture on myself? What was I thinking of? It would be my first day and the outcome was far from certain, and what I needed right there and then was stability and certainty, but here I was, an emotional spectrum, a flake, a mess. Except the colours were mine, muted and pastel rather than the primary colours of Pruda which I could only hope to emulate. At my interview for the care home, the questions came thick and fast. Would I fit in? Could I work as part of a team? Could I cope with the elderly and frail? I mentioned my last 18 months of caring for Pruda and surprised myself by providing convincing answers to all of their questions. But I just hoped that I could make a go of caring after my time with Pruda. Without CV or references, my only recent job was that of part-time waitress in the local seafront tearooms. The ill-tempered manager and shabby decor added to the drudgery of low-paid seasonal work.

I was actually relieved when I was laid off in the autumn. What little demand there was for seafront refreshment had already dwindled to an insignificant trickle by then. I needed to stave off the dark moods and depressive episodes just awaiting their opportunity to envelop me if left to my own devices. So I decided to bite the bullet and look for something less demanding such as local voluntary work. On a trip to the local Oxfam charity shop a few weeks earlier, taped carelessly to the window I saw a hastily written vacancy notice for a part-time sales assistant. It took me a while to pluck up courage, but I entered and enquired about the vacancy. However, it soon became obvious to me that they were looking for a particular type of person, one whose face would fit, probably a member of the local Women's Institute. They appeared to be looking for someone who could play bridge and knew their way around the Telegraph crossword.

As I waited for the manager's response, I overheard a staff member bluntly rejecting the donation of a t-shirt bearing a silhouette of Che Guevara. She was obviously appalled at the offer and waited for the donor to leave before condemning them as riffraff, while swapping disdainful expressions with the manager.

Without political opinion, having only ever browsed the tabloid newspapers in quieter moments at the tearooms, I was out of my depth again. I felt completely inadequate when faced with a privileged and exclusive minority. Snobbery was obviously still alive and thriving in 20th century Sussex. I decided against applying, noting that they were running a self-serving pastime, rather than charitable enterprise.

Although the charity shop remained my main source of clothing, if I thought no one was watching, I would peer in the window to see which volunteers were working before I plucked up the courage to enter. Even then, in the absence of the coven, I would feel self-conscious and rushed, whether making a purchase or just browsing. However, without routine or structure to my daily existence, I knew that I could not endure another winter of despair in my lonely and closeted world.

The Cranbourne Home for Veterans – 1999

As I reached the end of Seaward Lane, I paused to gather my wits. The freshly painted sign on the main entrance proudly announced 'The Cranbourne Trust – Care and Respite for Our Veterans', with 'Visitor Parking at the rear' apparently added as an afterthought. The care home was at the other end of Seaward Lane from my place. I had lived in that flat for several months, and I suppose it was okay but served only as a retreat, somehow, not quite home. I hesitated when confronted with the doorbell on the frame of the glass-panelled entrance. The wind blew the first drops of rain in gusts from the leaden and forbidding sea. I felt sure the late autumn storm had deliberately followed me along Seaward Drive, waiting to announce my arrival on the doorstep of the care home. I prepared myself, checking my featureless reflection in the opaque glass of the entrance door while attempting to adjust my unkempt, wind-ruffled hair. My index finger wavered an inch from the bell push, as I waited for my gloved hand to stop its nervous tremor. Finally, summoning the last vestiges of my resolve, I pressed the button.

I remember that it was Clare who answered the intercom. Glancing through the partially frosted glass door panel, she released the catch with a metallic buzz and gestured for me to come in. In late middle age, a loosely buttoned cardigan worn over her carer's uniform, Clare carried the smell of recent tobacco smoke. Her warm smile revealed irregular and yellowing dentistry as she let me in. Pausing to remove my leaking boots, I was immediately struck by the warm and informal atmosphere. I was embraced by the comforting smells of fresh baking laced with freshly brewed coffee. Rich aromas drifted in from the kitchen, marinating the atmosphere from reception to the garden room. The entrance lobby was an imposing sight.

A Dartington vase of fresh cut flowers sat on a polished mahogany counter-top, and a crystal bowl overflowed with apples and oranges, strategically positioned, fresh and inviting, on a side table. An ornate highly polished grandmother clock overlooked the entrance lobby and reception desk. I felt that I had fallen down the rabbit hole or walked into a still life watercolour painting without realising. I marvelled that such a well-maintained, clean and spacious establishment existed at the end of my lane, the same lane as my untidy modest apartment. The contrast was stark. The modern, spotless care home which I had passed many a time without even a glance. Then there was my drab home at the other end, separated by less than a quarter of a mile in distance, but half a century in time. Stepping through the entrance hall with my escort Clare, I was confronted with a spacious room that seemed empty at first glance. The majority of the residents had apparently been taken on a day trip to a local garden centre. They were not expected back until afternoon tea, which was, according to Clare, a daily ritual that would not be missed by either staff or client.

Removing my coat, and brushing drops of rain from my sleeves, I was struck by the vacant atmosphere in the spacious conservatory, despite its warm and welcoming presence. As I sat in the reception area, waiting for Clare, I surveyed the scene in front of me. Whether it was my mood that day or whether it was the reminder of how lonely, vacant, and fragile human existence can become; maybe it was the cold weather; I'm not sure – but I felt a tear trickle from my right eye which I dismissed as I removed my gloves.

Shaken from my reflections, Clare smiled at me politely asking if my name was spelt with a 'Y' or was it two Ns and one E, or one N and two Es. Shortly after, I was presented with a hastily written nametag of white card, which announced my name as 'Coney', but it was my first day, and I could not feel more proud. Pinning the tag to my jumper, I signed the visitors' book and was offered coffee, which I readily accepted.

Apart from an elderly gentleman who was absorbed in his jigsaw of the Mallard steam engine, and a frail couple equally engrossed in their crossword, there was little activity. The large windows offered views of the beach beyond the esplanade and reflections of flickering images from a television which murmured to itself in the far corner of the room. The passage of time was marked needlessly, by the resonant pendulum beat of the grandmother clock, its occasional, and somewhat mournful chimes echoed in the main lobby.

As I entered the garden room carrying my coffee by the saucer, Clare asked me in a confidential whisper if I would mind talking to the gentleman in the far corner. "He's been with us now for several weeks and seems to have no family or visitors." Clare confided that social services brought him here as they couldn't accommodate him elsewhere. "He doesn't seem to join in with the others very much, he just seems to keep himself to himself.. His name is Don... We've all tried sitting and chatting to him, but whatever we say, we can't get much out of him..." Then she added, "... He had a bit of a fall recently which seems to have been a bit of a setback for him. Anyway, see how you get on. By the way, the GP is supposed to be coming sometime today to change that dressing on his arm."

I began to wonder if I had been set some sort of initiation task – perhaps they did this to all new staff members, a test to see if a newcomer was up to the job. Or perhaps the other carers were watching from behind the kitchen door, sniggering at my naïve efforts on my first day.

Either way, I decided that I would do my best and settled myself to the task.

For the first time, I sat down beside Don as I knew him then. I judged him to be in his late 70s or 80s, and even when seated, he appeared quite tall, a gaunt listless figure. He reminded me of pictures I had seen of great renaissance sculptures – blank unseeing eyes gazed out, unfocused, pensive, and impassive. Lifelike yet lifeless. Although traces remained of a once boyish and innocent appearance, finely lined features suggested hidden depths, a man both older and wiser than his years. Despite the warmth of the central heating, he wore a non-descript grey cardigan over a threadbare Argyle pullover which hung loosely on his frame. Silvered hair in unkempt strands, and his skin was weathered, taut, opaque and discoloured. A well-used supermarket shopping bag containing his few meagre daily trappings lay on the carpet, casually propped against a leg of his chair.

If he had noticed my approach, he did not react, apparently content to continue reading his well-used copy of the Daily Mail. I asked him if he would mind me sitting next to him, a request which prompted an open-handed gesture which I took to be an invitation. After an awkward silence, Don turned towards me slowly, regarding me with rheumy, but perceptive brown eyes.

Lifting the cup slowly, he took sips of lukewarm coffee, his hand trembled, cup clattered softly against china saucer, spilling droplets of coffee onto the dressing on his left forearm. When offered a digestive biscuit, he politely declined, his gaze distracted and vacant. Was he watching those white-capped waves on the grey ocean beyond the shoreline, or was he distracted by the patter of the first heavy raindrops against the conservatory windows? In those fleeting moments, a verse from a half-remembered poem surfaced in my head.

"The Parson commands us to silence, and struggles to lead us in prayer, but half of the room has forgotten the words, like the man with the thousand-yard stare."

Don truly was the man with the thousand-yard stare, his gaze had become distant and transfixed. I watched each iris move and dilate, opaque cataracts surrounded the rim of each pupil as miniature reflections of the garden room, danced, vanished, and reformed with each infrequent blink.

I eventually plucked up courage and in a hesitant voice introduced myself, uncertain as to whether to expect an intelligible reply. After a prolonged pause, Don cleared his throat and uttered a response in a voice clouded and indistinct through lack of use.

In the awkward silence which followed, I listened to myself relate a dreary monologue consisting mostly of a complaint about my car, and my own trivial experiences over the last week. Even while the words were leaving my lips, I realised that my efforts were so tame and uninspiring, why would anybody respond. I suppose I was secretly hoping that I would not receive some incoherent reply. Although glimmers of a polite smile of attentiveness crossed Don's features, I was convinced that his mind was elsewhere. He shifted posture slightly as he absently adjusted one heel in his well-worn slippers with the extended fingers of his right hand.

That was the first time I met him, although, with hindsight, it was more of an encounter rather than an introduction.

When I arrived for my shift the next day, I was met at the door by Clare again, who seemed agitated but otherwise relieved to see me. As she guided me into the garden room, she told me that after his last session with the speech therapist, Don had mentioned my name and said he would like to talk to me... Adding that she thought that he had taken a liking to me!

"We are trying to encourage him by prompting his memory which seems to be troubling him. It is as if he has memories that he either wants to talk about or maybe hide. He's with the nurse at the moment, who has come to remove his dressing and fit a new arm splint, but I'm sure he won't mind seeing you."

I kept my distance initially as the nurse was in the process of renewing the dressing on Don's left arm. When I watched more closely, I was struck by the image of a fading blemish on his forearm. Apparently satisfied with her work, the nurse replaced the splint and was preparing to leave. Still distracted by the blemish on Don's arm, I asked the nurse if it was the result of his recent fall, but as she left, she dismissed my enquiry, assuring me that it appeared to be an old tattoo of some description.

During my conversation with Don, which was more animated than my previous visit, I could not dismiss the image of that tattoo. That evening alone in my flat, the same image kept replaying in my mind like some half-forgotten tune, persistent and distracting. Although indistinct, there was something vaguely familiar about it – was it actually a tattoo or just a bruise? The mental picture haunted me, no matter what I did, the image stubbornly refused to go away.

Chapter 3

THE RED TIN BOX

The prospect of another Sussex winter prompted me to act, so I resolved to get the heating fixed, as the late autumn chill arrived uninvited in my draughty flat. After months of unsuccessful protesting, I had finally persuaded the landlord to repair the troublesome central heating boiler. During this process, the plumber needed access to some floorboards in the second bedroom. I used the unwelcome upheaval as an opportunity to de-clutter. After all, I had had plenty of practice at Coronation Lane in my time with Pruda. So I would attempt the same in my cramped flat, where space was very much at a premium. I would rid myself of accumulated years of knickknacks and out-dated memorabilia.

Still the image on Don's left arm haunted me, mottled and indistinct but nevertheless significant. Was I missing something? If so, I could not for the life of me think what.

But I needed to focus if I was going to get this place tidied up, so I told myself to be ruthless: just get rid of all the junk. It was during this process that I came upon it. After many years of neglect, the old faded and rusting red metal box taunted me

251

with its unanswered questions and accusing stare. Although I was familiar with its contents, these days I rarely took the trouble to inspect them. In fact, I probably hadn't even bothered opening it since I lived in York. Releasing the rusting metal catch, I lifted the lid and considered whether I should just ditch the whole thing. I didn't like its contents the first time I opened it, but now it seemed even more irrelevant. Perhaps if I just got rid of it altogether, it might help my mood. Over the years, the contents of that tin would have inevitably deteriorated, and the prospect of opening it up again didn't appeal to me. Years earlier I had searched through its contents looking for something that just wasn't there; I decided that there was little of significance inside and consigned it to my growing junk heap. But, hesitating, I decided to open the old tin one last time before ditching it forever. The rubber on the child's gas mask was flaking and perished, and now smelled stale. Its two round opaque glass lenses stared back at me with a baleful gaze. Its sinister red nose valve must have looked comical on the wearer in an era when fear and doubt was more commonplace than humour and frivolity.

Other items in the box meant little to me: a silver metal whistle on a chain and an embossed metal lapel badge. Trinkets, they were the only mementoes of fleeting lives and a family that I had never had the chance to know. Yet another reminder of my lost family. I tried not to think of the tin as Pandora's box, but on the few occasions when I did open the lid, it unleashed emotional turmoil, doubt, insecurity, and loneliness, judgement from my very own gods. At least Pandora was left with hope, and I needed all the optimism I could lay my hands on. I think I needed a cathartic experience and perhaps this was the ideal opportunity.

It was at that moment that I remembered the photograph. The one thing missing from the tin's original contents. I remembered putting the photograph aside for safekeeping. Without doubt, it was the most significant relic from the red tin, which is why I was careful to look after it. But where had I put it? It had been in the envelope that I returned to Pruda, but where was it now, what did I do with it?

Distracted, I smiled as I remembered that little dishevelled and irritable person—Pruda, who else would I have allowed to take over my life at that critical stage. Even in her lounge, she was a breath of fresh air, despite the twilight aromas of Rothmans and cats. I could not help but admire her courage and conviction. I had never met anybody with such an abrupt and forthright manner, she could praise and condemn in the same breath without giving it a second thought. She was a 'one-off' whose company I still desperately missed.

I smiled as I thanked God that I was able to spend those few priceless years with Pruda. Even if the photo I was searching for was black-and-white, Pruda would certainly have lent the image some of her colour.

Then I remembered.

The Catholic Anthology, that's where I had put the photograph, it had been kept in Pruda's envelope for all those years, but after I returned the envelope to her, I didn't want to leave the photograph loose without any protection, so I had tucked it away in between the pages of the anthology. I admit that I don't pray very often, but I did pray for Pruda after I visited her in hospital the very last time. Despite my upbringing or maybe as a result of it, I couldn't conjure up a prayer on the spot, so on the rare occasions when I needed the words, I always had the anthology to fall-back on. I left the photo in the section entitled collected works of spiritual poets, the book that the sisters had given me at the convent, I had placed the photograph safely inside, as a bookmark but mainly for protection. It was still there on my bookshelf, with its blue binding and embossed silver lettering. The Anthology was the only reading material allowed when locked up or confined to the cloister in the convent. I can't say I had paid much attention to the book since, and I had memorised only one poem from its pages. But there were other words, not those included by the publisher, but words which helped me through my solitary days confined in the convent, and words which have guided me through my darkest days ever since.

On the flyleaf inside the front cover, I found a single sentence, a simple line of handwritten prose inked in neat script, by somebody who identified herself as Sister Magdalen.

"Two men looked out from prison bars, one saw mud and the other saw stars."

Only 15 words. But words of hope and optimism passed on from one of the sisters at the convent. I wondered if Sister Magdalen had noticed the Star of Fortune as she gazed heavenwards, or had she intended the words as spiritual guidance, absolution for sinners. Perhaps she had suffered the same fate as me, perhaps she too had been incarcerated for her own sins. If she had, I felt absolved; it wasn't just me, there was no escape from the retribution of the convent. Denunciation, where the sisters were even prepared to judge and punish their own.

Whatever their original intent, those 15 words from Sister Magdalen became my salvation.

CHAPTER 3

The Anthology had kept the photograph safe, hidden, shrouded in its pages. I had looked at it ages ago and last time I had the impression that the image was out of focus and faded. But today somehow it was as clear as if it were taken yesterday. I studied it more closely. I couldn't say that it was crisp or even sharp, but I saw it now with new eyes. Six young men in RAF uniform were crowded together in what looked like a shop doorway. Each was pointing at their bared forearms. Each bore the same tattooed image, an upright horseshoe surrounding a five-pointed star. Rangy and handsome with his cap askew, one of the group pointed to his left forearm whilst the others pointed to their right; midway between the elbow and the wrist was the tattoo. Was this the same tattoo that had distracted me so much the previous day, or was this just a product of a romantic, overactive imagination?

Typical of that era, the picture looked like one of those taken by a Brownie camera, then developed and printed somewhere like Timothy Whites, an otherwise unremarkable monochrome enprint. On the back of the photographic paper was the watermark 'Velox'. But in smudged and fading blue ink was written 'Lefty and the gang, Mar 14th, 1942' in an anonymous freehand script.

I slept fitfully that night. Obviously the photograph was important enough for my mother to keep it in a safe place. The tattoo on Don's arm certainly looked similar to the picture. There was the tantalising possibility that Don and my father had been in the same RAF squadron in the war. If so, he may even have known or come into contact with my mother, Mary.

The next morning, with stiffened resolve, I brought the photograph with me to the care home, in an attempt to animate Don, perhaps trigger his memories. At the same time, I would secretly try to explore the possibilities of my own links with the

255

past, however tenuous. If there was a connection, I was determined to find it; after all, I had nothing to lose except for my new job!

Don was dozing, mouth open, snoring softly, in the same winged fireside chair as when I had first met him. As I approached, he stirred and gratefully accepted his afternoon coffee with a fleeting smile. In an attempt to control his fatigue levels, the GP had reduced the dosage of his medication. Roused from his nap, he welcomed me with a warm and engaging smile, his eyes had lost their tarnish, and his expression seemed brighter now.

I arranged my duties so that I could sit and help Don. Clumsily, I asked him about the Cranbourne foundation and its connections with the RAF. He had read the notice board which gave details of the Foundation's history but seemed unable to offer more. I started the conversation again by asking him if he had any connections with the RAF. He smiled hesitated then mentioned 'one of the few...'

"Battle of Britain?" I offered hastily without thinking.

Apparently amused by my enquiry, he eventually replied that he had been in Canada from his childhood and that was 'one of the few' clear recollections that he had.

I resolved to listen to him more attentively, be patient and avoid the temptation to jump in and complete his sentences for him. Determined to pursue my line of enquiry, I asked him if he had ever flown. His gaze turned wistfully to a nearby painting in pastel colours on the garden room wall depicting a Second World War bomber on a misty morning entitled 'The Lincolnshire Ghost'.

I was unaware that Don and I had an audience until Clare's voice interrupted us from behind. She continued without preamble or apology, "Well you know, those memories of his come and go, don't they, luv?" Adding in the same breath, "...By the way, Don, your favourite programme, Antiques Roadshow, will be on in a few minutes."

For the sake of the assembled company, she added, "They are only repeats but he never misses it, y' know."

Unaware of her unhelpful and untimely interruption, Clare sighed as she settled herself into a vacant armchair, a cup of coffee in one hand and TV remote in the other. She complained at length about her 'barking dogs', while removing her shoes and rubbing her feet. Throughout the entire performance, Clare still managed to broadcast her practised smile to an audience, each indifferent to her sufferings. For the residents, the only urgent topic of conversation was how to get an extra helping of tea and biscuits. Judging by the audience in the garden room, those who weren't dozing off or negotiating their next refreshments were not residents at all. It soon became obvious that the Antiques Roadshow was actually the staff's favourite, especially Clare, who traded gossip with Pauline, the tea lady, throughout the entire episode.

I was acutely aware of the time and the obvious distractions. I knew that I would soon have to abandon my efforts for today. I decided to persevere and make one final attempt to attract Don's attention. Maybe it was already a lost cause. Reflected TV images danced in the windows of the garden room, early shadows in the gathering afternoon gloom, distracting us both. The more I tried to ignore it, the more the unblinking eye of the Cyclops demanded our attention with its flickering images and unheard dialogue... I plucked up the courage to ask him about his tattoo but instantly remembered that I had fetched the picture with me. I fussed through the contents of my handbag and finally withdrew the photograph in its protective Manila envelope. I passed it to Don, studied his reaction closely, and then asked him if he saw anybody he knew. He took the picture from me, glanced at it and was at once distracted by the television. I must have sounded like some sort of interrogator as I asked him again if he recognised anybody in the picture.

Wearing an expression of distracted indifference, he reluctantly reached down for his carrier bag, finally producing a small rectangular plastic magnifying glass. Don inspected the picture, alert hazel eyes widening as he studied the image more closely. A pool of light fell across his lap as I drew the nearby standard lamp closer, adding that it may help him to read what was written on the back of the picture.

At that crucial moment, he was distracted again, raised voices from viewers in the garden room, fingers pointing at the television. There was a buzz of excitement and conversation caused by a particular lot on Antiques Roadshow. What now? I thought in frustration. Subtitles on the TV announced that the item of interest was an antique Lalique glass vase. In a loud voice, one of the residents claimed to have a similar item in her room, prompting everybody's attention, including mine. According to Hugh Scully, the vase was "highly collectable, and may well attract £700 or £800 at auction".

A sound investment, I'm sure, but none of my vested interests at that moment could be so readily quantified. For me, any relationship with Don would be priceless and may well turn out to be invaluable. I resolved to continue my questions to Don the following day. I would have to sign in as a weekend visitor on my days off, as my duties did not resume until Monday. I was impatient, not sure that I was prepared to wait until then; I felt that Don and I were on the brink of a precipice, a revelation, an epiphany for both of us.

Chapter 4

1998 SOUTHEND
"THE ROCHFORD INCIDENT"

Recently employed by the Southend Reporter as a trainee journalist, young Ned Ellis was hungry, intelligent, and ambitious. He had graduated earlier in the year and saw himself as something of a sleuth who aspired to greater glories. He was only a few months into his probationary year, so Ned was keen to make a good first impression on the chief editor. He made no secret of the fact that he aimed to be the youngest investigative journalist in the business. Always looking to the main chance, an opportunity to 'hold the front page', Ned was undeterred by the lack of earthshattering revelations or celebrity scandal in the fleshpots of Southend. The Reporter's small editorial team was preoccupied with such exclusives as the reopening of a local bowling alley, the controversy surrounding the proposed building of a new casino complex, and the even weightier issue of the town being renamed 'Southend-on-Sea'. Okay it was only a small local paper, but it was a start, he enjoyed the work, and his jokes and pranks had become an office hallmark.

Eager to find a channel for Ned's enthusiasm, the editor gave
him the task of producing a weekly mid-page article entitled
'Southend Past and Present'. In the only way he knew, Ned set
about the task with diligence and enthusiasm, accompanied by
his own brand of scepticism and humour. It was not long before
Ned stumbled upon an old article which had been archived
many years earlier. The report included details of an incident at
RAF Rochford airfield on the outskirts of the town, which had
since been renamed Southend Municipal Airport. During his
research, Ned discovered a black-and-white photograph of an
RAF Anson aircraft which had crash landed at the airfield during
a thunderstorm in 1946.

Apparently, over the years, the incident had passed into local
folklore. The story abounded with half-truths and conspiracy
theories not to mention rumours of a spy. Intrigued by the
50-year-old mystery, the young reporter decided to delve deeper
into the incident and asked readers to contribute any information
that they may have. It had been a slow week in the office, and
there was precious little other newsworthy copy in Southend
to distract him. Ned interviewed those who responded to his
enquiry and managed to accumulate several credible first-hand
accounts. Significantly, a member of a local metal detectorist club
and a dog walker who had discovered a brass 9mm cartridge
case from an area of long grass close to the original crash site.
If there was a story here, maybe this was it, a piece of evidence
that had apparently been overlooked. An original newspaper
report from the time of the incident stated that following the
crash, the runway had been closed, so priority was the recovery
and removal of the aircraft wreckage so that the airfield could
reopen. The significance of the 9mm cartridge would not become

apparent until several years after its discovery. Delving into the local authority ambulance records of 1946, Ned searched for any reports or even a mention of injuries involving an aircraft. This, in turn, led him to search archived records in the dusty basement of Southend General Hospital. Convincing the primary care trust that he would not breach patient confidentiality, Ned's methodical search revealed an intriguing entry in Southend district hospital casualty department records. On the night in question, a patient had been admitted with a gunshot wound to the left leg. No weapon was mentioned in connection with the injury. Although the patient himself was unarmed, hospital notes record that the victim was wearing an empty leather shoulder holster at the time of his admission.

During what was described as a 'complicated procedure', a 9mm bullet was removed from the patient's thigh. The injury had caused trauma to both bone and femoral artery, resulting in serious blood loss. The report also noted that it had been necessary to establish the patient's blood group in order to perform a successful transfusion. Unfortunately, the patient had been given more than one dose of morphine to ease his pain. While he remained sedated, the mystery patient could only be persuaded to divulge number, rank, and name. A search of his belongings revealed a service ID card which suggested that he was some kind of plain-clothed military policeman. The hospital recorded his name as Richard Knight, blood type B positive, and his employer as HM government service; discoveries which added yet more fuel to growing speculation. The more Ned discovered, the more he became intrigued and determined to get to the bottom of the mystery.

With the editor's blessing, Ned ran an article entitled 'The Rochford Incident' in the Southend Reporter, along with the black and white picture of the aircraft, and the enprint of the 9mm empty cartridge. The article included details of the mystery patient with an empty shoulder holster, prompting a new wave of speculation. Where was the missing weapon? Why did the aircraft make a forced landing in the dark at an airfield that was closed, and what was the purpose of the mission? Ned deliberately worded the article to prompt comment from readers. He knew that involving the public in a local mystery might get him noticed, and may even improve the circulation of The Reporter at the same time.

The story was eventually sold on to the Essex Mercury, which appeared as a centre spread of their popular weekend edition, earning young Ned professional kudos along with a well-earned bonus, as the story went countywide.

Chapter 5

CONNIE AND DON 1998

I was not rostered to work at the Cranbourne centre until the following Monday, and staff were discouraged from visiting residents during their off-duty time. But when I felt lonely at home, the centre was an attractive proposition with its warm rooms and ample supplies of coffee and tea. The temperature in the care home contrasted so much with that of my flat that it made me shiver just to think of it. At least my place was less of a winter icebox since the central heating boiler had been fixed.

Now I had time to spend relaxing in the warmth, now I could concentrate my thoughts on my next move and how I would get through to Don.

Up until now, my time spent with him had been a mixture of success and frustration.

Last Friday I had made some progress, albeit limited and hesitant. Apart from that, I was aware that I had spent more and more of my shift with Don and, consequently, less time with my other duties. I was told that it had come to the attention of the senior carer. I knew that she would have the word neglect ready to write on my report when my probation came up for review. I was called in to see Sheila, the manager, who reminded me of my duties and responsibilities as a carer, warning me that all employees were kept under review during their probation period. They may also receive a formal warning, especially if a resident filed an official complaint against them. On the report, Don was listed as vulnerable with suspected dementia. If he or anyone else made a formal complaint it would be instant dismissal for me and a black mark for Sheila from the Cranbourne foundation. If it came to the attention of the Health Care Commission, we would be put on notice, which would be bad for all concerned. Apparently, there had been cases before where carers had become inappropriately involved with residents. If I did not mend my ways, there would be consequences, and from now on, my work would be closely monitored by Clare.

I was being watched, but I could not help that; my quest was too important to abandon now. Was I imagining things all over again? Was this really worth risking my reputation, along with my job? The job that I had come to love. I valued every moment that I spent in Don's company.

I had the whole weekend to consider my next move, and which questions I would ask Don. I could not believe that he was suffering from dementia, he was just being ignored. During the week, I tried to hide my disappointment. I was sure that we were on the verge of a breakthrough, but the moment was lost. No sooner had I triggered a memory in Don, it had been snatched from us both by the invasive presence of the television. I loved working at the care home, but there were too many distractions – nobody gets the time to even think or converse in a meaningful way. I did wonder if the manager actually appreciated the value of silence? Just run-of-the-mill peace and quiet. An opportunity for reminiscing and conversation, time to hear and more importantly, time to listen. An allotted time without interruptions from GMTV breakfast, Pebble Mill or Hugh Scully.

I was determined to have another attempt on Monday. I would show Don the photograph once more, at the same time taking care to avoid Sheila or Clare, but I felt sure that some of the other carers were watching me as well.

Monday, 14ᵗʰ December 1998.

Arriving for my next shift at the Cranbourne care home no sooner was my foot in the door and my coat on the hanger, when I was confronted by Clare who seemed to have adopted panic mode.

"Sheila, the manager, has gone off sick, I have got to do doctors' run this afternoon, we are rushed off our feet.

"I am now officially in charge. You need to avoid talking to Don, he won't give us a minute's peace at the moment..." adding with a frown, "... he keeps asking for you but don't go wasting time, we are short-staffed. Remember that Mr McFarland has dementia."

"Dementia? Has he been formally assessed and received a diagnosis?" My tone must have sounded wrong.

"Look, I haven't got time to argue with you now, dementia was on his personal file when he arrived from the social. There are others who need help, Cheryl will take care of Mr McFarland for the moment, so I'm putting you in the kitchen for the time being. Keep your head down, no more time-wasting, Sheila may have put up with it, but I won't."

Heeding the warning, I made my way to the kitchen, deliberately avoiding Don. I found it extremely difficult to ignore him with his left arm extended, trying to attract my attention from the other side of the room.

After lunch, I was called into the garden room by the late shift supervisor, who said that Don keeps asking to speak to me. Aware of my warning, I was cautious, but I had spent all weekend thinking about Don, and was not about to delay my quest any further, so I obediently followed the shift leader into the lounge. With a knowing smile and a sideways glance, she reminded me that Clare would be back from the surgery soon, as the coffee break would be in about 15 minutes, suggesting that I use the time wisely.

I spoke to Don for the first time since the previous week and he seemed overly anxious to talk to me. He had probably noticed that I had been avoiding him all day, but if so, there was no hint of accusation in his tone, only urgency.

Don looked much brighter than he had the last time I saw him, more animated, much more alert since his medication had been adjusted. To my amazement, he asked to see the photograph again. His eyes narrowed as he moved the smudged magnifying glass slowly up and down the image, this way and that, tilting and turning it at the right angle to catch the light from the lamp by his left shoulder. As I watched in silence, I became aware of what appeared to be a distant recollection on his features. The trace of an enigmatic smile crossed his brow. It lingered, tugging at one corner of his mouth, slowly migrating to occupy the rest of his face. But then to my complete surprise, Don began to stand. He pushed down on the arms of the fireside chair, expanding his tall frame slowly like an unfolding pocketknife. But the expression stayed with him. He slowly put down the magnifying glass and became transfixed by an image on the television showing a black-and-white picture of a World War II bomber with the crew standing proudly by its nose. I supported him by his left elbow, his gaze fixed on the television image as he shuffled forward slowly, trying to get closer to the television for a better view.

I decided that if Antiques Roadshow was more important than my box of tricks, I would have to give up any hope of continuing with my quest. Resigning myself to the television, still supporting him by his left arm, I accompanied him as he sat back down in his chair motionless. I felt completely deflated; I turned to my coffee cup, the brown fluid tepid and uninspiring, just how I felt at that moment. As I sat punishing myself for my thoughtless and selfish actions, projecting my own indulgences onto a complete stranger, Don turned slowly towards me, a new expression on his face, one which I had not seen him wear before. Not the features of somebody who had finally completed a jigsaw or that difficult crossword clue from yesterday. It was a look that was at once wonder, bewilderment, recognition, and revelation.

He asked me to get the black-and-white photo which he had dropped as he stood up. The six young men in the picture stared back at him across the decades... He knew them or at least seemed to have recognised someone or something. Ever present, Clare immediately stepped in, asking him if he was okay. But Don was busy, scanning my photograph with his magnifying glass.

He muttered something, I listened closely to him as I tried to ignore Clare's urgent tones. I was sure he said he knew them, the picture on the television and my photograph, both had triggered some long-lost recollection, or so it seemed. After further inspection, I suggested that he turned the picture over and read the faded writing on the back. Smudged by water and faded with age, the writing was difficult to interpret, but he read the words aloud 'Lefty's Gang'.

As if responding to an alarm, he put down both magnifying glass and photograph and turned to Clare, then turned again to look at me as he grasped my hand, wrapping it in his left. I think that was the point when each of us knew that something significant had happened, something intuitive, unique. Prompted only by ghostly black-and-white images, memories from another era began to surface, old memories that had remained dormant for too long, lost in the mists of time. In his excitement, Don removed his splint and exposed his left forearm again, pointing at the fading tattoo exactly the same way as shown in the photograph. Then in the fading afternoon light, he said that he remembered Lefty, he was sure that he knew Lefty. Then after a long pause, he hesitantly pointed his left forefinger at the photograph and said, "that's me!".

Locked away in that old red tin box for over 50 years, was the photograph along with the whistle, the lapel badge and the envelope. But the photograph was the key—the key to Lefty's past. Now all that remained was to open the door. But Lefty's mental labyrinth contained many doors and just as many locks.

Chapter 6

CELEBRITIES SHEILA RETURNS

In the following days and weeks, representatives from the RAF Association and British Legion were introduced to Lefty and Connie. For the first time in their lives, Flight Sgt Donald 'Lefty' McFarland formerly of the Royal Canadian Air Force, and his daughter Connie became celebrities. The media was eager to get to know the couple; together at last after five decades of separation.

The local newspaper 'The Sussex Star' interviewed Lefty and Connie and ran an article with a photograph of *'The man without a past, now hero of the hour'*, reunited with his daughter.

But Lefty and I would need plenty of one-to-one time if we were going to reveal more, the story which remained elusive in the inaccessible recesses of his memory. Lost in time, events buried so long ago that exposing them would be a drawn-out and painstaking affair.

I decided that it would be better for him to spend more time away from the care home.

So I came up with a plan that I hoped would allow us to make more progress with Lefty's recall. But it would need the blessing of the care home manager. I thought that our newfound status of father and daughter might open the door now, but our family links were still unconfirmed. We were waiting for results from the paternal DNA test, which I thought would lend more weight to my request.

In Sheila's absence, Clare had taken on the role of manager with an unfortunate mixture of authority and over-enthusiasm. Nevertheless, I knew that I would need to tackle Clare if I was going to make any progress with my plan.

I needed to take Lefty out for visits, days out to improve the quality of his life.

Too late, I realised that asking Clare was a mistake. I should have realised it was pretty obvious from her abrupt manner and patronising tone. She had become envious of my newfound popularity, and I'm sure she resented the fact that Lefty and I were stealing her limelight.

As acting care home manager, Clare reminded everybody that her decision was final. She was not prepared to even consider my suggestion; she dismissed me with a look at her watch, saying, "You remember what I said – haven't you got work to do? You know the rules, I don't want to have to tell you again!"

I was waiting to hear it, but she didn't need to say the words, I got the message:

it was more than her job was worth.

Nevertheless, I had become used to it, Clare always had the last word.

Despite my warnings I spent more and more time with Don as we reviewed the contents of the red tin box. But progress was slow, perhaps my prompts were misguided, I needed to distract him from his recurring memories of boyhood escapades, but that would take more patience. I would need to allow Don to develop his more recent recollections rather than early ones which continue to surface as if to deliberately confound every attempt at recall. Late in December during one of my visits we were off down memory lane again, which I was beginning to think was becoming something of a cul-de-sac. Perhaps they were right all the time, could this be the first signs of dementia? Until the cold snap, one of those which seemed to turn up just when you thought that winter was over. I was having coffee with Don who was in one of his thoughtful moods again. Snow flurries brushed against the window before resting on the sill, forming small accumulations on the concrete path, and settling on the privet hedge, green shoots from the shrubbery protruding from the white mantle.

Lefty had not been known to react to snowfall in the past, but I feared that just the mention of it would lead us back down the path of childhood memories rather than those of more recent times. I began to notice that he had become easily distracted and more than once had been tempted to abandon my futile quest. But once again Lefty had a surprise in-store for me, in fact for us both. He spoke of being buried in the snow as a child playing in the winter fields of Québec. Then very gradually, his tone changed. He remembered being injured, helped from a snowdrift by a kindly man who spoke neither English nor Québécois. As if in a dream, he remembered the farmer with his husky who helped him shelter in a storage shed. Lefty recalled staying in the freezing woodshed overnight. In the morning, he was taken into the farmhouse and given hot drinks while his injured head was bandaged, and the burn on his hand treated. He raised his left hand, exposing his forearm as confirmation.

I grabbed my pen and jotter from my handbag, I listened intently to Lefty as the half-forgotten story dormant for so long began to unfold, long lost recollections, echoes which now claimed a voice of their own. With renewed enthusiasm, I encouraged Lefty to continue, as I scribbled in my notepad. With its constant interruptions, the care home was not the ideal place to record a memoir, so I produced an alternative plan. Lefty and I needed to concentrate if we were going to build on the progress with his memory. We needed time, space, and elbow room. However, as I walked home that night, I had a renewed spring in my step, and new tingling optimism; I began to hope that I would never be alone again.

It was early spring before I plucked up courage and knocked on the manager's door; hesitating, I asked if she could spare some time to talk. Sheila, the care home manager, adopted the manner of an overworked matron, whether dealing with staff or residents. Those of us who were a bit older could see through the act, but decided to go along with it anyway, anything to keep the peace. But some of the younger carers found Sheila quite intimidating at first. They too were learning to indulge her, choose the easy option. Go with the flow, all part of the job.

Anyway, Sheila reluctantly agreed to see me. Without bothering to disguise her impatience, she gestured for me to close the door and sit down. I began my appeal, which I delivered with an appropriate level of solemnity.

I managed to control myself as I began.

"Most residents receive visitors and trips out, but Don would always be left in his fireside chair; alone with only yesterday's newspaper and his thoughts for company."

I watched her as I spoke. I didn't think that Sheila was actually listening to me, she seemed distracted or disinterested, or both. Nevertheless, I had plucked up a lot of courage to do this in the first place, rehearsed my speech several times over the last 24-hours, there was no turning back now. I was committed to staying with Don, I had decided that nothing or no one was going to stand in my way. I surprised myself as I continued my plea. At one point, my tone did begin a nervous waver as I attempted to avoid being over critical, but I was on a roll. "No one is permitted the time to engage with him, and when opportunities do come, they are few and far between." I finished my speech by suggesting that I took Don out for regular visits, adding that I would always be contactable, and would take full responsibility for his care during his absence.

Adopting full matron mode, Sheila propped each elbow on her desk and slowly removed her reading glasses. With a pained and weary expression, she exhaled long and hard, pinching the bridge of her nose while considering her response. I waited patiently, hoping that I would not be dismissed on the spot. She finally spoke, warning me to be careful. I must have looked puzzled by her words and asked what she meant. Sheila emphasised, "I said, be careful, Connie."

I think that was the first time she'd ever addressed me by my first name, only to have it thrown back at me as a warning.

"Have you heard of Florence Nightingale syndrome?" She didn't wait for my reply. "... It's not uncommon for a caregiver and patient to become romantically involved." She watched me closely, awaiting my reaction. I was so dumbfounded that I couldn't think of anything to say in reply, but I didn't care for the insinuation.

I looked at Sheila with new eyes. She wore a pained expression as if she was carrying the entire weight of her mahogany office desk on her lap. I didn't think she looked well. I knew she was quite a bit younger than me, but she certainly seemed older than her years. Her restless hands looked almost opaque, blue veins conspicuous beneath taut skin. I noticed that she never wore a wedding ring on her unmanicured fingers, or any other jewellery for that matter. I decided that she was not qualified to pass judgement on matters of romance. Manager or no manager, I was not about to be lectured on relationships by such as her.

It didn't matter, it was too late anyway, Sheila was in full flow. She launched into a sermon about relationships or 'getting involved', exploiting the 'vulnerable' as she put it. Her speech ended with the warning: "As a junior carer, you are still on probation, and remain under close observation. Any inappropriate action on your part, which comes to my attention, will mean instant dismissal. Do I make myself clear?" She went on to remind me that my status and privileges within the care home were entirely superseded by the trustees' house rules, to say nothing of health and safety regulations. Most important of all, she emphasised her own obligation to the aged and vulnerable in her care, to their families and relatives. A level of responsibility which could not and would not be delegated to a junior staff member.

I suppose I hadn't expected an instant acceptance of my suggestion, but there now seemed little scope for negotiation. The subject was closed.

I prepared to stand and leave the office, saying, "If I had my choice, I would be quite happy to continue working here, but you seem to criticise me in particular for some reason."

After rubbing her eyes with her knuckles, Sheila replaced her reading glasses and sat in silence, her unspoken reluctance obvious. In a last-ditch attempt to redeem myself, I said that I would only take Don on short visits reminding her that I only lived at the end of Seaward Lane, it only took 10 minutes to get there. But Sheila was busy, delving into the drop files in the cabinet behind her desk.

I felt sure that she hadn't heard a thing I had said, but I decided to carry on anyway. Then, without as much as a glance in my direction, she raised her right palm to stop me, interrupting me in mid-flow. Sheila removed a typed A4 sheet with the heading Mr Donald McFarland, leaving the rest of the file open in front of her. She adjusted her glasses for effect, then read the doctor's report aloud in her practised Middle English accent, one of Sheila's mannerisms which had become a source of amusement to her staff, several of whom could do very passing impersonations. But it was yet another of Sheila's forced affectations which she adopted especially when encountering officialdom.

The lecture began.

"After a full physical examination including full blood test, psychometric and cognitive examination, my diagnosis is that there is nothing organically wrong with Mr McFarland. There is no evidence of mental impairment or symptoms frequently associated with dementia. The best therapy for his condition is incentive and stimuli greater than those he would experience if left to his own devices. I recommend frequent trips out such as visits, a greater exposure to real-life encounters, and opportunities for one-to-one dialogue. I believe that my recommendations are in the best interests of both Mr McFarland and the Cranbourne care home. - Yours Aye

Capt Kendrick MD DSO ret.
Consultant, the Cranbourne trust"

During the ensuing silence, Sheila removed her glasses, looked over the top of the typed report and made eye contact with me at last.

This was my chance to exploit the fleeting opportunity which hung in the air. I seized the moment, and she finally began to listen.

After replying to every argument which she could throw at me, my integrity, and my motives, she asked me what exactly I had in mind. Without mentioning my own interests, referring only to Don's welfare, I suggested that I could bring him to my ground floor flat once or twice a week where I could help him one-to-one. I would include him in my day-to-day routine. I suggested that as agreeable as they may be, Don needed a break from the same four walls. Sheila appeared to be searching for more objections than concessions to my request, but she finally agreed, on the understanding that Don's welfare came first, and there was no breach of trust.

From the start, I had not even considered that he might have dementia. The care home had accepted the social services assessment as a diagnosis without checking until now. I had grown attached to Don, all the time I had resolved to release the enigmas of the red tin box, helping him in the process. So began the next steps in the pursuit of lost time, the recall of distant memories and catharsis for both Don and me.

As winter finally released Sussex from its icy chill, the lengthening days held the promise of spring. My frequent excursions to the end of the Lane with Don seemed to revive his flagging spirit. He walked more confidently and seemed to enjoy the tang of salt that blew across the shingle beach. Hour by hour, slowly and deliberately, we began to unravel the long-forgotten knots of Don's memory. In the process revealing more and more of Don's wartime past, convincing me that he was indeed the key to my family link, however vague it may seem.

Brick by brick the wall of his past became inextricably linked with my own. As time passed, I came to regard him increasingly with something akin to parental or at least kind-hearted warmth.

As with many organisations, there were wheels within wheels. At the care home, the wheels were beginning to turn, some predictable, others less so. Only time would tell if the roulette wheel of fate would begin to spin in my direction.

The care home was beginning to feel like a second home for me, but circumstances were about to change, to move me out of my comfort zone. It started as a perfectly normal day at the care home, so I don't think any of us were prepared for the bombshell about to fall from on high.

The only indication that the foundation was short of funds was a greater reliance on volunteers rather than employees. So with appropriate ceremony, the manager called us all to the garden room for an announcement. I had always found Sheila difficult to fathom – what was she hiding behind that veneer of invincibility? Part of me felt sorry for her. I thought she was probably insecure, or even unwell; last month she had certainly been on leave of absence for two or three weeks.

From the start I found Sheila to be either haughty or patronising, depending on her audience. She could be openly critical of her staff, the very staff who ran the place every day.

But today was different. Sheila's announcement of the care home's closure was received with gasps of disbelief from all present. She requested that staff and volunteers alike would help in the administration and relocation of the residents in the few remaining weeks before all employees would have their contracts terminated.

It was obvious to all that the numbers of residents had declined over the years, and inevitably, several of the more frail had died over the harsh winter. Only six of the original residents remained, and one of those was spending extended periods in hospital. The cost of upkeep of the care home meant that the Cranbourne trust had finally run out of funds. They were broke.

For me, there was no question, I would provide whatever care and assistance I could over the few weeks left of the home's licensing and tenure. Social services' dithering, and local authority bureaucracy meant that the process of rehousing and relocating the residents became very lengthy and complicated. I resolved to apply to be Don's guardian.

My suggestion would mean an immediate if interim solution while other options were considered. In the relaxed and sociable atmosphere of my flat, Don and I would have all the time in the world. We would need peace and quiet if we were going to join the many remaining pieces of the jigsaw as the strands of our past lives converged. To satisfy the trustees and social services, I had applied for a DNA test to comply with sibling paternity requirements.

In just over two years, I had come to record and document Lefty's increasing awareness, resulting in restored memories.

But now seems an appropriate moment to relate the story as thoroughly as possible. This is his story which he related to me bit by bit over the years since we first met.

Part 4

Chapter 1

1999 – An Investigation

On 2 August 1947, an Avro Lancastrian airliner belonging to British South American Airways, disappeared on a routine passenger flight from Buenos Aires, Argentina to Santiago in Chile. Despite widespread searches along the aircraft's presumed flight path, no wreckage was found and no trace of either passengers or crew.

In 1998, two amateur mountain climbers stumbled upon an unexpected discovery. Amongst the moraine at the foot of a retreating glacier in the Argentinian Andes was what seemed like wreckage, corroding metal fragments and other debris. On their return, the climbers reported the location of the suspected crash site to the local police in Mendoza. After further investigation, the Argentinian army dispatched a recovery team which reached the crash site the following summer. Amongst a jumble of human remains, clothing fragments, and twisted aluminium debris was an engine identification plate bearing the initials RR and a serial number. That one discovery allowed investigators to positively identify an engine from the lost Lancastrian. Despite close examination of the wreckage, personal belongings, and accumulated debris, there was still no clue as to the cause of the crash. The incident would need further investigation to establish a cause. So far, it had stubbornly refused to provide any solution and remained a mystery.

Responding to pressure from UK relatives of the Lancastrian crash, in 1999 the Home Office re-opened the formal investigation into the circumstances surrounding the crash now that more evidence was available. As the aircraft bore a UK registration, the team responsible for conducting the inquiry included a semi-retired investigator with many years of experience in criminal and civil cases. So it was that a copy of the file landed fairly and squarely on the desk of a man with tenacity and focus, a single-minded individual, keen to resolve any mystery which came his way.

An investigator

James Carver had become something of a recluse since he had retired from full-time employment. But he enjoyed his routine, it was familiar, comfortable, and predictable. Tilly had reminded her husband that he was becoming less tolerant of intrusions and petty distractions. He remembered the first time that she had mentioned it, suggesting that as he was spending more time at home, he might consider becoming a little more outgoing, more sociable, especially with the neighbours.

However, solving intractable mysteries was James' passion, second only to his attempts at writing his memoirs. Neither activity was conducive to mundane chitchat or other social interaction. Each passion required long quiet periods for uninterrupted research and reflection, according to him.

But James knew that his wife was right; Tilly's words hung in the air, reverberating, the echo yet another distraction. James shook his head as he tried to dismiss the suggestion, wondering if, at 57, he was too old to change. Still deliberating, he continued with his Sunday routine, bringing order and meaning to his world. James often considered that the world might be losing its way. Perhaps he was right. Hadn't the turmoil of the 20th century been evidence enough? There were promises of a new dawn, a new age of enlightenment, the anticipated utopia of the new millennium. But what if it all just turns out to be yet another pipedream? Hadn't the brave new impatient world of the 21st-century already taken its first tentative steps on the dreaded slippery slope? Perhaps it was the destiny of every civilisation; first a decline into mediocrity, then anarchy and chaos, followed by the inevitable apocalypse.

Suddenly roused from that particular quandary, he was interrupted by a familiar and unwelcome voice, the intrusion punctuating his Sunday routine. He had been enjoying the solitude of his sun-drenched patio, scanning the leader in the Sunday Times while enjoying his morning coffee. James had always planned to retire somewhere in the Home Counties. He knew he needed to be within easy reach of the City, far enough to be out of the rat race, but close enough to the capital, with its cultural influences, infinite resources, and archives vital for one whose life had become defined by a passion for detail. James Carver was now able to continue his work at his own pace in a less pressured environment. However, the investigator was not one to be trifled with, especially by somebody who insisted on addressing him as "Jim". Ignoring the interruption, James absently swatted away an inquisitive wasp as he studied the garden over the rim of his coffee cup. Perhaps he would cut the lawn tomorrow. The forecast looked good for the next few days, so there was no urgency. He might even be able to fit in a round or two of golf later.

As a ministry of transport investigator, James' speciality was aviation.

A problem-solver by nature, he was about to tackle the crossword, when the familiar, insistent and unwelcome voice intervened again. His privacy was invaded by the arrival of his neighbour Des, who seemed overly animated about an article in the Essex Mercury.

Takewell was a quiet, well-to-do village, James reflected, but it only took one oddball, like Des, to upset the delicate balance of the genteel neighbourhood. His neighbour's loud voice, coarse mannerisms, and tactless nature were well-known in the street. James often wondered how on earth he had managed to retire next to the former owner of a used-car business with an estuarine accent to rival that of Harry Enfield. Des had apparently sold his business just outside Billericay several years earlier for what he would frequently describe as 'a handsome return'.

Although he did not regard himself as a snob, James found his neighbour's oafish demeanour and coarse humour offensive. Many in the village avoided Des and gave him a wide berth, especially those with more delicate Middle English sensibilities. But, as Tilly often reminded James, their neighbours could also be kind and well-intentioned. James knew that his wife was right, but still found it amusing that those same words had once been used in Crippen's defence.

Des was standing next to the investigator, hovering now, so tactful as ever, James put those deliberations aside for the moment.

Knowing the investigator's reputation for solving aviation mysteries, Des extracted a centre spread article from the Essex Mercury, leaving it by James's coffee mug for the investigator to read at his leisure. Initially irritated by the intrusion, James feigned interest, knowing that Des's politeness was often camouflage for a request of some sort, so he braced himself for the catch, the payback.

Nevertheless, the investigator politely offered to read the article while hiding his lack of enthusiasm at the prospect. After exchanging niceties about the unpredictable weather and James's manicured lawn, Des asked if it would be okay for him to run the engine of his vintage sports car. James was not the only person who had complained about the deafening noise of the V8 engine, but as the neighbour's garage shared a border with James's garden fence, it was he who bore the brunt of the noise. But with an air of resignation, James reluctantly conceded on the understanding that he would be in the garden for the next half hour, enjoying the peace and quiet. After that, James would reluctantly retreat to the conservatory until the din subsided. Des's pet restoration project, the 1964 vintage AC Cobra, was his pride and joy. Rarely making an appearance on the street, thankfully the car remained in his garage which almost overlooked James Carver's garden.

Everybody in the neighbourhood had become accustomed to the noise, which resounded way beyond the limits of the cul-de-sac. Recently, Des had been replacing the exhaust muffler on the Cobra, a period during which the engine's unattenuated roar would send ripples of vibration across the surface of James' coffee mug. Matching ripples which furrowed their way across the inspector's brow, his teeth clenched in tight-lipped suppression of anger and hostility.

Agreeing to allow James his solitude for the time being, Des placed the article from the Essex Mercury on the table as he left, and order was temporarily restored to the investigator's Sunday routine. After finishing the crossword, James glanced absently upwards, noting the scattered fair-weather clouds, and hoping that they were not warning of rain to come. He shivered as a cool breeze snatched at the Essex Mercury news sheet, threatening to blow it off the seasoned oak table and add litter to his manicured garden. Retrieving the paper, James reluctantly scanned the article. The uninspiring black-and-white photograph and matter-of-fact journalistic style did little to dispel the investigator's indifference.

But James's mind was elsewhere. Preoccupied with his work on the Andean crash, he was becoming frustrated at the slow pace of the inquiry, painfully aware that the relatives needed closure. On their behalf he needed to establish cause, the circumstances which culminated in the death of all those on board the Lancastrian, how they died and why. James was following his instincts, focusing on the origin and significance of the 9mm pistol, convinced that it may hold the key to the entire incident. The puzzle was never far from the investigator's thoughts, even on his weekend off.

He pictured the scene and the crash site in Argentina, the Lancastrian, and her appointment with fate, a monochrome movie replayed over and over again, a haunting daydream. So far, the investigation had only proved that the Rolls-Royce engine plate recovered from the wreckage was indeed that of the missing Lancastrian. Any other evidence had been hidden, entombed in snow and ice for more than 50 winters in its glacial descent from the sheer precipice. Each item recovered from the crash site was tarnished and corroded, finally released from a frozen embrace and exposed to fresh alpine air. Each item was tagged and recorded, the jetsam of the doomed; pitiful remains of human flesh and bone, shoes, together with other personal items including a leather wallet, its contents either destroyed in the crash or stolen by alpine opportunists. Amongst other remnants, glistening in the Andean sunshine were three wafer ingots of gold, partly obscured in the seam of what was once a stylish woollen overcoat.

In the lining of an inner pocket, water-stained and barely legible, was an embroidered ribbon label bearing the tailor's name 'Zaremba'.

Further investigation established that the coat was made of high-grade wool by an exclusive manufacturer in Warsaw. Apart from that, the remnants stubbornly refused to give up any further information regarding ownership.

Along with the gold ingots and remains of other personal items, carefully hidden in what had once been either a towel or blanket, was a Browning 9mm pistol. The stock was stamped with the familiar British government crow's foot benchmark. Still loaded, the weapon appeared to be in good working order. Although a full magazine would have held 12 or 13 rounds, only seven remained, strongly suggesting that the weapon had been discharged more than once.

In particular, the gold ingots were in surprisingly good condition, having been exposed to the elements after 50 years in the glacial deep freeze. There was no sign of oxidisation or any other blemish on the wafers, a testament to their purity.

In order to officially determine their properties and provenance, it was necessary to submit the gold ingots to forensic investigation, after which they were dispatched to London for further examination. At the assay office in Goldsmiths' Hall, it was determined that the 40g ingots contained alloys of high quality 22 karat gold, one of which was found to have a high platinum content, an unusual amalgam often used in dental prosthetics. Although the gold bore no obvious commercial hallmark, when inspected by jewellers' eyepiece, each bar carried a small metal stamp impression. The distinctive imprint was similar to small gold ingots recovered from a secret Nazi hoard, hidden in a vault at The Reichsbank in Berlin.

The suggestion of a Nazi origin came as a surprise to the investigators and raised yet more questions. James remembered hearing witness testimonies at the Nuremberg trials after World War II. Anything of value was 'harvested' from concentration camp prisoners, including hair and dental work. Gold fillings, crowns, and bridgework, torn from the jaws of corpses, was melted down and formed into anonymous ingots whose origins could never be positively established. This discovery prompted further investigations regarding the identity of the owner. More evidence was needed. Inch by reluctant inch, the retreating ice obliged, revealing its secrets, a coy and hesitant bride slowly shedding her cold white gown.

For the time being, the investigation would have to wait.

The proclamation of the seven virtues in the Middle Ages, listed *patience* as number five after *diligence*, but any investigator worth his salt knew that he would need both, especially when attempting to solve the insoluble.

James had been here before; he knew that he needed a breakthrough. A reward for hour upon hour of diligence, searching for the missing part of the jigsaw, but where was that perplexing piece of evidence to be found? Or was the answer staring him in the face? Were his powers of deduction not up to the task anymore? Perhaps he had finally lost the knack that potent mix of intuition and perspiration which had served him well throughout his career.

Only time would tell.

Chapter 2

THE SMOKING GUN?

After being 'made safe', the Browning 9mm pistol was returned to the UK by diplomatic pouch, which inevitably attracted the attention of the security services. Once they had consulted their records of missing weapons and satisfied that the Browning was not on their watchlist, the pistol was finally released and made available for further investigation by James and the team. They watched intently as a qualified armourer deftly ejected the magazine from the pistol grip after checking that the breach was empty. He then placed each 9mm round on a bench, each round in sequence, recording the individual identity and position of all seven. The newer rounds on the top of the magazine would obviously be the most recent additions but the three older rounds from the bottom of the magazine must have been original. When studied closer, each of the older rounds bore the rim marking 'G B'. The newer shells were Spanish-made parabellum rounds, originally designed for Luger style pistols.

Their position in the magazine suggested that they were top-ups added to the Browning at a later date. Perhaps this was the missing clue to the cause of the crash – could one of the passengers have threatened the crew or even hijacked the aircraft? With this proposition in mind, the formal investigation into the fate of the airliner, its passengers and crew regained new impetus, more than 50 years after it had vanished.

In the UK, questions were asked again: how could a highly experienced crew fly a passenger aircraft into the side of a mountain? The evidence was perplexing, the unusual gold amalgam strongly suggested a dental link. So who could the mystery dentist be, and why on earth would he be in possession of a British military issue pistol while wearing a coat made in Warsaw?

Aside from weather phenomena, there was still no material evidence regarding the fateful moments after departure from Buenos Aires, finally leading to the crash. But the inspector's instincts were driving him; it was time to consider cause and effect. He began focusing on the next phase of the investigation, determining the origin and history of the Browning service pistol.

Bearing a UK war office benchmark and serial number, James discovered that the weapon was one of a batch of Browning service pistols originally ordered in 1944 by the Ministry for Economic Warfare. This particular batch was reserved and was only to be issued to security service operatives. But documentation referring to so-called special operations remained closely guarded secrets. However, following a freedom of information appeal, limited access was permitted to certain declassified documents.

Previously marked 'Secret', but downgraded to 'Restricted', was a Home Office armoury logbook dated 1945/6. The document had been transferred to microfiche, archived, and forgotten. In a partly redacted logbook entry, a loose-leaf page for February 1945 shows the issue of a Browning 9mm pistol, bearing the same serial number. The weapon had been issued to an individual, whose name and identity were completely illegible. Frustrated, the detective sat pondering the document as he moved it back and forth across the screen of the microfiche viewer. Suddenly his attention was grabbed when the slide was exposed to the highest magnification level, with maximum backlight. Although indistinct, faintly visible through the black oblong of the redaction were the initials 'RK' accompanied by a reference to MEW and 'Box 500'. However, the coiled script of the individual's signature remained illegible.

From previous experience, the investigator knew that the onerous task of redacting countless pages of classified material was usually delegated to a junior clerk in the archiving department. The work was detailed, tedious and messy, but nevertheless vital as each document was declassified and consigned to microfiche. It was not uncommon for a clerk to allow the level of ink in the redacting pen to drop during the process, making it less effective and slightly opaque.

Although the countersigning in the logbook remained indistinct, the next entry did reveal a blank column suggesting that the pistol had never been returned to the armoury following its issue. Another dead end for the investigation, or so it appeared.

Hence the investigator was reluctant to have his train of thought broken by reading an article about a totally unrelated historical incident in Southend from a local tabloid not generally noted for journalistic merit. Knowing that he may well be questioned by his neighbour, the investigator replaced his reading glasses and began reluctantly scanning through the half dozen paragraphs with the scepticism of a practised analyst.

The black-and-white image was of an RAF Anson aircraft. A buckled propeller suggested a wheels-up landing to James, not an unusual occurrence even now. Looking closely at the image, it appeared that the propeller on the left-hand engine had been feathered, suggesting that it had been shut down before landing. If it was *his* investigation, one of the first questions he would ask himself would be was this incident the result of engine failure? But it was *not* his investigation, just another distraction so he shook that notion from his head and reluctantly resumed reading.

Then, unexpectedly, the reference to a 9mm round and a shoulder holster leapt out at him from the tabloid. He smoothed out the pages of the article, studying the text with renewed interest and intense concentration, horn-rimmed glasses carefully balanced in front of the text.

But there was a further small black-and-white image, credited to 'Friends of Rochford Airport'. It was difficult to read at first, small and indistinct, a black-and-white photo of a spent 9mm shell case with distinct rim markings partly obscured by a matchbook, intended to give scale and proportion to the image.

James Carver sat back; a smile of intrigue occupied his face, his fingers drummed to a vague but familiar rhythm, soft against the oak veneer of the table. His instincts were aroused. Coincidence? Conjecture? Yet another red herring, or something else? But where to start? He knew that he would need much more information before he could even think of establishing a link between the pistol, the empty cartridge case, and any other incident. Nevertheless, James Carver found it intriguing and resolved to track down the source of the newspaper article.

Although James was familiar with ballistics and firearm forensics, he knew that he would need an expert to examine the shell case in detail. But the image stayed with him, constantly resurfacing in his dreams.

After a restless night, James had already woken before the radio alarm clock sounded. He silenced it as it was about to announce the headlines of the day. Sipping his early morning coffee, he resolved to ring the editor of the Essex Mercury in Chelmsford as soon as they opened. Fortified by a slice of toast and marmalade James lifted the receiver and dialled the number from the phone book. Only to discover that the article in question had been provided by arrangement with their business partners, The Southend Reporter.

He noted the number for the Reporter and thanked them for their help. After listening to musical wallpaper for several minutes, James hung up, resolving to make one last attempt to contact the editor of The Southend Reporter before lunch.

Tilly appeared in the conservatory carrying two steaming china mugs and placed each carefully on matching floral coasters.

"While you were on the phone, James, Des came round for the newspaper article that he gave you yesterday. Apparently, it had the weekly horoscope on the back. I said you would drop it round to them before lunch."

James took his first sip of coffee, rolled his pupils upwards and assumed a vacant expression, his silent gesture revealing far more than mere words.

Wondering vaguely who on earth in the 20th century would take a horoscope seriously, James was still mulling over the matter of the 9mm cartridge case and the image in the weekend newspaper. He mustered as much enthusiasm as he could before pressing the ornate bell push on his neighbour's door. As usual, James was greeted with enthusiasm and invited in, while politely declining the offer of a single malt, now that the sun was "over the yardarm".

James often entertained himself with comical cameos about his neighbour. Perhaps the consumption of sufficient single malt conferred on you the honour of becoming a solar astronomer, or maybe a soothsayer. There must be something to it – Des always seemed to know where the sun was in relation to the yardarm, whatever a yardarm was.

Des returned with his own crystal whisky glass charged while James returned the newspaper article neatly folded, deciding to forget The Rochford Incident. James was annoyed with himself, irritated by allowing himself yet more distraction, so he resolved to concentrate his efforts on his own enquiry while heading for the kitchen door.

"Are you sure you won't have a snifter before you go, Jimmy boy?" insisted Des, adding for good measure. "... Did you like Ned's article?"

James had prepared his escape plan in advance and glanced at the fading cockerel on the kitchen clock. He wanted to say that lunch was on the table, but he stopped short in his tracks at the unexpected question.

"Ned?" said James, putting on his polite while disinterested tone.

"Yes, Liz's sister's eldest, he wrote the article originally for the Southend Reporter. It's a first for him, getting the article published in the Essex Mercury; the sky's the limit now!"

"You mean you know the journalist who wrote the Rochford article?" said James, dumbfounded.

CHAPTER 2

"Of course..." came the reply. "... you've probably seen him here, longish length hair, little slip of a lad, done well for himself, can't believe he's going to be 21 this year!"

"Does he live nearby?" said James, hoping the reply would not prompt another of his neighbour's complicated explanations. "Benfleet" came the response. "If you like, I will ask him to speak to you next time he comes over."

Just then the voice of an eavesdropper joined the conversation from the kitchen. "E's got his own car now, Des got it for him, didn't you, luv?"

"Thank you, Liz, I'm talking to Jim, we can't hear you in there."

Undeterred, the disembodied voice continued ... "E's got one of those new-fangled mobile phones as well, Ned 'as, because of his job, e's really come up in the world, unlike his mother, the lazy good for nothing mare "

Des interrupted with "Thank you, Liz, I'm sure Jim doesn't want to hear your family's life history, love".

Grateful for the interruption and becoming more animated, the inspector politely enquired, "Could I have his number; please? Just so I can fill in a few gaps in his story – most interesting and informative," James added, annoyed at his own exaggeration.

Chapter 3

A REPORTER

The VW Golf was badged as a GTI model, but Ned was unconvinced; he had probably paid over the odds for a high mileage motor that had obviously been clocked at some time. But Ned enjoyed the comfort of the grey leather upholstery. He smiled to himself over the padded steering wheel, reflecting that the Golf was rather like Uncle Des: overrated, and overpriced, definitely a case of form over function.

On the passenger seat of the Golf, Ned's mobile phone had rung twice before he managed to find a space in the car park. Just why parking at the Southend Reporter had become so difficult was a mystery to Ned, but he enjoyed a good mystery. Handbrake on, this time he answered the insistent Nokia tone on his latest acquisition.

Identifying himself as James, the caller asked about Ned's article 'The Rochford incident' and seemed overly interested in a 9mm pistol and the spent shell case, rather than the article itself. Hoping that James was genuine, rather than yet another nuisance call, Ned was impressed; there was something about the well-spoken sincerity of the caller. He sounded educated and well informed, someone who would study the broadsheets rather than jump to conclusions. Intrigued, Ned hoped that James may be a fellow sleuth, a meeting of minds.

They arranged to meet later that week for lunch at the Fox at Benfleet. James introduced himself as an investigator and with a firm handshake, offered to buy lunch. After ordering half a Foster's for himself and black coffee for James, Ned settled at a convenient table overlooking the pub car park.

The waitress brought the drinks and carefully placed a beer mat under Ned's glass. He watched her leave while he surveyed the bar and its customers, as James sat down opposite him. He thanked Ned for the drink and released a nervous sigh as each took their first sip.

"I planned to send you the print earlier in the week but by the time I managed to escape from the 'Friends of Rochford' gang and sent the negative to be processed, the enlargement only arrived yesterday..." said Ned, faking the trickery of a spy, while surreptitiously offering the investigator a 7 x 5 photograph in a folded foolscap envelope.

"... Anyway, I hope this is what you're looking for, James, a much better close-up."

"I wonder if this could be the solution to my little conundrum?" asked James.

From behind his infectious smile, Ned whispered, "You're not a cop, or a spook or, even worse, some sort of crank, are you, James?"

James was not sure what to make of the young reporter in front of him, but decided to give him the benefit of the doubt.

"What a strange introduction, what on earth makes you ask, Ned?"

"Well, you have just answered both of my questions with a question."

"Have I?" replied James, enjoying the moment.

"And there you go, that's three; no wonder I am suspicious!"

They both laughed as Ned continued. "In my job so far, I've met a lot of strange people, I think it is an occupational hazard! But since I wrote 'The Rochford Incident', it has attracted them like a magnet. I don't just mean ordinary run-of-the-mill-strange, we are talking seriously *weird*." Ned rotated a forefinger at his right temple for emphasis. "I just wanted to make sure that you were the real thing, you are, aren't you, James? Please tell me you're not another X-Files nutter!"

Feeling slighted by the question but undeterred, James smiled. "Well, Ned, if you mean am I a time-waster, I assure you that I certainly am not. To my professional clients, time is money not to be wasted on either whims or wild goose chases."

Ned glanced at his watch. "Neither do I as it happens. I need to be back at my desk in less than an hour." Ned's smile returned.

"So, tell me, who are you, Mr James Carver? All I know so far is that you answer questions with more questions, you live next to my mad uncle, and you bought me lunch in an attempt to convince me that you are not a crank!"

It was James's turn to smile. "Well, my original job was with the CID, but I retired from that many moons ago. Now I work for the government as a semi-retired crash investigator. My latest case has turned into a bit of a mystery, a plane crash that took place in Argentina in 1948 and I seem to be getting nowhere fast...

"... So, sorry to disappoint you, Ned. Yes, I *was* a cop, as you journalists put it but, no, I have never been a spook, and hopefully not a crank!

"What about you then, Ned?"

"Well, quite a lot of my time was spent as a layabout and general dogsbody, I helped Uncle Des with his business in Billericay for a while after leaving the air cadets. I graduated from Sheffield earlier this year, and here I am, back in Benfleet working for the Southend Echo!"

Starting to enjoy the banter, James smiled. "No more questions, your honour!" Knowing full well that there would be, whilst he extracted the 7 x 5 black-and-white print, from its protective envelope. Obviously impressed, he enquired, "How did you get this, Ned?"

"I know the guy who found the bullet..." came the reply. "... I met him when I did the research for the original article. I know the Rochford incident story was quite popular, but when it was sold to the Essex Mercury, it attracted conspiracy theorists and nutters out of the woodwork, even some who claimed that the crew of the aircraft must have been abducted by aliens!"

For effect, Ned attempted his terrible rendition of the Twilight Zone theme tune; his grin became a beam as he sipped at the foam on the top of his lager. "The brass cartridge has received cult status as sort of a trophy find for the metal detectors club.

"So I just did as you asked, James, I used a macro lens on my Pentax to bring out the detail on the shell case."

Initially irritated by Ned's antics, the investigator surprised himself as he began to warm to Ned. Unaccustomed to juvenile banter, Tilly's advice echoed in James' head just as he was about to dismiss the young reporter and his flippant approach to what he regarded as a serious subject. James became aware that he had been guilty of prejudging a relative of his neighbour, expecting little from the budding reporter, but he soon began to take Ned more seriously.

"So, Sherlock, what makes you think that an old brass shell case from Rochford can have anything to do with your investigation from the other side of the world?"

"Well, that's what I thought when I first read your article. That was when I looked more closely at the pistol and ammunition from Argentina."

"So what? They look the same, could just be a random coincidence, couldn't it, James?"

"Well, it could, Ned, that's why I decided to get a friend in ballistic analysis to examine the weapon and the ammunition."

"And...?"

"Well, if I am right, Ned, each round was fired from the same pistol. Not only that, but it appears that each round is from the same batch marked 'GB'. It seems that the rim markings, ejector scrape marks and firing pin strikes on the cap of your friend's cartridge, and those found on the ammunition from the Andes, were, to all intents and purposes, identical. What's more, I am assured by forensics, that these marks are unique, like fingerprints."

They both smiled, James at his dramatic revelation, and Ned at his jovial best, alert for the opportunity for improvised comedy.

Ned spoke first. "Do you mind telling me what this is all about...?"

Unconcerned, Ned continued "... So you have these two old brass shell cases, which look similar, mine from Southend and yours from God knows where in the Andes, so what, Sherlock? You are starting to sound like a member of the Metal Detectorists club , especially the one who had either been inhaling some household adhesive products, smoking oregano hemp or worse!"

His smile widening, James explained the Lancastrian investigation and possible links to the Rochford mystery. As he spoke, his doubts began to resurface – was this just another dead end? But James had warmed to Ned – the shrewd young man with a mischievous smile reminded the investigator of himself at that age, big on enthusiasm but short on experience. James continued. "There is a distinct possibility that your Rochford incident could be connected with my case," said the investigator. "But I am in need of a little help. Would you be interested in a bit of freelance follow-up research, Ned?"

Nodding enthusiastically, Ned enquired while draining the last of his lager, "What sort of research were you thinking of?"

"Well initially, further evidence of the 9mm pistol requiring deeper research into the Rochford incident and exploring any similarities and connections with the Lancastrian, but it's going to take a lot of time-consuming footslog, and painstaking sifting through archives."

"Sounds just up my street..." said Ned, "... but please don't build up your hopes too much on the Rochford incident."

"Really, why not, Ned?"

"Well, first of all, it is no longer my story now that it has been sold on, and second of all I didn't think there was much mileage left in pursuing it any further, with interest waning. No currency, a cold story dead in the water in my opinion."

"But, if I am right, Ned, this could be a fascinating follow-up and an exclusive for you. You must have found it intriguing at the time, didn't you, Ned? Where is your sense of adventure, young man? How about solving 'The Rochford Incident' and bringing the story up-to-date? I think we should join forces – I'm up for it if you are!"

"Well sure, I did find the original research fascinating... I tell you what, James, I will see if I can get my editor interested, he's big buddies with the editor of the Essex Mercury. If he agrees, I can do some legit research at work. Once I am on the case, if there is anything more to know, Sherlock, I will find it, trust me."

After agreeing to meet again, Ned hastily wrapped up the remains of his ploughman's in a pub napkin, adding, "Sorry, got to get back to work now, James, but I will give you a bell later in the week. You can keep the picture, by the way, it's of little journalistic significance, now that my article has been sold on." Then, tapping a forefinger against the side of his nose. "Besides, I've got the negative! One of the first things I learned about journalism is to always keep your own copies of everything!" he said, with his secretive smile.

Driving back home, James was pleased; he would continue to work on the Argentinian investigation with Ned concentrating on links with the Rochford incident. Although James had become accustomed to working alone, he felt relieved. His lack of progress with the Lancastrian had become frustrating, to say the least, but now he had an ally. James and Ned had agreed to actively pursue their own investigations while searching for further evidence of a connection between the two incidents.

Back at Takewell, in the quiet and orderly confines of his study, James took stock of the investigation so far. He compared the picture of the shell case from Argentina, with a one given him by Ned. He began to realise that the mystery of the gold had overshadowed the entire investigation until now. Obviously, the gold was material evidence, but James knew that the 9mm pistol just might reveal vital clues that the ingots may not. The gold would be of circumstantial importance, but on its own, could not provide a direct link to the identity of an owner or shed light on the fate of the Lancastrian.

Tantalising as the evidence was, the inspector knew that all investigations involving firearms would need to be scrutinised by an independent specialist, corroboration from a second forensic expert. With this in mind, James rang his contact at the Home Office and arranged for the pistol in question to be re-proved, tested, and test fired with another of the original 9mm rounds from the Browning's magazine. Each cartridge bore the initials 'G B'; there was no doubt that both rounds were from the same batch, and the same pistol had fired each round.

Each cartridge revealed its own secrets, its own evidence, the firing pin impression, the ejector scrape mark, and breech face impression all matched. Silent but unerring, the small brass cartridges bore witness to two separate incidents, each 50 years ago, and 7,000 miles apart.

A semi-retired investigator and the novice journalist, an unlikely team...? Maybe. Chalk and cheese...? Possibly. Only time would tell

But today, James had lost track of time. Absorbed in his task, he had skipped lunch and had spent hours scouring armoury records for any reference to a 9mm pistol bearing the same serial number as the one recovered from Argentina. It was almost 5 pm on his second day at the Public Records Office when he suddenly found it. As clear as day, the document leapt out at him from the microfiche monitor. Issued to an individual with the initials RK and cryptic reference to Box 500 in 1945. James printed a hard copy from the microfiche, just as the archives department was closing for the day.

Putting two and two together doesn't always add up to four, but, older and wiser, James had learned the hard way how to temper enthusiasm with caution. During his time as a police detective, the investigator had acquired finely honed instincts. Over the next few days, the more he thought about it, the more he became convinced of the connection.

With his editor's agreement, Ned had spent his time following up references to a 9mm round while delving deeper into the records at Southend General Hospital. At their next meeting, James and Ned eagerly compared notes over a pint at the Fox. The empty shoulder holster, the subsequent hospital admission of the mysterious R Knight all started to make sense now.

If James's research was correct, the incident at Rochford and the fate of the Lancastrian in Argentina were inextricably linked. But how could a British military pistol, issued in the UK during World War II, suddenly turn up on a mountainside in Argentina more than 50 years later? How could there be any connection with the Rochford incident? Was the answer staring them in the face, or was it just the product of two overactive imaginations? From the serial number of the Browning pistol, it seemed that they were one and the same weapon, that much was beyond doubt. But proof of ownership and intent would be a much greater challenge and might prove impossible. James was not one to be deterred by such difficulties, but he knew from contacts within the military that any attempt to contact the sponsors or crew of the Anson incident at Rochford in 1946 may be futile.

There were still a lot of ifs, far too many ifs for James' liking.

If the Rochford mission had been classified, *if* the crew members were still alive, and even *if* the individuals involved could be traced, they would probably have been vetted to a high-security level. That would put them beyond the scope of his investigation. They would effectively have been 'untouchables', it didn't take a detective to figure that out. From bitter experience, James knew the quickest way to jeopardise any inquiry was to rely heavily on conjecture and circumstance, at the expense of testimony and tangible evidence. Such an enquiry could only result in one outcome: an open verdict—wasted time both for the investigator and those who paid him for answers. James was not often given to doubt, but had the Rochford incident become just a sideshow, distracting him from his main task? He had not heard from Ned in the last few days either; yes, Ned was enthusiastic, but he also had a job and his own life to lead. James knew that if he was ever going to solve the Lancastrian inquiry, he would need a breakthrough – and soon.

Although thousands of miles away and 50 years ago, in 1947 it had been relatively easy to confirm the identity of those on board the ill-fated Lancastrian flight. Names of both crew and passengers were confirmed from the manifest which was still available in Ministry of Transport archives. The investigator knew that a name was one thing, but identity is yet another. The pathologists were doing their best, trying to match human tissue to each individual, but that part of the investigation proved much more problematic. Profiling human remains was time-consuming and complicated, especially when testing degraded DNA samples. Even then, the results from a so-called *mass casualty event* might well prove ambiguous and, therefore, inadmissible.

In Southend, Ned had spent the last two weeks making more enquiries, and digging deeper into the Rochford incident. He had been trawling the archives and followed up every lead in his investigation. However, his efforts to find any record or fiche documentation regarding the incident in 1946 at RAF Rochford were proving elusive. Later that year, the airfield had come under civil licence and was operating as Southend Municipal Airport. It seemed that this is where Ned's investigation would end.

Until it was that James discovered the transcription of a 1946 report in the Public Record Office in Kew. The document bore all the hallmarks of censorship, including some redaction. At the time of the report, unbeknownst to James, Lefty was still in the process of searching for his child. The transcript was in the form of a summary to a board of inquiry held in camera. The destination of the Anson had been redacted, but the departure airfield was given as CPH with no details of either crew or passengers. The report to special branch had been marked classified at the time, but since then, additional information regarding the flight was now in the public domain.

Under the 50-year rule and the freedom of information act, Ned had managed to unearth more information, including some relevant to Southend at the time of the Rochford incident. Digging deeper, Ned discovered an interesting but faint carbon copy of an official immigration pad for a flight which had originated in Copenhagen with the signature and name visible at the bottom. Although the ink had faded, a Mr Matthews had authorised the document and a declaration was countersigned by '478 F/S DP McFarland (RCAF)'.

Now he had names, Ned knew this is where the work really starts. James wasn't kidding when he had said "painstaking footslog". Ned decided at the outset that he would rule out Mr Matthews, the countersigning officer on the document. For a start, there was only a surname, no initials. Secondly, no one at Southend Airport could remember the name. That left Flight Sgt McFarland, who appeared to be Canadian. But from the start, Ned knew that tracing a Canadian national from 50 years ago may be all but impossible. Spending hour upon hour scouring UK telephone directories, he would never have believed how many D McFarlands there could have been in the UK. After 10 days of chasing up fruitless leads, Ned was about to give up. However, he reminded himself that perseverance was his middle name, and he didn't want to let James down. But he still had his day job at The Reporter to consider, and the work was piling up. He had been given a generous amount of leeway, but there was a limit to the amount of time that the editor would allow Ned for helping James Carver with his investigation.

It had been a frustrating morning In Takewell. James Carver had made little progress with either the Lancastrian investigation or the first draft of his autobiography. The more he wrote, the more editing he discovered. To make matters worse, the roaring of next door's car engine had gone on for far too long. James was about to confront Des just as the noise finished reverberating around the street. Peace returned to the sleepy village of Takewell. Grateful for the silence, James let out a long sigh, but just as he was about to take his first sip of morning coffee, the telephone rang. He allowed it to ring for several seconds, resenting the intrusion, then picked up on the sixth or seventh ring.

"Good morning, Sherlock, you're going to love me when you hear this!" Ned's animated voice was unmistakable.

"Tell me you've got good news, Ned, I've made no progress at all at this end," replied the discouraged voice of James Carver. "I really need your input, Ned, if I'm ever going to get this investigation report finalised. I haven't heard from you for over 10 days, Ned, I tell you, love was not the first word on my lips this morning."

"Now hear me out, Mr Grumpy!" came the reply, as Ned continued.

"... Okay, listen to this... In my junk mail this week came the monthly newspaper from the RAF Association. I'm not sure why I still get it, I must have forgotten to cancel my subscription, I haven't been an air cadet for years." Ned continued. "It normally goes straight in the bin, but before it reached the recycling, something caught my eye," said the young journalist.

"This had better be good, Ned," complained James, weary of Ned's frequent distractions, "... I have had over a week of nothing but dead ends."

Ned continued, "Pin your ears back, Sherlock. Inside the RAF newsletter was a photograph of a couple from Hastings, a middle-aged lady, about your age, or maybe a bit younger come to think of it. She was standing next to an elderly gentleman in an article entitled '*Father And Daughter Reunited After Five Decades*'..."

The weary sigh from James was audible.

"... Well, I read on, the article gave the name of the World War II hero... Wait for it!

"Flight Sgt DP McFarland (RCAF) and his daughter, Connie!

"It's him, James, I just know this is our man. The name, rank and initials and nationality, and even, RCAF, Royal Canadian Air Force, exactly the same as the name on the immigration pad from the morning after the Rochford incident."

"Great work, Ned! We need to meet up with him. Face-to-face."

"Well, Sherlock, it just so happens that I rang the editor of the RAF News and asked if it would be possible to meet up with Flight Sgt McFarland and his daughter. He said he would ask them and ring me back."

"You think that they will be prepared to arrange a meeting, Ned?"

"You haven't heard the rest, James. The editor returned my call this morning, and we are meeting up with Mr McFarland and his daughter Connie next week... How about that?"

Ned paused for effect, then added,"... My next question for you, Sherlock; are you free for a day out in Sussex on Thursday?" Ned was beaming from ear to ear.

"Brilliant work, Ned," said James, laughing with excitement and relief. "What an opportunity, the chance of solving both enquiries, two birds with one stone!"

"I'll drive, Watson," added James, cautious as ever.

"Sorted!" said Ned. "That's why I chose Thursday. I'm taking Uncle Des and Auntie Liz to Stansted. They are going to their timeshare in Marbella for a couple of weeks. I'll pick you up at the same time, we'll drop them at the airport, then Sussex here we come!"

"Bob's your uncle!" said James.

Ned couldn't resist responding with, "No, Sherlock, his name is Des!" adding "... some detective you turned out to be!"

Laughing could be heard at each end of the phone.

Chapter 4

JAMES AND NED,
CONNIE AND LEFTY

I openly admit that I was dubious about James and Ned when we first met. They were an unlikely pair and I wondered what they had to gain by meeting my dad.

They each had their own agenda, especially Ned, who was young, ambitious, and very bright, just setting out on a new career. Then there was amicable, reliable James, but he was preoccupied trying to solve some investigation in Argentina. But Lefty being Lefty, he was quite happy to accept them at face value. But me, sceptical by nature, I wanted to defend my father, to avoid undue attention from those who may try to exploit him and our story for personal gain. We had received quite a lot of publicity already, but so far it had been relatively low-key. Having finally found my father, the last thing I wanted was for our privacy to be compromised. I imagined Lefty and me as reluctant celebrities, hounded by the tabloids so that the world and his wife could own our story.

As usual, my fears were groundless. I soon discovered that James and Ned were very different; they were genuine, open, and engaging, and very soon felt like family to me. James as a long-lost brother, and Ned, the son I never had. All they asked of us was time, and in return were more than generous with their own.

It was time for the tale to be told.

Meeting Ned and James in the spare room at the Cranbourne care home would never have worked, but now it was closing we would have to meet in my flat.

Our weekend sessions with James and Ned were very productive, each recalling memories; joy and laughter, laced with tears of sorrow. The DNA test results had been confirmed, so I finally had legal status as a daughter. For weeks now I had practised in my mind calling him 'Dad', but I had spent so long at the care home, knowing him only as Don, I somehow still felt awkward when addressing him as Dad. We discussed it, and in the end, he was happy to be called Lefty by everybody, including me. The man that was Lefty, Don and now Dad, the face in the photograph. Waiting, searching for me ever since my birth.

He spoke to me with great affection and warmth, and the deep love he and my mother shared. He would often call me Mary by accidental slip, correcting himself quickly while absently shaking his head. We would share smiles; believe it or not I cherished that tiny mannerism of his far more than I can say.

Lefty and Mary were obviously very close in those unimaginably dark days of the war. Like many, they became victims of circumstances. Lefty surviving the perils of occupied Norway; Mary, my mother, plucked from life in a whirlwind of fire. My own miraculous survival due solely to the prompt actions of one warden, a man who later laid down his own life while saving others.

Lefty told me of Klara and her little cowbell. Although he got on well with her, he didn't like the way Klara treated Mary – after all, Mary was her niece, family, not slave.

We both laughed out loud when I told him about Pruda, and life in her house strewn with refuse, feral cats, and colourful language. I told him about my time caring for Pruda. I related the story of Pruda's rape in Poland, her escape to England with her sister and giving birth to her illegitimate son. My warm tears returned when I described her last few hours, holding her hand as life silently slipped away from the skeletal frame that once was Pruda.

Lefty described his activities in Norway during and after the war, both stories merged into one. Of course, I had never heard of Rathke, but his name was now in the public domain following the Rochford incident. Rathke certainly sounded evil to me, and I felt no pity for the man and his appointment with destiny in the Andean snow.

I received a letter from a solicitor who was working on the conveyancing of Pruda's house and personal effects, informing me that I'm the only surviving relative and entitled to the entire estate. Needless to say, I was not expecting any such legacy. I discussed it with Lefty, James and Ned and decided to invest the money in reopening the Cranbourne care home. I decided to contact some of the residents, especially those who had had to move out when Sheila left, and money from the foundation ran out. At the time I could only afford to open one wing of the home, but I intended to have it all redecorated and restored. I would find the best carers and invite them back. I was sure I would be able to comfortably accommodate up to eight residents in one wing, with the garden room for dining and leisure activities.

The property lease included a modern detached cottage which had been used as a manager's residence. As it was single storey it would be ideal for Lefty and me.

I was eager to proceed with my plan, but I could do nothing until Pruda's money came through. Tied in with the legacy was a quantity of Krugerrands that Pruda had acquired in South Africa, presumably hidden in Coronation Lane. There was to be a formal investigation to determine whether the gold coins were legally imported and whether or not they were subject to tax and import duty. But I was prepared to wait. Dear old Pruda. She did have gold after all, but I had cleaned number 43 from top to bottom and had no idea where she had hidden it.

Ned lent me a Dictaphone and a set of recording cartridges so that I could record my conversations with Lefty and not miss any crucial details. Each time James and Ned came to visit, they would drop off a batch of blank tapes and show Lefty and me their typed transcripts.

They would take the latest set of recordings with them and go through them back in Essex.

During one of these visits, there was a stern knocking on the front door of my flat. I wasn't expecting any visitors – I actively discouraged interruption of any kind during our sessions. The boys were relaxing with an afternoon drink and waited until I answered the door.

I was startled by the silhouette in the doorway. It was Gregory; I would know him anywhere. I hadn't seen him for at least two years, and I wasn't in the mood to welcome him now. I must've stood at the door in silence for several seconds, lost for words. He spoke first, his words slightly slurred just as I remember them; flushed features suggested recent drinking.

"Well, aren't you going to invite me in?" He pushed the door open and stepped across the threshold without waiting for an invite.

"What are you doing here? I don't want you in my flat or in my life ever again."

Alerted by raised voices, James and Ned appeared at the doorway. Gregory spoke first.

"So who are these, your new fancy men? One is not enough for you these days, obviously."

"Gregory, I just want you to leave now. I have nothing to say to you."

"Don't give me that, I know you have money, you have an inheritance; I think you owe me, don't you, Connie?"

"I owe you nothing, even if I did have an inheritance, you wouldn't see a penny of it; now get out of my house."

Gregory lurched in the doorway, reconsidering his next move as he eyed Ned and weighed up the opposition.

"I think the lady asked you to leave, sir," said James politely.

But Ned stepped forward, saying, "I'll handle this."

"And just who are you, Sonny Jim? She obviously prefers the youngsters these days. Does your mum know you are at an orgy?"

Ignoring the insults, Ned drew up to his full height saying, "You heard the lady, she politely asked you to leave twice now, third strike and you are out!"

In response, Gregory slammed the front door open against its hinges with a crash. Lefty looked up in alarm from the easy chair at the commotion.

His face an angry mask, Gregory snarled, "I know you have money; they say you have gold."

"Okay, you've had your warning," said Ned.

He stepped forward, dragged Gregory by the scruff and frogmarched him out to the car park, leaving him propped against the bodywork of his muddy Mondeo.

Gregory's shouting continued. "I'll be back for what is mine," he threatened.

"Don't even think about it, sunshine..." said Ned. "... You will have me to deal with, remember that."

In the car park, the echo of a car pulling away was accompanied by a screech of tyres.

James offered, "Well, I don't think he will be back any time soon."

"Not if he knows what's good for him," added Ned.

"How could he have found me?" I asked.

"Don't forget you have both had your 15 minutes in the limelight," said James.

"It was Ned who tracked you down after your story got the spotlight in the media."

"If we found you, it wouldn't have taken much for the likes of him to find you."

"Yes, I suppose you are right," I said. I thanked both James and Ned for their support, confessing that I had worried that he would try to find me, the past just has a way of catching up with you. I knew only too well that Gregory Pyle had a nose for money, and always held grudges. I admitted that I had been intimidated by Gregory who had threatened me in the past.

"Yes, well done, Ned, you can add bouncer to your CV now!"

They exchanged smiles as James said, "Now where were we up to before we were so rudely interrupted? Lisbon, I think."

All apart from Lefty was deep in thought, but before the question could be answered, Lefty said, "How do you know him? Were you friends with him, Connie?"

"No, he was somebody I knew in York, a mistake from the past, somebody I wish I'd never met.

"Gregory Pyle probably marks the lowest point in my past relationships."

"He said that you owed him something, what did he mean by that?" said James.

"Oh, his father tried to claim compensation after their property was bombed in the war. So help me. I wish I'd never taken up with him in the first place."

"What did you say his name was, Connie?" enquired Lefty.

"Pyle, Gregory Pyle, a name to forget. I think his father was sent to jail, so was not entitled to claim anything."

Lefty sat in silent thought. "I remember somebody of that name in York."

"Gregory rented a semi in Middlethorpe, but I think his father was from Osbaldswick."

"Do you remember his father's name, Connie?"

"No, it was an unusual name, but I don't want to think about him anymore if you don't mind."

"Does *Tobin* ring a bell?"

"Yes! That's him, did you know him?"

"Well, I think I have met Gregory and his father a long while ago, but we weren't formally introduced if you know what I mean!"

"I will tell you about that sometime, Connie." Lefty smiled, placing his hand on top of mine. He added reassuringly "It is not important, but it did bring back other memories of your mother, and 11 Laburnum Grove."

"We've got plenty to be getting on with, Ned," said James. Then looking at his watch, "We will have to get on the road soon, but we will be back in a few days after we have typed up the latest transcript. Give it some thought, and we will leave you in peace. We can pick up the story where we left off next week."

We were getting towards the end of the personal account from Lefty, and I was adding my own experiences. The transcripts from Lefty were all being edited and typed up. The rest was up to Ned and James now. After all, James was supposed to be working on his autobiography, although Lefty's memoir was growing day by day. In fact, if the chapter grew any more, it would qualify to become a book on its own. It wouldn't be too long now before the final manuscript could be submitted for publication.

About a month later, at long last, my copy of the confirmation of the leasehold document arrived in the morning mail. Lefty and I had moved from my flat into the manager's cottage at the Cranbourne home while painters and decorators worked on the East Wing of the main building.

I woke early that morning, enjoying the peace and quiet before the workday started. I put the kettle on to boil while I went over to unlock the main entrance to let the workmen in. I hadn't heard a sound from Lefty's room. He was always up and about early, but it was after 8 am and we had a busy day ahead of us. Normally he would never have food or drink in bed, but I decided to deliver his morning cuppa. He always kept his bedroom door ajar for ventilation, so I tapped softly on the door, drink in hand. The curtains were still drawn, a single shaft of sunlight was sufficient to reveal bed clothes undisturbed. Deep silence.

At times like this, well-meaning people trot out tired clichés about loss and grief, but my responses sounded equally clichéd.

Yes, I know that Lefty didn't suffer.

No, he didn't give in, no, it was not in his nature.

And yes, he will be sadly missed.

Choosing the right words takes great consideration and compassion, or maybe the right words are not written in any dictionary.

But if they do exist at all, they may have come from the pen of the poet John F McCullagh, deeply etched in the third verse of *The Man with the Thousand Yard Stare*.

The mourners pass by him in silence,
touch his hand or say meaningless words,
for his part he stares straight through them,
as if nothings felt, nothings heard.

As far as I knew Lefty had been his normal self, he was slowing up obviously but was still very active even in his 90s.

Looking back, if anything I think he was just plain exhausted. He often joked about death and choosing the best way to go. When I suggested dying in your sleep, he smiled and disagreed, insisting that the best way was in the arms of a lover!

That was Lefty, the man who saw humour and opportunity when others saw only misery and despair.

Epilogue 1

DRAINING THE CULVERT
AND FINDING LUCIA

O peration Culvert was the name given to a joint Allied post-war investigation tasked with tracing Axis war criminals in Europe and Scandinavia. In the form of an inquiry, the operation was concluded in 1949, its findings remained classified until released under the Freedom of Information act.

Buried in the depths of that particular report were the final pieces of the Osprey jigsaw. Although Lefty had been the official witness in the identification of Rathke, the report does not include the number, rank, or names of those involved.

Although the report relied partly on anecdote, it is supported by the facts as known to date. Evidence was collated from trusted sources and what little documentation was available, including transcripts of official statements and personal accounts. Under the provisions of the Official Secrets Act 1911 to 1939, information regarding the identification, repatriation, and detention of any agent of interest remained highly classified, especially those deemed a threat to the security of the United Kingdom. It would be 50 years before any documentation regarding the activities and detention of the double agent Osprey would be released for public scrutiny.

Conclusions

The following report is a summary of information obtained after cross referencing and collating details of the Lancastrian enquiry and the official report of Operation Culvert. Both reports were released in 2000, the latter having been declassified and in the public domain 50 years after its conclusion.

After an in-depth study of the evidence, the report concluded that the gunman on the Lancastrian was Rathke. Travelling under an assumed name, he was one of the passengers who perished in the Andean crash. Although bound for Chile and liberty, he only made it as far as Mendoza, Argentina, and his appointment with fate. And there he remained, entombed in the glacial ice of the Andes only one hour from freedom but 50 years too late.

The identity of RK is believed to be a Richard Knight, an operative who signed for the pistol as a personal sidearm in 1945. In 1946, Knight was detailed as one of two armed escorts assigned to detain Rathke and escort him on the return flight from Denmark, culminating in the forced landing of the Anson in Southend. All attempts to find Richard Knight were again dead ends, but the report was a catalogue of pseudonyms and Knight was probably just another. James had traced the serial number of the pistol from the armoury ledger, and we know the same weapon was issued to Knight. The empty 9mm shell case recovered from Southend bore the same 'G B' markings and batch number as those from the Browning pistol recovered from Argentina. That batch of ammunition was not British as first assumed, but was purchased by sources within the UK from the Bolivian Government. That particular consignment of 9mm ammunition was recalled in 1946 after reports of too many stoppages and misfires. The entire batch was subsequently destroyed as it contained inferior quality primer and propellant.

Although they would not confirm or deny involvement, the report refers to Box 500 as the official sponsor of the Copenhagen flight that crashed at Rochford. The sponsors held an internal inquiry which, although classified, returned an open verdict on the Copenhagen-Rochford flight. Box number five hundred was none other than MI5.

What is known is that following the forced landing of the Anson at RAF Rochford, emergency services were eventually alerted to the incident. In his written report, the fire officer from Southend on duty on the night in question recorded that they attended an incident at RAF Rochford after being summoned by an official at the airfield. Arriving at the scene of the accident, the Chief fire officer stated that the aircraft was substantially intact, with minor damage to the port wing and a buckled propeller, but no evidence of fire. The accompanying ambulance retrieved one civilian who appeared to be suffering from a gunshot wound or wounds. The crew of three suffered only superficial injuries and were treated locally at a first aid station.

At the time of the incident, RAF Rochford was in the process of being transferred to the local authority by the MoD, so there is little official verification. However, significantly, what few reports there were of the incident mentioned three crew and only two civilians. Neither crew nor passengers' names appeared on the declaration of immigration. The document gave only the date and location of the occurrence and was signed by a F/S DP McFarland (RCAF), in the presence of Matthews, the deputy airport manager.

Following the incident, the Home Office went to great lengths to trace Osprey's whereabouts to no avail. The three crew members, including Lefty, were ordered to talk to no one in connection with the incident, and any enquiries were to be referred to the ministry press office in Whitehall. Rathke had disappeared off the face of the earth.

Immediately after the Anson's forced landing at RAF Rochford, Osprey grappled with agent RK in a bid to snatch his weapon. In the ensuing struggle, the weapon was discharged twice, injuring the agent who received a bullet wound to his right leg. Threatening the second escort at gunpoint, Osprey grabbed his own overcoat and snatched items from his Gladstone bag before making off at the height of the storm. Armed with the pistol, he knew that he would need to flee the scene before the emergency services were alerted.

In the ensuing confusion, aided by the cover of darkness, Osprey fled the scene, making his way to the nearby port of Tilbury. Armed with the pistol and what remained of his wherewithal, he would have been able to either threaten or bribe his way out of the country.

Rathke had covered his tracks well. Along with the origins of the pistol, the dental gold wafers, and other articles discovered in the Argentinian Andes, very little of this story would have come to light at all.

At Tilbury it is believed that Rathke sought passage on the freighter 'Bohemia' which set sail on the early morning tide, bound for Lisbon.

Whilst in Portugal, Osprey could easily obtain counterfeit passports and other documentation, relating to German, Polish and/or British citizenship. From there, he sought onward passage to either Uruguay or Argentina, eventually arriving at Buenos Aires. With forged documentation, the dentist joined the British South American Airlines flight bound for Santiago and refuge in Chile. Beyond reasonable doubt, the gold ingots and the pistol placed Osprey at the scene of the crash, the dentist's journey finally ending in the snow of the high Andes, to the west of the scenic pampas of Mendoza, Argentina.

However, there was a surprise in store; subsequent arrests of those suspected of war crimes revealed an agent in Uruguay known only as Lucia. Motivated by either misplaced loyalty or personal gain, Lucia acted as go-between for ex-Nazis and arranged onward travel to Argentina and beyond. When questioned, Lucia stated that he met Rathke in Montevideo in 1947. He said that Rathke claimed to have been on the run for many months and was now desperate.

"I offered to do whatever I could but told him it would take time. He threatened me with his pistol and demanded my help, what else could I do?"

"... I managed to organise onward passage to Buenos Aires and arranged for him to collect a ticket to sanctuary in Chile. For a big man, Rathke was fearful, always looking over his shoulder, convinced that he had been betrayed and Allied agents were watching him. He said that he needed to keep moving to avoid arrest...

"... He said that he had no money, but he is dangerous man, he paid me nothing, but it is easy to obey a man with a gun.

"I hope you caught him, Montevideo was no longer safe for us, because of people like him. The country officially supported the Allies throughout the war, who am I to judge who but was right and who was wrong? All I know after Germany surrendered, there was little sympathy for fugitives in post-war Uruguay. If Rathke was being tracked by Allied agents, he may well lead them to me, that was a risk I could not afford to take...

"... To be honest, I just wanted to get rid of that man. I too was about to flee to avoid capture, but Rathke didn't care about me, he cared only for himself. I was sure he would probably betray me if he didn't kill me first, anything to save his own neck."

Asked if he was sure that it was Rathke, Lucia replied that Rathke had valid identity documentation including a photograph proving sanction by German authorities. When questioned further, Lucia admitted that the documents could have been forgeries, but insisted that when challenged, Rathke answered the authentication question correctly, as final confirmation.

When asked what the security question challenge was, Lucia replied in perfect German:

"Wann werden die Flaggen gehisst?"
"When are the flags raised?"
And the response was:
"Die Flaggen der Morgenröte."
"The Flags of Dawn."

From written statements to the war tribunal, it was established that others including Rathke attempted subversion of former

Norwegian resistance agents. One in particular known to Lefty as 'King'. King had been coerced by Rathke into leading Lefty to the trap, the hideout with the Rascal, and onwards to the rendezvous at Hitra. The plan was to subvert Shetland bus operations, capture as many agents as possible and deny the Allies clandestine access to occupied Norway. The second phase of the operation would be to round up any remaining resistance members and SOE agents. Despite repeated attempts, the true identity of 'King' was never established.

On the night of Lefty's journey to the rendezvous point at Hitra, the lucky star was certainly in his heaven.

Had the authorities at the *Luftwaffe* base at Vaernes been informed of the revised timing of the SOE operation, King would not have been detained for 24 hours by airfield security at Vaernes and mistaken for a member of the resistance. Had the *Kriegsmarine* been fully aware of the urgency of the plan to trap the Shetland bus that night back in September 1942, they would have positioned their fast patrol craft hours beforehand. The 40 mm Bofors guns on the S boat would have made short work of the *Røta*, the crew would have been captured and interrogated by the Gestapo. But one boat was out of service, and a second vessel which should have been pre-positioned close to the rendezvous point at Hitra was mysteriously absent. The only available vessel capable of pursuit was dispatched to deal with an incident at the north-eastern end of Trondheim fjord, a pre-planned diversion staged by the resistance. By the time the vessel joined the hunt it was too late. The bus had escaped by the narrowest of margins.

The great Aryan reputation for precision and coordination was certainly not in evidence that night. The following morning, after first light, a *Luftwaffe* SIG North Sea air patrol search commenced. Again, the mission was hastily planned and poorly executed, an opportunity missed. An HE115 seaplane had been dispatched to intercept, land beside *Røta*, and capture the crew along with any evidence, before sinking the vessel. Nevertheless, the crew of the seaplane was misdirected. By the time they received the correct coordinates, the weather conditions in the North Sea had begun to deteriorate significantly. The pilot, observing the sea state in the search area, decided that the heavy swell was beyond the limits of the seaplane, abandoned the chase and returned to base.

Eventually, the hunt for the *Røta* was joined by a separate *Luftwaffe* air group based in Hurdla near Bergen. The main thrust of the low-level bombing attacks on the *Røta* was poorly coordinated. Again, both raids were restricted by a lowering cloud base, rain, and poor visibility. Although she had sustained considerable damage, the lucky star still accompanied *Røta*. Ironically, the same storm which had been the ship's salvation was to be her undoing. In the next 24 hours as the weather deteriorated further, the Valkyrie of the storm abandoned her namesake. From then on, the *Røta*'s fate was sealed.

The Rinnen gang members and other Nazi officials and collaborators were now in the custody of the Norwegian authorities as part of their post-war legal purge. Those who avoided execution were imprisoned in the notorious Grini prison near Oslo. The gang leader Rinnen, convicted of 12 counts of murder, was, without doubt, responsible for many more deaths and other atrocities. He was executed by firing squad in February 1947.

Rathke had made his escape, but after being pursued and harried, he finally fled in desperation, joined the British South

American Airways Lancastrian bound for Santiago, only to meet his destiny in the high Alpine ice fields of the Andes.

The name on the nose of the aircraft was 'Starlight', which for Osprey became the star of destiny rather than the lucky '*Étoile Chanceuse*'.

Adorning the entrance of a driveway leading to the remote family-owned farm adjacent to Lake Hoklingen in central Norway is a mature evergreen shrub. Were you to linger on the spot and inspect beneath the well-worn pot, you would find that it is supported by an unusual circular metal stand. If you were to brush away the accumulated dust, you would discover the British military benchmark symbol followed by a series of numbers stamped on its rim, identifying this as the tailwheel of 'Lucky Georgie'. The tyre which permitted the wheel to float to the lakeside, many weeks after the crash, has long since perished, revealing the wheel, the only tangible evidence of her presence. Were you invited into the farmhouse, you might be offered a warming glass of homebrewed Akvavit as the local farmer owner, Erik, relates to you his grandfather's experience on that fateful night on 26 April 1942.

As for Lefty and Mary, their story has now been recorded for posterity. Connie continues in her role as a qualified carer and manager of the care home in Sussex. She decided against settling in York, but visits Stonefall cemetery whenever she can. On anniversaries and other special occasions, she can be seen laying a single white rose beside a well-kept headstone. She still wears the small metallic lapel badge whenever she visits and still keeps the old red tin tucked away in a cupboard in Sussex. 'Lucky Georgie' remains embalmed, undisturbed for eternity in the depths of Lake Hoklingen, which became her final resting place.

Epilogue 2

STONEFALL MEMORIAL
CEMETERY 1999

I t's appropriate, the right place. Memorials of Canadian servicemen from the war are laid out in neatly regimented rows in Stonefall Commonwealth War Graves cemetery, just outside the town of Wakefield. The wrought iron gates stand ajar and welcoming, headed by 1939-1945 picked out in gilded scrollwork. If you were to follow the narrow well-tended memorial path to the adjoining municipal cemetery, you would find a simple gravestone in a quiet corner.

Were you to look more closely, you would find a name upon that stone:

> *Mary Collins*
> *1921-1942*
> *Rest in Peace*

In the small chapel, a book of remembrance is left open annually on the appropriate day, listing names of those killed in the infamous York air raid of 29th April 1942, described as 'The overnight slaughter of innocents'. Included were testaments to the courage of the air raid wardens who helped rescue many that night in the face of the onslaught.

In another of the great ironies of war, Lefty and Mary are reunited, kindred of the county's soil where they had first met so long ago.

Standing by the freshly turned earth, a chilling breeze tugging at her fedora, Connie McFarland stood alone as brittle snowflakes melted on touching her shivering frame, the pure whiteness forming contrasting speckles on her black quilted overcoat.

Partly hidden by a white rosebud was the small round pewter badge with the embossing 'EE' fastened safely in her buttonhole. She thanked the Chaplin from the Commonwealth War Graves Commission who offered to be presiding minister. As he left, his gown and stole fluttering in the breeze, he blessed her and wished her well. Adjusting her neck scarf against the elements, she tried to think of an appropriate spiritual appeal. But Connie felt that in her darkest times the few prayers she had offered had fallen on deaf ears. If it was the God of the Convent, he was fearsome indeed, but perhaps now was the time to follow Him, just in case. She summoned up all her resources, then remembered the words of the poet John F McCullagh; she silently whispered that verse from "The Man with the Thousand Yard Stare".

> *"The Parson commands us to silence, and struggles to lead us in prayer, but half of the room has forgotten the words, like the man with the thousand-yard stare."*

The short service and committal had been rather a bleak experience. Apart from the priest, the only others in attendance were a rather dour representative from the local branch of the British Legion and a small knot of anonymous onlookers with nothing better to do.

Beyond them, Connie recognised two familiar figures standing beside a dark blue Lexus in the car park. A smart young man looking rather uncomfortable in a new suit. Beside him, the distinguished and ruggedly handsome investigator. It seemed ages since she had seen them. In the preceding months, she had spent many happy hours with them, listening to Lefty's story and getting it all down on paper.

Keeping at a respectful distance, James and Ned smiled as Connie approached, a warm handshake from Ned, and a heart-warming hug from James.

"I'm so sorry, Connie," offered James, "he was a truly remarkable man."

Connie sighed and smiled, greeting them as long-lost friends.

"Thank you, James, that means a lot... and Ned, look at you, you look *so* smart!" said Connie "If I'd known you were coming, I could have laid something on for you both."

James said, "We can't stay anyway, Connie, Ned has got to get back to work, and I've got a new project that I am up to my ears in!"

"I'm just so pleased that you could come, Lefty would have loved it!"

James turned to Ned saying, "Actually, we've brought you a gift, Connie." Ned opened the passenger door on his new Lexus and withdrew a paper bag, which he handed to James, who in turn passed the package to Connie.

"Is this what I think it is?" She smiled, withdrawing a brand-new book from its paper bag, admiring the dust jacket, and feeling the satisfaction of hefting an unopened text. "Well look at this! ... *Cause and Consequence – a life of inquiry*'," she said, reading the title aloud.

"Well, it's all yours, just have a look at the flysheet inside."

She read it aloud: "For Connie – in memory of Mary and Lefty."

Choking back a tear, Connie hugged them both as James said: "All three of you are in there, you, Mary and Lefty, you have your very own chapter! I hope you enjoy it; young Ned here and I have loved every minute of committing your words to paper, getting to know you and your incredible parents, we will never forget you."

"It's a big book. How will I know which chapter is about Lefty?" she asked.

In reply, James said, "Although the book is quite long, it was a lot shorter before we met you and Lefty!"

James made his apologies and said he had to get on the road, he and Ned each had commitments the following day.

Connie raised a gloved hand before she spoke again. She addressed them both.

"Before you go, I just wanted to say that the trustees of the Cranbourne foundation want me to write a history of the charity, but I'm not good at writing and not sure where to start. I'm definitely going to need a good author or researcher... can you recommend anyone?"

As they got into the car and prepared for the drive home, James turned to Ned and said: "I'm not sure, Ned, you know anyone?"

Fastening his seatbelt, Ned turned to Connie, wearing a wry smile, and offered: "I know of two pretty good researchers in Essex. One is a grumpy old man, but the other one is keen, young and handsome; I could put in a good word for you if you would like?"

They laughed and waved through the open window as the Lexus crunched its way across the gravel drive towards the exit.

"I'll call you next week, Connie." James smiled from the open passenger window.

She returned the gesture, beaming in the late afternoon sun, watching the red brake lights blink as the car paused. Then pulling smartly away, the Lexus joined the early evening traffic on the main road, leaving only a white plume of exhaust, a hovering wraith, lingering, watching for a final farewell.

Connie stood on the spot watching after them as Ned, James, and the Lexus disappeared from view. The sun was low on the horizon. It would be a full moon at sunset that day, a delicate silver orb suspended in a beautiful twilight glow. If Connie looked above, she may have been able to spot the lucky star; it was still there observing, watching over them from its lofty perch in the heavens – the *'Étoile Chanceuse'*. There would surely be a frost in the early hours, but nothing now could chill the warmth that Connie felt within. Her life would always have meaning now, alone again but accompanied by enduring memories and the prospect of meeting up with new friends.

Clutching the book in her left hand, she brushed away a single tear. The air had a distinct chill, with the prospect of a fine evening ahead.

She looked again at the glossy dust cover, no regrets, no hollow and meaningless memories. Unspoken words just murmurs on her lips:

He's still with me now and always will be, we had the privilege of those precious remaining years where I helped Lefty become that 20-year-old again and relate those missing years... Lefty had found his home now and would always remain here, father, friend, and hero as one.

The End

Appendix

"And lo, already on the hills
the flags of Dawn appear,
gird up your loins, ye prophet souls
proclaim the day is near."

SONGS of Solomon

Acknowledgements

To all those who inspired and encouraged me when I was tempted to give up.

My sister Frances
My parents
Rosie Travers
Sue Hiscock
Jo Foley
Lloyd Brown
Mike Wilman
The RAF Museum
The crew of 'S for Sugar'
The Public Records Office at Kew
Not forgetting Dim, without whose intervention I would have finished this at least 18 months earlier!